Thanks to a lifelong fascination with Ancient Greek mythology, Jennifer Saint read Classical Studies at King's College, London. Since September 2022, she has been a Visiting Research Fellow in the Classics Department there. In between, she spent thirteen years as an English teacher, sharing a love of literature and creative writing with her students. *Ariadne* is her first novel, *Elektra* is her second, and *Atalanta* is her latest mesmerising mythological retelling.

Praise for Jennifer Saint:

'Jennifer Saint has done it again with the story of Atalanta, the only female Argonaut . . . Atlanta is one of the most complex but forgotten heroines of Greek myth and her story has so many parallels for any woman living in a world of men.'
Red

'Jennifer Saint brings Atalanta and her adventures to life in another exciting Greek mythology re-imagining.'
Cosmopolitan

'Jennifer Saint's latest mythological retelling
is brilliantly evocative.'
Woman and Home

'With her previous novels *Ariadne* and *Elektra*, Saint has
become much-celebrated for her sweeping retellings of
Greek myth. *Atalanta* is the equally spellbinding story of the
daughter of King of Arcadia, trying to make her way in the
world made for men.'
iNews

'Jennifer Saint you can do no wrong. This unstoppable
author bounded into the world of epic mythological
re-tellings with *Ariadne*, following up with the brilliant
Elektra. Her focus on women behind the scenes continues
with thistale of heroism and courage . . . Fans of this genre
will be delighted.'
Glamour

'A stunning retelling filled with breathtaking adventure,
Atalanta brings to life a heroine who stands tall among
the ancient gods and heroes of legend.'
Sue Lynn Tan, *Sunday Times* bestselling author of
Daughter of the Moon Goddess

'Jennifer Saint deftly draws the reader into the legends of
Atalanta, swift huntress and favorite of Artemis, bringing
the world of ancient Greece alive. The detail and description
is lush: you can hear the rustle of the green leaves and taste
the salty spray of the sea as the Argo rides forth on its
quest. A story of adventure and love against all odds,
this is an ancient tale limned with gold.'
Luna McNamara, author of *Psyche and Eros*

'Absolutely beautiful. This is a retelling that fully inhabits the magical realm of myth while losing none of its human heart. The way Jennifer Saint dealt with the ending was absolutely inspired - staying true to the mythology yet giving it an emotional twist that felt completely true to the heroine she had created. *Atalanta* is a lyrical, exciting and deeply poignant tale of one woman's remarkable life – and I cannot wait to read it again.'
Elodie Harper, author of *The Wolf Den*

'Through the eyes of a strong and unbending heroine, *Atalanta* weaves together some of the most exciting myths: the Argonauts' quest, Hypsipyle and the women of Lemnos, Hippomenes's footrace. Beautifully written and crafted with magic, this is an unforgettable retelling.'
Costanza Casati, author of *Clytemnestra*

'*Atalanta* is an absolute joy of a novel. As always Saint brings Ancient Greece to life with deft story-telling and lyrical imagery, but with her third outing we are drawn into a truly empowering story - a novel of strength and resilience, love and friendship, skillfully enthused with the addictive magic of timeless myth. A beautifully written retelling.'
Susan Stokes-Chapman, author of *Pandora*

ATALANTA

JENNIFER SAINT

WILDFIRE

First published in 2023 by
WILDFIRE
an imprint of HEADLINE PUBLISHING GROUP

First published in paperback in 2024 by
WILDFIRE
an imprint of HEADLINE PUBLISHING GROUP

1

Cataloguing in Publication Data is available from the British Library

ISBN 978 1 4722 9217 9

Typeset in Sabon by CC Book Production

Printed and bound in Great Britain by Clays Ltd, Elcograf S.p.A.

HEADLINE PUBLISHING GROUP
An Hachette UK Company
Carmelite House
50 Victoria Embankment
London EC4Y 0DZ

www.headline.co.uk
www.hachette.co.uk

For Bee and Steph, my Northern writers' group,
who loved this novel from its earliest incarnation
and cheered it every step of the way

Atalanta: From the Greek Ἀταλάντη *(Atalante)* meaning 'equal in strength'.

'Atalánta was exceeding swift of foot . . . she exposed not her self to view, unless accidentally in following the chase, or defending herself from some man; in which action she broke forth like lightning.'

– Thomas Stanley, translator (1665),
Claudius Aelianus His Various History: Book XIII
(pages 258–87)

PROLOGUE

When I was born, they left me on a hillside. The king had given his decree – *if it's a girl, expose her on the mountain* – and so some unfortunate soul was dispatched from the palace with this unwanted scrap of humanity: a baby girl instead of the glorious heir the king desired.

Left on the bare earth, I suppose I might have howled for as long as my little lungs could bear it. Or I could have lain, whimpering and fearful, watching as she came closer. The mother bear, her cubs still blind and damp-furred, attracted by the plaintive sound of a desolate newborn, her maternal anxiety still at its peak.

I'd like to think that I looked up at her, the mother bear, and held her gaze. That I didn't flinch away from her hot breath or the rough caress of her paw. She must have been too solicitous to leave me, unable to stand the sound of a hungry infant, and so she scooped me up and took me back with her.

I grew strong on bear milk. I learned to wrestle with my bear siblings, the rough and tumble of our play with no quarter given. I never cried when their claws or teeth scraped my skin or when they growled and pounced. Rather, I twisted my fingers into their fur, pulled them to the ground, buried my own teeth in their flanks and bit as hard as I could. By night, we curled up together, a tangle of limbs ursine and human, the soft pads of their paws resting on my sun-browned flesh in our warm nest of leaves and earth, the damp rasp of their tongues against my face.

Seasons passed and, weaned from their mother's milk, they learned to hunt for themselves, tentative at first, perched precariously on slippery rocks in the fast-flowing river that rushed through our forest. I would sit cross-legged on the grassy bank, watching the water for the shining dart of fish scales like they did, laughing at their clumsy swipes, the splashes that left them bedraggled. At first, their mother stayed close, intent upon them, but as their confidence swelled, she started to wander further away. She sniffed the air, her eyes drawn to the sloping hills, her attention drifting from us, caught by something else.

The cubs knew it before I did. They made themselves scarce before he appeared, the huge male in search of a mate. They hid themselves in the trees when he came shambling out of the mountains, from some faraway cave where the scent of the mother bear had carried on the fresh spring breeze. An irresistible summons to this monster, who seemed to rear up to the height of the trees themselves. The rumbling in his throat sounded like the thunder that had shaken the branches while I'd lain safe among the sleeping cubs all winter.

She sensed it too. In the space of a moment, the time it took for the wind to turn, she changed; swift, abrupt and inevitable. Her loving caresses turned to snarls and swipes; if any of her young looked back longingly before they scattered to the safety of their high branches, she leapt to chase them away. I trembled from behind a boulder, feeling the hot blast of air as she roared her warning. The only mother I had known in my short life was gone, replaced with something terrible.

She let him follow her. From where I hid, I saw his great head butting against her neck, and her answering nuzzle.

The cubs were agitated at first, but after a while they calmed, and one by one, each of them at last climbed down. I watched as my brothers and sisters made their own separate ways through the forest, quickly swallowed up by the towering trunks and verdant branches.

Disorientated, I went too, wandering without direction among the trees, but in time my tears dried up and my gasping breaths slowed. I knew where I was, and the familiarity of the forest was soothing as I walked. The air was golden-green, filtering through the leaves, rich with the scent of pine and cypress and soft black earth. A fat spider squatted in the centre of her web between two branches, her hairy brown body and striped legs almost disappearing against the bark. A snake darted forwards, coiling swiftly into a protective circle, the diamond sheen of its scales glittering where the sunlight fell across it. Where the trees thinned out on the higher slopes of the mountain, lions prowled, sleek and soundless through the ragged bushes and rocky outcrops. A forest sharp with fangs and claws, trickling with venom, pulsing with life and beauty. There were a thousand interconnected threads criss-crossing through it: from the ancient roots soaking up water deep beneath the earth so that the trees could lift their mighty crowns towards the sun, to the insects that burrowed into the deep crevices of the bark, to the birds that nested in the boughs, to the deer that trotted lightly and the stalking predators ready to pounce.

And in the heart of it all, there was me.

PART I

1

She came to me in the forest after the bears had gone. She would have been an imposing sight to anyone, taller and stronger than any mortal woman would be – although I didn't know that then – with a gleaming bow in her hand, a fierce glint in her eyes and a pack of hounds at her heels. Even as a small child, however, my curiosity was more powerful than my fear. When she held out her hand to me, I took it.

I remember my first sight of the grove where she led me, stepping out from the cluster of cypress trees behind her. I squinted, dazzled for a moment by the golden light reflecting back from the shimmering surface of the pool before us. I screwed up my eyes, opened them again and blinked.

Across the water, set into the sloping mountainside, was a wide cave with large rocks dotted about in front of the entrance. And perched on the flat planes of the rocks were women – nymphs, as I would come to know them. The air rang with their soft chatter and gentle laughter. I looked up at the woman who had brought me here and she smiled.

They gave me berries, ripe and sweet. I remember the taste

of the cold, clear water they gave me to drink, how clumsy I was with the cup they held to the mouth of the spring for me. That night, I did not sleep next to the bears' shaggy warmth, the heavy thrum of their hearts beating in my ears, but on a bed of animal skins, and I woke to the sound of a woman singing.

It was Artemis who had come for me, I would discover, and it was to her sacred grove that she had taken me. Artemis, the goddess of the hunt, to whom the forest and all its inhabitants belonged. We all fell under her silvery gaze, we all bowed to her might, from the worms slithering in the earth to the howling wolves. The forest of Arcadia shimmered with her power.

She gave me to the nymphs to raise. It was their task to teach me what she found too tedious; for them to guide me to understand how they talked, and to learn, haltingly at first, how to respond; for them to show me how to weave the cloth from which they made the simple tunics they all wore, and how to honour the other gods and goddesses whose names they taught me, though none of them ever came to our forest. They taught me where to gather berries, how to avoid the ones that would make me sick, warned me against the innocuous-seeming fungi that would drain the life right out of me. I saw that their lives were dedicated to Artemis; they kept the forest for her, nurturing its springs, its rivers, its plants and all the life within it. In exchange, they lived there, loved and guarded by her.

At first, her visits seemed sporadic, unpredictable to me. From the cave where I slept beside the nymphs, I would watch the passage of the moon across the sky, chart its progress from slender crescent to shining orb. I learned that it would never dwindle back to a sliver again without her coming to us. Wandering through the forest, I would keep a watchful eye all the time. The dogs that had waited patiently at her side when she'd first found me would follow me into the trees, as though they looked for their mistress too. There were seven of them, and at first I found it easier to be with them than the nymphs. Their soft fur reminded me of the bears and their sharp teeth never frightened me. Every rustle of branches or snap of twigs as we walked would catch my attention, root me in place, searching in between the clusters of gnarled trunks for any sign of her return. I was eager for her to come back and see what I'd learned each time in her absence. Whenever she stepped out, as startling and unexpected as a sudden rain shower in spring, I felt my heart leap.

She would call out for the nymphs to follow her, and they would leave me behind, fleeing lightly through the trees and returning with the dusk, their prey bundled over their shoulders. Those evenings, the grove would be rich with the mouth-watering scent of roasting meat. I yearned to go with them, for the day she would think me useful enough to take with her.

Five more winters passed before she came to me one dawn at the start of spring, when she whispered 'Atalanta?' at the mouth of the cave, and I leapt to answer. Her cheeks were flushed, her eyes shining, her tunic loosely belted around her waist, and the smoothly curved bow in her hand. She greeted the hounds, then inclined her head for me to follow her into the forest depths, indicating for me to walk as soundlessly as she did, and to pause and look around with quick, darting movements at frequent intervals. I felt the pressure building up inside me, the gleeful joy at this new sport threatening to explode into giddy laughter, but I swallowed it down, setting my chin as firmly as hers and placing my feet exactly where she did on the soft earth. The dogs streamed ahead of us, ears pricked as they sniffed the air eagerly. When they caught the scent they were searching for, she pulled me down swiftly beside her, crouching behind a fallen log, peering over the velvety moss as she narrowed her eyes and took aim with the bow.

The stag broke through the trees, panicked by the hounds. It was a majestic creature, the antlers spreading wide and tall from its broad forehead, perhaps the most magnificent one I'd seen. Her arrow pierced its throat in an instant, before its liquid brown eyes could register the danger it had run into, and it slumped down, a trickle of red sliding down below the slender wooden shaft of her weapon.

She caught my admiring glance and smiled. The next time, she showed me how to hold the bow, its weight seeming to thrum in my hands, quivering with power.

From then, I lived for the days that Artemis would arrive in the grove, when she would beckon me out into the stillness of dawn with the bow in her hand. Her voice, low and urgent in my ear as she breathed her instructions: how to watch for the movement of the deer hidden deep among the ferns, how to render myself motionless, invisible, eyes fixed on the target, the bow strung taut in my hands until there was nothing left in the world but me and my quarry. I'd exhale as the arrow flew straight for its throat, just as she'd shown me. Under her tutelage, I shaped a bow of my own and never went anywhere in the forest without it. There was nothing sweeter to me in the world than the sound of her delighted laughter when I hit the mark.

As well as the thrill of success and the satisfaction of the kill, I wanted to please her. As the nymphs had told me, it was under the protection of Artemis that I had the chance to grow free and joyous. She didn't live as the other gods did, and my life was like no other human's either. Artemis shunned the golden halls of Mount Olympus, the grand cloud-cloaked palace where the other immortals lived. She chose a life in the forest instead, preferring to bathe in the pools by silver moonlight and run through the trees by day, swift and graceful, a quiver of arrows slung across her body and her bow always ready. I saw that it pleased her to have a mortal grow up in her image, and I was glad of it too, even if I didn't quite understand just how much gratitude I truly owed her.

I had never known a human hearth; I had no conception of how rare a thing it was to be the protégée of a goddess, to spend my childhood in the wild simplicity and raw magic of the woods.

Artemis may have chosen to shun her fellow Olympians, but the Arcadian woods were full of her companions. The nymphs who cared for me were dedicated to following her: dozens of ageless daughters of rivers, springs, oceans and winds, young women who ran and hunted and bathed alongside the goddess.

They told me stories. At first, I liked it best when they recounted my own – how I'd been left on the mountainside and rescued by the mother bear and later by Artemis. It kept the memories of my earliest life vivid in my mind. I didn't want to forget who I was before I came to live with these gentle, laughing women. I didn't want to lose the way it had felt, the exhilaration I'd known clutching the mother bear's fur, holding on tightly as we ran through the forest, her powerful muscles shifting beneath me and the trees flying past.

I was full of curiosity, though, watching my new companions from my vantage point perched on a boulder by the pool, shaded by the delicate sweep of willow branches. There was Phiale, who, in the summer months when the water ran low, could always coax more to flow from the springs even if they had dwindled to a trickle, while Crocale drifted gracefully across the earth, flowers blooming in her wake. When the ground dried and hardened, baked beneath the sun, Psekas could conjure a sprinkling of rain from the air to nourish the thirsty soil. I wondered how they'd learned such tricks. 'Have you always been in the forest?' I asked them.

'Not always,' Phiale told me. 'Some of us are the daughters of the Titan Oceanos, the mighty river that girdles the earth. Our father sent us to Artemis when we were children, and we've dwelt here ever since.'

It raised another question for me: though I was growing swiftly all the time, and was almost as tall as the nymphs were already, why did they never seem to change?

'Like Artemis, we grew from childhood to take this form and this is how we will stay,' Phiale explained. 'While the goddess will never die, we can be harmed by wild beasts or ... in other ways.' She paused. 'Nymphs can be killed, like the creatures you hunt in the woods. But the ravages of age won't ever touch us.'

'What about me?' I asked.

She cupped my cheek in her hand, stroking back the wisps of hair that had escaped my braid. 'You're mortal, Atalanta. Not like any other mortal who has ever lived, but you will grow and age like every human does.'

'Don't frighten her.'

Approaching from the far side of the grove, her hair coming

loose from its braid and her face smudged with traces of dirt, Callisto was returning from a hunt. She tossed her spear aside, letting it land with a clatter against a rock, and sank down on the ground beside the boulder I was sitting on.

'She doesn't frighten me,' I said. I reached down and plucked a leaf from Callisto's tangled curls.

'Of course not.' She leaned her head back, closing her eyes against the gentle sunlight.

'Are you weary?' Phiale asked her.

Callisto reached up her hand and caught my fingers in hers. 'I've been hunting with Artemis, but she ran so far ahead. I can't keep up with her.' A wry smile lifted the corners of her mouth. 'Not like Atalanta here, who can already run across the mountainsides with her all day and come back refreshed and ready for more.'

Phiale laughed. 'Atalanta is only young, that's why she's so full of energy.'

'Don't you think she'll be even more formidable when she's fully grown? I do.' Callisto squeezed my fingers and then she opened her eyes, looking up at me. 'You'll take my place as her closest companion before long,' she said. There was no bitterness in her tone, no hint of jealousy. She said it simply and sincerely, with the affection she always showed me. It made my chest swell with a surge of pride and I looked away, not quite sure how to respond.

We felt it at the same moment, the sudden tingling in the air as though the forest itself was alert with anticipation. It meant only one thing. Artemis was here.

She strode out into the clearing, nymphs jumping up to attend her. She stood in the centre of them all, head and shoulders taller, holding a javelin stained with blood. She was still glowing from the thrill and exertion of the chase. She handed off the spear, her bow and her quiver of arrows to a couple of nymphs standing ready, and they laid them carefully at the sides of the cave. While they did so, Crocale slid the tunic from Artemis' shoulders and swept up her hair as the goddess stepped naked into the water.

Artemis sighed with contentment as the midday sun caught her in its glow, highlighting her upturned face, the curve of her shoulders and her breasts. It was a moment so beautiful, so harmonious, that I think all of us were suspended in it.

'There were men out hunting this morning too,' Callisto said. There was something significant in her tone, some kind of meaning that passed between her and Phiale as they glanced from each other to Artemis, still blissfully bathing.

I sat up straighter. 'How close did they get?'

Callisto laughed. 'Not very.'

'They never do,' I said. Men, hounds and horses. They intruded on our forest every now and again, horns blaring and the thunder of their shouts startling the birds from the treetops, but in all their noise and chaos, they never knew for a moment how close they might pass to me, a nymph or the goddess herself.

Phiale's face was unusually stern. 'Don't be so sure,' she said. 'They've made it deep into the forest before.'

I shrugged. 'They aren't fast enough to catch more than a glimpse of us.'

'You can't let them catch even a glimpse.' Phiale shook her head, and I felt a flicker of irritation at her caution.

'Truly, you mustn't.' Callisto stood, reaching into the cave to retrieve a wide-mouthed cup that she dipped into the stream of water constantly replenishing the pool.

'A hunter did once find this sacred grove,' Phiale said. Callisto was standing half in the shadows of the cave, so I couldn't see her face, but Phiale's gaze was intent and serious, fixed upon me as she spoke. 'He got separated from his companions and, searching for them, stumbled right on to the banks of the pool.'

'Really?' I wasn't sure whether to believe her or not. Perhaps it was a joke or a story she was telling to test my credulity.

'Artemis was bathing, just as she is now,' Phiale went on. The laughter and soft splashes as nymphs joined Artemis in the water meant her story wouldn't be overheard, but still she kept her voice so low that I had to strain to hear her. 'The nymphs flung themselves into the pool, clustering around the goddess to shield her from his view, but it was as though he was frozen to the spot, just staring.'

Despite myself, I felt a stirring of unease. 'What did she do?'

'He had two dogs with him,' Callisto said. 'Artemis was furious – more so than I had ever seen her. I remember her face, how she looked at the dogs and then back at the man. It was silent, no one moving, and then at once her hand struck the water, and droplets flew at his face. Her voice – it wasn't like Artemis' voice, it was deeper, terrible. She told him to go and tell his companions how he saw the goddess naked.'

Phiale took up the tale. 'He tried to get away, he scrambled back towards the trees, but I could see where his hair dripped with water that there was something forming on his head, something that made no sense. I stared, not able to believe what I was seeing, but as he screamed, I saw it taking shape – two antlers twisting out of his skull.'

'Antlers?' I gasped. 'But how . . .?'

'He fell, and all across his body, fur was growing. He was

convulsing, over and over, his screams ringing into the sky, and then he rolled over on to four legs – no longer a man but a stag.'

'The dogs . . .' Callisto said, and she swallowed.

'He tried to flee, his legs tangling underneath him. They leapt on him at once, and the whole grove rang with the sound of their snarls.'

'I couldn't watch,' Callisto said.

I was fascinated and repelled in equal measure. 'But isn't this a warning to the men to stay away? Why does it mean I should avoid them? If they follow us here, they'll meet the same punishment.'

'Imagine if Artemis hadn't been here that day.' Phiale pushed her hair back from her face impatiently. 'Imagine if a man found one of us here without her, came across a nymph bathing alone, disrobed and vulnerable? If they knew we were here, what do you think they would do?'

'I don't know.' I could tell from her tone it was something awful.

Callisto came forwards, into the light again. 'Of course you don't, and that's because of how we live, just us women and Artemis.'

'Artemis keeps us safe here,' Phiale said. 'But in exchange, we've all made the same vow: that we have nothing to do with men.'

'His dogs were howling all through the evening, searching for their master,' Callisto said. 'They wanted his praise for the kill they'd made. We heard his friends in the distance shouting his name, Actaeon, over and over. It took hours for them to give up.'

I thought about it. 'He came to hunt. He found something

stronger than he was.' That was the way of the forest. Artemis had taught me that when we'd stalked our prey through the woods, bow in hand. We had to be able to take on whatever we encountered, to be strong enough to come out the victor every time.

'That's right,' Phiale said. 'But Artemis isn't always here, and we aren't all as fast as you are, Atalanta.' Her mood was lightening now; she laughed as she said it, already back to playfulness.

'Nor do we all have as much skill as you already do with the bow,' Callisto added, kissing my forehead.

But I would be there, even when Artemis was not. I'd only regarded the hunters as a noisy nuisance, but now I resolved that if any came as close to us as Actaeon had, I would make sure they fared no better. I had been tempted sometimes to dart ahead of them, to see if any of them could ever manage a fleeting glance at me. Now when they thundered through with their horses and their dogs, I would turn away from their noisy intrusion and head deeper into the heart of the forest, where they could never manage to follow.

I was determined to keep growing stronger and faster. I worked harder, practising every day at shooting my bow, perfecting my aim. When Artemis came for me, I would show off my skills, bringing down stags and mountain lions alike. I would race her across the steep slopes of the mountains, my legs pumping, my breath sharp and desperate, always just a fraction behind her. I was young enough to think I might one day beat her, that I could be faster than a goddess. I wanted her to trust that I could protect us all, just like she did: I, who had grown up in the rough and tumble of the bears and stalked the woods silently with my bow and arrow. She was my sister, mother, guide and teacher all in one, and just like her, I wanted to fear nothing.

2

We came upon a meadow full of flowers, their delicate red heads nodding among the lush grass. I thought it was a beautiful place to rest, but Artemis frowned when she saw it, and the displeasure on her face only deepened when the breeze carried a rich, sweet scent over to us and we saw the garland left there. It was a wreath of pink roses, twisted together and laid among the other flowers, their petals brushing together. I glanced at Artemis, bewildered by the sharp distaste that pinched her features together.

'What is it?' I asked. 'Who left it here?'

I couldn't see what there was to offend her here. Soft tufts of white cloud drifted across the sky, the sun shone mellow and golden over the gently waving grass, the flowers proliferated bright and blooming, a poplar tree spread its wide branches to offer shade.

'Roses,' Artemis said, nudging the garland with her foot and stirring its heavy, sultry perfume. The movement shook a few petals loose, and they fluttered to the ground. 'Left here by some foolish mortal, some lovestruck hunter perhaps, in offering to Aphrodite, in the vain hope that she'd ever dare to return here.'

I held my breath, not wanting to interrupt her with the slightest movement. Artemis rarely spoke of the other gods. She'd never given any indication that one of them had ever been in our forest, her realm, where her power was unquestioned. It was the nymphs who taught me the worship of those others so that I could avoid accidentally neglecting or insulting one of them. I knew of Dionysus, who taught mortals how to make wine from grapes; Zeus, who wielded the thunderbolt and split the heavens apart with his stormy rage; Demeter, who blessed the earth so that it bore fruit and nourished us; Poseidon, who ruled the seas I had never seen and could only imagine. Deities of war, of song and poetry, of strategy, wisdom, marriage, of all kinds of things, some of which touched my life and some of which never came close. Aphrodite was definitely in the latter category.

Artemis turned her face away from the roses, looking back at me instead. She smiled, her annoyance lifting. 'It's ten years since I found you wandering in the woods,' she said. 'Already, you stand taller than all of the nymphs, and you're still not a grown woman. You're brave enough to want to protect them, even if you aren't always sure from what threat.'

Her eyes darted back to the roses on the ground and she pursed her lips, seeming to come to a decision. 'This forest used to be under the dominion of Rhea, the mother goddess. She ruled before any other; the gods were born from her and so were these mountains. Lions slept by her throne; when she set forth through the trees, they would pull her chariot, the strongest and most ferocious of beasts tamed by her alone. The forest passed from her to me, and no other Olympian dared to interfere in my lands.'

Around us, birds chirped merrily from the treetops. The scent of the roses hung in the air, thicker now and cloying.

'When Aphrodite came, it was in pursuit of her lover, of course. A mortal named Adonis, who loved to hunt. For a while, she amused herself with it too, chasing after hares and birds and thinking herself brave. She begged him to stay away from the bears, the wolves and the lions, entreated him never to stalk a wild boar and risk so much as a scratch on his handsome flesh.' Her lip curled. 'They used to lie together here, in this meadow.'

My eyes widened.

'In my forests, Atalanta, the place where I brought my nymphs to live in peace.' She shook her head. 'It was this meadow where he came with the mortal wound he got when he disturbed a wild beast in the woods – a creature more savage than he, the kind she'd warned him against. He died in her arms, his blood streaming on to the earth where it mingled with her tears.'

Artemis took a deliberate step forwards, crushing a clump of red flowers beneath her sandalled heel. 'These sprang up where he died,' she said. As she lifted her foot, I saw the broken stems, the scattered petals. 'She never came back here again.'

I nodded as though I understood completely. I always hungered for more, but when a conversation bored her or she had said enough, there would be something so utterly forbidding in her eyes that I never ventured to ask any questions. Only later did I go back over what she'd said, trying to prise out any meaning I might have missed.

She was always abrupt, unpredictable, gone in an instant and returning without warning. That evening, when she was gone again, I joined the nymphs sitting around a fire, thin curls

of smoke streaming upwards to the starlit sky, the notes of
their laughter and chatter mingling harmoniously in the quiet
dusk. Psekas swirled a jug between her hands, sending ripples
across the dark liquid within. The smell of it reminded me of
the roses, heady and sweet. Smiling, she took up a jug of water
and poured some of it in, letting the two mix together. As she
started to hand it around, I surprised myself by reaching for
a cup.

Usually, I preferred to drink the cold, fresh water from
the springs. Tonight, I was intrigued by the fragrance of the
wine. I breathed it in, looking at the deep, rich colour, and
took a sip. It had a tang to it, a sharp taste of fruit and spice
that made me wrinkle my nose at first. But I felt it warming
me from within and I took another sip, feeling that warmth
radiate through my body.

Crocale leaned back, resting against the gnarled bark of
the oak tree whose branches spread above us, the leaves fluttering against the night sky, the stars glimmering between its
limbs. She ran her fingers idly through the tiny white flowers
that grew around her. There was something so languorous
and relaxed about the evening. It wasn't that it was better
when Artemis wasn't there, but it was different. When she was
with us, everything felt more alive, more vibrant. I would sit
straighter, more alert, listening more intently. With her away,
I let the conversation flow around me, until I remembered the
meadow we'd found that afternoon and I interrupted with a
question that seemed all at once to be pressing.

'How long ago was it that Aphrodite left the forest?'

Psekas looked askance at me. 'What do you mean?'

'Artemis showed me the meadow today, where her flowers
grow. I wondered how long ago it was.'

Psekas shrugged. 'I don't know.' She cast a quick glance around and took a long sip of her wine. 'She came here to tryst with her lover. Artemis hated that she was here at all, but we'd never really have known about it if she hadn't told us – she was furious, of course. But I think the goddess was seeking somewhere hidden, away from the eyes of the world.'

'This forest belongs to Artemis, though,' Callisto interjected. She took up the water jug, stirring a little more into the wine.

Crocale leaned forward, holding out her cup to be refilled. 'Aphrodite learned that clearly enough, I think.'

'Artemis said it was an animal that killed Adonis,' I said. 'A hunting accident.'

Crocale nodded, though I saw her catch Psekas' eye for a moment. She took a long sip and leaned back again. 'Artemis hadn't forgiven Aphrodite for interfering with a favourite of hers. She couldn't tolerate her presence here. Her anger was constant; it clouded every day.'

'No doubt she wanted to protect all of us,' Callisto said. Her tone was mild, but I could detect a note of warning.

'Why, what happened to her favourite? Was it a nymph?' I asked.

Crocale sighed. 'A girl to whom Artemis was devoted. They were dearest friends. Her name was Persephone.'

'Persephone, the queen of the Underworld?' I asked.

Crocale nodded. 'They were girls together, their most cherished place the island of Sicily, where they would play in the meadows and gather violets. They had both sworn to a life without men, like all of us have done.'

'But Aphrodite had other plans.' The moonlight shimmered on the wine in Callisto's cup as she tilted it one way and then another, her eyes sad as she spoke. 'She wanted to prove her

23

power, to show that there was no corner or cavern of the world where she didn't have influence. Even the Underworld.'

'She sent her son Eros after Hades,' Crocale said. 'She wanted the cold king of the dead to burn with desire. So Eros fired his arrow, and Hades was seized with a longing for Persephone that he couldn't resist.'

'So Persephone was married to Hades?' I asked.

'And Artemis lost her beloved friend,' Callisto finished.

'It made the insult of Aphrodite bringing Adonis here even worse,' Psekas said. 'She really couldn't bear it.'

I thought of Artemis crushing the flowers beneath her feet. 'That makes sense.'

Crocale stretched her arms above her head, letting them fall back by her sides with a slight shudder. 'But just as Artemis didn't forgive what happened to Persephone, I'm sure Aphrodite hasn't forgiven the loss of Adonis either.'

'How do you know?' I asked.

'There is a world beyond the forest,' Crocale said. 'We came to live here, with Artemis.' She glanced at Psekas again. 'Our sister, Peitho, went to serve as handmaiden to Aphrodite instead.'

'There are nymphs all across the world,' Psekas agreed. 'Some who live like we do, some very differently.'

I frowned and swallowed the last of my wine. 'Did your sister have a choice?'

Psekas laughed. 'She did.'

'And is she your enemy now, like Aphrodite is to Artemis?'

'Not at all. She's our sister; we love her just the same as always.'

I opened my mouth, but Callisto stood up. 'I think it's time to sleep,' she said.

I was tired, a pleasant heaviness weighing me down. An owl hooted softly from a treetop, the dark shapes of the mountains rising behind the shadowy silhouettes of the trees like familiar friends. *How unfathomable,* I thought to myself as I made my way to bed, *that anyone would choose a different home than here, a protector other than Artemis.*

Other nymphs had come to join us over the years, sent by immortal fathers seeking a home for the numerous daughters for whom they found themselves responsible. It wasn't long after that evening that Arethusa came. Her father was Nereus, an ancient sea-god, I heard her telling the others as I slipped out through the trees with my bow and arrows to hunt. I tracked through the forest, my feet light and soundless, until Helios began the downward slope of his mighty arc and the sun began to sink once more. I came to the banks of a river. Gratefully, I stripped off my tunic and submerged myself, washing away the dust and grime that clung to my skin. I broke the surface and let myself float, the gentle currents washing away my fatigue and soothing my aching muscles. I was not the only one there; the chatter of a small group of nymphs on the bank drifted on the breeze, and I lifted a hand to them. Callisto stood up from the group, shrugged off her tunic and slid into the river too. We often swam together, swapping stories of the day's hunt. Waiting for her to reach me, I closed my eyes in blissful satisfaction, letting my hair fan out around me. But as I luxuriated in the memory of the day, I felt a tugging at my scalp. My eyes snapped open, my skin prickling at the unmistakeable sensation of fingers sliding through my hair.

I looked about me and saw that Callisto was still near to

the opposite edge, nowhere near me. It was no nymph that had hold of me. Something else was in the river.

I twisted about in the water, jerking myself free, and splashed frantically towards the shallows, taking hold of the long grasses to pull myself out on to the safety of land, scrambling my tunic back over my head and seizing my bow. I stood panting at the river's edge, searching the ripples for what had seized me. Across the water, Callisto had leapt out too, seeing my panic, and our eyes met. The nymphs on the other side sat up, puzzled but wary in the shattered peace of the gathering twilight.

And then Arethusa screamed. Arethusa, who had leaned too far over the river that all at once seemed composed of a dozen watery hands, all of them slithering over her flesh. She twisted away, squirming free on to the slippery mud, screaming again as we heard his voice gurgling from the depth, a thick growl of rushing water shaping the words, 'I am Alpheus, god of this river.' A shudder ran down my spine. Artemis was the goddess of our forest, but these minor gods sprang up at every brook or pool. Most would not dare to incur her wrath, but some were brasher and bolder.

Arethusa dragged herself to her feet and ran, but as I watched, a flurry of bubbles broke the surface and a shimmering, dripping form began to rise. Without thinking, I plunged back into the water, swimming to the other bank, where I yanked myself up on the muddy edge and tore after her. But he was following her too, his footsteps squelching at her back. If I fired my arrows, they'd slice right through his waters into her flesh. My breath was sharp and ragged in my lungs, but I called out to Artemis as he reared up over Arethusa like a wave, the emerging moon reflecting in his glistening crest.

The air stilled. My heels scraped against the earth as I halted. I could feel Artemis' rage pulsing in the silence. She must have been near enough to hear my desperate cry, or else she had sensed the presence of Alpheus herself. And before Alpheus could descend, the exhausted Arethusa disappeared, replaced in an instant by a cloud of mist. He turned his great head from side to side, searching for her. A steady patter of water dripped from the centre of the massed fog where she had been. Then, all at once a cleft opened up in the earth beneath and the cloud collapsed in upon itself, a torrent of water cascading into the ground.

Alpheus roared in frustration, foam bubbling furiously into the dirt as he dived after her, but I heard Artemis laugh softly behind me and I whipped my head around. 'Will he catch her?'

The goddess shook her head. 'He will try. He will pursue her as far as he can, but she is a fast-moving stream now, flowing all the way beneath the earth to the Underworld itself. He can't follow her that deep; he will have to come back to his own waters.'

'The Underworld?' I asked. 'Then is she dead?' She had been laughing on the riverbank only minutes ago.

Behind Artemis, I could see Callisto, her hair dripping and her tunic damp against her skin, her eyes wide with shock. She must have chased after us and seen what happened.

'Not at all,' Artemis said. 'She will flow back up to earth, to an island far from here. She will be a sacred spring, blessed by me.'

The glint in her eye stopped me from asking anything more. I looked behind her, seeing that Callisto had been joined by the other nymphs. I saw her sweep her arms into the air, tracing the shape of the cloud that had been a girl and the dawning comprehension on their faces as they listened. I didn't go back to them. I followed Artemis instead, my racing heart beginning to slow. Her stride through the trees was graceful, sure and confident. Her hair, as always, was caught up in tight braids at the back of her head, her legs bare beneath the knee-length hem of her tunic, her bow gleaming gold on her back. We passed the river from which I had fled, its waters as dark as the sky. The soft rush of the inky waves lapping against the bank sounded peaceful. The other nymphs had not returned. Perhaps Alpheus sulked somewhere in the depths, not daring to challenge Artemis. Calm had descended over the forest again. She stopped, perching on a rock to fasten her sandal, the strong line of her jaw and cheekbone silvered by the moonlight.

I couldn't let it go. I had too many questions and, wary as I was of angering her, I had to know more. I tried to keep my tone even as I spoke. 'So Arethusa is gone,' I said.

Artemis leaned back on her elbows, tilting her face to the sky. 'Ortygia is a beautiful island,' she said.

'It can't be as beautiful as here.'

'Well, if she wanted to stay, then she should have run faster.' Her tone was mild despite the cold finality of her words. 'It's a mercy to her that I didn't let Alpheus do what he wanted.'

I felt as though his fingers were still tangled in my hair. I shuddered.

'You've been hunting today,' Artemis said. 'I've taught you to be careful, warned you about the mountain lions and wolves that might want to tear into your flesh and eat you while you're still alive. But if one of those river-gods gets his hands on you . . . it's something different.'

I watched the fractured darts of moonlight play on the water. The grass brushed against my heels, the air soft and cool on my skin. 'So she's better off as she is now than if he'd caught her?'

Artemis sighed. 'She's free of men forever. So, better off than most.' She rolled over on the rock, resting her chin on her hands and looking at me squarely. She could have been any young woman: simply dressed, not weighed down by precious metals or fussy ornaments. Only her fearlessness marked her out, the steady determination of her gaze, her ease and her unapologetic confidence. 'You know I only leave the forests and go into cities for one reason,' she said.

I nodded. 'To answer women's prayers there.'

'Women's prayers in childbirth,' she said. 'There are so many of them, more than Eileithyia, goddess of labour pains, can help alone. I attend when I'm called, when they're desperate.' She shook her head, her eyes darkening. 'It's not something you'd ever want to see, when it gets desperate.'

'How bad is it?'

'Terrible. It's the first thing I saw: my mother, Leto, seized with labour pains. She was a Titaness and she was raped by Zeus. His wife, Hera, was furious – the last thing she wanted was more of his bastards in her way – so she cursed my mother so that she would never be able to give birth on either land or water. She roamed every inch of the world, her babies stuck, desperate and exhausted, until she found a floating island where at last she could bring me into the world. My twin brother, Apollo, though, he was a problem.' She laughed. 'No surprises there. It took her another full day, panting and sweating and screaming that she'd be torn in two. Fortunately, I was born clear-eyed and steady on my feet. I could see what the trouble was, and I helped her guide him out of her womb to safety. He didn't stay long with us, of course. He wasn't interested in helping her recover – he had a world to explore and conquer. I looked after her, nursed her broken body back to health. I gathered our food – that's how I learned to hunt.'

'Did Hera ever come after you again?' Artemis had never told me any of this before. If I'd thought about it at all, I'd assumed she'd sprung fully formed into the world, like her sister Athena, who stepped forth from Zeus' brow already clad in armour and ready to fight.

'No, she didn't dare. Zeus was pleased to have such skilled twins, so he put his foot down. I've never been interested in spending much time with the rest of them anyway, and Hera wouldn't care to come into the forests. I made a bargain with him: if he'd let me have the mountains and my girls, then I'd keep out of Hera's way. But the main thing I wanted was to live untouched by men. I wasn't going to find myself in my mother's position if I could help it.'

'What did he say?' It still felt like Artemis was telling me fanciful stories. She was so much a part of the forest, I couldn't picture her in a golden throne room, bargaining with the king of the immortals.

'He thought it was hilarious. A life of chastity is something he couldn't even begin to understand, but he agreed and let me alone to do what I want.' She smiled, satisfied.

Leaves rustled on the other side of the riverbank. As I watched, the foliage parted and a bear shambled out from under their cover, making her leisurely way to the rocks at the water's edge. Settling herself down, she cocked her great, shaggy head at us for a moment, then lowered it to drink. I felt the peace rippling out from Artemis, a moment of harmony so pure and perfect it felt like this was the world entire: us, the river and the bear. 'I wish I could have saved her,' I said. 'Before Alpheus got too close.'

'She is saved.'

I tried to imagine Ortygia; a faraway island with its lonely spring. What it would be like if that was me, if I had been easier prey for the river-god, like Arethusa was.

Artemis looked contented. I leaned back, trying to arrange my body the same way she did, hoping I had the same easy grace. Her words echoed in my head – *She should have run faster* – and I vowed that I would always be fast enough. Whatever dangers lurked in the forest, I could never let any of them catch up with me.

3

I didn't talk of Arethusa with Artemis again, but I thought about our conversation many times. It preoccupied me while I was out hunting alone, along with the memory of what Phiale had once told me about the nymphs never changing, never dying of old age. After Arethusa was lost to us, I understood a little better what the other harms were that could befall them. But I was a mortal, not a nymph, and I was changing. As I grew, I found myself yearning for something else – not to leave them or to change my happy life, but for something. I didn't know what it was that I was craving until I found a cave right in the heart of the forest, hidden deep in a valley, surrounded on all sides by a drop so sheer I was sure no other mortal could ever scale it, not that any would be likely to find their way so far into the woods. A ring of laurel trees encircled the cave, their trunks blanketed in velvet moss. Soft grasses sprang up across the earth, sprinkled with fiery orange crocuses and rich blue hyacinths, and a cold, clear stream flowed past the cave entrance.

I went back to the nymphs' grove and told them I had found

a home for myself. I was as surprised by my own words as Callisto was.

'Don't you want to live among us anymore?' she asked.

'I'll still be in the forest,' I said. I didn't know how to explain the urge I had to make a part of the forest mine alone. I'd shared everything with the nymphs from the day they had adopted me. Now I wanted something that belonged only to me.

Even though I couldn't explain it, Callisto seemed to understand. 'Don't stay away too long,' she said, and I promised that I wouldn't.

I soon learned every foothold on the steep slopes, how to drop lightly through the tree branches, testing the springy resilience of each beneath my weight, the distinct trills and chirps of every bird, the place where the streams met in a roaring surge and the currents would tussle against one another, dragging any unsuspecting swimmer under. I kept my promise to Callisto and joined the nymphs each day when they gathered at the banks of the shimmering brooks to drape themselves across the rocks, plaiting each other's hair and laughing in the sunshine. Sometimes I'd spot the darting shadow of a dryad, the rarely-seen guardian deities of the forest, not bold enough to join in the chatter, watching wistfully instead from the safety of the trees. Every evening, I was glad to make my way back to the cave alone, relishing the quiet.

Seasons passed, several cycles of them, and I grew stronger and more skilful with every year.

We never bathed in Alpheus' river again. But the memory of what happened to Arethusa had faded over time. I was fully grown, still a shade shorter than Artemis but taller than anyone else, and I doubted the river-god would have dared to grab at my hair in the water now anyway. The languorous, hazy days of summer stretched out; slow afternoons where the sun bore down and the pools we did visit were mirrors, still and shining. I joined the nymphs, lying on the rocks, sliding into the water when the heat became too much. Artemis was among us all the time, it seemed, laughing and singing, carefree as any of us. Only occasionally did I notice her gaze slide to the horizon, suddenly watchful, before the light came back into her eyes and she would smile at us again.

I always tried to go hunting early in the day, before the sun had risen. If I lost track of time, the heat would build while I was out on the sloping mountainsides, sending rivulets of sweat running down my spine, and however many skins of water I carried with me, it wouldn't be enough. On one such day, I found myself in a thickly wooded part of the forest, thirst pounding in my temples and the knife blade of the sun slicing through the leaves overhead. I tried to listen out for the tinkling of water over rocks or the splash of a nearby stream, but there was nothing. I pushed through the trees, finding a clearing scattered with heavy boulders but only parched, dried ground where I was sure there had once been a spring.

I glared at the heavy spear I carried, the one I'd carved myself, whose weight was now an encumbrance. I unhooked the empty skin that had held water from my belt, turning it inside out in the hope of finding a single drop to wet my lips, but there was nothing. I imagined filling it in the stream that ran by the entrance to my cave, scooping up that cold, fresh water. Dry air hissed between my teeth and, in a rush of frustration, I flung the spear at one of the rocks.

The sharpened point hit the stone with a resounding crack and I felt satisfaction flare up inside me. I turned around in a circle, getting my bearings again. I squinted through the ivy-clad tree trunks, trying to remember where the nearest stream would be. I pressed my thumbs to my forehead, feeling my pulse thumping thick and heavy through my skull. A relentless *drip, drip, drip* was distracting me from concentrating.

My eyes snapped open.

My spear lay on the ground where it had bounced off the hard rock, and I could see a trickle of water snaking down its length, dripping on to the earth when it reached the end. I followed it to its source: the crack where I'd hurled it, where the point had split the rock in two. Now a tiny spring bubbled up through the cleft, the water sparkling in the sunlight. Only tiny, but enough.

I threw myself on my knees beside it, pressing the empty skin to it. The water began to flow in earnest, spilling over the sides and soaking the earth around. I took long, grateful draughts and refilled the skin again. The heavy fuzz in my brain dissolved into clarity, the pain squeezing the sides of my head loosening with every gulp. At last, I knelt back up, feeling the satisfying stretch in my thighs, the delicious relief of tension and the tingle of exertion. I wiped my mouth with my hand and looked around the glade. The sunlight was slanting through now; it must be late afternoon. Rocking back on my heels, I grabbed my spear and stood up. I felt a little swell of pride as I glanced back at the spring; testament to the strength of my throw, to how I could make water flow from rock.

I made my way back to the nymphs. I decided it was too hot for hunting after all. Instead, I gathered wildflowers and let the nymphs plait them into my hair.

*   *   *

The heat built steadily for weeks, the weight of it becoming almost unbearable. There was no respite, even at night; my cave felt airless, not so much as a breeze to ruffle the trees outside.

When the storm came, it was a relief. Sheets of lightning tore the sky apart, thunder growled from the east and fat raindrops spattered into the pond, distorting the reflection of the stars. I laughed out loud, delighted by it. Impulsively, I jumped from my bed, desperate to feel the rain on my skin. Alone in the dark, unafraid, I twirled outside, bare feet on the damp earth, face upturned to the wild skies, letting the rain drench me. It ran down my hair in rivulets, soaking my thin tunic, deliciously cold, shocking the heaviness from my limbs at last.

I didn't hear her approach; the sound of her sobs must have been carried away by the winds. The clouds gathering over the moon obscured her from sight, the shape of her scrambling down the steep slopes towards me. The first I knew of her presence was when she barrelled into me and I grabbed her shoulders instinctively, my fingers tightening on her flesh as she tried to twist away. Her dark hair was plastered across her face, her breath coming in harsh, panicked bursts, and she felt like a fragile bird in my grasp.

'Callisto?' I asked.

She couldn't form the words to answer me. All that came out was a high, keening cry.

'Come inside, out of the rain.' She was still writhing, still fighting to be free, and I wondered if she knew me at all. Only that day we had swum together in the river, but she seemed to have lost all her senses to blind and desperate fear. 'It's me, Atalanta,' I said, trying to guide her into the cave without hurting her, making my voice as soothing and tender as I could. I thought of Artemis when one of the nymphs was hurt, the calm compassion in her voice as she bound up feet torn by unseen rocks, ankles bitten by abruptly awoken snakes, forearms clawed by the swipe of a bear foraging for the same berries. I tried to make myself sound like her, firm and gentle at the same time.

It worked, a little. Callisto stopped pushing back against me, and although her shoulders were still rigid with tension, her chest still heaving, she let me take her in. I gathered up the animal skins I'd cast aside before the storm, and wrapped them around her shoulders, wringing the water from her hair. Gradually, her shivers subsided and the awful gasps quieted.

In the darkness, I sat beside her, not sure what to do next. 'What happened?' I asked.

She hesitated. I couldn't make out her expression. 'The storm,' she said. Her voice was thin and ragged. 'It was the storm.'

'Did you get caught out in it? Couldn't you find your way home?'

She dipped her head. Behind her, at the cave entrance, I could hear the rain slackening off to a light patter. The wind was dropping, the branches swaying gently now and the clouds dissipating, the moonlight casting ghostly beams on the dark ripples of the pool. 'I got lost.' She was quiet for a long moment. 'I thought Artemis was there, but she wasn't. She wasn't there.'

I could feel the unspoken question hovering between us – *Who was there instead?* – but the way she folded her body in on itself, clutching her arms close to her chest, her head half-turned away from me, made the words die in my throat before I could speak them aloud. 'You're safe here,' I said instead.

37

Her hand clutched at mine. 'Thank you.'

'Sleep here tonight,' I told her.

Callisto was silent while I laid out the skins, but she nestled into them, another half-sob gulping out as she pulled them close around her. I stroked her hair, wondering what else to say. I didn't know how to give voice to the gathering suspicion in my mind of what she had encountered out there in the storm, or if I even should.

I cast a glance at my bow, leaning ready against the cave wall. The long spear at its side, the knife I sharpened daily against the rocks. Then back to the cave entrance. There was nothing to be seen out there; the storm had died away and the usual quiet peace was resuming.

Never had I feared to sleep alone. Since finding my cave, I had never shared it with anyone. I was surprised to find that the sound of her breathing, uneven at first but slowly steadying, was comforting.

I wrapped furs around myself and lay down beside her, watching the dawn seep through the darkness until my eyes grew too heavy and I slept.

The sunlight woke me, vivid and disorientating. I sat up, squinting against its harsh brightness, much higher in the sky than when I usually awoke.

'Atalanta.'

I whipped my head around. She was a silhouette against the dim interior of the cave. 'Callisto, are you feeling better?'

'Much better, thank you.' She sounded stilted. In the daylight, the events of the night before seemed unreal, tinged by doubt. I wondered if it was possible that she was simply embarrassed by her fear in the night, her foolishness in getting lost in the storm. For a moment, I basked in that idea, reassuring in its simplicity.

I yawned. My eyes were refocusing, adjusting to the light. I took her in. The brief moment of warm hope was draining away with the last remnants of sleep. 'Your tunic,' I said. 'It's so torn.'

'I must have caught it on the branches when I was running down here,' she said.

I looked more closely at her, at the long rips in the fabric and the bruises blooming on her upper arms. 'Artemis will have a poultice, something healing.'

I couldn't mistake the panic that flared in her eyes as she shook her head vehemently. 'I don't need anything. There's no need to tell Artemis.'

I opened my mouth, but the imploring look she gave me stopped me short. A long moment passed. 'Are you hungry?' I said instead.

She shook her head. 'I'll go. Thank you – for giving me shelter.'

There was something behind her words, a shadow in her eyes or something about the way she was holding herself, so unlike the carefree girl I was used to seeing running through the forest. But I didn't know how to ask her. I watched her leave, cautious on the uphill climb as though she was guarding an injury, mindful not to hurt herself more.

I looked for her by the pools, in the glades, out in the quiet places in the woods. For a few days, she didn't appear at all, but when she rejoined the others, it was with the same smile on her face as ever. Only rarely did I see her falter, her lips trembling for a moment or her eyes glazing over, staring at something I couldn't see. It was always so fleeting I could wonder sometimes if I had imagined it entirely.

There were no more storms. The leaves began to turn golden and burnished bronze, drifting from the trees, gathering in heaps of vivid, glowing colour. Cold breezes began to whistle through the depleted branches, and every morning I woke to drifting mists, dissipating into drizzle in the weakening rays of the sun. In the afternoons, before the light faded, I stitched together deer pelts and draped them over my shoulders for warmth. The forest quieted; the chorus of buzzing insects and chirping crickets that heralded the warmer months gave way to silence, the bears retreated to their mountain caves and the highest peaks were dusted with snow. When we gathered, all of us were snuggled in furry cloaks, the cold making roses bloom on our cheeks. I loved the snap in the air, the sparkle of frost, the bare skeletons of the trees, black against the soft white sky.

Artemis was often pensive when winter drew in. 'She grieves for her friend,' Callisto told me as we walked together. 'Her childhood companion, Persephone.'

'You told me about her once,' I said.

Callisto nodded. 'Artemis still misses the time they shared together, before the day that Hades split the earth in two, caught hold of Persephone and dragged her down to his world.' Her voice cracked and I glanced at her, surprised.

'I didn't know she was taken like that.' They'd told me Hades had fallen in love. I felt a spasm of pity for the laughing girl picking wildflowers with her friends before the ground tore open beneath her feet.

'You've heard of Persephone from the nymphs,' Callisto said. 'Not from Artemis. She doesn't speak of her now, but if she did, she would tell you differently.'

'What would she say?'

Callisto looked meditatively into the distance. 'She'd say that Persephone loved to be in sunlight. That the days they spent together among the flowers were the happiest she'd known. That she let those days of freedom slip away like the glass beads of a necklace dropped carelessly to the floor, never knowing how they would shatter.'

I kept my face very still, hardly daring to breathe in case it interrupted her. It was the first time she had spoken to me like this since the night of the storm.

'Demeter plunged the world into its first, most brutal winter when she learned what had happened to her daughter. She swore she would never allow the earth to bring forth grain or crops or flowers again, that everything would wither away and die, and every living creature would suffer in grief along with her. The other gods forced Hades to give Persephone up for part of every year, to let her return so that her mother will bring the world to life each spring. She only renders it barren when Persephone descends again.'

'Then Persephone wasn't lost forever,' I ventured.

'Those innocent days on Sicily were ended.' The bleakness in Callisto's tone forbade any further reply. 'Persephone's vow was broken. Everything changed.'

I knew her meaning for certain when the crocuses peeped up outside my cave again, when buds sprouted and swelled on the trees, when the trilling of birds greeted the dawn and the starkness of winter was swallowed up in the profusion of life that accompanied Persephone's annual ascension. The nymphs shrugged off their thick furs, returned to the bathing pools. Only Callisto hung back, reluctant, still swathed in a heavy dress, until Artemis grew impatient and commanded her to join.

I saw it in Callisto's face, the resignation, the defeat as she pulled away the draped fabric that hid her shape. The stunned silence in the grove as she stood before us all and we saw it at last, the rounded curve of her belly. I cast my eyes around the circle of nymphs and back to Callisto, pinned in the centre of their horrified gaze. I didn't dare look at Artemis.

The goddess strode towards her, spear flashing at her side. 'What's the meaning of this?' Her voice was cold.

Callisto lifted her chin. I felt a pang of sympathy for her, but more powerful was the churning dread at what would happen next. 'The storm, last summer,' she said, and the final piece fell into place in my mind. 'Zeus, the wielder of thunderbolts. You didn't hear his approach, you didn't know he came here, concealed in the chaos.'

Artemis snorted. 'So you welcomed him here, in our forest?'

'I thought he was you. He took your shape, your form. In your voice, he called to me, urging me to follow, to take shelter from the rain. Thinking it was you, I went where he told me, and when he took hold of me and I saw who he truly was, there was no way I could escape.'

I swallowed, remembering the dazed, panic-stricken girl that had scrambled down the banks to my cave. The bruises on her arms, her torn dress, the blankness in her eyes.

'All who follow me must abide by one condition,' Artemis said.

'I had no choice.'

But we all knew there was nothing to be gained by pleading. Callisto knew it as well as any of us. Tears sprang up in her eyes, her arms wrapped around her swollen body as she sank to her knees, weeping bitterly.

Artemis laid her hand on the girl's head. Her expression

was hard, unmoving, as she stood for an agonising moment, then stepped away.

And, before all of our eyes, Callisto's shuddering shoulders seemed to cave in, her body contorting. I saw her hands fly up to her face, but her fingernails were lengthening into curved claws. Her arms bristled with dark fur and her sobs became growls, any words she could have grasped at to defend herself lost to her forever. Where there had been a desperate girl, there was now an animal, a beast of the forest, a bear like the one who had taken pity on me when I was a newborn, but there was no pity in our goddess for Callisto. Only a harsh determination as she watched the desperate creature take in its transformation, look at us from one to the other, and then turn and flee the grove.

4

All of us grieved for Callisto, even Artemis. I noticed how sometimes she would look into the distance, lost inside herself for a moment, and I was sure she thought of Callisto. Of Persephone, too, perhaps Arethusa and others. Although Artemis had the face of a young woman, who was to say how many she'd lost in all of her immortal years?

Sometimes at night, I looked out at the patch of sky visible through the sloping arch of my cave and tried to trace Callisto's shape in the stars. I wished I'd been out on the night of the storm, that I could have been with her, that I could have helped her run.

My sadness lingered and I couldn't seem to shake it off. It dragged at me all through that spring, while the flowers bloomed around me in a riot of colour, while the forest awakened to glorious life. When I was out hunting, my aim faltered or my quarry outran me altogether; worse, I didn't even care. The days felt flat and the afternoons long and tedious, though somehow they would spill through my fingers with nothing accomplished at all.

It was on such an afternoon that I found myself far away from my cave, the light draining from the day altogether. Cursing, I squinted through the trees and forced myself to focus again. To listen carefully, to feel the direction of the breeze, to notice the markers by which I navigated: a fallen trunk cloaked in moss, a tumbling brook, a cluster of violets. I took a long, deep breath and let it all flood in, all the instincts ingrained within me, the memories imprinted in my muscles that I relied upon, that had never let me down before. I set off with confidence, sure I'd reach home. I cast a glance at the sky, the indigo edges softening to pink, and picked up my pace, the familiar feeling of it humming through me, the comforting rhythm of who I had always been.

As I'd predicted, I found the pool, lined with rocks and surrounded by ferns, its soft green depths reflecting distorted tree trunks and a shimmering sky. Ruffles whispered across the surface of the water, a darker shadow leaning out across the opposite bank, and I felt her eyes upon me before I saw her. The bear, her face lowered to drink, but her attention seized by my appearance. The cub nuzzling into her side. Her eyes fixed on mine, dark and deep and steady.

I stopped, suspended in her gaze. I stared back, searching those big black pupils for something else, something more. I felt the desperation yawning inside me, but she shook herself and turned away, back into the undergrowth, her baby safe against her flank.

I didn't move again, didn't trust my legs to carry me. The shadows grew long, the sky bruising overhead and the flame of the sun dipping below the trees, swallowed up in the dark pool.

Dusk had settled and I was still so far from home. I pushed

down my loneliness, my longing, resettled the quiver of arrows and the bow strapped across my back, and stepped away from the water. Even in the dark, I knew this forest.

Above, in the gaps in the canopy, the stars began to glimmer. The thin crescent of the moon hung pearlescent, and I heard the long, mournful hoot of an owl. Dark silhouettes fluttered through the branches, frogs croaked and fireflies flashed here and there.

Then, for a terrible moment, I thought thunder cracked through the skies again, but the sudden tumult I heard came from the forest, not the heavens. A crashing of heavy bodies, snapping twigs, the rumble of deep voices and laughter. And fire, a sudden surge of flames leaping high, the smoke hot and thick and choking. My eyes streaming, I backed against the wide trunk of an oak tree, my hand pressed over my nose and mouth as I looked for the source.

Their bodies didn't make sense to me at first. I'd heard of centaurs, but I'd never seen them for myself. There were two of them, lurching through the trees, great boughs twisting and breaking as they forced their way through. They held pine torches, huge limbs torn down from mighty trees and set ablaze in their fists. One of them clutched a spear, too, crudely fashioned but sharp enough.

I could smell the wine before I saw the skins they carried, the dark liquid slopping out of the open necks. I was amazed they hadn't set themselves alight, though behind them, I could see trees burning where they had swung the torches.

They were taller than any man I'd seen, as tall as Artemis herself. Their torsos were thick and corded with muscle, their beards tangled over their chests, and, at their waists, the inexplicable join where man became horse. But something I might have marvelled at in curiosity by day was altogether more menacing in the smoke-filled dark.

I saw recognition dawning in the drink-glazed eyes of the centaur closest to me, and he swung a fist at his companion, knocking him clumsily in the chest. 'Hylaios,' he said, his voice a heavy rumble. 'Look here.'

The second, Hylaios, peered at me, and I saw excitement grip him. 'A girl, Rhoikos, all alone in the woods.' He took a long swig, his gaze wandering up and down my body.

My fists curled. I had come face to face with snarling lions and hungry wolves, and while these two beasts might have the same ravenous spark in their eyes, I could see how the wine made their legs totter and sway beneath their weight.

As intoxicated as he was, Rhoikos seemed to sense my disdain. 'She doesn't look very pleased to see us,' he said. They had come to a halt a few paces away, but now he stepped closer to where I stood. He moved more smoothly than I'd expected, horse flanks rippling in the moonlight, powerful and mesmerising. I felt a stirring of fear for the first time, a flutter of realisation as I sized him up. My fingers twitched as I thought of reaching up behind me for the bow and arrows strapped to my back. He'd close the gap between us before I could do it. His torch crackled, casting shadows across his craggy face, and I held myself completely still, not flinching at the reek of his breath.

'Pass through this forest,' I said, keeping my voice low and steady. 'It belongs to Artemis.'

He smiled.

It was Hylaios who grabbed me. While I was focused on Rhoikos, Hylaios leapt forward, threw down his wine skin along with his torch, and wrapped his meaty arms around me, wresting me from the tree. The shock of it forced the air out of my chest; for a moment I was immobilised, pressed against the heat of his body, both of them laughing. The fire from his discarded torch caught a hanging branch, flames leaping up behind them.

'Let her go!'

Their heads turned at the sound of another voice. Even in the chaos, I knew it wasn't Artemis or even a nymph. It was a man's voice. I took advantage of the centaurs' distraction, pulled my arm free and jammed my elbow hard into Hylaios' chest. He staggered back, and I saw a fleeting glance of the man's face – the horror in his eyes, his mouth wide as he looked at them – just as Rhoikos swung his fist right at the intruder's head and he reeled back, collapsing on the ground. Rhoikos turned back to me, his face triumphant, but I was ready now. I ducked, slipping under his arm so that his grasp closed on thin air, and I darted away, jumping over the prone figure of my would-be rescuer as I sprinted back along the riverbank. My feet were flying over the ground, dodging every root and boulder, but the centaurs gave chase, trampling everything in their path, Rhoikos' torch igniting the trees in their wake.

The noise and the tumult might attract the attention of others, my innocent companions, and as I fled up the sloping sides of the mountain, that thought slowed me down. It wasn't enough to outrun my pursuers; they'd only find slower prey. I wasn't going to let it be another girl.

I swung around, yanking an arrow from the quiver at my back and unhooking my bow in one smooth motion. Without pausing for even a second's hesitation, I bent back the string and let the arrow fly, right at Rhoikos' throat.

He tumbled in front of Hylaios, who reared back and

crashed to the earth beside his stricken friend. The breath was harsh in my throat, my chest heaving, but my fingers were steady as I reached for a second arrow.

'Please,' Hylaios said, raising himself up on his elbows, looking between me and his companion, at the blood gushing out around the arrow lodged deep in Rhoikos' neck. I narrowed my eyes and took aim. 'Please, don't—' he managed to say, but my arrow sailed through the air before he could finish begging. He looked down as though astonished by the sight of it protruding from his chest, before his eyes rolled up and his head fell to the earth.

I watched them for a few moments, until I could be sure that their breath had stopped. Then I took a long breath of my own, feeling the air cool and fresh in my lungs. Down the sides of the mountain, smoke rose from the fires they had set, flames dancing at intervals to mark their path. I seethed at the wanton destruction, the carelessness and the brutality.

But the man, I remembered, the one who had attempted to intervene. He had been knocked to the ground; he might still be lying there unconscious. My eyes traced the path back down, the pockets of fire. He might have inhaled too much smoke already; he might not have been able to pull himself clear. He could already be dead. I gritted my teeth.

My arrows were no use against fire, and if the smoke overwhelmed me, my speed and strength would count for nothing, either. It wouldn't be my fault if he died, if he wasn't dead already; it would be his for interfering where he wasn't needed. The pang of my conscience told me that wasn't true before I could begin to try to convince myself otherwise. He'd tried to save me; I couldn't leave without trying to save him.

I yanked at the bottom of my tunic, ripping a length of it

free, and I dipped it into the river. Further down, the water glowed orange, reflecting the inferno. I pressed the damp cloth to my mouth and nose and, not giving myself time to think any more about it, I ran back the way I had come. My eyes streamed in the thick, black smoke, branches toppled about me, and I didn't know if I could even retrace my steps to the clearing. Panic threatened to crest within me, and I forced it down. I kept the river to my side, following it down the slope, and, without realising I was nearly upon it, I burst through into the clear space between the oak trees. He lay in the spot where he had fallen, but when I dropped to my knees at his side, I saw that his chest was rising and his eyelids fluttered open. He focused on me, bleary confusion clouding his eyes, and he moaned.

'You need to get up,' I said.

He must have seen the flames then, for he jolted up, his face full of horror.

'Now. There's no time.' I looked at the side of his blood-streaked face, where the centaur's fist had struck him. The blood here was thick and clotted, not pumping from the wound.

He grimaced as he twisted himself over into a crouch. I held out my hand for his, pulling him to stand. He stumbled a little, but he was upright, and I felt a surge of relief. Too soon, for he sagged against me.

'My shoulder . . .' he gasped.

He clutched his hand to the opposite shoulder, wincing in pain. Blood was streaming through his fingers.

'. . . spear . . .' he managed.

Rhoikos' spear. He must have plunged it in before giving chase to me. I braced myself. 'It's lucky he missed your heart or your throat,' I said. 'Lean on me, I'll help you to walk.'

I took his other arm, looping it around my shoulders so that I could hold him steady. The flames reared up on every side and I turned around, suddenly uncertain. The heat felt like a solid wall, pressing in against us, the relentless crackle drowning out all other sound. I couldn't get in enough air, my chest was tightening, and the fear was creeping back in, twisting and treacherous.

I searched frantically for a gap, a dark space between the burning trees.

'This way,' I told him, and plunged forwards.

The fire raged around us. Every buckling step we took, every lurch forward, I was sure would be the moment that we succumbed to the suffocating heat. I could see nothing in front of us, the fire obliterating everything, but I dragged him onwards. I wasn't going to die here, and I wasn't going to leave him to die, either.

We staggered through a clearing and I saw what I was hoping for: a wide stream, gushing over rocks. Our saviour.

We splashed through it, over to the other side. The smoke still billowed in thick clouds from the fire we left behind us, but for now, the water held it back. I scooped some up in my hands, splashing it on his face and then mine. He coughed violently, retching, then he dropped to his knees and cupped some water in his hands, gulping it down. At last, he rocked back on his heels and looked up at me, his eyes less glazed.

'Can you walk?' I asked him.

He nodded.

'Then come now, as fast as you can.'

I led him towards the quiet dark, away from the noise and the ravaging fire, looking for familiar landmarks. I was intent upon the route, the dissipating smoke, the fresh, clean scent of the trees. As peace descended, the path illuminated in the soft light of the moon rather than the livid glare of fire, I saw that we were not far from the steep bank that led down to my cave. I stopped and he came to a clumsy halt alongside me. 'I can't go much further with you,' I said. 'Can you go on alone?'

He was panting, exhausted, his face drained of colour. Although his hand was still clenched hard over his shoulder, the blood had stopped pouring. I hoped that meant the wound wasn't too deep.

'Go where?' he asked.

'Wherever you came from.'

He looked confused, and so young. I wondered what on earth had possessed him to stand up to a centaur.

Tentatively, he drew his hand away from his shoulder, flinching as he did so. He shuddered, looking at the raw edges of his torn skin and the dark stain across his ripped tunic. But he drew himself up, standing without my support.

Now he looked at me for the first time, taking me in; my short tunic, ragged and soot-smeared, my scratched and grimy limbs, and the bow and quiver tied to my back.

'What were you doing in the forest anyway?' I asked him.

'I got separated from my companions,' he said. 'It grew dark, I was walking in circles – and then I saw the torches. When I came closer and saw what they were and that one of them had seized you ...' Reflexively, he touched the wound on the side of his head and winced.

'I didn't need you to help me.'

'Clearly not.'

'You need to keep going, up on to the ridge there. You can follow the downward slope all the way. There are settlements at the bottom; some huntsmen live there.' I glanced around us. Now that the immediate danger of the fire had passed, a different anxiety was prickling at me. The flames couldn't escape Artemis' notice for long; she would be back, and when she returned, she would be furious. I wanted this man gone before she arrived.

'Is that where you live?' he asked.

I shook my head.

He nodded, as though I'd confirmed an answer to a question he hadn't asked. 'Can I ask your name?'

'Atalanta.'

'Mine is Hippomenes,' he said.

'Good luck, Hippomenes. Get out of this forest as quickly as you can. Don't linger.'

Trees encircled us, towering shadows tipped with silver moonlight far above our heads. The sky that was visible through the leaves was clear and starlit. Here, it felt as though the fire was a distant nightmare. I wondered if, by morning, he would doubt that any of this had ever happened. Only his pierced shoulder would confirm that it had.

He drew in a long breath. 'Goodbye, Atalanta. And . . . thank you.'

I stood back, not wanting to start towards my cave in case he turned around. I wouldn't want him, or anyone else, to know its location. That's what I told myself. That was why I watched him climb, unsteady still, but with a lithe agility that surprised me. I stepped back among the spreading branches of the oak behind me, but I kept my eyes on him as he swung himself up on to the high ridge, a beam of moonlight falling on him as he looked from side to side before turning down in the direction I'd told him, swiftly swallowed up by the thicket of trees.

I stayed a while longer, just to make sure he'd really gone.
'Atalanta.'

My knees buckled.

She stood tall, unbowed and imperious. Her perfect face more incandescent than the glow of the inferno, her fury burning hotter than a thousand fires ever could.

I tried to speak, to tell her what had happened, but she waved her arm to silence me.

'I saw the bodies of the centaurs,' she said. 'It was well done, Atalanta. Slaying two of them would be beyond any other mortal.'

'The fire . . .' I said.

She tossed her head. 'The forest is mine,' she said. 'I wouldn't let it burn.'

I saw behind her that the forest was no longer aflame; no crimson halo above the trees, only the quiet dark of the night. Had she seen Hippomenes? Did she know that I'd helped him? She gave no sign of it if she did.

'You can go,' she said. 'Sleep now, you've earned it.'

Relief and gratitude washed over me. 'Thank you,' I said.

She smiled. Then she darted back into the depths of the forest.

But I didn't leave the shelter of the oak, not straight away.

I wondered if Hippomenes would make it safely to the hunters' cottages. If they would welcome him when he arrived, sore and tired and full of incredible stories. If they would take him in, give him warm broth and wrap him in animal pelts, bathe his cuts and give him ointments for his bruises. Out there, on the fringes of the forest where the trees gave way to rolling plains and then to hamlets, farms, villages and cities, all beyond the reaches of the world I knew, places that I had never been. All I knew came from Artemis' descriptions, from the scraps of stories she would share of where she'd travelled.

I plucked a leaf from a low bough, rubbing it between my fingers to release the fresh, sharp scent of it. The oak was sturdy, familiar and reliable beside me. It could have been here since the formation of the world, standing steady through battles of Titans and gods, witness to the start of everything. I stayed there, in its embrace, and it was long after Hippomenes and Artemis had vanished that I made my way down to my cave in the misty, rose-tinged light of dawn.

5

My dreams were full of smoke and fire, confused fragments of chaos and shouting, mocking laughter and the hiss of my arrows. I jerked awake, my throat raw and my pulse racing.

My cave was the same as it always was, silent and peaceful. I drew in a long breath, shaking off the vestiges of the panic that had awoken me. The centaurs were dead and I was the one to have killed them. I let the thought settle. The danger had passed and it was thanks to me.

I wanted to see Artemis and hoped she was still close, not hunting on the furthest edge of the forest or answering the pleas of desperate mothers in the cities. I made my way as fast as I could to the riverbank where the centaurs had found me. It was easy to follow the trail; scorched circles of bare earth marked where they had been, and flakes of ash still spiralled in the breeze. Never mind the ruin they had caused, I reminded myself. They wouldn't have the opportunity to rampage again. I wondered for a horrified second if I would come across their bodies, but there were only crushed flowers and bent stems where I had left them. I could see the flattened path where

Artemis must have dragged them, and I could imagine her slender frame and how she would haul their vast weight as though it was nothing. A heap of freshly turned earth a little distance away suggested she had buried them there. I looked at it for a moment and then turned away. I didn't care about where they were, only her.

I wandered distractedly, glad to move away from the bare, burned sections of the forest, further into the leafy glades. I heard her dogs first, the excited barking and then two of them bursting out on to the path in front of me. I smiled to see them, patting their great heads and scratching their ears. 'Where is your mistress?' I asked them, but their eyes were closed in bliss and I laughed until the first pulled back and loped away, cocking his head back at me to see that I followed. I and the other dog followed him to the grove where the unfortunate young hunter had surprised her once before. She wasn't bathing today; she sat watchful and poised on a boulder at the water's edge, surrounded by the nymphs.

Her eyes were steady on me as I approached. I found it hard to lift mine to meet hers, something like guilt gnawing at me, restless and inexplicable. But when she spoke, there was no disapprobation in her tone, only a warmth that surprised me. 'Atalanta, come closer. Sit here,' she urged.

My shoulders loosened, the tension in my body unlocking as I pulled myself up on to the flat surface of the rock beside her. 'Last night—' I began.

'Last night you slew two centaurs,' she said. 'You, a mortal girl, against the strength of creatures more powerful than any man.' She laughed. Her cheeks flushed pink and her eyes sparkled; her hair was pulled back from her face and her knees drawn up with her arms looped around them. She was the picture of youth and radiance. There was nothing of the seething anger I had seen in her as she surveyed her burning forest, no hint of the ancient power and immortal rage she possessed. 'You stopped them before they could harm you or do any more damage to our home. If they had made their way further in, found my nymphs . . .' She let the silence conjure up a vivid image. 'But you, Atalanta, they were no match for you.'

I dipped my head, heat spreading across my chest, not sure what to say.

She nodded, satisfied. 'You proved yourself,' she said. 'Your prowess is a testament to my teaching, everything you're capable of, having grown up here, under my tutelage, in my forest.'

I felt the glow of her approval like sunshine on my skin. Somehow, I had thought she might reprimand me, that I might have erred in letting them cause what damage they did, or in my mercy to Hippomenes, if she'd seen it.

'It was very impressive,' Psekas chimed in from the river-bank, where she dangled her feet in the water, turning her head to smile at me.

'We knew you were strong, but—' Phiale swooped in at my side, handing me a cup of water.

'This surpasses anything we thought,' Crocale finished.

I paused. I realised now that all the nymphs were looking at me, and there was something different in their expression – more than just the warm friendliness I was used to, but a new admiration. There was a seriousness in the air, a quiet acknowledgement of what could have been, had I not averted it.

I sat taller, my spine straight and my head lifted, as more voices rang out, their happy tones mingling together in an excited stream of congratulations commending my bravery, my accuracy, my fearless instincts and selfless actions.

I wished so much that Callisto could have been there to share in it. Only one consolation lightened the sadness I felt when I thought of her; I had made sure no other nymph last night had suffered like she had done.

I let them coax the story from me, enjoying their gasps and delight as I described it. I didn't mention Hippomenes. I felt it turn into something else, sitting at the centre of the group in the sunlight, shaping it into a tale of suspense and excitement, one that captivated the nymphs and even Artemis herself. As I related how the second centaur fell to my arrow, I felt the last remnants of horror and revulsion at the memory of their grasping hands on my body dissolve. It was my story now, and it would live on in the legends of the forest, something the nymphs would tell again and again. But this one wouldn't be passed on in hushed tones, with meaningful looks and heavy warnings. It was a victory, clear and joyful, and one that would define me. *That was Atalanta*, I imagined them saying in years to come, *slayer of centaurs*, and the listeners would be as riveted as they were now.

I think it was the sweetest moment of my life so far.

I was always alert when I stalked the forests, always looking for tracks in the earth and listening for the softest flutter of leaves to tell me that my prey was close or that a hungry mountain lion might be prowling nearby, intent on the same quarry. But it was different that summer. When I saw something move in my peripheral vision, when I darted my head to see, I knew what I hoped the fleeting shape I saw might be.

I searched for bears and cubs. Of everything in the forest, no one knew better than I to leave them alone. In the early months, there was nothing more ferocious in these woods than a protective mother bear. Still, I lingered on every riverbank, combing the ferns on the other side with my eyes, waiting to see if she stepped out again. If I could look into her eyes again and be sure – well, of what? I didn't know what I would do, but it didn't stop me looking.

I watched for Hippomenes too. Surely he would have learned his lesson, not to wander recklessly out here again. He would keep to the hunters' cottages, the far-flung villages and settlements that men had made on the edges of our world, and not risk crossing over.

The loops I took got wider. I'd always kept close to the wild heart of the woods, intent upon the secrets that belonged to Artemis and us, her companions. Now I found myself skirting the unmarked boundaries, the outer edges and high ridges where I could crane my neck and peer over to where I could sometimes see thin spirals of smoke or hear the distant blare of a hunting horn. Perhaps I was patrolling our territory; perhaps it was the sensible thing to do, after such a violent intrusion.

That's what I'd say to Artemis, if she asked.

Summer took hold, but already I was thinking of winter. Callisto's voice came floating back to me; Persephone stepping into the shadowy caverns below. The world above held fast in cold, silent grief.

When Callisto had told me the story, I'd heard in it hope, a confirmation of what I'd always known. The forest lived in cycles, it came back new and nourished, always dependable and always the same. I had never wanted anything to change.

I thought ahead to another spring, another summer. A tiny

hunger had opened up inside me, a gnawing sense of dissatisfaction.

I pushed ahead, hunting with zeal, bringing back the carcasses for the nymphs and going out again. Piling up wood for our fires, sharpening my knife, carving more arrows and watching the quiet forest as dusk fell, looking for blazing torches, listening out for thunder.

Artemis noticed my busy industriousness. High up on the slopes, in the territory of the mountain lions, she told me to sit. 'But the sun is still high.' Surprised, I gestured to the sky.

'Sit,' she said again, swinging herself up on to a rock. 'Look, Atalanta, even the hounds are exhausted.'

Around her, the dogs had flung themselves to the ground in the patch of shade provided by the jutting rock, their flanks heaving and tongues lolling. A restless impatience rolled through me, but I did as she said. From here, I could see the forest laid out beneath us, dense and green and seemingly endless.

'Things are happening out in the world beyond here,' she said, her abruptness startling me. 'The gods are talking about it – a voyage unlike any other, a new quest. It's caught their attention on Mount Olympus. A king of a city called Iolcus has given his nephew a quest: to gather together the greatest band of heroes from across all of Greece to sail with him on his ship, the *Argo*, from Pagasae harbour in search of a Golden Fleece.'

I felt the world fall still. Artemis had never cared about the preoccupations of the other gods or what was happening in the mortal world. A sense of anticipation flickered to life inside me.

'You have power and courage, speed and skill far beyond what's needed in this forest,' she said. 'And you're better already than any warrior out there. You're greater than any man laying claim to the name of a hero. The world should know the name Atalanta. They should see what you can do.'

Artemis laid one hand on top of mine and, with the other, drew my chin up so I looked directly into her face. As light as her touch felt, it was impossible to turn away even a fraction.

'The nephew, a man called Jason, is going to bring back the Fleece,' she went on. 'He wants to prove himself worthy, make himself a legend. He has the backing of Hera, who wants a hero to glorify her name, not another that is the son of Zeus or Poseidon, but one who owes his loyalty to her,' she said. 'All that sail with him will earn fame and glory along the way.' Her eyes looked steadily into mine and she smiled. 'I want my share.'

'How?' I breathed.

'You go, in my name. You are stronger than them, you are fearless, and there is nothing that any one of them can do that you cannot. I want you to show them all who you are, what you have become.'

I hesitated. 'I've never been to sea. I've never been outside this forest. I don't know where Iolcus is, or Pagasae either.' The unfamiliar names felt pleasing to say.

'It doesn't matter,' she said. 'No one learns more quickly than you.'

I could feel a response to her challenge creeping in. A straightening in my spine, a wash of energy.

'Go, Atalanta.' Her stare burned into me. 'Board the *Argo* as my champion. Be the best of them all.'

I let the seductive promise of it fill my mind, sweeping aside any doubt or uncertainty. She'd put a name to the tiny glimmer of yearning I'd felt before, and now it yawned open into a desire more urgent than any I'd ever known. 'I'll do as you command,' I answered.

Her eyes shone with satisfaction.

If I could have leapt off that rock and run to the *Argo*, I would have done it. It would have been better to take advantage of the impetuous thrill of it, and plunge in without hesitation. But Artemis said I needed to wait, that there were preparations to make first of all. She was gone for several days, seeking advice from the oracle at Delphi, and my impatience grew. I couldn't see what there was to do. I paced the forest, practising my aim, bending back my bow and letting my arrows fly, the instinctual action of it helping to push down any niggling thoughts I had: how I would navigate unfamiliar terrain, what it would be like to be among a band of men, what terrors we might face along the way. Without Artemis there to bolster my confidence, I had to tell myself that I would succeed, that there would be nothing I couldn't handle, no foe that could run faster or shoot with better accuracy than me.

Still, I was glad when she appeared in my glade just as twilight dimmed to a soft violet, her tread so gentle over the bright flowers spread before the cave entrance that she barely disturbed even one of their drooping heads.

'Are you ready?' she asked.

I pressed my hand against the stone arch of the cave entrance to steady myself. 'Now?'

'You will set off at dawn,' she said.

I nodded. 'What more do I need to know before I leave?'

The air around her smelled of earth and fresh green shoots; a stillness charged with energy, as though she was poised in the instant before a hunt begins, when the world hums, alert and alive and intent upon the chase.

'A prophecy,' she said.

'About me? What does it say?'

She hooked back a stray curl that had sprung loose from the braids coiled around her head. 'The oracle at Delphi speaks my brother Apollo's words. He can see into the heart of everything; what is to come is laid out before him, and he chooses what to share. You must listen carefully to his warning and abide by it or suffer the consequences.'

I could hear something ancient breathing through her, a timbre in her voice that thrilled with ageless knowledge.

'My followers make the same vow as I did,' she went on. 'We all swear to a life of virginity. We are safe and free to live unencumbered, to hunt and be self-sufficient away from the rest of the world. But you didn't choose to join me, Atalanta; you were left in my forest as a newborn baby.'

'I live as you do, though,' I said. I had never questioned the condition that came along with being one of Artemis' devotees.

'You have never been among men.' Her lip curled a little. 'You have never had your resolve tested.'

'I've seen enough of men, even here in the forest,' I interjected.

'Hold on to what you've seen.' Her tone was low and passionate. 'Don't forget your sisters, what became of them. When you board the *Argo*, keep them at the forefront of your mind. Remember that when the adventure is done, your home is here with me.'

'I will.' I felt flustered by the doubt implicit in her words. Why wouldn't she trust me to hold fast to the fundamental rule she had always taught me?

'Good,' she said. 'For it isn't my decree alone, Atalanta. The prophecy that comes to you from the oracle is that marriage will be your undoing. If you take a husband, you will lose yourself.'

I shook my head. 'I'd never take one anyway. I've never dreamed of it.'

'You're so much luckier than you know,' Artemis said. 'Outside my protection, for other girls, there is no choice in it at all. It's another of your gifts, Atalanta, your freedom. It's one you must never give up or toss away carelessly.'

A flush was rising in my cheeks now. I straightened up, folding my arms across my chest. 'I will board the *Argo* as your champion. I'll honour you in everything I do. And then I'll come home.' I looked around my little cave, the peaceful grove, the star-strewn sky and the comforting black shapes of the trees all around. I'd hold the memory of it close to my heart.

'Then sleep now.' Artemis looked behind her and whistled. I heard the rustle of her dogs in the ferns up on the ridge above and saw them emerge, silhouetted against the moon, ears pricked up eagerly in response to their mistress. She turned lightly, springing off her back foot to run up towards them, casting a glance at me over her shoulder and calling out, 'I'll be back at dawn!' The fleeting shapes of goddess and hounds were visible for a moment before they disappeared into the smudge of trees.

I let the breeze cool the stinging warmth on my face, the rush of indignation I'd felt at the suggestion that I would ever go in search of a husband. There was much I hoped for from this quest, more than I could put into anything but vaguely formed dreams. But I certainly didn't need an oracle to tell me that marriage was no part of it and never would be.

I made my way to the nymphs' grove. Artemis had told them of the quest already but I had been putting off my goodbye. Although I'd been pulling away from their company more than ever this summer, I felt sorry to be leaving them altogether.

'You'll soon return, full of stories for us,' Psekas told me, drawing me into an embrace. Her hair was soft against my cheek. She smelled of oak and earth and home.

'I will,' I promised. Their warm words of farewell and encouragement followed me all the way back to my quiet cave.

I was awake before sunrise. There was so little to do. The cave had been my home for years, but the only trace of myself I was leaving was a pile of animal skins folded in the far corner and a circle of ash where I had built my fires. I wore a tunic in the same style I did every day; just the same as Artemis wore, belted at my waist and falling to my knees so that I could run smoothly and unhampered. I braided my hair and strapped on my bow and quiver of arrows. There was nothing else that I needed. I stepped out into the pearl-grey light and heard the sound of clattering hooves. At the top of the slope, Artemis stood in her chariot. A surge of excitement rose through me.

Two does were tethered to the front of the chariot, the breath huffing from their velvety mouths, their dark eyes watchful. I reached out a hand to fondle the nearest, stroking her soft neck and feeling the flutter of her pulse beneath my palm. They were taller and stronger than any deer I had seen scampering fleet-footed through the forest before, and there was a golden sheen to their coats that was brighter and more dazzling. They had the same delicate grace, though, their limbs slender and elegant and their posture proud, as though they knew who it was they served, and they were glad to do so.

The sky behind was brightening, wreathed in rose and amber, and the warm light struck the gilded body of the chariot, illuminating the ornate swirls and intricate patterns. I stepped up beside Artemis and she shook the reins. The deer responded at once, moving smartly along the twisting path. I kept my eyes on my cave for as long as I could. As full of excitement as I was, I felt a tugging homewards even as the does pulled us away. The forest was all I'd ever known, and I had no idea when I would see it again.

The chariot ride was swift and fluid. Artemis' deer never stumbled over rocks or tree roots, only trotted smoothly as though running over meadows. The sun rose steadily ahead, setting the sky aflame, and birdsong trilled from every tree we flew past, a triumphant chorus in our wake. I had never travelled like this before. If sailing was as joyous as this, I had nothing to fear from the voyage ahead.

'When we arrive at Pagasae, what can I expect of Jason and his heroes?' I asked.

Artemis looked thoughtful. 'They'll be shocked by you,' she said. 'They won't be used to a woman of your prowess – they will never have known one before. Where they live, women don't hunt and run and live alone.'

'I'm grateful I was left to the bears,' I said. I couldn't imagine what life I would have led if I'd grown up behind palace walls, sheltered and veiled and never handed a bow or the means to manage my own survival.

Artemis laughed. 'That's the spirit you need to show them.'

'What about Jason, the leader of this quest?'

'Like you, he wasn't brought up by his parents. He was

born to the King and Queen of Iolcus, but they were ousted by the king's brother, and Jason was given to the centaur Chiron to be raised.'

'A centaur?' I was horrified.

'Not like the two you slew in the woods,' Artemis said. 'Chiron is a centaur quite unlike any other. He is wise, learned and gentle. Boys are sent to him for training in battle skills. I don't know what kind of man Jason has become, but he had a good teacher. His uncle fears him enough to send him on this quest, believing it to be impossible. King Pelias thinks that Jason will never retrieve the Golden Fleece and so never prove himself worthy of taking his kingdom back.'

'Why does Pelias want the Golden Fleece anyway?'

'I doubt that he does. He wants his nephew dead, or proven a failure, so that he can hold on to his power. But the Fleece is a valuable thing; many men would want to steal it. Not even because they want to possess it, but because it's so hard to get. It is held by Aeetes, the powerful son of Helios, in the land of Colchis, and it's guarded by a huge serpent, with many perils along the way to anyone who seeks it.'

I wouldn't betray any nerves. 'Where did the Fleece come from?'

'That's a sad tale.' Artemis pursed her lips. 'It began with a king, Athamas of Orchomenus, a city far from here. He was married to a goddess, Nephele, who was sculpted of cloud. She was beautiful, ethereal and kind, and she bore him a boy and a girl, Phrixus and Helle. But Athamas grew bored of Nephele and abandoned her, marrying a woman called Ino instead. In her sadness, Nephele fled the city, and now that she did not summon the clouds, the land was beset by terrible drought. The crops withered and died, and the farmers prayed and begged the gods for rain. Ino resented her husband's children and wanted them gone so that hers could inherit the throne. So she persuaded Athamas that the oracle had demanded the sacrifice of his children in exchange for rain.'

'He believed her?'

'He was a fool,' Artemis said shortly. 'Nephele discovered what was about to befall her beloved children and she sent a winged, golden ram to rescue them. They jumped on its back and flew away from their weak father and jealous stepmother. But the little girl, Helle, she fell. The strait where she drowned is called the Hellespont in her memory. Phrixus made it safely to Colchis, where Aeetes took him in, and he sacrificed the ram in gratitude. He gave the Fleece to Aeetes, who hung it from a tree in the sacred Grove of Ares, protecting it from thieves with magic and monsters, and Aeetes gave Phrixus his daughter, Chalciope, in marriage.'

I watched the trees fly past us, flashes of sunlight and clear blue sky between the tangled leaves.

'Aeetes believes that no one can ever steal it,' Artemis said.

'But you think it can be done?'

'Prove that it can. Come back here a victor, as glorious as any of them. Hera boasts that she is the immortal patron of Jason, so smug about what he will achieve in her name. Show her what my champion can do, a woman fighting in the name of Artemis.'

The trees began to thin impossibly soon, the forest's easternmost edge reached quicker than any mortal's chariot could have brought us. I stood taller, my skin prickling as the deer swept out from between the final cluster of trunks. I looked about, eager to see a new landscape, the sky a wide blue bowl ending in a distant horizon, not fringed by the forest canopy or hemmed in by mountains. The deer surged forward with another bound of energy, almost knocking me over as Artemis laughed in pure exhilaration.

I squeezed the wooden rim of the chariot so tightly that my knuckles whitened, but I was determined not to betray any alarm. And at last, in the low golden light of the late afternoon, we slowed and came to a halt on the crest of a high peak. I let myself adjust to the stillness, wondering if my legs would hold me up if I tried to dismount.

Sweeping down the hillside, a forest sprawled green and familiar. But beyond that, I could see fields dotted with slow-moving animals, and buildings that seemed even from here more uniform and stable than the ramshackle huts where huntsmen dwelt at the edges of the Arcadian woods. Further still lay the wide curve of a bay and my first real sight of the sea. I stood, mesmerised. The shining blue waters stretched on forever, the light playing across the waves. Here and there, the dark shape of a ship glided across it, and I felt giddy thinking that I would board one of those, that the ocean would carry me away from the safety of land.

'What do you think?' Artemis asked softly. The sound of her voice made me jump; I'd forgotten she was at my side at all.

'It's magnificent,' I breathed.

'That city is Iolcus,' she said. 'Jason and his heroes are gathering at the harbour of nearby Pagasae. Many will be travelling to present themselves and claim their place. I won't go further with you; you will make the rest of the way there on your own.'

I nodded.

'Rest at nightfall in the woods. Enter the city by daylight. Don't let them turn you away or deny you a place. Don't forget the warning of the oracle, and remember that you go in my name.'

'Of course.'

'Then, this is goodbye, until you return,' she said. She was brimming with anticipation, and I couldn't help but feel it too, a current running through my veins.

'I'll do my best,' I promised.

'And that will be better than the efforts of all the other heroes combined.' She swung herself back into her chariot, the deer somehow as alert and lively as they had been at the start. Framed against the sky, her golden bow shining, she was so fierce and wild, and I thrilled to think that she had chosen me to bring her glory. Her eyes met mine. A mutual understanding flared between us. There was no need of any more words.

The deer arced around, gone in an instant. I didn't linger, taking in one last glance at the city below before I began to run. After a day of travelling, even in the comfort of Artemis' chariot, it felt so good to stretch my limbs and feel the energy crackling through me. I didn't have long before it would be too dark to make my way, so I plunged into the woods, keeping a watchful eye on the position of the sun.

It wasn't my forest, but I wasn't hampered by any fear. I ran until I could see that twilight was near, and then I cast around for a suitable place to spend the night. An oak tree with wide-spreading branches reminded me of home, and I settled beneath its leafy shelter. Between the gently swaying branches, I caught glimpses of the stars scattered across the sky, the same stars that would be shining over Arcadia, steadfast guardians of the night. I thought of them twinkling above my empty cave, the home that awaited my return, whenever that would be, and, comfortable on the soft earth of this strange forest, I closed my eyes and gave in to sleep.

6

I woke up ravenous, dry-throated and momentarily confused. It was not yet dawn, but I was immediately alert and tingling with energy. I could sense the coming of day as though the light was crackling at the edges of my vision, setting my senses aflame.

I jumped up, pushing the overhanging branches out of the way so that I could get to the stream. I splashed my face with cold water, cupping it in my hands and drinking it down greedily. Drops splattered across my tunic, the shock of it bringing goosebumps. I felt another surge of energy and smiled in the shadows.

Shivering just a little, I made sure my bow and arrows were firmly tied across my back and I made my way through the trees, my footsteps soft and silent. The forest slept, its peace undisturbed.

I was well practised in finding berries; it was the same here as it was at home. As the light of the morning crept through the sky, filtering through the boughs, I came upon some and stopped to gather a couple of handfuls. It took the edge off my appetite, though not quite enough. I tried to calculate how far I'd come and how much further Pagasae might be from where I was.

I kept going, following the twists and turns down the hillside. It was a smooth, easy sprint, and I was confident I'd be at the city before nightfall. What I'd do then, I didn't know. I wasn't sure what to expect, and Artemis hadn't given me much in the way of guidance. I'd have to work it out when I got there, act in the way I thought she would expect, in a way that would be befitting to her champion.

I'd heard nothing all day but the chirping of birds, the occasional dart of a snake's coils as it felt the vibrations of my approach and dodged away, the rustling of the leaves in the breeze and the sound of my own feet hitting the ground. I was absorbed in the rhythm, my eyes fixed on the path ahead, when a deer exploded from a thick cluster of ferns just in front of me, its ears flattened to its head in panic. It raced away, long legs scrambling in a frenzy of movement, and before I had even consciously decided, I gave chase. It was instinctual, a change in direction that my legs decided upon before my mind could catch up. As I ran, I was reaching behind for my weapon, taking aim and bending back the string of my bow in one fluid movement.

The deer crumpled to the ground. My arrow quivered in its throat.

I paused, feeling my heart thundering in my chest. It wasn't just the rush of blood I could hear, or the sound of my breath. Something had been chasing that deer, something had frightened it into my path, and whatever it was, it was gaining ground behind me. I swung around to see what it was – wolf, lion, bear, whatever wild beasts stalked these woods. I had another arrow poised and ready to fire.

He hurtled through the branches, a spear held aloft in his fist, searching for the prey. I saw him take in the scene, the stricken deer and me, and he slowed to an abrupt halt. He stepped back, letting his spear fall at his side, his other hand raised as if to say he meant no harm.

The silence between us was like a bright crystal we both feared to shatter.

He dropped his eyes first, bowing his head. Not looking at me, he spoke. 'Are you – a goddess?'

I narrowed my eyes. 'No.'

He breathed out. 'I thought for a moment—'

'What?'

He cleared his throat, raising his face again. 'I wondered if I had blundered into the path of Artemis.'

I looked down at my plain tunic, the smears of dust and dirt, and the scratches on my legs from the thorny stems I'd run through earlier. I'd never seen Artemis look anything less than pristine and unmarked. 'Artemis is taller,' I said at last.

I saw his eyes flick to the top of my head, equal in height to his. 'Of course.'

I eyed him coolly. 'Your quarry,' I said, indicating the deer. 'I didn't realise that I was intercepting a hunt, I thought it was an animal chasing behind.'

He raised an eyebrow. 'You got into the path of – what, a lion, maybe? On purpose?'

I shrugged.

'Well, it's your kill,' he said. 'An offering to you, though really it's your rightful prize.'

I might never have been in this situation before – only Hippomenes came close – but I had a fairly good idea of how Artemis would want me to behave. She would want me to take my kill and leave, not make conversation. So the words that came out of my mouth were a surprise to me, a reckless impulse. 'Why would you make an offering to me? I told you I'm not a goddess. I'm no spirit of the forest, not a nymph or any other kind of deity either,' I said. 'I'm a mortal woman.'

'Out here alone?'

'I have hunted in the woods alone every day since I was old enough to hold a bow.' I was realising just how strange I must seem to him. 'Not these woods; I've travelled a long way to be here. I'm on my way to Pagasae.'

'I've come from Pagasae this morning,' he said. 'Why are you travelling there?'

A tingling began in the base of my spine, a presentiment of what I was suddenly certain he was going to say. 'What's your business there?' I asked, too cautious to give my own reasons first.

He was still guarded, but I could tell his curiosity would overcome him. Now he knew I was a mortal, he was more intrigued than afraid. 'I'm part of a crew,' he said. 'Sailing on a ship called the *Argo*, in search of treasure.'

I stiffened. 'Then you're exactly who I'm looking for.'

'Why?'

'I've come to join,' I said. 'I've come here to find Jason, to take a place among you.'

He'd been taken aback before, but this utterly dumbfounded him. He stared at me for a long moment. 'You want to join the *Argo*'s voyage?'

'I do.'

'Well.' He started to speak, then stopped himself. I could see so many questions wrestling in his eyes, but instead he said, 'My name is Meleager.'

'Atalanta.'

He nodded. 'Do you want to come with me? To the harbour?'

It went against every instinct that Artemis had trained into me. But on the other hand, she was sending me to join a whole crew of men, so why be reluctant to spend time with one now? Perhaps it would help my cause to arrive with an established member of the group rather than make my petition alone.

'Sorry if that offends you – if you don't wish to go accompanied by me.'

'There is no one else to accompany me.' I was used to the way that the nymphs and I made our way freely through Artemis' domain, though I knew from what she'd said of the villages and cities that such freedom was rare. I could see that it made this man nervous, but if I gave any thought to the conventions by which the rest of Greece lived, I would never have taken a single step on this journey to begin with. 'I attend in the name of Artemis,' I said. 'I'm under her protection.'

He nodded. 'Then I can show you where they're gathered. You can make your case to Jason.' I wondered what lay behind those words. He didn't sound convinced.

'Which way?'

He began to give directions, much more at ease now that he was on familiar conversational ground. I listened carefully. I had sketched out a route in my mind that adhered generally to what he described, but I stored away all the details of where streams flowed into uncrossable torrents, where the ground was rocky and treacherous, where to loop around and take the easier path, and where to forge ahead. 'And the deer?' I asked.

He smiled. 'Tonight we will feast on the beach and make

our offerings to the gods, that's why I came hunting. The *Argo* sails at dawn tomorrow. We might encounter some of the others in these woods as we go.'

I wondered if he preferred to hunt alone, like me.

'I'll carry it back,' he said, inclining his head towards the deer, and I stepped aside to let him pass. I watched him swing the animal up on to his shoulders, its head hanging limply at his back, its glassy eyes empty and staring, the forelegs caught easily in his fist.

'Do you think there will be much of a case for me to make to Jason?' I asked.

'I think . . . he won't know what to think.' Meleager's tone was wry. 'The rest of them – the Argonauts, that's how we refer to ourselves – I mean, they won't be expecting you, that's certain.' He laughed. 'I'm looking forward to seeing their reaction when you arrive.'

There was something in his tone I didn't like. 'Then I suppose I'll just have to show them what I can do.' I adjusted the position of the bow on my back, sank into a crouch and felt the long stretch of my thighs as I sprang forwards.

I heard him exclaim; then, without hesitation, his footsteps pelted behind me. I let him draw up beside me, cocked my head back at him, and then shifted into a higher speed, the ground disappearing beneath my feet. I recited his directions in my head as I ran, keeping an ear out for the distant sound of him running in my wake. I always loved to run, but this was different. Knowing that Meleager was behind me gave it another edge, a thrill not unlike that of the hunt but more playful. This wasn't going to end in bloodshed; this was racing for the sheer pleasure of it and the glee of winning.

I stopped at the crest of the final hill. The city spread

beneath my feet. So close, the sight of it robbed me of what breath I had left. There were more buildings than I could ever have imagined, some of them so vast and sprawling I couldn't make sense of them. What would it be like to walk through one of those great squares, hemmed in on every side, jostled by people in every direction? I let my pulse return to normal, my gaze drawn past the city to the curve of the bay and the ocean, dotted here and there with boats.

I stood there, transfixed, until at last I heard Meleager reach the top, panting hard. I turned to see him just as he threw the carcass of the deer to the ground and flung himself down, too, resting on the grass beside it. He dragged his forearm across his face, wiping away the sheen of sweat, and then rolled over on to his back.

'I forgot you had the deer.' I felt a little guilty, the joy of my victory dissipating.

He propped himself up on his elbows. 'It wouldn't have made a difference,' he said. He tipped his head back, his eyes closed against the sun, his hair hanging down in thick, dark waves. It looked so soft, and it summoned up a memory – a flash of sensation, rather – the feel of a bear's fur between my fingers. Then he sat up a little, opened his eyes and looked at me. 'I've never seen anyone run so fast in my life.'

'I wish I'd taken the deer.'

He laughed. 'You would have outrun me even if you carried two of them.'

I hadn't expected such good humour. I'd wanted to show him my prowess, impress him with my skills so that he could vouch for me to the Argonauts. But I'd thought he might take some exception to it, that his praise might be won grudgingly. Instead, he seemed to take it as an amusing joke.

'You're faster than anyone I've ever seen, too,' I told him. *Anyone mortal*, I didn't add.

'Thank you.' He scrabbled at a knotted cloth sack he had tied at his belt, pulling out a cask of water and taking a long draught. 'I stopped to fill this up on the way,' he said. 'At the stream at the foot of this hill. You didn't appear to need any sustenance, but perhaps you're thirsty now?'

My throat felt like it was closing up just looking at the droplets of water sliding down the cask. I hadn't noticed my thirst or even the stream in my desire to push ahead, but now it was all I could think about. 'Please,' I said fervently, reaching for it. I gulped down what was left before it even dawned on me what a strange intimacy this was, to put my mouth where his had been.

He retrieved a dense hunk of bread and tore it apart, handing me half. The berries I'd found that morning seemed like a very long time ago. Although the bread was dry and tasteless, nothing compared to the ripe juiciness of the fruit, any food to my growling stomach seemed delicious.

I wondered with a slight lurch what Artemis would think of this. I had an uneasy feeling that what I was doing might be wrong. But then, I had found an Argonaut, a way on to the ship. And Meleager seemed to accept our odd situation without question, which made me hope that he might not be the only one to take me at my word. 'Tell me about the others,' I said to him. 'The rest of the crew, what they're like. I want to be ready.'

He looked thoughtful. 'I arrived only two days ago, from Calydon. Heralds brought the news of Jason's call for heroes from all across Greece, and men have travelled great distances to join. More than forty have come.'

'So many?' I hadn't expected that.

'The bards will sing of this quest for years,' Meleager said. 'That's what Jason has promised. The men who go with him will be famous, their names known in every corner of the world. Or some of them, at least. It's impossible to steal, the Golden Fleece, everyone knows it. To be one of those that takes it, that achieves the unimaginable . . .'

'So who has made their mark so far?'

'Heracles is the best known already.' He plucked at the grass, rolling the broken stems between his fingers. 'He's exactly as the legends tell him to be – a son of Zeus who has already accomplished more than any other man who's ever lived. His strength is unmatched, he's a giant of a man. Everyone looks to him before Jason, as though it's him that's the leader. Even though it's Jason's quest, some of the men argued it should be Heracles who takes charge. It could have come to blows if Heracles had wanted it to, but he didn't.'

'Why not?'

'He wants to fight and drink, not make decisions.' Meleager laughed. 'He preferred for Jason to take on the responsibility.'

'So what's Jason like?'

'Unproven.' He looked up and our eyes met. 'Very determined, but he has no experience.'

'Who else is there?'

'Well, there's Argus, who built the ship – hence the name, though his hands were guided by Athena. Tiphys, the helmsman. Orpheus, a musician.'

'A musician?' I interrupted.

'Not like any you've ever heard before,' Meleager assured me. 'There are sons of gods – Zetes and Calais whose father is Boreas, the North Wind. Euphemus and Periclymenos, sons of

Poseidon, and Echion and Erytus, sons of Hermes. There are Castor and Polydeuces, famous warriors of Sparta and sons of Zeus, and more kings and princes among our number, too; more names than I've learned yet myself.'

'And you?'

'And me.' He didn't look away, and I had the feeling he was enjoying my curiosity about how he fitted into this impressive roll-call. 'My mother is the Queen of Calydon,' he said.

'And your father?'

'Oeneus, the king, has raised me as his own,' he said slowly. 'But there are those who say my true father is Ares.'

My eyes widened. Ares was never in the nymphs' stories, but they'd told me of all the Olympians, and so I knew enough to know he was the god of war, whose battle-cry struck terror into the hearts of the bravest warriors. The most savage of the gods, with an immortal lust for bloodshed and carnage. Artemis relished the chase, the clean purity of the hunt, but Ares loved the sweat and dirt of the battlefield, the desperate violence of the struggle to survive. It made me look at Meleager again. I'd noted his strength already, and now I considered the polish of his skin, his handsome vitality, everything about him so different to the rough huntsmen I'd caught glimpses of in the woods. Nothing about him was what I would have expected; nothing of our encounter so far matched what I'd heard and seen of men, but I didn't know if that made it any more likely that he was the son of a god. He'd graciously accepted his defeat in the race I'd made him run; there was no rage or wounded pride in his reaction, and his dark eyes sparkled with warmth. They weren't the hollow pools I imagined exulting over clashing armies.

'But now there's you,' he said, cutting through my thoughts.

'Atalanta, chosen by Artemis, the only woman among the Argonauts.'

I felt his words awakening something within me, opening up a vision of myself alongside the catalogue of demi-gods and heroes. I saw myself, as though from the outside. A baby opening her eyes to the savage bear, a child running free through the forest, a young woman loosing arrows at rampaging monsters. It felt as though every moment of my life had been building up to this: my destiny.

Any vestige of doubt I might have harboured evaporated. The other Argonauts might be more resistant than Meleager, less willing to accept a woman in their ranks, but I didn't care what they might think or how they might protest. I was as worthy as any one of them. I would get on board that ship, I vowed. I would take my place, not just in the name of the goddess. It was for the sake of my name, too. Atalanta, an Argonaut.

PART II

7

We walked down the side of the mountain together. The names of heroes resounded in my head as we neared the city, my anticipation growing. Guards flanked the entrance, but when they saw Meleager, they stepped aside, swinging open the heavy oak gates to let us through. I was aware of their eyes sliding over me, idly curious, resting on the bow on my back, lingering on my bare calves. I was ready for a challenge, but none came.

Inside the gates, there were more people than I had ever seen. The ground was dusty, sun-baked mud, hardened to a dull brown. No flowers, no greenery, no swaying trees to span the horizon. The air rang with shouts and laughter, a dizzying swell of noise. And the smells mingling on the warm breeze – salt and meat and the sharp stink of so many bodies together – made my eyes water and my breath catch in my throat, disorientation overwhelming me.

'We need to get through the markets, down to the harbour,' Meleager said. 'It's this way.'

I took a slow, careful breath. 'How far?'

'No great distance,' he said. 'Why? You aren't tired, surely?'

I shook my head. 'Of course not.'

He looked at me closely. 'Then what?'

'I haven't been in a city like this before.' I chose my words carefully, not willing to betray my confusion.

He nodded as though I was confirming something he already suspected, and I bristled. I much preferred it when he was admiring my speed; I didn't want him to feel superior now, shepherding me through this unfamiliar place. I drew myself up and looked around. It was a great crowd, that was true, but I could see over nearly all the heads. The choking atmosphere was an assault on my senses, but there was no danger anywhere. I was sure that in the churning mass of people, there were plenty with ill intentions, but I had taken down two centaurs in a fire-ravaged forest. A bustling town square in daylight should be nothing to me.

'Lead the way,' I told Meleager, and we walked on. Most of the faces I saw were male, though some women darted here and there, mostly on the edges, buying from the stalls, surveying the shining green olives, ripe purple figs, crumbling blocks of salty cheese and jars of golden honey. It made my mouth water to pass by, my eye caught by other things I'd never seen before. But as I absorbed the details around me, I felt the burn of eyes staring at me, just as the guards at the gate had done. The women I saw wore dresses that draped over their bodies, belted loosely at the waist and falling all the way to the dusty earth, while mine ended at the knee. Among Artemis and the nymphs, who attired themselves the same, it was natural, but here it clearly sent a stir through the onlookers. I narrowed my eyes at anyone whose gaze was too brazen, but it did little to deter any of them. As much as the city was a revelation to me, I could see that I was a strange sight to its inhabitants, too.

I was relieved to pass through to quieter streets. I took a long breath, though the air here was still fetid with an animal stench so different to the fresh, leafy scents of home. There were no grand, towering buildings here; the dusty track widened out and there was clear space between the huts and tumbledown taverns. The strangers that passed still turned to stare, a cool suspicion hovering between us, but whether it was the bow at my back, Meleager's spear, or our purposeful stride, their misgivings stayed unspoken.

We rounded a curve, passed a screen of cypress trees and, all at once, the ocean was before us. The bay was a wide crescent, a jagged ridge of tree-covered mountains behind it that made my heart ache with longing for a moment. I gazed out to the waves lapping the shore, their crests foaming. I had been so impatient to get here, to begin the task that Artemis had set me, but now I had arrived, I found that I wasn't in a rush after all. Maybe it was a flip of nervousness in my stomach that held me back, though I chose to call it excitement. But I felt strangely reluctant to cast my gaze further down, to where an immense ship floated at the shoreline, its mast piercing the sky, its wide sail billowing majestically. And gathered on the beach before it, a group of men, some of them busy building a large fire, others chopping wood, carving animal carcasses to load meat on to spits, sparring with fists or swords, though the shouts of laughter made it clear this was for practice.

There were women too, I noticed. Some with downcast eyes, carrying jugs of wine to groups of men; some bearing loads to take to the ship, piles of folded fabric and crates, supplies for the journey.

'There's the *Argo*,' Meleager said.

I swallowed and nodded, keeping an expression of studied calm.

'It's the biggest ship that's ever been built,' he went on. 'It takes fifty men to row it.'

I didn't know how many men would ordinarily be required to row a ship. I wondered fleetingly if Artemis should have told me more, prepared me better for this. I was sure that I could match any of the crew, but I didn't want to betray my unfamiliarity with a world of knowledge they took for granted. 'Tell me which one is Jason,' I said, 'so that I can present myself to him.'

Meleager nodded. 'Come with me,' he said.

Just as in town, I felt the weight of stares, as one by one the men noticed me. I didn't cast my eyes down or look away. I wanted to see who these heroes were, what kind of men I had come to join.

I searched for distinguishing features among them, some way of separating them out from the homogeneous mass of brawn and beards and insolent eyes. That one sitting on a boulder, his fingers brushing the strings of a lyre, a shiver of melody that raised goosebumps on my arms, must be the musician Meleager had mentioned, Orpheus. He alone didn't look over at me; his expression was dreamy and soft, lost in the music spilling from his instrument.

Further down the beach, unmistakeable even from Meleager's brief description, a hulking mountain of a man sprawled on the sand, a lion pelt draped across his shoulders. Heracles, he'd said. A son of Zeus, already famous. He was almost preposterous in his size, more like a bear than a man. He looked at me directly, taking long swigs of wine from the flask he clutched in his meaty fist. There was something in his gaze, something like a challenge in the way he looked at me, a call that I couldn't keep from answering. I held eye contact, determined not to be the first to look away. After a long moment, he laughed mockingly and tipped his head back to drain the flask, breaking our gaze. Let him laugh, I thought. I still felt a flush of exultation: my first victory among the Argonauts.

Next to Heracles, an extraordinarily handsome young man poured more wine. Meleager had said that there were sons of gods here, and I was sure he must be one of them.

Two men sparring, ox-hide thongs wrapped around their knuckles, turned briefly to look at me and then went back to what they were doing. I stifled a gasp. They were dodging so fluidly, their movements graceful and swift, that it had taken me a moment to see the little golden wings fluttering at their ankles, their feet hovering slightly above the pebbled ground.

Another man, wrapped in a heavy bearskin although the sinking sun still warmed the air, held an enormous double-headed axe, the blade glinting. More of them, sitting about the fire, a pile of rich crimson cloaks heaped up behind them. More of them, turning spits of roasting meat, the scent of it mouth-watering, sparks flying into the sky.

And at last, standing before us, a man with a doubtful expression on his face. He looked younger than most of the others, less roughened and not so powerful, with no other characteristic that singled him out. His features were handsome, if fairly unremarkable, and his dark hair was thick and wavy. He was a little shorter than me.

'What's she doing here?' he asked Meleager sharply. 'The women are coming later, when we feast.'

'Jason,' said Meleager. I gave a start of surprise that this man was Jason, the leader of the quest. I thought I saw his mouth thin a little at my reaction. 'May I present Atalanta, the champion chosen by Artemis to join the Argonauts.'

'Join us? A woman?' He looked from side to side as though expecting a reveal to the joke.

Anger began to rise inside me. 'I intercepted Meleager's hunt. I shot his quarry under his nose and I outran him across the mountains.' A laugh ran around the circle of spectators who were drawing in closer, watching our exchange.

Meleager shrugged. 'It's true. She is as fast and as skilled as any man I've seen.'

I felt my cheeks burn under the heat of all their scrutiny.

Jason looked incredulously at Meleager. 'You admit that she beat you?'

'There is no sense in lying,' he said.

'You want the Golden Fleece,' I said. 'Why turn away anyone who can help you get it?'

Jason was shaking his head before I finished the sentence. 'A woman can't join the Argonauts,' he said.

My jaw set. 'Why not?'

'He's right.' This new voice was deep and rumbling. 'There's no place for a woman among us.' It was Heracles who spoke, having hauled his great frame up from where he had been reclining. He towered above us. 'It's dangerous.'

'Dangerous how?' I eyed him warily. His beard was level with my face; I could see where the wine had soaked it.

'A woman alone among men is always in danger.' His gaze ran up and down my body as he opened his arms wide to the others, eliciting mutters of agreement.

'Haven't you chosen men of honour to fight alongside you?' I ignored Heracles, aiming my question at Jason instead. I saw that it landed, sure as one of my arrows.

'Of course I have.' He frowned at Heracles. 'My Argonauts are the best men that all the lands of Greece have to offer.'

'She's a distraction.' Heracles took another long swig and frowned, tipping his goblet upside down. The last remaining drops splattered on the ground. 'Hylas,' he said, and the young man leapt to his feet, ready to fill it again.

I bristled. 'How can you rely on your men to fight the battles ahead if you can't trust them? Artemis herself sent me here. I come in her name. I have no interest in anyone here, or anything but the quest. I want to fight beside you. And I'm as good as any one of the men you've gathered here.'

'Don't be a fool, Jason,' Heracles warned.

Jason's eyes darkened. 'You said you didn't want to make the decisions. That you would follow me as the leader of the *Argo*.'

Heracles gave a bark of laughter, so loud I saw some of the others flinch.

I held my ground.

'You can't be considering it.' Heracles' voice was thick and slurred but mocking, the challenge unmistakeable.

Jason looked me up and down again. He tugged at his hair, his face twisted with indecision. 'Our voyage is blessed by Hera and Athena,' he said. 'We have sons of Zeus and Poseidon, of Hermes, of Ares among us.' His eyes flicked to Meleager.

'Then why risk the wrath of Artemis?' I asked. 'When you could have her strength behind you, too?'

'And you're a sworn devotee of the goddess?' he asked.

I nodded.

'It's my choice,' Jason said. 'I decide who joins us, no one else.'

I wondered, if that was really the case, why he felt the need to say it out loud.

'I won't offend the goddess,' Jason said. 'I won't insult her chosen champion.'

Meleager glanced at me, smiling.

'If you join us, no one here can protect you,' Jason continued.

'I need no protection. I can defend myself. I killed two centaurs that tried to attack me. I don't fear any man here.' I looked defiantly at the Argonauts to see how they took my words. None looked impressed.

Jason let out a long breath. I could see he wasn't certain, but he looked again at Heracles and I could see his stubborn intent fighting against his doubts. 'Then, for the glory of Artemis, you can join.'

'We won't sail with her.' It was one of the others who spoke now, his features heavy and sullen. 'If you want a woman, there'll be plenty on the way. We won't make ourselves a laughing stock taking one with us.'

I felt a new flush of heat, a tingling in my muscles as my fists curled at my sides. 'I'm here to fight, just like all of you.' I kept my voice low and calm, even as the inferno built inside me. I couldn't let my instincts take over here.

The man sneered. 'She's either insane or a liar.' He didn't even address me, talking only to Jason, as though I hadn't spoken. 'You know what centaurs are, are you really going to believe she could take one on?'

'I'm the leader, Peleus!' Jason's words were forceful, but I could see he was rattled. He'd backed himself into a corner now; either he backed down from his edict in front of them all or he overrode them. He was anxious to assert his authority, but he hadn't wanted me to join in the first place, and now he had to defend a choice he already regretted. 'Stay here if you're afraid to sail with her; lose your chance to come on the greatest quest there's ever been. Follow me and make your name, or let everyone know you're too cowardly to join.'

Peleus looked incredulous, but as he opened his mouth to argue further, Heracles clapped him on the shoulder. 'If she's lying about what she can do, she won't last long,' he said. He let out a bellow of laughter, and I flinched. I had been ready for a fight; I was tensed for it. 'A woman Argonaut!' He laughed again. 'What would your wife make of it, Meleager? A slave-woman is one thing, but this . . .'

The lascivious glee in his voice turned my stomach.

Jason's face twitched. 'No one touches her,' he said. 'And no one helps her either. If she can't keep up, it's not our problem.'

Meleager slung the deer he carried off his shoulders. 'Atalanta's contribution to the feast,' he said. 'I'll take it to the fire.'

The men began to disperse, Heracles and Hylas walking off together. I was trembling with rage. The only thing that held me back was that somehow, I'd won. I was an Argonaut, on the path that Artemis had set out for me, against the wishes of every single one of them except Meleager. As satisfying as it would be to give vent to my fury, as clouded as my mind was with images of me pounding the arrogance right out of Heracles and Peleus, I'd have my chance to show what I could do when we sailed. Starting a fight now would jeopardise everything – and besides, I wasn't so blinded by anger that I couldn't see how formidable Heracles' massive bulk was. *I'll wait*, I told myself. *He'll see soon enough how wrong he is.*

No one approached me. Of course, no words of welcome or greeting were forthcoming. I was left with Jason, grim-faced and preoccupied. I looked over towards the great ship, held in place by thick ropes, and the wide ocean behind it.

Heracles' final words gnawed at my composure. It felt as though he ascribed another motive to Meleager bringing me here. I wondered if I should have come here alone, if I should have declined Meleager's offer to escort me.

'The overseers have returned!' A shout went up and Jason turned. Several herdsmen were coming down the beach towards us, driving two oxen before them.

'Let us build the altar!' Jason called, hastening away from me. The Argonauts swung into action, several of them hauling up shingles from the beach to make an altar, others piling up wood for a bigger fire than any of the smaller ones burning around us. I watched the smooth, coordinated motion as they worked. At last, Jason summoned everyone forwards. I stayed back, watching.

Jason stood, outlined against the sunset, the mighty ship silhouetted behind him. Although I hadn't found him impressive before, I couldn't help but be drawn in by the power of the moment as he began his prayers to Apollo, beseeching the god for a fair wind and lucky passage while he sprinkled barley at the altar. The oxen stood by, quiet but for the gentle huffing of their nostrils. When Jason's prayer drew to a close, Heracles came forwards, along with the man I had seen earlier with the double-headed axe. In one swift swing, Heracles struck the first ox with his club, the powerful animal swaying under the blow and sinking to the ground. The other man dispatched the second ox with his axe, and then others hurried to slit the beasts' throats, cut out the thigh bones and wrap them in fat to burn on the altar so that the smoke and savour would be carried up to Mount Olympus.

A giddy thrill of celebration descended as the sacrifice was completed and the rest of the oxen carved up to be roasted alongside the other meat. There was an abundance of food, fat hissing from the flames and the rich aroma drifting into the twilight skies. Although there were broad smiles on every face, I couldn't relax. I was braced for more hostility from Heracles, but he didn't look at me at all. Most of the Argonauts followed suit. Peleus glared at me across the sand, his face livid in the shadows. I stared back at him, lifting my chin in defiance, but before either of us could take a step forwards or say a word, Orpheus drew out his lyre again and began to play, a rousing tune this time. He was on his feet, his head thrown back as he began to sing, his voice as captivating as his lyre. The anger between us dissolved in the spell his music cast.

I had heard Artemis herself play and sing on the riverbank at home. I had never heard anything like this.

'Here.' Meleager was at my side again, handing me a skewer of meat.

It felt easy to be next to him. The steaming meat smelled too delicious to resist, even though it burned my mouth. Another of the Argonauts proffered wine, not meeting my eyes as he passed it over. I drank deeply. It was sweet and heady and delicious, stronger than the nymphs had mixed it back at home. This was so unlike the nights in the forest, the air thick with smoke and deep, male voices and laughter, the unearthly song of Orpheus, the tang of salt and the splash of the waves on the shingles.

The women that Jason had mentioned began to arrive, painted eyes flashing, arms bare in the firelight, dresses slipping low over their breasts. I looked away. I had heard from Artemis about the kind of lives women led in the cities, the ones who called on her for help. I felt a swift pang of longing for the forest and the easy chatter of the nymphs.

'Will you miss your home?' I asked Meleager. 'While we're at sea, do you think you'll feel nostalgic for it?'

'I might miss some of the comforts,' he said drily. 'When we're getting lashed by storms or sleeping on the hard ground. What about you?'

I thought about it. 'There are no luxuries for me to long for.' I pictured my cave, my pile of animal skins, the mirror-flat surface of the pool outside, the croaking of the frogs and the trill of birdsong.

'And family?' he asked.

'My father left me on a hillside to die when I was born.' I didn't want to talk about the nymphs or Artemis. Certainly not the bears. I didn't know how to begin to explain it all. I was starting to see what a gulf lay between me and the others. Princes, heroes, demi-gods. They'd know nothing of what it took for a girl to survive in the forest.

'But you lived,' he said. 'And grew up to become the scourge of centaurs.'

I laughed. I drained my cup and let it be refilled, the pleasant buzz of the wine fogging my head, washing away my uncertainties. We were all strangers to each other, most of us from faraway places, brought together for the same purpose. No doubt they didn't trust me; I didn't trust them, either. Not yet. But they would see soon enough. By the firelight, it was easy to cast aside my doubts.

When the feasting was done and the fires had died down to glowing embers, men peeled away from the centre, some finding places to rest, spreading out thick cloaks or animal hides to keep them warm, others disappearing with the women. I slipped into the darkness, so that no one could see where I went. I would be careful to keep my guard up.

I walked all the way to where the trees fringed the edge of the beach. In the pitch black of their cover, I felt my way to the spreading roots of a great oak. I made myself a place to rest, my movements practised and quick, and I kept my hand firmly on my bow as I let myself drift into sleep.

We would sail at dawn.

8

Most of the crew were only just stirring as I made my way back the next morning. There was a lightness in my chest, a tingle of excitement spreading throughout my body. The rays of the rising sun sparkled on the waves, their frothy crests lapping at the wooden sides of the *Argo*. I was seized with an urgent desire to board it, to find where it would take us.

As my crewmates heaved themselves up, I glanced back towards the town so that I could fix the image of the land in my mind before I left it. To my surprise, I saw a gathering of townsfolk, a small crowd waving from the top of the beach. Well-wishers, I supposed, come to see us off. From the long dresses rippling in the breeze, I could see there were several women – wives, perhaps, of Argonauts, come to bid their husbands farewell, or anxious mothers grieving to see their sons sail away for who knew how long, to face who knew what dangers.

The rest of the Argonauts noticed the crowd too, calling out their thanks and farewells, waving back to the cluster of women. I caught sight of Meleager, his smile broad and carefree as he raised his hand towards them. I wondered fleetingly what his goodbye to his wife had been like, if she woke this morning and wished him well from her faraway bed in Calydon, if she cried and prayed for his swift return. I wondered if the nymphs of the forest felt my absence, too, or if the rhythms of life carried on seamlessly without me.

Shouted instructions echoed along the beach. Tiphys, the helmsman, directed us to the ship, wading through the surf, securing a wide plank for us to climb aboard. I followed, my heart full of the momentousness as I set foot for the first time on deck, the blue water below, the swaying motion and the unsteady feeling that the ground was not solid beneath me. As though I was a skittish foal, suddenly unable to trust my own balance. I gritted my teeth and forced my feet to move. I wouldn't let anyone see.

The *Argo* had looked so imposing from the beach, but now that I was on board, it felt confining. The main body of the ship was lined with wide benches, long wooden oars tied to each side. There was a small raised deck at either end, and the tall mast in the centre. The crew were taking their places on the benches, and I hurried to sit too. My stomach rolled as I looked over the edge, out towards the deep waters. Hastily, I looked behind me, where Jason was taking up his place at the front – the prow, I'd heard Meleager call it. In front of me, as the final Argonauts took their seats on the remaining benches, Tiphys took up position at the steering oars at the stern.

The ropes were hauled in, the ship freed from its mooring, and I watched as libations were poured into the sea, prayers going up to the skies as the Argo began to move. I felt as though I were fixed to my bench, clutching my oar, as the ship carved a line through the waves. On the beach, the crowd had run down towards the shore, and I caught sight of a woman holding up a baby, her face wet with tears and fierce with pride, and then we gathered pace, a heavy drumbeat keeping time as we pulled on our oars. Meleager turned briefly around from the bench in front of me, smiling his encouragement as the ship began to turn smoothly towards the horizon, guided by Tiphys, propelled by our collective strength. In the centre of the ship, Orpheus began to play his lyre, the beauty of his song strange and ethereal. I gave a little gasp that was half-laughter, half-sob, lost in the wind, and pulled harder on my oar. The land receded, and we rowed on.

It was hard, repetitive work. I was used to exertion, but not to sitting still. The unfamiliarity of the action made my shoulders ache, and I was glad when the sails were unfurled and the wind carried us forwards. Now I could look around; now I could see the grey backs of dolphins diving through the waves around us. On the benches, there was laughter and chatter, a sense of excitement and purposefulness. The constant motion of the ship made me queasy, but I was still as swept up in the feeling of adventure as anyone else. Maybe more so. This was my first time at sea, my first heroic quest. For someone like Heracles, seated on the middle bench so that his massive weight didn't tilt the ship, there was probably little novelty left in such a journey.

I was attentive to everything that happened over the first few days. I watched quietly and learned quickly. Each night, we found land and camped ashore. I got used to the way Tiphys steered the great ship directly up on to the beach, how the keel would grind and shriek as it slid from the shallows to solid earth. Then we would secure the ship with ropes and find food, perhaps wild goats or sheep to roast, along with the barrels we had on board of grain and olives, nuts and grapes, or fish plucked out of the sea, the skin crisping and blackening, and the firm, white flesh flaking over the fires. At sunrise, we'd roll the *Argo* back out to sea on logs, Heracles pressing his shoulder against the prow, his strength matching that of a dozen men. I slept well those nights, under the stars, my body pleasantly exhausted from each day's labour.

I started to be able to tell my crewmates apart. There was Peleus, of course. It was his baby son who had been held aloft as we launched. That baby, Achilles, was the subject of divine prophecies, a hero destined to be greater than his father. I'd overheard Peleus speak proudly of the child and disdainfully of the mother who had left them both. I didn't know who the woman holding the baby had been, just that when Peleus mentioned his runaway wife, his face would darken and he would spit contemptuously on the ground. I kept that bit of knowledge close, aware that there were many on board who had not forgiven Jason for granting me passage. I noted it, just like I had always catalogued in the forest which plants were toxic, which berries to avoid, where the lairs were of the prowling mountain lions, and the favourite hiding places of the snakes.

I was determined to gather as much knowledge as I could on my fellow Argonauts, and Meleager seemed happy to answer my questions. We'd only been sailing for two days, but all our time was spent in each other's company, and I could see how friendships on board formed quickly, an intimacy born of intensity. I was so used to spending long swathes of time alone that it was strange to me, and I preferred to stay out of the bigger groups, to steer away from the raucous confusion when so many of them were talking at once, each one eager to share the stories of what they'd accomplished before this voyage.

The two brothers I had seen sparring above the ground, wings fluttering at their ankles, were Zetes and Calais, the sons of the North Wind. The Spartan brothers, Castor and Polydeuces, were so attuned to one another they seemed two halves of the same good-natured whole, always eager and ready to work. Prince Acastus, Meleager told me quietly, was the son of Pelias and cousin of Jason. He accompanied us on his father's orders, to witness that Jason fulfilled the task Pelias had set – or not. There was axe-wielding Ancaeus, and fleet-footed Euphemus, whose speed in running was famed, so Meleager said. 'He might even be able to keep pace with you.' His tone was light, but I could feel how he studied my face when he said it and I made sure not to give any reaction. Inwardly, I vowed to take the opportunity to prove otherwise as soon as it arose.

Of course, there was Heracles, whose personality overwhelmed all the others, and who seemed so much more present than our leader, Jason. Always at Heracles' side was the impossibly beautiful Hylas, the young man I'd assumed at first sight must be born of a god. 'His father was a king, not a god,' Meleager told me when I asked on the second evening as we set up camp. 'He was slain in battle by Heracles. Hylas has been Heracles' companion ever since.'

I stared. 'Heracles killed his father?' It made no sense. The devotion between Heracles and Hylas was clear to see. The two were never far from each other, and the only time I heard Heracles' booming voice soften to tenderness was when they were deep in conversation, as though they were the only two people in the world.

'That's right. And he took Hylas away with him. Instead of planning his revenge, it seems Hylas fell in love with him.'

'Fell in love? With his father's killer?'

'Maybe his father was a cruel man.' Meleager shook out a thick bundle of furs, spreading them out on the shingles and gesturing for me to sit. The others were building a fire further back, and I was glad he sat beside me rather than joining them. 'Maybe Hylas was glad to escape. I don't know.'

I frowned. I felt like I was getting the measure of the others, piece by piece, but Heracles only threw up more questions in my mind. 'Why do you think Heracles didn't want to lead the expedition?' I asked. 'He seems like the obvious leader of the group. Is it really that he didn't want the responsibility?'

'He has other tasks,' Meleager said. 'He has labours to carry out for his cousin, the King of Tiryns. I think perhaps he couldn't pass up the chance to sail with the Argonauts, but his energies are reserved for those.'

'What labours are they?'

A shadow passed over Meleager's face. The seawater frothed and foamed around the pebbles on the stony shore. I could lose myself staring out at it sometimes; something about the emptiness of the horizon was unsettling as well as inviting.

'He performs the labours in punishment for a crime he committed.' Meleager sighed, his usual good humour dampened. 'In a fit of madness, rage, I don't know what – he murdered his wife and children. The tasks that King Eurystheus sets him are his penance, to absolve himself of the guilt.'

My eyes widened. The *Argo* rang every day with the booming of Heracles' laughter, his shouting conviviality to everyone but me. I knew he was powerful, his strength formidable, but I hadn't imagined that he would use it against victims so defenceless.

'He's hated by Hera—'

'Hera who's blessed this voyage?' I interrupted. 'Hera who loves Jason?'

Meleager shrugged. 'Well, supposedly, that's the case. He's a son of Zeus. He says that Hera sent the madness to him, that he didn't know what he was doing.'

He was the greatest hero among us, surely the most famed in all of Greece. I had no doubt that the price of that glory was blood. None of us could afford qualms about slaying the enemy. Meleager could be right in supposing Hylas' father was a tyrant. But the deaths of an innocent woman and her children, his children – even with the excuse of Hera's wrath – were harder to reconcile. 'These labours, though, they'll only make him more famous,' I said. Each one would carve his name more indelibly upon history. 'What was his wife's name?' I asked. 'Does anyone remember her?'

Meleager looked at me, surprised. 'I don't know.'

I didn't say anything more. There was a quest ahead of us, and Heracles was an asset: strong, effortlessly capable and jovial all the time. He kept the spirits of the other men high, while Jason was more reserved. I knew that Jason fretted still over his decision to include me; indeed, he seemed anxious about everything. He was always distracted, staring out to sea, unsure at every turn.

I had no doubt that some of the others still resented his decision. *Let them boast about themselves and pretend I'm not here at all*, I thought. I didn't want to be among them when we left the ship, drinking on the shore, singing loudly and tunelessly. They were heroes, I kept telling myself, on the same quest as I was, but if I didn't remind myself of that, I would have thought of them as no different to the huntsmen that I and the nymphs protected our territory from.

On the fifth night of sailing, we put in on the rugged, rocky shore of an island Tiphys told us was Lemnos. Dusk was settling, and we bounded on to shore, eager to make camp before nightfall. On the previous nights, we had found empty beaches, with no sight of any inhabitants. But as we descended from the high sides of the *Argo*, a glint of light flashed in the distance, and then another and another. The low, slanting sunlight was bouncing off metal: an army of bronze-clad warriors streaming towards us.

I swung my bow round, steadying my back foot, training my first arrow towards the onslaught. Beside me, I registered the change in Heracles, at once silent, drawn up to his full height, his lip curled in a snarl that made him more ferocious than the lion whose skin he wore about his neck. It was the first time I had seen him like this, the first time I began to understand the legends that abounded about this man.

All of us were poised and ready, armed with bows, spears, axes, clubs and swords. A battle was coming, just as I'd been anticipating for days. Now was my chance. I watched them come, urging them closer, ready to let my arrows fly.

Jason held up his arm. I felt a moment of irritation, but I saw that the onslaught had halted and that the fighters were holding themselves in a line some distance from us. They stood and we stood, all of us wary. From their line, a figure detached itself and came forwards, bronze helmet catching the dying rays of the sun. Jason stepped forwards, then changed his mind and gestured for Aethalides, our herald, to go forth to meet the enemy. The two met in the centre of our opposing lines.

I waited, holding my breath as I held the taut bow string. But no hostilities broke out. Rather, the other warrior reached up to pull off the shining helmet and, to my astonishment, a tumble of long hair cascaded down from beneath it. One by one, the other warriors behind her did the same. Every single one of them was a woman.

I strained to hear as Aethalides and the woman spoke, but I couldn't make out the words. In our line, I saw the men relax. I wondered that the surprise didn't make them more uneasy. After all, what kind of a place was defended by a female army? Somewhere like the forest from which I had come, but perhaps ruled over by Athena rather than Artemis? That would explain the military appearance of the women, but it would bode no better for the Argonauts than it had for any of the hapless men who had strayed into Arcadia.

At length, Aethalides stepped back and beckoned Jason over. The armoured women turned away, retreating to the interior of the island. I was disappointed to see them go, and keen to hear what conversation had taken place. Jason nodded tersely to Aethalides, then signalled for us all to draw nearer.

'The woman that spoke is the queen of this island,' Jason announced. 'Lemnos is defended by women since all the men-folk deserted them. They brought slave-women from Thrace and preferred them so much to the wives they had at home that they deserted Lemnos and went to live among the Thracian women instead. The Lemnian women you just saw feared that their former husbands were returning, that they might want to claim the island for themselves and their new wives, and drive out those they had abandoned. That's why they rushed out, ready to fight if necessary. But since Aethalides explained that we are here only to seek food and shelter, Queen Hypsipyle welcomes us to their shores. She invites us to share their hospitality tonight.'

I stared at him. While many of our crew were exclaiming their pleasure at such welcome news, eagerly anticipating the luxuries of a banquet, I was sceptical of the offer.

Meleager shifted from foot to foot at my side. I was glad he wasn't joining in with the clamour to follow the women into the city.

'What do you think of this?' I muttered to him.

He shook his head. 'It seems . . . odd.'

I noticed that Heracles was listening to us. 'Do you think it's wise to go?' he called out to Jason.

Jason bridled. 'I hardly think a town full of women poses us a threat,' he said. 'They have offered hospitality; they won't dare to break the sacred tradition by attacking us. I am sure they mean us no harm, and even if they did, we are stronger than they are. But feel free to stay and guard the boat if you're concerned.'

I was taken aback by the sharpness of his tone. I'd seen the conflict between Heracles and Jason back at Pagasae. But while Jason seethed, resenting the easy respect that Heracles commanded, I hadn't heard him issue anything as close to an open challenge as this, and I didn't know how Heracles would respond. I was fairly sure he wasn't a man used to controlling his temper. But he only barked with laughter, a response that made Jason bristle more.

'I will stay here,' he said. 'Good luck to the rest of you.'

Jason turned on his heel and strode away. Although some of the crew looked between us, clearly torn between their natural trust in Heracles and their desire for wine, good food and the company of women, the latter won out for all but me, Heracles, Hylas and Meleager.

The four of us exchanged glances. Heracles' gaze was cool, and he soon looked away as though uninterested.

'Do you think it really is a trick?' I asked.

Heracles shrugged and spat on the ground. 'Maybe it is, maybe it isn't. It's a distraction anyway. We should sail on at dawn, not linger here.' He let out a long, rumbling sigh. 'Come, Hylas, let's get some wood for a fire.' He stalked away towards a copse of trees, Hylas at his side.

'Why didn't you go with the crew?' I asked Meleager.

'It might be suspicious,' he answered. 'It makes sense to stay here, for us to wait and see what happens.'

'Perhaps they'll return quickly,' I said. 'Jason will want to keep going. This is his expedition, his quest for the Fleece. Surely he won't want to waste time.'

'I hope so. Come on, let's see what we can find in those woods to eat.'

I followed him into the trees. At least I would get to use my bow for something.

Night fell, and though it was strange to sit with Heracles and Hylas, the four of us managed to eat companionably enough by the fire. Heracles told his stories as usual, draining cups of wine at a far faster rate than any of the rest of us. I let his anecdotes wash over me, focusing my attention elsewhere. The moon glimmered above the crest of the hill, her beams casting a faint illumination on the track where the women and our crew had disappeared earlier.

'What are you thinking?'

I jerked my head back.

Meleager's eyes were intent on me. 'Are you wondering if you should follow them? See what's happening?' He'd seen exactly what was on my mind.

'Don't you want to know?' I asked.

He was leaning back on his elbows. The jug of wine at his side was almost empty, a drop of wine tracing a glistening, crimson path down the side. On the other side of the fire, Heracles sat with one arm resting on his drawn-up knees, the other loosely draped over Hylas' shoulders. The atmosphere was somnolent and hazy. Except for me. My fingers drummed on the ground, my feet twitching to run.

Meleager yawned. 'I'm sure they'll tell us everything in the morning.' He looked apologetic, but not enough to want to accompany me.

'You won't be able to rest until you've seen them,' Hylas said, looking shrewdly at me through the flames.

It was true, I wouldn't. 'I'll go.'

'Wait, I'll come with you.' Meleager started to struggle to his feet, but I shook my head.

'You'll only slow me down. I'll be back before you know it.' I smiled to soften any sting my dismissal might carry, but he didn't look offended.

It amused Heracles. 'So, the entire army of Lemnos is no match for you, Atalanta.'

I met his gaze steadily. 'I'm not going to take on an army,' I said. 'I'm just going to see what they're doing.'

9

The path wound its way between two peaks, the dark shapes of the mountains rising up on either side of me as I jogged along. The soft sounds of the night whispered around me: the rustling breath of the wind through leaves, the darting scamper of a small creature and the heavier tread of something bigger, quietly stalking, hidden in the shadows. It felt like home.

My way was lit by moonlight until I rounded a bend and suddenly, there before me, were the lights of the city. Torches burned around the outer walls, a brighter blaze where the glow of a dozen flames merged into one incandescent halo around what must have been the palace. That would be where they were, I thought, narrowing my eyes as I surveyed it, searching for a way in.

As I drew closer, however, I saw the tall wooden gates of the city were unguarded. They creaked in the breeze, swinging slightly on their hinges, the bolts left undone. Despite the defensive front the women had mounted when we arrived, they clearly were unconcerned about an attack now. That gave the lie to what they had told us before, that they feared the return of the Lemnian men, that they were ready to fight to protect themselves.

I crept closer, keeping out of the pools of light cast by the torches. I could hear music spilling through the wide arched doorways to the palace. The streets that led to it were empty; everyone must be in there, all the women of Lemnos and all the men of the *Argo*.

I passed through a great colonnade at the front entrance to the royal building. The vivid hues of the paint and the polished sheen of marble were dazzling to my eyes, unused as I was to artifice. And somewhere, deep in the heart of this palace, my crewmates feasted. The scent of roasting meat mingled with the sounds of their laughter. It was clear there was no fighting taking place. I hesitated, tempted to turn back now I knew that no hostilities had broken out. But I was curious to see more, intrigued by the unfamiliar grandeur. I wanted to reach out, to run my hand over the gems inlaid among the tiles, to breathe in the rich fragrance of the crushed petals that floated in wide, shallow bowls, perfuming the air.

'Atalanta?'

I jumped. How had I allowed myself to be so distracted that someone could creep up on me? I whirled around.

It was her, the woman who had spoken to our herald. I recognised her by the thick fall of her hair, though now it was topped with a crown rather than a war-helmet. She wore a long dress of dark blue, stitched with golden thread, like stars shining in the evening sky. Before, she had been hidden behind her armour; now, she was soft and graceful. There was a certain hardness in her expression, though; something imposing in the way she stood.

'How do you know my name?' I asked.

'I've heard about you, from the others. It was easy to recognise you from the description – the only woman among their number.'

'And you are queen of this city?'

She nodded. 'Hypsipyle. Have you come to join us?'

'No.'

'Then what?'

I gave her a long, cool stare. I noticed how her eyes flickered over me, her covert assessment of my height, my stance, the bow fastened to my back.

'Did you think we plotted against your men?' she asked. 'Lured them here, into an ambush of some sort?'

I held my silence. Her face stayed smooth and calm.

'We respect the laws of hospitality here,' she said. 'And we would gain nothing from harming them.'

'What do you want from them, then?' I asked.

A flurry of notes plucked from what could only be the lyre of Orpheus tumbled through the air like shining coins.

She sighed. 'Do you want to walk with me, Atalanta? Out in the city?'

I hesitated.

'Don't be suspicious,' she said. 'I can swear to you now, by any immortal that dwells on Mount Olympus, that we won't hurt a single member of the Argonauts.'

'I'll go with you.' I was intrigued. I didn't trust her, but I was drawn to know more, too. I suppose she reminded me of Artemis, this warrior queen, with her self-assured composure and the display of strength she had put on for our arrival.

Outside, the sound of the revels dissipated. As we walked away, all I could hear was the crunch of our footsteps on the stony tracks and the song of crickets, punctuated by the occasional hoot of an owl.

'You know that our men didn't leave us,' she said. 'I could see it on your face the moment you heard what I'd said to Jason.'

'Why would they go? Leaving their city behind, to go to a foreign place, the home of the women they'd stolen to be their captives?' Saying it out loud, I couldn't believe Jason had accepted it so easily.

'It didn't occur to any of your crew to look for reasons to disbelieve me. Perhaps they wanted it to be true. A city full of women, welcoming them to our shores.'

'What did you do to them, the men? What happened here?'

'I asked about you,' she said. 'Where you had come from, how you came to join such a voyage. They told me you have lived in a forest, devoting your life to Artemis. I don't suppose you know much of what men are like.'

'Men would come to the forest. To hunt. To search for the nymphs they'd heard stories of.'

'Then you do have an idea.' She took a long breath. 'Our men were seafarers, always going on long journeys. We were used to being self-sufficient, to running Lemnos in their absence when we had to. They always came back. It was a harmonious life. But things changed, all at once.' She stopped walking. 'Perhaps we neglected our worship of Aphrodite, I don't know. Perhaps it was simply our way of life that offended her. But she struck us with a horrible affliction.'

'A plague?' I asked.

'No. Something much simpler, much more humiliating and vile.' She swallowed, and I could see that it pained her to talk of it. I waited for her to go on. 'We didn't know what caused it, not in the beginning. At first, we thought it rose from the earth; a dank, mouldering sort of smell, so foul it could have come from the very caverns of Hades. We crushed flowers into oil to fragrance the air, then, as the reek only intensified, we would dip rags into the perfumed liquid and press them to our faces for some respite. The men were away, breathing the fresh salty air that blows across the ocean. Here, we set our wits against defeating this foul stench. But, as time passed, we found it harder to look one another in the eye. We found it impossible to speak out loud, the truth we couldn't deny.'

'What was it?'

'The smell that was driving every one of us to the frayed edges of our sanity wasn't from the stagnant depths of a festering pool or some undiscovered animal carcass rotting in the hot sun. It was us, the women, from the smallest of our girls to the oldest of crones. Each one of us somehow was afflicted.'

'And it was Aphrodite?' I asked. 'A punishment?'

'So it seemed.' She turned to the side, angling her face away from me as she struggled over the next words. 'We were scalded with shame, praying to Aphrodite and burning offerings at her altars, begging to be forgiven for the transgression we had unknowingly committed. But – when the men returned, they were unaffected. Only we were cursed.'

'And so, did they leave you because of it?' But I suspected this wasn't what had happened at all. From the way she wrapped her arms around her body, the slight tremble in her voice, I knew there was something much worse to come.

'One by one, they withdrew from us. The most devoted of our husbands did their best, turning their faces away, finding every excuse they could to be outdoors, to roam the furthest corners of the island. But to a man, they couldn't tolerate the hideous miasma that had settled on us. They boarded their boats, took to the seas again.'

'But they came back?'

'We thought they were leaving us. The only man who stayed was my father, the king. He wouldn't go; he wanted to do whatever he could to help us. But he was as mystified as we were. And then' – she seemed to steel herself to go on – 'then they returned, but they weren't alone.'

'The slave-women?' I imagined the scene, the sickening realisation.

'We trusted them. They were our husbands, fathers, brothers, even sons. They had left us, unable to bear being anywhere near us. And while they were gone, they had resolved to bring back new women instead.'

My blood boiled to think of it. Not just on behalf of the spurned women staring from the shoreline, but the captured women, torn from their own families, their own homes, taken on the selfish whims of men. 'What did you do to them?'

'What would you have done, Atalanta?'

'When centaurs came to my forest, looking to ravage, I shot them both dead with my arrows.'

I saw her smile in the dim light. 'Well. We didn't turn on them in that moment. We were shocked by what they'd done. These were men we thought we knew. Instead of helping us to make amends to Aphrodite, or helping us to shoulder the burden, bearing it alongside us, they had gone to find other women to satisfy their needs. Whether they'd hoped to seek willing consorts at first, we didn't know, but it became apparent that they had sailed to Thrace and waged war, kidnapping the women to take as slaves. Now they set their faces against the sobs and the pleas, not a shred of pity in their hearts for any of us. Only glee at their conquest.' She was quiet for a long moment. Then she seemed to shake herself out of her distant reverie. 'We gathered together the evening that they returned, out on the peninsula. The winds were vigorous there, buffeting us from all sides. They would cloak our words from anyone trying to overhear, carry away the worst of the smell.'

'There is no trace of it anymore,' I said, not wanting to interrupt but not able to suppress my curiosity either. 'Did you find a way to appease Aphrodite?'

'Later – afterwards – her anger waned,' Hypsipyle said. 'As soon as we had become afflicted, we had been building more altars to her, we had made more sacrifices and given her more praise. If our men had been prepared to wait with us, to bear it for a while longer, then perhaps we would never have had to do what we did. But they weren't. They didn't wait to see if she relented. They didn't give us a chance.'

Afterwards, she'd said. Aphrodite had lifted her punishment too late, after whatever it was they'd done to the men. I stayed silent, waiting for her to continue.

'It was me who suggested it.' Her voice was low. 'Me who asked the women how we could ever go back to our lives, shoulder to shoulder with those men, knowing what they were capable of doing. We couldn't break bread with them, let them into our beds, bear their children, not now we knew the monsters that dwelt behind their human faces.'

The fierceness that simmered in her even now was impressive. It was easy to picture her, standing in the centre of the women, rousing them to anger.

'We knew they'd be drunk, stuporous soon enough from the celebrations to which they treated themselves in honour of their victory. They thought we had been crushed and defeated, that we'd slunk away. I knew that if we were to strike, it had to be at that moment, when they believed us to be beaten. Our hearts were hardened against them. We crept back in the depths of the night to their houses, where they lay drunk and snoring in their beds. Beds they had defiled.' Her voice trembled with remembered rage. 'We gathered up their weapons. Knives, swords, daggers, any blade we could find. Heavy pots from the kitchen. When the Thracian women realised what we were doing, they were eager to join us.'

So this was the secret. 'Did you really kill them all?'

She paused. 'My father was blameless. He had taken no part in it; it wouldn't be fair if he paid the price as well. I knew he couldn't stay though; the women would never allow it. There was a savagery among us that night, a pent-up ferocity that had built inside us since the moment we realised we were cursed. All the horror that had overwhelmed us, it was like a crashing wave, a storm of righteous anger.'

Artemis had told me once of the rites of Dionysus. His maenads, who gathered beneath the moon, unleashing all that they held inside them. Tearing through flesh, smearing their faces in blood. An ancient passion, a shared frenzy. Hypsipyle's story made me think of it now.

'I crept away from the other women. I stole to the palace alone, hurrying through the dark corridors to find my father. He was sitting up among his pillows, confused by what he'd heard. His confusion turned swiftly to fear when he saw me, my hair loose and my dress stained with blood. I knew I had to hide him; I tried to persuade him to climb into an oak chest. But then, the women might tear the palace apart, and I couldn't bear the thought of them discovering him cowering inside.'

'Did you save him?' I asked.

'Something about the wildness of the night imbued me with more strength than I knew I possessed,' she said. 'With my father following me, I dragged that chest across the tiled floors, right out into the open air. I could hear the women shrieking at the gates, ready to rid the island of its final man. Although my muscles screamed with agony, I pulled the chest over the rocky ground, dragging it all the way to the shore. He didn't want to get in – he wondered if it would be better to die the King of Lemnos in his own palace – but I convinced him. He trusted me. I felt as though I was sealing him in his own tomb as I fastened the lid shut. I could hear the footsteps of the women racing from the palace, searching for him. I had no time. I pushed the chest into the water, a cry breaking from my throat as I watched it dip beneath the water and then bob again to the surface. It drifted on the current, away from the shore. I watched it for as long as I could until it was swallowed up by the night. I offered a fervent prayer to any gods that were listening to take pity on my father's gentle heart and spare him, bring him to safety somewhere far from here.' Her voice softened. 'They found me down on the shore, the women of Lemnos and the women of Thrace. They never suspected what I had done. The frenzy of violence lifted from us as the dawn broke. We held each other close, bathed each other's wounds and, as the sun rose, we rinsed the blood from each other's hair.'

'Have you all lived here alone since that day?' I asked.

She raised her eyes to meet mine. 'No man has set foot on Lemnos since my father escaped. Not until the Argonauts arrived.'

10

I'd known there was something darker in the history of Lemnos, something she had been holding back. Even so, wholesale slaughter was more than I could have guessed. The palace seemed far away from us now, out on the edges of the city where we stood together. The palace where my fellow Argonauts were drinking and feasting, much like the doomed men of this island on the night of the massacre. Had she lured me here for a reason, distracting me with her story to get me too far away from my crew to defend them?

'We aren't killers for the sake of it,' she said. 'Believe me, Atalanta, that not one of us wants to relive that night.'

'Then what is it that you want from us?' I paced away, then back again. Should I run to the palace, or to the shore to summon Heracles and Meleager?

'Isn't it obvious?' she asked, a flutter of amusement in her tone.

'Why would I ask if it was?' I was annoyed by her continued evasion.

'Atalanta, we are an island of women now. Not one man or boy survived our vengeance.'

'So?'

'So, all was well at first. As I said, we were used to fending for ourselves. But now . . .'

'Now what?'

'Now our elders grow older still. Our daughters are women with no babies of their own to cherish. If we stay as we are, the years will pass and they will become old themselves, and who will care for them? Who will plough and hunt when there is no one young and vigorous to take over? We will die and our city with us.'

'But what can we do about that?'

Hypsipyle reached out and I sprang back, poised to counter any blow. But she only tried to take my hand in hers. Without thinking, I shook her away. It didn't ruffle her dignity at all. 'You can join us, Atalanta. All of you.'

'Are you mad?'

'We know of your quest, we have heard of the reputations of many who sail with you. We've invited your men to feast with us this evening and been impressed with their courtesy, with their conviviality . . .'

'We only arrived on your shores this evening. And you want – what? For the Argonauts to abandon their quest, to join your city, to stay here with you in place of the men you killed?'

I could see the flush spreading across her cheeks. 'You are a band of heroes, the like of which the world has never known. The stories abound already. But the Fleece that you seek, it's a trick. No one could retrieve it; it is guarded by powers even your crew could never match. I could see it plainly enough when Jason explained it to me tonight. It's a doomed venture – why waste such men on it?'

'It would be a far greater waste of men to spend our lives here!'

'We ask for a season, perhaps, not the rest of your lives. Time to spend here, to train together, to consider how such an impossible task could be achieved – rather than sailing off with no strategy, no idea of how to accomplish it. Perhaps we can help you. And then if, somehow, you can find a way to steal the Fleece, perhaps some of you would return here afterwards, to the children that might be born from the stay, to wives and homes here. There is a place for you too, Atalanta. I think you'd fit in very well. There is no other city like this, nowhere else we know of where the women live as we do.'

'Is this another collective insanity? How could you decide to make husbands and fathers of these men? How do you know they would be any different from the ones you had before?'

'There will be no other opportunity like this for us again,' she said. 'What else do we do? Wait for fishermen to wash up on our beaches, take in any stray survivors of nearby ship-wrecks? We won't leave our home, and even if we did, where could we go? Who would accept us, if they found out what we've done?'

I was shaking my head. 'It isn't for us to fix what you did. We have our quest, we won't be delayed. The gods are behind us. We don't need time to devise a plan.'

'But why the hurry? Come, see the feast, see how your crewmates are enjoying the comforts of a rich palace. It's better than casting out again on an unpredictable sea, to endure the lashing rain and freezing winds, to sleep on hard ground and forage for your food. You can have weeks here with us, building up strength before you sail again.'

'We have all the strength we need,' I said.

'Well. I had hoped to persuade you, Atalanta. When I saw you among them, I thought I saw a woman like us. But I think your men take a different view to you, anyway.'

'They might enjoy your company tonight,' I said shortly. 'But we will sail tomorrow.'

She inclined her head. 'We'll see.'

I didn't bite at the challenge in her words, though I was more riled than I wanted to admit.

'Will you come back with me now, at least?' she asked. 'There's really no need for you and your other companions to sleep out on the beach tonight. We can offer you warm beds and shelter.'

'That's of no interest to us.'

'Of course. Whatever you prefer.' Hypsipyle's eyes were unreadable in the dark. 'Sleep well, Atalanta. Perhaps you will accept my invitation tomorrow – or another day.'

I ground my teeth together. 'We will be gone before then.'

She touched my arm, and this time I didn't pull away. I held my ground, sure and steady. 'Goodnight.' Her skirts rippled in the breeze as she turned, the fine fabric fluttering behind her. I wasn't fooled by the soft femininity of her appearance now.

She was right to think that she recognised something in me. I felt it too, the call of something fierce and untamed. But something of her repelled me too. I'd killed before and felt no regret. I hadn't wept across the bodies of the centaurs who sought to attack me. But then, I'd acted to defend myself. It was a different thing to steal up on a sleeping man, a different thing to slaughter a city full of them. These women hadn't just killed their faithless husbands; together they had murdered their own brothers, their own sons. Could every last one of them truly have been so wicked as she said?

I watched her go, her light tread across the dusty earth, the ripple of her hair like a dark, polished jewel, everything about her so rich and fine. I did believe, at least, that she meant the Argonauts no harm. They could give her something, some hope of a future for the city she ruled. I was sure they would be safe in Lemnos tonight.

But tomorrow, I resolved, we would leave this place.

I waited until she was out of sight and then I ran, all the way back to our camp.

Dawn broke misty and damp over the bay. Meleager was already awake when I rose, but Heracles and Hylas still slept. They had made their bed further away, but the air carried the faint sound of Heracles' snores.

I had stayed by Meleager, sheltered from the wind by a line of boulders but in full view of the *Argo*. There seemed no need to find a secret place, to hide myself away when there was only us two. It was strange, though, to see his face when I opened my eyes. He was sitting on the beach, his knees drawn up, his eyes on the ocean. I watched him for a moment before sitting up. He looked lost in thought and I wondered what it was that preoccupied him so. Worries about our errant crew and how well they might resist the charms of the Lemnian women, perhaps. I'd shared everything that Hypsipyle had told me when I'd returned the night before. Heracles had seemed unsurprised, even by the lurid details of the massacre. I suppose it took a lot to shock a man who had seen and done the kinds of things he had. He was sceptical that we would be on our way today. Perhaps Meleager was thinking of that, longing to be back on board, heaving the oars and slicing through the waves again.

Or maybe he looked out at the horizon thinking not of where we were going, but what he had left behind. Did he think of his family, wishing himself back in Calydon?

I sat up and he looked around at me. 'You're awake,' he said. He smiled, the same as ever, but his eyes were serious.

'No sign of any of the others?' I asked, not hopeful that there would be. He shook his head. My hair was beginning to come loose from the tightly coiled braid I kept it in, wisps fluttering over my face, obscuring my vision. Irritated, I pulled it all free, yanking my fingers through it to pull out any tangles.

Meleager looked away.

'What's that in the distance?' I asked.

Something was rapidly moving along the mountain path, taking clearer shape as it got closer to us.

'Euphemus!' Heracles' voice boomed out. I was surprised I hadn't heard his heavy-footed approach, but I was distracted by watching Euphemus' swift stride as he hurtled towards us. In a matter of seconds, he was standing before us.

'Heracles,' he said. He nodded to the rest of us. He wasn't out of breath at all, I noticed. 'The queen extends her invitation to you all to join us at a feast tonight.'

'Tonight?' I stared at him. 'I thought you must be coming to tell us to start readying the ship to leave.'

Euphemus shrugged. 'That's the message Jason told me to deliver. What answer shall I take back?'

Heracles snorted.

Euphemus nodded. 'As you wish.' He darted away, sprinting back along the path before we could say anything else.

I itched to follow. I'd been waiting for my chance to see this legendary runner and I was sure I could beat him if I wanted.

But Hypsipyle might be waiting for his return. I didn't want to see her again.

'They should all have come back,' I said. 'Jason should be rounding them up and bringing them here.' I started to plait my hair again, my fingers deftly twisting it back into place, out of my way.

Meleager looked contemplative. 'A longer rest might not do any harm,' he said. 'A day or two perhaps, to replenish their spirits, renew their resolve.'

'We've barely begun!' I protested. 'Surely no one's resolve can be flagging already.'

'Meleager's right,' Heracles said. 'Give them a day, another night here. They won't want to go just yet, and from what you said, Atalanta, the women here will do what they can to persuade them to stay. But they'll remember why we're here, what we're going to do. Now's not the time for dallying, not at the very start when we're eager still to see what comes next. No one is jaded yet; no one's tired of fighting and questing.'

I wrapped the finished braid around the crown of my head, fastening it tightly. 'So we just have to wait?' It didn't seem like Heracles to be the patient one.

'Leave them tonight,' he said. 'But tomorrow, if they don't remember themselves, then we'll remind them.'

I bridled. Tomorrow wasn't soon enough for me.

The day was desultory. I fired arrows at a gnarled tree for practice until I grew tired of the tedium and flung myself down by the charred remains of the previous night's fire.

'I didn't know you were so eager for the Fleece,' Meleager remarked.

I frowned. 'Why not? It's the whole reason we're here.'

'Maybe.'

'Well, why else?'

He seemed perfectly content, sprawled out under the warm sun, watching the waves glittering. 'Adventure. Excitement. Discovering new lands and making a name for ourselves.'

'I never wanted to find anywhere other than my forest before.' I turned my face up to the sky, closing my eyes. 'But then, I've never known a day to drag so slowly as this one.' I felt a flash of worry. Meleager seemed so assured that making a name for himself from this quest would be simple, but how much harder would it be for me to be remembered? The other Argonauts' names were known already. Mine still had to be forged.

'I can't wait another night,' I said. 'We need to remind Jason of his duty, so that he orders them to come back.'

The impatience in my tone got through to him and he propped himself up on his elbow, his eyes more serious now. 'We can go together this time,' he said. 'I'll come into the city with you. I want to see it.'

I eyed him with suspicion. 'You don't want to join them, do you?'

'I wouldn't dream of it. I want to leave here too. I expected battles – I thought we would have one here when we saw their army. But instead, we got the queen.' He paused and I wondered if he was remembering the moment when she pulled off her helmet and we saw her face for the first time. 'A woman who ordered the deaths of all her men . . . that's something I never imagined.'

I hesitated. 'She intrigues you?'

'No, I didn't mean that. Rather – I want to see for myself if our crew are at any risk.'

'I thought you were confident they could take care of themselves.'

'They can. But if she is plotting anything, it's better that we know. Besides, I can talk to Jason.'

'You don't think he'll listen to me.'

'We can present our case together.' His smile was disarming.

I wavered, but perhaps Meleager was right. His words would carry more sway with Jason. Though it rankled, it was better that he came to argue alongside me. The sooner we were gone from Lemnos, the happier I would feel.

'Tell me about Calydon,' I asked Meleager as we set off. I found myself interested to know what it was like, the place where he had been born and lived his life. Now that I knew a tiny piece of the world beyond the edges of my forest, I wanted to be able to picture more of it.

'It's ruled by my father, King Oeneus,' he said. 'Rich in vines, which thrive in our soil. My father says they're a gift from Dionysus, that he came to Calydon and, in thanks for my father's hospitality, gave them to us so we would always have plentiful wine.'

'Dionysus stayed in your father's palace?'

'He did.'

'And?' I could tell there was more to this story.

He sighed. 'My mother is very beautiful. She has borne my father many children ... but when Dionysus honoured my father with his presence, it was obvious that he was very taken with my mother's beauty. When my father realised this, he went away for a night, claiming that he had to perform some sacred rites, leaving the god with his wife.'

I raised an eyebrow.

'My sister, Deianira, was born nine moons later.'

That explained the gift of vines, then. I remembered Meleager saying that some thought his own true father was Ares, and wished I could see just how beautiful his mother really was, to attract so much attention from the gods. I thought of Callisto, the shame and condemnation she suffered when Zeus seized her in the forest. And now Meleager was telling me that Oeneus hadn't blamed his wife, but had accepted the children she brought him. It felt like a little splinter lodged in my heart.

'As well as wine-making, we hunt,' Meleager went on. 'Our forests are full of wild boar. I have been out with my hounds ever since I can remember.' He laughed. 'I'm not sure any quarry ever escaped me before you appeared.'

'And were your parents worried when you left to join the crew of the *Argo*?' I asked.

'They have no need to worry about me.'

'It's a dangerous venture. The sea alone is full of perils.' The thought of the salty, choking depths of the ocean made the base of my spine feel cold in a way no monster could.

'Really, they believe they have no need to fear for my life,' he said.

'Why not?'

'After I was born, my mother had a dream,' he said. 'She heard the Moirai talking – the three Fates who spin and cut the thread of every human life. They said her baby would live only until a log in the fire burned to ash. She woke, terrified, and saw the log from her dream burning in the hearth. She pulled it out, not caring about the burns or the blisters on her hands. She flung a woollen blanket over it to smother the flames and she has kept what's left of the log locked away in a box. She believes I won't die unless it's set alight again.'

'Do you believe it, too?'

'It's tempting. I wish I did, but – I can't help thinking it might have only been the dream of an anxious mother.'

'So it doesn't make you yearn to put it to the test?'

He laughed again. 'Not necessarily, no. But you were chosen by Artemis to join this voyage; do you feel safe knowing that she watches over you?'

'It's not like that – not completely, anyway,' I said. I saw what he meant, that he had no more guarantee of safety than I did. 'She rescued me as a baby. I was left on the side of Mount Parthenion to die.' I glanced at him to see how he reacted. His eyes were warm with sympathy, inviting me to go on. 'She has her sacred animals in the forest and they do as she commands. It pleased her to have me taken up by a mother bear and raised with her cubs for a time. When I was no longer a baby, her nymphs took charge of my education. The bears never harmed me, and when they left me, she made sure I was cared for by the nymphs. But I learned to defend myself. In the forest, it's the only way to survive.' I thought of Arethusa, and Callisto. 'If you make a mistake there, you bear the consequences. It's the natural order of things.' *Even if that mistake was simply to trail your fingers in a river or stay out in the woods after dark*, I didn't add.

He nodded. 'I can see that in you.'

'What do you mean?'

'Well, there's no other woman who would have joined this quest,' he said. 'It's taken them so much by surprise. Most of them don't know what to think of you at all.'

'I'm here because I'm good enough.'

'That's what confuses them the most.'

We walked in silence for a while. I wanted to ask him more about his home, about his wife too. The questions hovered on my lips, but every time I opened my mouth to ask, I found that I couldn't.

Clouds drifted over the moon, casting us into a deeper darkness. Up ahead, the lights of the city gleamed.

'I think rain is coming,' Meleager said, glancing up at the heavy skies.

I picked up my pace and he matched it. I could feel it in the air too, the stillness before a thunderstorm. But it held off as we rounded the final curve and reached the sloping track that led to the city gates.

Again, they were left undefended, and we slipped through, into the deserted streets.

'This way to the palace,' I whispered. We darted through the shadows between the circles of light cast by burning torches. Great bowls of fire burned at the base of a statue, fresh flowers heaped at its feet. I looked up at the smooth stone curves of her body, the blank and beautiful face. Aphrodite, the goddess of love. I took note of the recent offerings; clearly the Lemnian women were honouring her enthusiastically now. Were they calling on her to help them detain our men, to keep them from our quest? I felt my lip curl, almost a snarl.

'Here?' Meleager said. He was ahead of me, by the columns that stood at the palace entrance. He stepped back, taking it in. 'Let's try this way.' He gestured down the side of the imposing façade. 'We'll see where they are, how we might be able to get Jason away to speak in private.'

I thought of hunting, how I would track my prey, stay hidden while I assessed the best strategy. Before, I had allowed myself to be wrong-footed by my surroundings, by the unfamiliarity of the gold and jewels, the dazzling finery and the maze of corridors. But I had no need to be intimidated. There was no one to match me in the forest, after all; why would it be different here? And it added another layer, having someone with me. A little thrill of enjoyment, not stalking silent and alone as I was used to.

We slipped down the side of the palace, the noise getting louder as we went. The lyre, clear and melodic as always, joined by a haphazard drumbeat. Voices raised together in rowdy song. Clearly, the Argonauts were enjoying themselves. Meleager stopped, his face intent, listening hard. Then he seemed to relax.

'Let's just go in,' he said. 'I don't think we need to be too careful about being seen. There is so much revelry going on, I doubt any of them will notice us.'

As long as we didn't encounter Hypsipyle prowling around again, I thought. 'Fine,' I said.

We peered through the great arched doorway into a hall packed with long tables. Our comrades lounged on benches, surrounded by jugs brimming with wine and platters piled high with food – roasted hunks of meat, olives, cheese, bread and fruit. The women of Lemnos sat between them, shining curls and sparkling eyes, full of vivacity and high spirits. I felt mine sink a little at the sight and saw Meleager's face mirroring my own.

'Look, Jason is there,' he said, pointing to the furthest bench, one that sat higher than all of the others at the end of the hall. While the other benches were grouped together, a cluster of Argonauts and Lemnian women at each, Jason sat alone – with Hypsipyle. She was leaning in close to him, a curtain of hair obscuring her face from where I stood, but I could see his. He gazed at her, enrapt, utterly intent on whatever she was saying to him. He looked more comfortable and content than I had ever seen him. He'd struck me so far as unremarkable, but now, his easy smile and relaxed demeanour made him seem more handsome, more appealing than I'd considered him before. I sighed, frustrated.

'I'm going in,' Meleager said.

'What?' The horror I felt must have rung clear in my tone because he rushed to reassure me.

'Not to join them – though they'll think that's why I'm here. I'm going to get Jason, make him come out here so we can talk to him together.'

It made sense. If I went in, I was sure it would alert Hypsipyle's suspicion, but Meleager could easily be one of them. I watched him go, sure and confident as he greeted the crew, brushing off their roars of welcome and the drunken shouting, making his way directly to the leader. At the swell of noise, Jason tore himself away from the queen, looking around to see what the disturbance was. I watched Meleager lean in, Jason listening and Hypsipyle turning away, her displeasure at the interruption clear. I wondered if she would try to keep him at her side, but she waved an imperious hand and he stood, looking a little uncertain but following in Meleager's steps.

Meleager led Jason swiftly through the crowded hall and out into the corridor where I waited.

'What is this?' Jason asked.

'We have come to find out what the delay is,' I said. 'Why you dally here, in this city, while the *Argo* languishes on the shore.'

His brows drew together in a frown.

'We wanted to know what was happening,' Meleager said. 'If the crew had become recalcitrant, if you needed our assistance in reminding them what we set out to do.'

'The queen has offered us hospitality for as long as we want to stay.' Jason's eyes were hard. I suspected that he didn't like being asked to explain himself.

'We are rested now,' I said. 'Why stay any longer?'

He glanced back into the feasting hall, the sweet aroma of wine mingling with roasting meat, the music and all the women; bare, slender arms, dresses held with a single glittering clasp at the shoulder. 'They are seeking new husbands,' he said. 'A future for their city.'

'But we aren't seeking brides,' Meleager said. 'That's not what we sailed for.'

'She's offered me her father's royal sceptre,' Jason went on, as though Meleager hadn't spoken. 'The queen, Hypsipyle, she has said that she would make me king if we stay. If I marry her.'

Really? I mused. The woman I had met, so full of fire and determination, a woman who would mastermind the deaths of every man who had wronged her and her sisters, she would be content to marry *Jason*? 'But you don't want to be the King of Lemnos,' I said. 'You don't want to rule over a distant city, on an island far from your home. You didn't embark on the greatest voyage the world has ever seen in order to settle here and oversee the farming and settle disputes and have an insignificant realm like this under your control. Would that bring glory to the goddesses Hera and Athena who blessed our journey?' I watched his face carefully as I spoke. 'You didn't come here to win a foreign queen. You set out to achieve the impossible, to take the Golden Fleece, so that bards will sing of you forever. How will that happen if you stay here?'

'Of course, I don't plan to stay,' he blustered. 'I haven't given up our quest. I would never do such a thing.'

'Then why stay any longer? Every day that passes only keeps us from our goal.'

'We have stayed only to rest, to replenish our spirits.' A raucous shout of laughter burst from the hall, echoing down the corridor. 'And to show gratitude to the queen for welcoming us here. But I intend to leave tomorrow; I have always planned it to be so.'

I kept my face as still as possible, determined not to roll my eyes.

'I am glad that you both came, however, to make sure of it. Your loyalty to our quest is admirable.' He was puffing himself up as he spoke, convincing himself, at least, of the truth of his words. 'Will you come in now, share some wine with us before we make our farewells?'

'Thank you,' Meleager said swiftly, 'but we will go back, prepare the ship and make sure all is ready for us to sail in the morning.'

I breathed out. 'We'll let Heracles know to be ready, too.'

Jason's eyes darkened a little. 'Why hasn't he come?'

'He prefers to stay outside. To stay focused,' Meleager said, his voice smooth. 'You know how he can be, how much he can drink. If he were here, we might never be able to make him leave again. It's better that he stays away, with Hylas.'

Jason shrugged, a jerky movement. 'Make everything ready for dawn,' he said. 'We will be there.' He turned and strode back into the hall and I saw Hypsipyle lift her face towards him, like a flower opening towards the sun. But her eyes caught mine as she smiled. I saw the coldness in them, and I hoped we had done enough to persuade him.

The rain began to fall on our way back to our camp; great fat drops, a shock after the warmth of the palace. It quickly became torrential, cascading in huge sheets from the skies, and

Meleager and I didn't even have to speak, dashing together under the branches of a wide-spreading oak tree at the side of the track to take shelter.

'Do you wish you'd taken Jason up on the invitation to stay?' I asked, squeezing water from my braided hair.

'Not in the slightest,' he said. 'I'd rather be here.' He stopped, an abrupt halt in whatever it was he was about to say.

I could sense the heat from his body, how I instinctively moved closer to him, the fresh scent of the rain on the leaves, the giddy feeling of release. In the city, the Argonauts and the Lemnian women would know they were spending their final night together, that the sunrise would herald their separation. Back at the camp, Heracles and Hylas would have stolen away from the beach together, Heracles' lion skin draped between branches to hold off the rain, its ferocious head frozen in a warning snarl to ward away any intruders. Meleager's face was level with mine; the twisted boughs of the tree were all around us, hiding us from the rest of the world, even from the eyes of Artemis, I was sure.

A bolt of lightning shattered the darkness, a simmering rumble of thunder the barest moment after.

'Come on, we should run,' I said, and without hesitation, he grabbed my hand and we hurtled out into the downpour. I gasped as the cold rain engulfed me, the wind buffeting us and the thunder rolling over and over. I glanced back to see the lightning strike again, its forked tongue darting into the forest where we had just been standing. The tree that it struck seemed to glow, sparks flying in a wild halo around it.

My heart was racing. I pulled my hand free of Meleager's and ran all the way back to the beach.

* * *

To my great relief, and surprise, the rosy streaks of dawn illuminated the most welcome sight – a stream of Argonauts coming back from between the hills. They looked tired, reluctant and grim, a muted contrast to the men I'd seen the night before.

Jason was at the forefront of the procession, and my breath caught as I realised who walked at his side. Her crown glimmered in the soft light, reflecting back the wreaths of pink and amber clouds. She cast me a brief glance, her eyes indifferent, as they reached us.

'Remember us,' she said to Jason. 'May the gods speed your passage across the ocean and bring you back with the Fleece that you seek.'

Jason took her hands in his. 'When I have the Fleece, I will return,' he said. 'I promise I'll come back to you.'

She smiled. I wondered if she believed him, or if she cared. I hoped she had what she wanted from him, that the women might bear some children from the Argonauts' visit, but I was sure she wouldn't be pining for him when we left. 'The kingdom of Lemnos will be yours if you do,' she said.

Some other women had accompanied the men and were bidding farewell to them as we gathered up what we needed. I saw one of them, tall and beautiful, pressing a cloak into Polydeuces' arms. Her hair swung behind her, long and thick and dark, as he pulled her into his arms and kissed her deeply. I looked away. Heracles and the others were launching the *Argo* back on to the water. I was almost buckled by the sense of relief of climbing back aboard.

Hypsipyle watched us go, her figure shrinking as we began to row away. Whatever her final words, I knew that as long as she lived, Lemnos would only ever belong to her.

11

The atmosphere on board that day was sullen. Jason stood at the helm, scowling at the horizon as we sailed away from Lemnos. He gave no rousing words to urge us on as we heaved on the oars, and silence settled over us like a cloud. Usually Heracles could be relied upon to shout across the deck, bellowing some coarse aside that would elicit laughter and an eager clamour from the others. But he barely glanced at our crewmates, contempt in his gaze as he rowed effortlessly, his powerful strokes churning the water into furious white foam.

I felt the burn of a dozen eyes staring at my back as I rowed. Peleus strode over the benches, approaching Jason, who waved him away peevishly. As he returned to his seat, Peleus glared openly at me, his eyes dark with resentment.

The injustice of it enraged me. His eyes had slid right past Meleager at my side – Meleager, who had argued for us to leave Lemnos just as much as I had done – and fastened only on me. Heracles had been no more in favour of staying, but no one dared direct their ire at him either.

The grumblings of the crew drifted over the galley. *My*

shoulders ache . . . no time to rest . . . the sting of the salt spray, the cold wind, the endless lurching of the waves. Peleus' low tones overlapped with the other complaints: *What do you expect with a woman on board? . . . an insult to their hospitality, disdain for Aphrodite . . . a mockery of our quest.* I gripped my oar tightly, my knuckles stretched white and thin. I was about to stand up, to demand they explain why it was a mockery to insist that the quest continued, to insist that the foolishness came from those so bitterly yearning for the comforts of the Lemnian women. What kind of heroes were they to gripe about the weather and the exertion of rowing? But before I could, Orpheus and two of the others had got to their feet and begun to haul on the ropes that held the sail in place, shaking it down to its fullest extent so that it billowed in the wind, obscuring my view of Peleus, giving a welcome surge to the ship and some respite to our shoulders.

It was Idas and Idmon, two of the younger Argonauts, who helped Orpheus, I saw now, and Idas was calling out to the others. 'Come on,' he declared, his jovial tone at odds with the Argonauts' mood. His eyes were overly bright and he flung his arms out expansively. I wondered if he was still animated from the wine he'd drunk the night before. 'Forget about those Lemnian women's beds – who knows what else we have in store on our journey? Our voyage is blessed; there could be better ahead than we've found already. There has never been a ship like this one or a crew like ours. Nothing can hold us back: not beautiful women, not any obstacle or disaster, not even the gods themselves.'

I heard Idmon gasp as he seized Idas' arm roughly. 'Don't be such a fool!'

Across the benches, the Argonauts drew themselves up, alert

and watching. The tensions of the day felt poised to burst into flame. Jason looked over from the helm, alarmed, and Heracles made as if to heave his massive frame up from the bench. As I looked from one angry face to another, I caught Orpheus' eye. For an instant, I felt like I was back on the beach at Pagasae, looking at Peleus' sneering face across the fire, and I remembered what had happened next. Just as it had done then, a wash of serenity rippled out from Orpheus. He took up his lyre, his meditative gaze falling on each Argonaut in turn as he began to play.

The melody was all there was. It was impossible to think of anything else, or to remember the animosity of only a moment ago. Orpheus the man no longer existed; he was the conduit through which the music came, as though it flowed from the roots buried deep in the earth up through his lyre and out towards the heavens, sweeping us up along with it. He sang of the world's creation, how the sky and the earth became separate realms, how the mountains and oceans were formed, the stars were born and the world took shape, and how Zeus took up his thunderbolt and led his Olympian brothers and sisters to victory over the Titans so that they could rule. When at last he reached the end, I could see my crewmates shaking their heads in surprise, faces rapt with wonder, as we found ourselves still on the ship, still gliding over the waves when the world had seemed to come to a complete stop for his song.

The threat of dissent had drifted away with the last notes Orpheus plucked from the lyre. Idas and Idmon took their seats again, and we all pulled together on our oars as Tiphys hauled on his at the stern to steer our course.

It was the first heavy droplets of rain that dissipated the last remnants of the dreaminess Orpheus' song had bestowed upon us. I felt them striking my face, scattered shocks of cold water that quickly gained pace. I glanced up, saw the heavy bank of dark clouds gathering above us. At the same time, Meleager turned his head, and our eyes met in a moment of shared panic.

'A storm's coming,' he said and I felt a giddy sensation, like I was falling through air.

The skies blackened, the sun extinguished like a torch plunged into water, and the wind began to keen, a hollow note of mourning that made me shudder.

Until Callisto, a storm had been something to relish from the safety of my cave, an exhilarating chaos that thrilled my heart. At sea, it was a different thing altogether. The waves rose around the sides of the ship, crashing against the wood. The mighty *Argo* was tossed between them, nausea cresting inside me with every lurch and crash. Heracles was shouting orders, his booming voice almost lost in the noise of the wind and the growl of thunder.

'Help, Atalanta!' Meleager was shouting. He grabbed my arm, pulling me from the bench, and I saw he was gesturing towards the sail in the centre. The winds were hammering it, threatening to tear it apart. The deck was slick under my feet as we scrambled towards it, other hands reaching out to yank at the ropes with us to furl it again. I could see Heracles grimacing, the muscles of his arms and back rolling beneath his skin, veins standing out like corded ropes as he rowed against the storm, and when I twisted around to see behind, Orpheus was at Tiphys' side. He was gesturing towards the waves, helping Tiphys lean hard on the steering oar to turn the ship.

Slowly, inexorably, the *Argo* tilted, and briefly I thought the nausea would overwhelm me. But as the ship sailed on, the waves began to calm and the storm receded in our wake.

My forehead was clammy, my hair drenched from the spray, but as I looked at the soaking, shaken Argonauts around me, I saw we shared the same sense of relief.

'We're through,' Jason announced. He looked dazed.

Peleus clapped Heracles on the back. 'Thanks to your strength,' he said.

Heracles shrugged. 'What land is that ahead?' he asked, squinting at the rocky shores of an island looming larger into view.

Orpheus stepped forwards. Above us, the clouds were clearing and the sun was streaming right behind him, making the tips of his hair glow in a strange halo and shadowing his eyes as he spoke. 'That,' he said, 'is the island of Samothrace.'

It was Orpheus who guided us in, giving quiet instructions to Tiphys as we drew closer to the mountainous island. Usually, I was eager to be one of the first to climb down, to help drag the ship up the beach and take in our new surroundings. This time, I held back, waiting for Orpheus.

'What you did, before the storm,' I said.

'Yes?' It was the first time I'd spoken to him. Up close, I could see how young he was, how soft and smooth his skin looked. I'd never heard him join in with the other men's boasting or jibes. He seemed at odds with us all, a musician among fighters, and it made him easier to approach.

'How do you do it? How do you play like that, so it calms everyone?'

'I don't know. It just comes, as though it's meant to be.' The sky behind him was tinged with violet, a single bright star shining above as the dusk gathered. He picked up his lyre and started to walk down the rapidly emptying deck. He moved with a liquid grace, a lithe dancing motion in his every step.

'Well,' I said. 'If Peleus starts again, next time don't get in between. I'd like the chance to silence him myself.'

Orpheus laughed. Although I'd meant what I said, a smile tugged at the corners of my mouth, too. As we jumped down on to the beach, an efficient group of our crewmates were already handing down the smooth round logs we used to roll the ship up on to land. Meleager was among them, and I saw him notice Orpheus and me together. He didn't smile. I wondered if he was annoyed that I wasn't helping as I usually would, or if there was something else amiss.

I joined them in hauling the ship up and when it was secured, Orpheus strummed his fingers over the lyre strings. Everyone looked round, their shouts dying down.

'I've brought you to Samothrace,' he said, 'a sacred island.' His voice was low, but carried effortlessly over the sands. He looked up towards the mountain and I followed the direction of his gaze. Down a winding path, I could see a small procession coming towards us, priests identifiable by their long flowing robes. Orpheus went on. 'I have visited before and been initiated into the rites they practise here. We can pay our respects to the gods that protect this island and beg their favour to keep us safe out on the seas.'

I noticed that Idas looked shamefaced, staring at the ground. The weight of the Argonauts' stares had fallen on him, though Idmon put an arm around his shoulder, his own anger clearly forgotten.

The procession had reached us, the foremost of the men opening his arms wide at the sight of Orpheus. They greeted one another as friends and Orpheus gestured to us all to follow. 'Thyotes will lead the way,' he said.

No one was going to argue. After our brush with the storm, no one wanted to risk angering any gods. Hera might have given the voyage her blessing, but if another immortal wanted to wreck our ship, they could do it. Besides, it could be that Hera's favour extended no further than Jason. I knew better than to hope Artemis would save me if it came to it. I was here to prove my strength.

We followed. Night was falling and the path took us inland, towards the centre of the island. At its heart, a high mountain rose to a dramatic peak, dominating the landscape around it. The robed priests led us towards the mountain. The atmosphere among the Argonauts was unusually solemn as we walked. There was something heavy in the air, a quiet anticipation stirred by Orpheus' words, or maybe by the earnestness of the tone in which he'd delivered them. Perhaps it was his poise and certainty.

As the path curved around the mountain, I could see it began to slope downwards into a valley. The distant sound of music, the rhythmic throbbing of drums and the melodious hum of chanting drifted up from it, getting more distinct as we walked on. Torches lined the path as it sloped more steeply. I felt my pulse quicken, beating in time to the pounding drums as they grew louder and we drew closer.

We stopped when we reached a courtyard, a wide paved circle of stone sunk into the earth. It was lined with statues, the light from the torches jumping from each bronze face, casting strange shadows. Someone handed me a wide-mouthed goblet, ornately carved, brimming with wine. The sweet scent made my stomach growl, reminding me how long it had been since we had eaten. I took a long sip, savouring its richness, and looked up at the dark mountain against the sky. Somewhere nearby, the sound of rushing water. Another sip of wine. The music was louder now, the snaking beat of the drums seductive. More wine and the stars were wheeling overhead.

'Walk on,' someone was saying, and there were steps down from the courtyard, taking us closer to the music and the chanting. My goblet was empty now, and my head was spinning.

Later, I would try to remember what the sanctuary looked like. It was a blur of torches sweeping in long, fiery arcs and dancing bodies silhouetted against the flames. The hypnotic lure of the drums, the noise drowning out my other senses. And then darkness, black and absolute, a soft blindfold wrapped around my head. Chanting, swallowing up the drums, the words pounding and insistent, the praise we offered to the dark gods of Samothrace. And when the cloth was lifted away from my eyes, the sun was rising over the sea. We were on the beach where our ship waited for us, the dawn fresh and exhilarating as I looked from face to face and saw the same baffled expression on each, until my eyes came to rest on Orpheus. His face was contented, lifted to the breeze as he spoke. 'We'll sail from here cleansed,' he said, 'renewed and ready to face what lies ahead.'

I didn't know if it was the rites themselves or the sense that we had shared something inexplicable, something no one else would ever understand, uniting us in an experience that only we had known, but the mood had lifted and the ill will that had threatened to erupt after leaving Lemnos seemed forgotten. The crew loaded the *Argo* in good spirits and we sailed away from Samothrace with a harmony that Orpheus did not have to conjure with his lyre.

We sailed on for several days, sometimes through treacherous channels and then across open water. We found hospitality again, this time from the Dolionians, whose king invited us to his wedding feast. There was no division like there had been on Lemnos. Meleager and I, as well as Heracles and Hylas, feasted alongside our fellows and enjoyed the comforts of warm beds, fine food and good wine, with no threat to the rest of our adventure.

It wasn't only Meleager I could talk to now. I felt comfortable sitting at Orpheus' side, too, and while I still felt hostility emanating from some of the crew, there were other Argonauts who were more conciliatory towards me. I began to know Idas and Idmon a little better, the former impulsive and unguarded in his speech, while his friend was more reserved and careful.

On the long tables at the wedding feast, we were all shoved close together, pressed up against one another on the narrow benches, great jugs of wine placed at intervals before us. Opposite me, Peleus was taking long swigs, his face reddening as he held forth to Ancaeus and Acastus. I could hear snatches of his conversation as his voice got louder and louder, until I couldn't block it out at all. He was talking of his own wedding, the sea-nymph Thetis who had been given to him.

'She took on every shape she could think of to try to wriggle free,' he was saying, his speech slurred. He took another swig and wine dribbled down over his beard. 'One moment a fluttering bird, then a tiger, then fire – I held on tight through it all.' He raised his goblet to Acastus. 'You know I'm a champion wrestler, there's no one who could beat me. Even when her claws tore my skin and her flames burned me, I didn't let go.'

I stared at him in appalled fascination as he continued.

'What happened?' said Ancaeus, and Acastus laughed. There was an ugly edge to his laughter that made my skin crawl.

'She gave in, in the end. She'd put up a good fight, but she couldn't get away.' His lips were wet and glistening. The others craned in closer to listen more intently. 'After that, the gods all came to the wedding. It was a prophecy – something about the boy. She was never any kind of mother to him, though. I caught her trying to throw him into the fire. She ran away after that, back to the sea. But I had my son; what did I need her for after that?'

My fingernails were digging into the wood of the table.

'Why don't you come outside, Atalanta?' Meleager's voice was low in my ear and his hand firm on my shoulder.

I wanted to be out of the press of bodies, the stifling heat of the hall. I let him lead me out into the courtyard.

'Are you all right?' he asked.

I could feel hot acid in my throat. 'What do you want?'

'I thought it was better if you didn't kill Peleus at the table right in front of everyone.'

'Do you think it's funny?' I glared at him. 'Why do we have someone like that on board at all? Do you want to sit beside him, fight at his side? He doesn't deserve the glory of winning the Fleece with us.'

Meleager shrugged. 'He's strong. We might need that at some point.'

I shook my head, disgusted.

'This is a wedding. We're invited guests. We can't offend the king by fighting among ourselves,' he said. 'Plenty of the others like Peleus, anyway.'

'Do you?'

'I don't need to like him,' Meleager said. 'But I don't want trouble between us.' His tone lightened as he went on. 'Anyway, if you take on Peleus, where will you stop? Will it be Heracles next?'

I sighed.

'It's better to beat them another way,' he said. 'Everyone's here for the same thing. They all want the chance to prove themselves strongest or fastest or bravest. Wait until you get your chance.'

'When will that be?' I grumbled. 'It's been weeks, and the worst threat we've encountered was at Lemnos.'

'Apparently there are six-armed giants living in the mountains around here,' Meleager said. 'If they see invaders, they attack. I heard the king warning Jason about them earlier.'

'Really?'

'You sound pleased to hear it.'

It wasn't just the prospect of a battle that I relished. If what he said was true, we must be making progress, getting further away from the world the Argonauts knew and into the realms of monsters. It meant we were closer to the Fleece.

'I'll stay away from Peleus,' I told Meleager. 'I want to get to the Fleece, and if that means tolerating him for now, then I'll do it. But I won't go back in there tonight. I'm going to bed.' I paused and smiled at him. 'After all, we might be facing giants tomorrow.'

As it was, we made it all the way back to the *Argo* the next morning without encountering any giants. But somewhere up in the hills, they must have spotted us, and as we heaved on the oars to row away, the first of the boulders struck us. It smashed through one of the wooden benches in the centre of the deck, the impact sudden and violent, making all of us leap to our feet.

At first, I couldn't see them at all. They looked like parts of the mountain itself, like great branching trees sprouting from its rocky face. A rain of boulders came hurtling down upon us, most of them crashing into the sea, sending huge sprays of foaming water over us. The saltwater blinded me, my eyes stinging, and the ship lurched. My words to Meleager seemed foolhardy now, but I swung my bow around and, blinking furiously, took aim.

My first arrow struck one of them right in the chest. He swayed and toppled, the crash of his landing reverberating through the ground, sending a flurry of smaller rocks tumbling after him. Out of the corner of my eye, I saw Heracles hurling a spear, and I kept firing arrow after arrow. The Argonauts fell into order, the idle conversation of minutes before forgotten as together we focused on bringing the giants down. When the boulders hit, the ship tilted, and I caught sight of the boiling green depths of the sea. I steadied my aim. Out of the corner of my eye, I saw Zetes take to the air, the little wings at his ankles beating frantically as he hovered, throwing a spear with incredible precision. I made myself look away, not letting the impossible sight of him suspended above us distract me. Meleager was hollering as our hail of missiles overcame the giants and they fell, their heavy bodies tumbling down the slopes, rolling into the sea. When the last of them had toppled, I took a long breath. My hair hung in damp strings around my face, and my crewmates were similarly sodden. The attack had blindsided us, but now a ripple of elation passed from each of us to the next. I'd felt this kind of victorious glee before, but always alone. It was a different kind of sensation to look around and see my own feelings mirrored, to know we had conquered a foe together.

'Atalanta!' Meleager cried. 'You killed the first one, and with a single shot!'

Idas laughed, exultant, pushing his wet hair out of his face. 'And half a dozen after that!' Idmon was nodding in agreement, Orpheus' eyes were warm with approval, and, for a moment, I found myself at the centre of a circle of appreciation from the Argonauts.

On the edge, I saw Peleus' face twist with anger.

The conversation turned to everyone's exploits: Heracles' indomitable strength, hurling spear after spear; how effortlessly Zetes dodged every boulder and fired back upon the giants without faltering; the indefatigable power of Castor and Polydeuces; Meleager's rallying shout that had spurred everyone on to the final glorious victory. I found half the pleasure again in reliving it, in sharing each thrill and shock of the battle anew.

We brought the boat back on to the shore to take stock, collect our scattered weapons and repair the broken benches. Consequently, the sun was high in the sky by the time we could set sail again. Perhaps we should have waited another night, but triumphant at the outcome of our first battle, we left the fallen bodies of the giants behind us and sailed on.

12

I could still feel the lingering effects of the rites at Samothrace. If I closed my eyes, I could feel the reinvigoration of standing in that sunrise, bathed in the light of a new day. The battle with the giants had affirmed it again, the sense of purpose that held our group together despite the clashes of personality and the struggle of egos.

The fight seemed to have had an energising effect on Heracles. He was as rowdy as I'd ever seen him, the ship lurching as he stamped his feet and called on the others.

'A contest!' he was shouting. 'We'll have a rowing contest, see if any of you can last as long as me.'

The wind had dropped and the sea was flat in every direction. Heracles brandished his oar, a glint in his eye belying his eager grin. 'Come on,' he ordered, 'row as hard as you can and we'll find out if any man here can keep up with me.'

I crashed my oar into the water, rattling it hard between the slats on the side of the ship. Heracles smirked. 'There's Atalanta,' he called. 'Who among you will be beaten by a woman first?'

The Argonauts all started to heave as hard as they could, the oars churning up froth on both sides of the ship.

As determined as everyone was, it was mostly good-natured insults that were hollered across the deck as we rowed. Orpheus struck up a lively tune and the *Argo* sped across the sea as though we were flying.

Trying to keep pace with Heracles' strokes was impossible, but I ignored the agony in my shoulders and the sweat that was dripping into my eyes, driving myself harder and harder. Soon, there were no more friendly jeers going back and forth between the Argonauts, only grim silence from the rowers – except for Heracles, who grew louder and more insufferable all the time. He was laughing, singing along to Orpheus' playing and mocking the others as, one by one, the crew began to admit defeat. The wind was starting up now and we were fighting against it. Those of us still rowing were straining hard. When I glanced at Meleager, I saw his grimace; the veins in Peleus' forehead were bulging, and Ancaeus grunted every time he leaned back. Heracles was roaring with delight. He showed no signs of slowing down, his energy undrained. My lungs were burning for air, my arms begging for respite, and there was no way Heracles was going to surrender. The men that had given up were shouting their encouragement for Meleager, for Peleus and for Ancaeus, and it spurred Heracles on further.

Just as I thought I would have to stop, Heracles pulled so violently on his oar that the thick slab of timber smashed against the side of the ship and, to the spectators' disbelief, snapped in half. Heracles watched, his jaw hanging open in disbelief, as the wood floated away over the smooth waters.

A huge cheer went up around the deck while Heracles

stared. I stopped rowing, much to the relief of my exhausted muscles, hardly daring to believe this turn of events.

High spirits abounded among the crew, except for Heracles. Furious at the loss of his oar, unable to channel his energy into rowing and denied the sweetness of victory, he paced the deck, searching the horizon for land. When we stopped at what Tiphys announced was the Mysian coast, he leapt from the ship, striding up the sand towards the trees he could spy in the distance. I knew he would be seeking one to turn into a new oar.

Hylas watched him go and sighed. 'I'll fetch the water,' he said, picking up a large pitcher.

Later, Heracles came back down from the woods with a great pine slung over his shoulder. He started fashioning it into an oar, concentrating deeply on his task. As the moonlight shone across the breaking waves, he looked up at last. 'Where is Hylas?' he asked.

'He went for water,' I said.

Meleager frowned. 'Shouldn't he have returned by now?'

Heracles turned his great shaggy head from side to side, surveying the length of the beach. 'Polyphemus!' he called out, seeing the young man emerging from a nearby copse of trees. 'Have you seen Hylas anywhere?'

Polyphemus shook his head.

'Acastus? Peleus?' Heracles cast his oar aside and stood. 'You've explored this island, do you know where Hylas went?'

They responded with blank looks, and the question echoed around our whole crew, everyone as ignorant as the next man as to Hylas' whereabouts.

'Let's look for him,' I suggested. I was sure he wouldn't have come to any harm, but I felt a prickle of unease that he had been gone for so long. I was unnerved by how anxious Heracles looked, his massive fists clenched and worry writ across his usually jovial face. I'd never seen him fazed by anything.

'I'll stay here,' Jason announced. 'Orpheus, Tiphys, Echion, stay with me. We'll tend the fires and cook the meat so that we can all eat on your return.'

Heracles swatted away his words. 'Let's go.'

All of us whom Jason hadn't named set out, spreading across the long line of the shore and calling Hylas' name. 'I think he set out this way,' I said to Meleager, and we walked together. As we made our way through the thick clump of trees, I listened intently for the sound of water, a bubbling stream or gentle waterfall, the softest lapping of ripples against rock or the squelch of damp earth that would signify a nearby spring. I told myself there was nothing to fear, that Hylas must have simply become lost and wandered off course. I heard his name ricocheting from the solid trunks, from the rocky hillsides, echoing up into the dim skies from all across the island as the Argonauts searched. There was no way that he wouldn't hear it too, wherever he was, however far he had gone.

I saw the pitcher first. My eyes didn't make sense of it immediately, lying there at the bank of a wide pool in a clearing up ahead. It looked so innocuous, as though it had been casually dropped there, as though Hylas might be about to emerge from the dark water at any moment, shake the droplets from his hair and smile at us.

'Heracles!' Meleager called out, his voice booming through the trees.

I heard the pounding of Heracles' feet before he came crashing through to where we stood. He stared at the fallen pitcher.

'He must be nearby,' he said at last.

Meleager and I sprang into action. 'We'll comb the area, we'll find him,' Meleager said, and I nodded vigorously, leaving the crucial words unspoken. What, exactly, would we find?

In a way, it was worse. We found nothing at all. No sign that he had ever been there except the abandoned pitcher. There was no sign of a scuffle, no tracks of bears or mountain lions. It was as though he had been swallowed up by the forest and disappeared into nothing.

The night wore on and still we searched. I couldn't bear to voice how fruitless it was to stumble around in circles, barely able to discern anything in the dark. I thought of Hylas' sweet face, how gentle he was, how unlike Heracles in every way. I kept going.

The sky paled to a dull grey as we emerged back on to the shore. The rest of the crew were gathering up their belongings, loading it all back on to the *Argo*.

'What are you doing?' Heracles had lapsed into silence hours before. The sound of his voice now made me start.

Jason looked over from the prow of the ship, where he was in conversation with Tiphys. His expression was sombre as he leapt lightly down and made his way to us. 'Did you find any sign of him?'

'Only his pitcher,' I admitted.

Jason shook his head and sighed. 'He is a great loss to our crew.'

Heracles' face blanched with fury. 'We can't give up on him after one night! He could have wandered anywhere, but now it's daylight again, he'll find his way back.'

Jason looked doubtful. 'Was his pitcher far from here?'

Reluctantly, I shook my head. 'It was by a pond, not such a long way into the woods.'

'Why would he drop it and go further?' Jason asked.

We were silent. I glanced at Meleager. He looked weary, his mouth set in an unfamiliar line.

'Surely it's more likely that he dropped it when something came upon him, perhaps an animal,' Jason continued.

Heracles was shaking his head scornfully. 'A preposterous suggestion.'

Jason shrugged. 'He would have been back if he could – he has never wandered far before. Something has befallen him out there. We will honour him, make offerings for his safe passage to the Underworld. But we must sail this morning; we have no time to lose.'

Heracles' eyes burned with an unearthly fire. 'We haven't found his body. He isn't dead, and if he was, we couldn't go without finding him. If he died and we didn't give him the correct rites – if we just leave—' He broke off.

There was a determination in Jason's face that I hadn't seen before. I wondered why there was no time to waste now, when he might have dallied far longer with his Lemnian queen if it had been left to him.

'We sail now,' Jason said. 'We won't wait any longer.'

Heracles stared at him. If I were Jason, I would have feared his retaliation, but Heracles didn't strike him. 'I won't leave him here,' he said.

'Then stay.'

I gasped. Meleager's mouth fell open.

But Heracles simply turned on his heel and walked back towards the trees. In a moment, his massive frame was swallowed up by the forest and he was gone.

*   *   *

'Shall we stay?' I grabbed Meleager's elbow, yanking his body around so that he faced me. The crew were shoving the *Argo* down towards the water on the rolling logs. Without Heracles heaving it against his massive shoulder, they were stumbling and sweating, but still it was moving. Jason had resumed his position on the prow, his face turned towards the open sea so that I couldn't make out his expression. 'Should we help Heracles to find Hylas?' I continued.

Meleager sighed. 'If we let them sail without us, our part in this quest is over.'

I watched as Zetes and Calais clambered lightly up on to the deck. Only a handful of men were left on shore, shouting commands to one another, a hive of activity ready to go.

'Surely the rest of them don't want to leave without two of our men?' I asked.

'I don't know if they realise Jason plans to do this.'

'Let's ask them.' I started towards the boat, then realised Meleager wasn't at my side. 'What's the matter?'

'If we ask them to stay – we're defying Jason,' he said. 'He's made his decision and we'll be challenging it. Again.'

'Better that than marooning one of our number here.'

He didn't answer.

'They should know what Jason intends.' Decisively, I marched towards the boat and up the wooden ramp, swinging my legs across the railing at the top. I cleared my throat and spoke out before I could doubt myself. 'Heracles won't leave without Hylas.' I made my voice ring across the deck. 'If we go now, we leave him behind.'

There was an immediate clamour of voices.

'He isn't coming?'

'I thought he was on his way back?'

'We can't go without Heracles!'

'Does Jason realise?'

Meleager leapt lightly over the railing, landing at my side.

'Hylas is lost!' Jason's voice cut through. 'He has wandered away and met his fate. It's a tragedy, but we gain nothing by staying here to mourn.'

The clamour died away. All eyes were fixed on Jason.

'Heracles has made his choice,' he went on. 'He has decided to leave us.'

'He's grieving,' I said. 'He's not in his right mind. If we stay—'

'Then we waste our time, time we must spend in pursuit of the Fleece.' There was a new note of authority in Jason's voice, one that I was sure we wouldn't hear in Heracles' presence. 'Anyone who wishes to stay can stay,' he continued. 'But if you do, you give up on our quest.'

There was utter stillness. The only noise was the faraway shriek of gulls and the soft splash of waves.

'Hera has sanctioned this voyage.' Now, Jason's tone softened a little, became more wheedling and persuasive. 'She has given it her blessing. She visited me, and me alone, in the form of an old woman asking for my help in crossing the river Anaurus. When I carried her over, she made herself weigh as much as two centaurs, and still I held her above the rushing water, even when I thought the effort would drown me. She made herself known to me then, and promised me victory. She swore that I would have the Fleece and win glory for us all.' He looked at us, from one unsmiling face to the next. 'But we all know Heracles is despised by Hera, that she has set him his own labours so he might earn her forgiveness. He needs to return to those tasks, not dally with us. We don't want to lose her patronage in keeping him from fulfilling what he owes her.'

This line of argument seemed to be loosening my crew-mates' resolve. No one wanted to risk Hera's wrath, not out on the perilous expanse of the seas.

'Heracles has made his choice,' Jason said again. 'His loyalty isn't to us, to our quest. It's to his own interests, always. He never wanted to lead you. He doesn't care enough to stay now.'

I glanced at Meleager, seeing his uncertainty reflecting mine. It revolted me to think that we would leave one of our number behind. But Jason had made it clear: we could go with the Argonauts, or we could stay here.

'Can we leave the strongest out of all of us behind?' It was Acastus who spoke up.

Jason gestured towards the rows of men on the benches. 'Look at us. The strongest men that Greece has to offer.' He looked right past me. 'There are other sons of Zeus here besides Heracles, more of you who boast of other Olympian fathers. Don't you deserve to be known like Heracles is? There are other fighters here; why should it be Heracles who takes all the glory for himself? He's reckless and destructive; he cost us an oar, and now he threatens to cost us our journey. Without him, all of you have the chance to make your name.'

I cast a look back at the shore, wondering if Heracles had heard. I expected to see him come charging out of the woods, bellowing. But the beach remained empty, the trees undisturbed, the wind carrying us nothing but silence.

Jason's final argument was convincing. One by one, the Argonauts took up their oars. Meleager sat down among them, but I stood motionless in the centre of the ship, by the bench where Heracles always sat, where his mighty strength had shattered his oar only yesterday.

The ropes were hauled back on board, the ship freed from its mooring, and the oars began to beat the water in unison. Orpheus began to play a tune so sad and sweet that it made tears burn in my eyes. Only the sight of Jason leaning against the prow, a smile of satisfaction on his lips, made me blink them back.

13

The sun never fought through the clouds that day. They banked up in the skies, thick and grey and endless. Yesterday, the deck had rung with shouts and laughter at the rowing contest, but today there was a weary silence among the crew.

I longed for our arrival on whatever land we would find, so I could eat and then steal away to sleep. The fatigue from the sleepless night had set in. This time, though, no sooner had we beached the *Argo* at Bithynia, land of the Bebryces, according to Tiphys, than fighters were upon us.

'You will fight!' shouted the foremost of them. 'I challenge you now!'

Jason stepped forwards. 'We mean you no harm.'

'No one sets foot on my island without this challenge,' the man continued.

The men behind him were ranged in a semicircle, eyes fixed upon us.

'I have killed every man who accepts the challenge.'

It was Polydeuces who stepped up beside Jason at this. 'I'll accept.' He was already shrugging off his cloak, the parting gift I'd seen him receive at Lemnos. In the livid yellow light that filtered through the clouds, his muscles shone. He must have been the strongest of the Argonauts, after Heracles.

One of the men behind the challenger stepped forwards too. 'You are no match for King Amycus,' he said, placing long strips of rawhide on the ground before them both.

Amycus wrapped his hands in the coarse strips and Polydeuces did the same, binding them around his fists. I waited for a signal that the fight was to begin but none came. Instead, Amycus lowered his head and charged at speed, right at Polydeuces.

It was a brutal battle. There was no doubt that Amycus fought to kill and Polydeuces did the same. Polydeuces was more nimble, dodging many of Amycus' blows, but the sheer strength and ferocity of the king meant that when they connected, it was with a sickening thud of flesh and bone. The spectators behind Amycus began to jeer, shouting for their king, howling every time he hit Polydeuces. I ran my eyes along them all, calculating their number against ours. I could see some of the Argonauts doing the same.

But Polydeuces withstood every punch, rearing back and slamming his fist hard into Amycus' stomach. I saw the king's disbelief, felt the momentum of the fight shift, and Polydeuces took advantage, merciless and unstoppable. He forced Amycus to his knees, demanded his surrender, and the king shook his head, no. He tried to stagger to his feet, his arms wheeling, and Polydeuces hit him again. Amycus roared, hauling himself up, launching himself at Polydeuces.

But Polydeuces was a son of Zeus, like Heracles, and the blood dripping from his temple did not deter him; the hammering of Amycus' fists could not bring him down. Over and over, he asked for surrender, offered his mercy, and every time the king refused, spitting his teeth, his mouth frothing pink, but still insistent he would fight to the death.

Silently, I urged Polydeuces to finish it. In the forest, hunting was clean. An arrow through the throat of my prey would end it in a moment. It was how I'd killed the centaurs, a quick death, not this drawn-out beating, this hideous violence. On and on it went, the wind whipping against us, the skies desolate as Amycus was reduced to a heap of broken flesh. Polydeuces stepped back, took a long breath and then, with a precision that was almost merciful, landed the final blow to the king's head.

The crack of Amycus' shattered skull seemed to reverberate, a sound I knew I would never be able to cleanse from my mind. But it was over, at last.

Not for his men. With a howl of outrage, they came for us, fists flying, clubs and swords and spears brandished. There was no moment to brace ourselves; they were upon us the instant their king died.

It wasn't like the giants of the mountain. This fight was up close, meaty hands closing around my arms, bearded faces snarling into mine. I tore myself free, kicking back at them, wrenching the club from one who reared up above me and smashing it into his shoulder. They were furious, maddened by the loss of their king, but I could tell that the Argonauts were getting the better of them, just as Polydeuces had overcome Amycus. I saw them tumbling down under our onslaught. There was Peleus, his arm wrapped around a fighter's throat, squeezing remorselessly until the man's eyes rolled back in his head and his body sagged, limp and lifeless. Ancaeus whirling his axe above his head, Polydeuces and his brother Castor a formidable duo as they fought side by side, Zetes and Calais darting across the battleground, taking flight and swooping down on their terrified opponents. In the heart of the battle, I saw a man swing his sword at Meleager and then look down in stunned surprise to see Meleager's spear lodged in his stomach. The man's eyes widened and he swayed, toppling forwards like a felled tree in a storm. Meleager yanked his spear free and stood back, breathing hard.

Those that could were crawling away, not willing to die as their king had done. Those that were not so lucky lay scattered across the beach around him.

'Drag them away,' Jason said. He was breathless, blood blooming from a wound to his temple, but a light of victory shone in his eyes. We did as he said, two to each corpse, toppling them over the high rocks at each end of the bay, letting them tumble into the swirling waves below. I watched the water swallow them up.

And then, our usual duties: finding food and water, lighting fires, and making camp. No one else seemed tired now. Orpheus led the song, the fires blazed and the wine flowed. Jason's point had been proven more quickly than he could have anticipated: Heracles was gone, but we had won a battle and hadn't missed his strength.

For me, the flush of triumph from the battle mingled with guilt. As I drank, I thought of Heracles alone where we had left him. I didn't miss the sound of his booming voice or relentless bragging, but his presence had been so massive among us that his absence was jarring, the gap he left almost as impossible to ignore as he had been when he was with us.

The rain began to fall, causing shouts of good-natured protest. I took my moment to slip away. Before night fell, I had seen caves, hollowed out in the cliffsides. Perhaps I would curl up under the domed ceiling of rock and imagine, just for one night, that I was back where I had come from, that I was home again.

I made my way across the dark bay, a thick woollen blanket over my arm. I had gone so long without sleep, I felt almost delirious. It was as though I walked through a dream, hazy and slow, where nothing was real. My head was full of images from the day; every time I pushed one aside, another would take its place: Heracles disappearing into the woods, the long stretch of sea as we sailed further away, Amycus bleeding on the ground. The red-streaked eyes of one of his fighters, as I drove my club hard into his stomach.

I had reached the caves. The cool damp was so welcoming, so familiar and so safe. I placed my hand on the wall inside, felt my way in, letting my eyes adjust. There were no stars visible, and the moon was almost entirely hidden behind cloud, but what pale glow there was showed me that the cave was empty and undisturbed. I pulled down my rain-dampened braid, letting my hair fall around me, and laid the blanket down on the hard floor.

Then, sensing something behind me, I took a noiseless step back towards the cave entrance.

'Did you follow me?' I asked.

I couldn't make out his expression in the dark. 'Sorry.'

'Why?'

'I wanted to see how you were after today.'

'Don't stand out there in the rain.'

He didn't move.

'Aren't you going to come in?' I asked.

'I don't know.'

I didn't ask him why. I didn't need to. I was still dizzied by the memories unspooling across my mind, but now they went further back: the curious admiration in his eyes when I shot his deer, the sincerity with which he'd presented me to the Argonauts, how he'd fought at my side, laughed on the benches with me. I saw the tree, split by lightning, consumed by flames. 'I want you to,' I said, and I reached for him.

Far away in Arcadia, Artemis was presiding over her nymphs. Their faces would be lifted towards hers, the sharp perfection of her profile, her high forehead and eyes clear as moonlight. I remembered it so vividly, a vision as bright and flawless as crystal. I'd thought I would never want anything else but the life she granted me. The moon had only waxed and waned twice since we'd sailed, but it felt like a lifetime ago.

And in distant Calydon, a place I didn't even know how to imagine, Meleager's wife waited for her husband to return.

Here, in this cave, the scent of the rain mingling with his, both of those places seemed impossibly remote, as though they didn't exist and never had. There was nothing real except us, now, hidden within the mountain itself. The daze from the wine and the fog of exhaustion had lifted away, and I felt more myself than I ever had, my thoughts clear and true and undeniable.

I pulled his face to mine and I kissed him. It was nothing I had ever known before, nothing I had been allowed to know. A sunburst of colour, his hands tangled in my hair. A heat sweeping through me, his body pressed against mine. I had thought of this before, the image of it flashing in my mind before I could stop it, but I hadn't known it would feel like this.

The shock of the unfamiliarity made me dizzy, the sensation of clinging to a cliff edge, about to fall. I kissed him more deeply. He tasted like salt and smelled like springtime. The uncertainty and the fear gave way to something else, an urgency and a hunger. I thought of ice cracking across a river in the warmth of the new sun, the waters surging free after a long, frozen winter. Radiant light flared behind my eyelids, a leaping exhilaration as I forgot everything in the world that wasn't us, as I let it all disappear.

Soft sunshine filtered through the cave. I stirred, reluctant to wake. I wanted to stay there, hovering on the cusp of sleep, suspended between dreams and reality.

The image of Artemis swam into focus in my mind and, with a gasp, I opened my eyes, my skin prickling in anticipation of some punishment.

We'd fallen asleep in each other's arms, but at some point in the night, Meleager had rolled away. I stared at the smooth length of his back, his skin tinged with gold in the gentle light. Holding my breath, I reached out and traced my finger lightly down his spine.

The cave stayed still and silent, but almost at once, the unwelcome image of the Argonauts looking for us occurred to me, and I pulled myself upright. Meleager rolled back over, his eyes fluttering open and then fixing on me. 'We need to get back to the ship,' I said. 'Before we're missed.'

He smiled, the same broad, honest smile that had become so familiar to me, unencumbered by any hint of regret or anxiety. Seeing his face dissolved some of the worry needling at me. I called back the memory of my goodbye to Artemis. I'd vowed never to marry, I reasoned. And there was no danger of marrying Meleager.

I silenced the voice protesting against this. It wasn't in my nature to connive at arguments, to twist what was true. But then, Meleager wasn't like the men Artemis had warned against. And the truth of it was, she wasn't there. My reality had so quickly become the Argonauts, my life was bound with theirs. It was more pressing to me that Jason not find out about us.

'I'll go first,' he said, and I was relieved that I didn't have to speak my thoughts aloud. He rose, pulled on his tunic and, with a last glance back at me, disappeared through the cave entrance.

I was reluctant to step back into the world again. But the bright morning air seemed to sparkle, the day made fresh and new and beautiful, cleansed by yesterday's rain. The bay that had seemed so bleak and rugged when we'd landed was now imbued with magnificence, the sea a glittering jewel.

Artemis had done nothing to me. I imagined her, back in the forest, running with her dogs. She wasn't watching me. She was only waiting for me to return with glory in her name. If we won the Fleece, it would be enough.

She would never have to know the rest of it.

PART III

14

The Argonauts were in high spirits, still elated from winning last night's battle. No one paid me any particular attention as I took my seat on my usual bench behind Meleager. I glanced around, worried I would see someone's eyes on me, hardly able to believe that the warm glow radiating through me wasn't visible in some way, but no one seemed to notice anything different. I kept my gaze turned firmly out to sea, towards the horizon, where nobody would catch my eye and guess somehow at the tingling flush of heat that still swept through me, a restless pulse of desire that was so new. It was a revelation to me that the body I thought I knew so well could feel at once so different and unknown.

We would sail to the easternmost shore of the Propontis, Tiphys announced, and with a fair wind and the blessings of the gods, we would reach the Bosphorus, our gateway to the Black Sea. Colchis lay on the other edge of that sea, at the very end of the world. The Fleece was still many days of sailing away from us, and there would be more dangers ahead, but when we reached the Black Sea, it would feel, at last, within our grasp. We would aim to reach Salmydessus, he told us, home to a prophet named Phineus whose advice we could seek before we sailed onwards.

The winds were indeed friendly to us, the songs of Orpheus keeping pace with our swift progress.

'Have you heard of Phineus before?' Meleager asked me.

I shook my head.

'He has a kindly reputation,' Meleager said. 'I think we can expect a better welcome there than we found with the wrestler-king and his army.'

I was about to answer, but noticed Peleus turning his head slightly to listen. I clamped my mouth shut and turned my head to stare determinedly at the ocean. I was sure I could feel Peleus watching me.

If Meleager was surprised by my curt reaction, he didn't betray it. After a while, he fell into easy conversation with Euphemus. I rowed on, letting my thoughts drift, finding that however hard I tried to distract myself, they kept wandering back to the cave the night before.

Just as evening began to fall, we reached Salmydessus. Meleager was buoyant, jumping down to unload the *Argo*. He seemed entirely untroubled.

I lingered at the back of the group as we started to make our way down the shore, following on my own. I was careful to avoid walking alongside Orpheus. He was so observant of the mood, so shrewd to any changes in atmosphere, that I didn't dare invite his attention.

Ahead of us, I could see a large building standing alone on the coast. It looked pleasant, if a little run-down and ram-shackle. I saw that Meleager was slackening his pace, letting himself fall to the rear of the procession until he fell into step beside me. He smiled at me, and I couldn't stop myself smiling back.

'Phineus!' Jason's voice echoed through the squat columns at the dwelling's entrance. 'I am Jason of Iolcus, son of Aeson, here with my Argonauts to ask for your wisdom.'

No reply came. Jason continued forward, and we followed him inside.

Dust swirled in the dim air, glittering where the light struck. I wrinkled my nose, catching a sour whiff, one that intensified as we walked further in. There were tapestries hung on the walls at either side, but they were ragged, the frayed edges gaping open as though they had been clawed apart. I shared a dubious glance with Meleager as I felt our collective mood shift from celebratory to cautious.

The corridor was long and narrow, lined at intervals with statues, punctuated with bolted doors. I would rather take a battle out in the open than an ambush in this gloomy, claustrophobic place. Jason kept calling out for the king, but his voice was swallowed up by the silence, no answering shout returning.

We turned a corner and I was glad to see daylight, a wide archway opening up to a square courtyard. In the centre, there was a long table, and at the very end of the table, a man sat on a tall chair, tiny and wizened against the ornately carved wooden back.

'Phineus?' Jason said. Behind him, we filed out into the courtyard. Here, despite the fresh air, the stench was even worse.

The man turned his face towards us. His skin hung in wrinkled folds, sagging from his bones, not enough flesh on his frame to fill it out. Although the hot rays of the sun seared down from a clear blue sky, he was wrapped in a cloak. And his eyes – his eyes were milky and clouded, unseeing. 'So you are here, Jason, and your Argonauts too. I have waited for this day, for years now.' His voice wavered, cracking at the end. I could hear how dry and raspy his throat was.

'You prophesied this?' Jason asked. He sounded uncertain, frowning as he looked around the desolate courtyard. This wasn't what we had expected, not at all.

'It's been my only hope,' the old man said. I thought I could see tears gathering in the corners of his sightless eyes. 'All this time, I have held on to this.'

My heart swelled with pity for him. I had never known hunger in the forest; I'd never seen its cruelty. He was so wretched, so broken and alone. The bleak despair of this place touched something in me, a wave of sadness cresting as I thought of him clinging on to the hope of our arrival, day after day.

'We came seeking help from you,' Jason said. 'We didn't expect that you would need our service – what is it that you need from us?'

'You need me to tell you what lies ahead on your journey,' Phineus said. 'I can guide you, for I was given the gift of prophecy from Apollo himself. But I offended Zeus, and he cursed me to this existence – although I can see the future whole and entire, I can see nothing else. He blinded me and condemned me to starve in my old age.'

'We have food; we've brought supplies with us,' Jason said eagerly. 'And we can hunt in your lands, too, and bring you meat. Unless . . .' his face darkened a shade. 'Unless Zeus forbids it. We don't want to bring his punishment upon our own heads for interfering.'

Phineus shook his head. 'I'll swear to you, by the lord Apollo, that there will be no retaliation against you for helping me. But bringing me food won't be of any use.'

'Why not?'

The old man dropped his head into his hands. 'You will have to see it to understand.' He raised his face a little, his fingers pressing into his tired eye sockets. 'Bring a meal to this table, and you'll see for yourselves what happens.'

Jason glanced back at us. 'Meleager, Atalanta, go to the *Argo* – fetch food.'

I was glad to be out of that rotten air, back to the shoreline and the fresh salt of the breeze. Meleager and I hauled out a cask of wine, along with bread, olives and grapes that we had gathered from vines we'd found on another island, gorging ourselves on their sweetness and taking what would last us a few more days.

'What do you think will happen?' he asked.

'Something terrible,' I said. 'It must be – did you see how emaciated he was? And the strangeness of that place.' I shuddered.

Even though I braced myself for it, the sour stink hit even harder this time. I could taste it at the back of my throat, and I swallowed down the urge to retch.

In the courtyard, there was a swarm of activity around the table as Jason, Orpheus and Polyphemus laid out the food we had brought back. Meleager lifted the wine cask on to the table and there was a long moment of silence. Then, as Phineus stretched out a hand towards a hunk of bread, wincing as he did so, a veil of darkness blotted out the sunlight in an instant, and the air rang with a monstrous screeching sound. Two great birds swooped down, the wide span of their wings casting shadows over us, their stench thick and putrid, making my eyes water. All around me, the men were coughing, clutching their tunics over their faces, doubling over. Peleus was flailing his sword in the air, trying to fight them off, but he gave in, spluttering and gasping like the rest of us. Through my streaming eyes, I saw Phineus' face dulled in resignation as huge, scaly talons groped for the food that had just been laid out. I caught a glimpse of their faces, thin and pointed human faces, contorted with cruelty. Scavenging birds with the heads of women, squawking and grabbing, taking everything they could carry and leaving streaks of putrid filth behind them.

As they soared back into the sky, Phineus sat, his hand still outstretched, his fingers shaking as they reached for sustenance that had been snatched away.

It was Zetes and Calais who reacted. The rest of us were stunned. But those two, with their winged ankles, gave chase to the bird-women, rising into the sky after them. They soared higher than I'd seen them reach before, wheeling around in a wide arc that sent the creatures scattering away in different directions. For a moment, the bird-women rallied, hurtling back towards us, one coming so close that I felt the brush of wings against my head and saw her eyes stretched open, staring into mine, before they both swept upwards again. I heard a squeal of panic echoing from high above us as Zetes and Calais pursued them towards the horizon, spiralling into tiny dots in the distance.

'Every time I try to eat,' Phineus said into the shocked silence, 'they come. The Harpies. Every time, they steal the food and ruin whatever is left. Wherever I go, even if I hide in the deepest cellars of the palace, they follow.' I remembered the clawed tapestries, imagined the scrape of their hooked nails against the stone.

'The sons of Boreas have chased them away,' Jason said, his voice thin. 'Your monsters are gone now.'

Phineus' face seemed to collapse in on itself. 'Is it true?'

There were murmurings of assent all around the courtyard.

'Let's try again,' I said, and this time Meleager and I ran all the way to the ship, bringing back everything we could carry.

We returned to find the other Argonauts had dragged the old table away. We'd chop it to pieces, use it for kindling. They'd carried chairs and other tables from the unused rooms of the palace and put them outside the colonnaded entrance, away from the reeking courtyard. This time, when we set out the food, Phineus ate his fill, the light of rapture transforming his ancient face.

'I could only get tiny scraps,' he explained, leaning back with a goblet of wine, a haze of contentment settling over him. 'For so many years, only a fraction of a mouthful here and there. But I knew that when the Boreads arrived, they would vanquish the Harpies. I knew that however endless the torture seemed, it wouldn't be forever.'

'Where is everyone else?' Meleager asked, leaning forwards. He held a goblet of wine too, a golden one set with jewels. This palace must have been full once, of people who would feast from fine dishes, who would have drunk wine from these glittering cups. 'Why do you live here alone?'

'I told them to leave,' Phineus said. 'The curse was mine and mine alone. I couldn't make anyone else suffer for it. All my neighbours fled to neighbouring towns and villages. People come every day. They ask me for advice, for help with their problems and dilemmas. I give them the words of Apollo, tell them the future that I can see, and they bring me what they can. They have stayed loyal to me and always tried to help, but no one could overcome the Harpies.'

As the shadows lengthened into evening, some of the villagers he spoke of began to arrive. Fearful and tremulous at first, they approached with bowls and jugs, glancing up nervously towards the skies. I watched their faces slacken with disbelief as they saw the banquet in progress, the awful miasma displaced by the aroma of roasting meat, the smoke from the fires spiralling up to the warm, star-scattered heavens. As they realised that the land was rid of the Harpies, they joined the celebrations, adding their voices to the songs and pouring wine lavishly, praising the gods for their mercy.

We Argonauts sat in the centre of it all. The villagers kept pressing more food on us, more wine, earnest in their gratitude. I was surrounded by smiling faces, caught up in their happiness. I felt a flush of pride, looking around the table at my crewmates. Even Peleus holding forth about how he alone had tried to battle the Harpies didn't rile me too much. I ignored him, refusing to return any look of loathing he sent my way. I was reminded of sitting among the nymphs after I'd slain the centaurs. We had done something good for this place; our intervention had helped these people and their admiration was a warm glow.

At last, Zetes and Calais returned, descending gracefully back to the earth. They had chased the Harpies to the very ends of the world, they said, where they had been warned by the goddess Iris to leave them alive. In exchange for such mercy, the goddess promised that the Harpies would plague Phineus no more.

The cheers greeting this news were long and loud, yet more wine sloshing into cups. My crewmates were swept up in carousing, singing and drinking. No one was watching me, no one except Meleager. I looked across the fire into his eyes, and without a word, we both made our way to the fringes of the crowd. His hand brushed my arm as I tipped my head back to drain my wine, the finest that Phineus' cellars had to offer, dark and rich and dizzying. I felt Meleager's touch on the bare skin of my neck, beneath the neat swirl of braids, his fingers trailing heat down my spine. I turned to face him, reckless and free, the moon shining behind him, and I led him away from them, out of the golden halo of firelight into the cool dark of the neighbouring woods, where we could be alone.

The next day, the blind prophet was at the shore to bid us farewell. 'It is not so far now for you to sail to reach Colchis,' he told us. 'Though there are more treacherous waters between here and Aeetes' kingdom, and other danger besides.' He held out a wooden box, which Jason took obediently. I could see it had small holes in the surface, and wondered what it could contain. 'The first threat you'll face is the Symplegades,' Phineus was saying. 'Open the box and let her fly through them first; if she makes it through clear to the other side, follow at once – don't hesitate, or you will be crushed between them.' Jason was nodding, and I wondered if we had missed more explanation the previous night. Phineus gave more directions, and when he had finished, he turned his cloudy eyes to me. 'You have lost two comrades already,' he said, 'and there will be more. I see a young man of extraordinary beauty, searching for water in a pool beloved by nymphs. They were bewitched by his handsome face, and they reached up their arms and pulled him under so that he could be theirs.'

I remembered the pitcher, lying by the still water. No signs of a struggle. It must have been silent and quick.

'He can never return,' Phineus said, his voice gentle. 'But his lover, the one that couldn't leave him, he has more labours to complete. This quest was never for him.'

There was some comfort in knowing what had happened to Hylas, even if I couldn't imagine what kind of nymphs they must have been, so predatory, so unlike those I had left behind in Arcadia. The world beyond was such an alien place; I was learning every day how different it was.

And maybe I was different, too. I leapt lightly on board the *Argo*, at home on it now; I, who had never gone beyond the furthest trees of my forest. On days like this, I didn't miss my home at all, days when the sunlight was golden and the sea sparkled, when the world was laid out before us like a feast. I felt invulnerable, like it was all mine for the taking, with no consequence to bear.

15

We heard the Symplegades long before we saw them.

When they finally came into view, they were worse than I had imagined. The tumultuous sea narrowed to a channel barely wider than the *Argo*, all of its raging, frothing waters protesting in seething clouds of spray and foam. Rearing above them, towering over each side, were two walls of rock – not fixed in place to the ocean floor, but hurled back and forth by the frenzy of the waves. The crashing we had heard was the sound of the rocks colliding, smashing into one another with a terrible, reverberating force. Then they would wrench apart, torrents of saltwater erupting in their wake.

It was through this channel that we must somehow guide the *Argo*, and as we drew nearer, the ship careening through the waves, panic began to take hold of us all. The rocks clashed and sprang back at irregular intervals; we could no more predict their movements than we could guess from where the next great plume of seawater would burst, drenching our deck. The channel was shrouded in mist and spray, making it impossible to see ahead.

'The dove!' Tiphys was shouting from the stern, and I could see the muscles straining in his back as he desperately sought to control the bucking ship.

And then Jason was there, opening the box he'd taken from Phineus. There was a flutter of pale feathers as a pure white dove took flight. I gripped my oar tightly, the salt stinging my eyes as I desperately craned to watch the bird's path.

It flew directly at the rocks; I thought it would fly straight into their impenetrable face, but just as it reached them, they heaved apart. The bird zigzagged through them in a graceful, sweeping arc, and then the rocks slammed together again, but as they opened back up, I saw the dove soaring away, safely through but for a scattering of feathers caught in the stone jaws.

'Now, follow it now!' Jason was yelling, and as one, we pulled on our oars. My shoulders were screaming from the effort, my face stretched into a grimace of agony as the ship was carried forwards, between the brutal faces of the rocks. I kept picturing the disappearing shape of the dove, imagining it far away now in the distant haze over the horizon, free of this nightmare. I concentrated hard on the image, not letting myself think of the rocks coming back together, the fear that they were about to crush us at any moment, to crumple our ship as though it was a flimsy toy. The *Argo* lurched, tossed about on the currents, and I knew that we couldn't escape, that the world was about to go black – and then, all at once, the sky widened and the rocks slammed into one another, but we were through, we were past them, and the water was suddenly calm. We had survived.

*　　*　　*

Tiphys guided us to land after that; a quiet shore where we could rest our aching muscles. The terror had drained out of my body, and I felt so exhausted that I could barely keep my eyes open as I swung my legs wearily over the high side of the ship to climb down. We scattered across the long expanse of sand. I made my way inland as far as I could walk, finding a shaded spot on a winding riverbank. After the shock of the Symplegades, I wanted to be by myself. Despite the warmth of the afternoon, I was cold deep in my bones, and so weak I was absurdly close to tears. I wrapped my arms around my body, grateful that no one could see me in this moment of vulnerability. Meleager might be looking for me, but I was confident I'd been swift enough that I wouldn't be followed. I wouldn't allow any of the Argonauts to see me as anything less than fearless, not even him.

I slept the kind of heavy, dreamless sleep that disorientates you upon waking. The sun was lower in the sky when I opened my eyes again, the light hovering on the border between day and night. Something had woken me, a howl from deeper in the woods, and my first thought was wolves. But then I heard it again, a guttural scream of pain that I was sure was human. I jumped to my feet, running in the direction of the sound before I knew what I was doing.

The trees grew close together, arching over my head, the scent of moss thick and heavy, the earth a soft mulch that sucked at my feet as I ran towards the screams that were ringing in my ears. Wherever the rest of the Argonauts were, they hadn't heard it; I was alone, and no footsteps hurried in my wake to help.

The boar crashed through, right across my path, bellowing as it thundered past. Then it stopped abruptly and turned its head towards me, its small black eyes staring right at me, its huge upturned tusks yellow and pointed. The screaming had stopped, but from behind the trees where the boar had emerged, I could hear whimpering, gurgling sobs.

The panic was like a knife to my chest. Why hadn't I waited for Meleager instead of running off alone on this unknown shore? The boar was scraping its hooves against the ground, churning up mud, coarse bristles quivering across its flanks as it lowered its head to charge.

The world went still. There was a rushing in my ears, obliterating the sound of anything else. I moved like liquid, fast and sinuous, the bow stretched taut before I was even aware I'd pulled it from my back. My arrow whistled through the air, planting itself right in the beast's neck, and just as the boar squealed and stumbled, someone else launched themselves out of the undergrowth and the boar collapsed, a spear lodged in its chest.

'Idas,' I panted, realising who the spear-thrower was. I wiped the sweat from my clammy forehead. The relief hadn't hit me yet; I was still stunned from the ferocity and suddenness of the encounter.

'Idmon,' he said, 'it attacked Idmon.'

The truth pierced me. The screaming, the whimpering: it was Idmon who had met this boar first.

'Where is he?'

Idas was already staggering back across, pushing aside the branches, not seeming to notice the thorns that scratched his flesh. I followed, swallowing back the sick sense of foreboding that rose in my throat.

Idmon was near to death; it was obvious at once. I could see it from the pallor of his face, his agonised wheezing. He was clutching what must have been his cloak to his abdomen, but it was dark with blood, the smell of it salt and iron. Idas was weeping, holding Idmon's head as his eyes rolled back and he gasped and shuddered into stillness.

I drew closer, laying a hand on Idas' shoulder. 'I'm sorry I wasn't here more quickly,' I said.

He shook his head. 'It happened so suddenly. We were looking for water – the boar came upon us before we even knew it was there.' He tried to gulp down his tears, squeezing his eyes shut, but they streamed down his face.

I could hear more footsteps now, men's voices shouting. 'We're here!' I called, and after a moment, I heard one of them call back.

I rubbed Idas' shoulder, not sure what else to do. I had not counted either of them as particular friends, but I had come to know them a little. They were young, eager for adventure, pleasant and willing. I wondered who waited for Idmon at home, if his mother prayed for his safe return, if he had sisters who had woven that cloak for him.

'Atalanta!' It was Meleager calling.

'Here, beyond the trees,' I called back, and he was there in a moment, Orpheus and Euphemus at his side. The horror of the scene before them robbed them of speech.

'A boar,' I said, and they nodded. They must have seen its corpse where we'd left it.

'He was a brave fighter,' Euphemus said as he knelt beside Idmon.

'A good man,' Orpheus agreed.

Together, they lifted him gently from the earth. Idas rose with them. 'We'll give him the finest funeral rites we can,' he choked out, and they began to move, carrying Idmon with a tenderness that made me look away.

As soon as they were gone, Meleager put his arms around me, pulling my body close to his, pressing his face into my hair. I knew he felt just what I did, that shameful lurch of relief when he saw that the mangled, broken body on the floor was someone else's. That we hadn't lost one another.

I wrapped my arms around him, found his lips with mine, so guiltily glad that he was safe. That it hadn't been him wandering in the woods, searching for me and blundering into the boar's path.

He rested his forehead against mine; for a moment, we were suspended, standing still together before he spoke again. 'Where did you go?'

I hesitated. 'Just – after the rocks, I was . . .' I wasn't sure how to finish that sentence. What had I needed? Silence. Solitude. These were familiar to me. I'd never been afraid like I was when we were being tossed about in those churning waters, the unforgiving rocks ready to crush our bones to dust. I'd sought safety in a return to what I knew. The quiet peace of the empty woods, with only myself for company.

'I looked for you,' he said and I felt a swooping sensation, like tumbling from a precipice.

I stepped back from him. 'We should return. Idmon, we need to be there to bury him.'

'Not just that,' Meleager said. I'd thought his face was so grave because of Idmon's death, but there was more to come. 'It's Tiphys,' he said. 'He has a fever.'

All the way back, I tried to think of the herbs the nymphs would gather for illness, what plants they would crush into pastes and ointments. I scoured the grasses and the ferns that grew here; nothing looked familiar or useful.

Tiphys was worse than Meleager had described. He was ashen, moaning and delirious. Jason was at his side, frustration wrought across his face.

'There's nothing we can do but pray to the gods,' Orpheus murmured beside me as we drew near.

I saw Idas' face, hollow with grief, as he knelt beside Idmon's body. The gods had been far from the woods today. I looked up at the clouds, searching for the stars.

We clustered together on that lonely beach, waiting for the hours of the night to pass.

Tiphys' life ebbed away before dawn. We buried them both at sunrise.

It wasn't just the loss of two comrades that hit us so hard. Tiphys was our helmsman, he steered the ship. I think all of us feared we would be lost without his steady confidence and calm guidance. Jason wrung his hands and fretted. Who could replace Tiphys? The day passed and so did the night, and his anxiety only grew. 'No one has ever sailed so far,' Jason kept saying. 'There has never been a voyage like this. Without Tiphys' skill in sailing, his knowledge of ships, his navigation and his understanding of the sea, how will we reach Colchis?' He turned his eyes to the waves, as though they might give him an answer.

The rest of us poured libations on to the earth and sang songs for our dead. Meleager and I rounded up sheep from the nearby hills, and Orpheus soothed them with his music so they were placid when we sacrificed them in the shade of a wide olive tree. Jason's anxiety was a dark cloud above us all; his fear and worry tinging every face I looked at with doubt.

'Might we really not sail?' I muttered to Meleager.

'Who can replace Tiphys?' His seriousness troubled me further. 'There are those among us strong enough to steer, some who are experienced sailors but no one with his knowledge.'

I started to speak and halted. I remembered the crashing rocks with a shudder. It was Tiphys who had steered us through that peril. Jason was right that no voyage like this had ever been done before. 'Going on without Tiphys could be dangerous,' I said at last. 'But staying here would be worse.'

'Can you get us to Colchis, then? Are you adding ship's navigator to your talents?'

It could have been a good-natured joke. It could have been the kind of light-hearted, teasing admiration I was used to from Meleager. But his tone was sharp.

He must have noticed my surprise. 'I couldn't do it either.' Now he sounded defensive.

'The shock is still raw,' I said. My face felt stiff, and I was suddenly very aware of the space between us. The strain of the past few days had taken its toll on us all. 'Perhaps in a day or two, the way ahead will be clearer.'

He sighed. 'Perhaps.'

It was Acastus who suggested the funeral games the next day. I sat up, intrigued by the proposition. I'd never encountered such an idea before.

'How are we to hold funeral games?' It was Peleus' voice, marked with displeasure. 'Here, on this strip of land? There is no racetrack; we have no chariots. Where are the prizes? The horses, the women?'

'We can honour Idmon and Tiphys without such things,'

Acastus said. There was a placating tone in his voice, a note of weakness that told me he'd already lost. Peleus' scorn had drained the spark of enthusiasm right out of him, and the rest of the Argonauts had lost interest already, sliding back into gloom.

'Why not?' said Meleager. He jumped to his feet to stand beside Acastus, clapping a hand on his shoulder. 'We don't need a track, we can run without one. We can sword-fight. We can wrestle.' Here, he nodded at Peleus, and I recalled with distaste the story of how he'd won the sea-nymph Thetis as his bride by holding her down until she stopped struggling. 'The prize can be the glory of winning.'

I shook off the image of Peleus and the nymph. I was sick of sitting around with the others, lifeless and miserable. Funeral games might revive us all. But if I spoke up in favour of it, it was as likely to make the others more set against it – some of them, anyway.

I wasn't the only one to stir at Meleager's eager encouragement. Here and there, the men were looking at one another, considering it. Euphemus stood up, and Idas and others began to follow. 'An excellent idea,' Ancaeus called. Shouts of encouragement rang out, a clamour of voices in favour, many of them flattering Peleus, urging him to wrestle and show off his strength. Meleager was grinning, calling out to those who hadn't stood and urging them on. I watched how easy he was with them, how they listened to him without rancour. I wondered what that must feel like. To have their respect unmixed with resentment or suspicion.

The waiting and uncertainty had frayed all our tempers, but now there was a purpose, something to do other than grieve and worry. Under Meleager's direction, we marked out areas for each event, dragging lines in the sand and using rocks as markers. After the flat despair that had hung over us since the deaths of our comrades, I felt a lightness in my step, a heady excitement building up in me. The prospect of a footrace especially was something I'd been waiting for since Meleager had told me about Euphemus in the first days after we sailed from Pagasae. He was just as eager for it as I was, I could tell, and everyone knew it was between the two of us. The others who lined up gamely at the start fell behind us almost at once, and it was Euphemus and I sprinting along the headland. Beneath us on one side, the surf crashed and frothed on a long platform of rock worn smooth by the surging waters. We were racing uphill, towards the plane trees that grew high on the summit, curving around in a sweeping arc perilously close to the cliff edge. I felt giddy with freedom, the feeling I'd known in the forest all my childhood, only now the sighing of the sea mingled with the fluttering of the leaves, and there were no limits to hold me back any longer.

From the headland, we had a dizzying scramble down into the canyon, where the Argonauts waited on the other side of the river that wound its way through to join the sea. Here, I was at an advantage, finding my way deftly down the steep slopes. They didn't slant as sharply as those that led to my cave in Arcadia, and Euphemus was left behind as I hurtled ahead. It was only on reaching the river that I slowed, scanning it for the easiest route across. It was shallow and rocky, and as I paused to search for where the rocks were highest in the water, Euphemus raced up behind me and, without a moment's hesitation, launched himself forwards. I plunged in after him, the water icy around my ankles as I splashed through, but to my astonishment, he was skimming across the surface, his feet only brushing the ripples as he crossed over. The Argonauts on the other side were cheering as he reached them. I waded behind, furious.

My angry words evaporated as Euphemus turned to me, laughing with no scorn or triumph, only sheer delight. 'Atalanta,' he called. 'The race was yours. What I did was a trick, a gift given to me by my father, Poseidon, who rules the waves. You were faster than me on land.'

I was annoyed, but his sincerity made it hard to hold a grudge.

'On to the wrestling!' Meleager was shouting. As we started to make our way along the pebbled bank towards the stretch of sand where the wrestling ground had been marked out, the straggling runners still making their way down to the canyon, Meleager nodded to me. 'You were far faster,' he murmured.

'I know.' Our eyes met, and all at once, I felt a prickle on the back of my neck. I glanced around.

Peleus was behind us, watching our closeness. His mouth was curled into a smug smile.

I sped up, leaving Meleager behind and joining Euphemus instead, waving off the apology he started to make. Peleus shoved past us, barging me with his shoulder to get to the wrestling ground. He and Ancaeus were to fight first. They stepped forwards to oil their skin, muscles gleaming in the sunlight. The match began and they grappled for the cheering spectators. Silently, I urged Ancaeus to win, but it took only moments before Peleus brought him crashing to the earth and raised his arms in victory.

Ancaeus rolled over on the ground, grimacing. His defeat had been swift and decisive, and as Acastus hauled him up, there was a sense of disappointment among the rest of us that it was over so quickly. Peleus strode up and down, bellowing at us all. 'Who dares to fight me next?' He puffed up his chest, his muscles shifting and bulging.

The words were out of my mouth before I could stop them. 'I will!'

There was startled silence at first, then laughter and jeers, mostly aimed at Peleus – would he really allow a woman to challenge him? Some of the comments flew at me, barbed like arrows. Was I so desperate to press up against a man, was I such an animal that I'd roll around with him right here, in front of them all? I let them bounce off me like a spear glancing off a bronze breastplate. I shoved my way to the front and stood before Peleus, my chest heaving.

He looked surprised. Definitely wrong-footed. He didn't know how to react – accept my challenge and lower himself to fight a woman, or decline and suffer the taunts of cowardice?

Whatever the Argonauts thought of me, we'd hauled ropes together, hunted, fought alongside one another since the start of our voyage. I'd left the forest in the final riotous days of summer; by now, I knew the leaves would have fallen and the rivers swollen from the autumn rains. We had travelled so far together. But all efforts at camaraderie melted away, dissolving like mist in the sunshine. I was back on the riverbank, seeing Arethusa flee the river-god; back in my cave, Callisto turning her face away so I couldn't see the despair in her eyes. Pine-trees catching alight and toppling to the earth as the centaurs came for me. Peleus' eyes fixed on me and Meleager, his look of satisfaction, as if his suspicions were confirmed. I hated the thought of him knowing, of him thinking he had any idea of what the two of us shared. But here was my chance to silence him. 'I'll fight you,' I said again.

Something shifted in his gaze; it locked on to mine. 'I accept.'

The sand was soft, warmed by the mellow sun, trickling through my toes as I stepped on to it and flexed my feet. I could feel the anticipation humming in the crowd as we faced each other, circling intently. They probably wouldn't care which of us won; if I toppled Peleus, they'd find it hilarious, and if he beat me, they'd enjoy watching me humbled. But I wasn't arrogant. He was strong and better trained, but I could feel the energy, clear and sharp through my body. When he grabbed for me, I caught his forearm and shoved it away. I saw him reassess me; then he grasped my shoulders, pushing down with all his weight. I thrust him away and he spun backwards. The determination settled in his features and he came back, wrapping his arms around me and driving me down. I twisted, my back pressed against his chest now and his arm locked around my neck, squeezing out the air so that stars shimmered in the edges of my vision. I yanked his fingers back, and he yelped as the bones cracked in my grip. His hold loosened; I dodged away, and then I leapt on his back, his knees buckling. He stumbled, lurched forwards, pulled at my leg so I fell sideways off his body, my head tipping down towards the ground. He pulled my right arm back, twisting it above me, his other arm pushing me down further and further. My hair was coming loose, falling into my eyes, and I could almost taste the dirt in my mouth as my face came closer and closer to the sand.

He was strong, one of the strongest among us since Heracles' departure. But I knew, even as his weight bore down on my back, that there was no way he was going to win. I closed my eyes for an instant. I had been tussling with bears when he was cosseted in his crib.

Gritting my teeth, I summoned up every ounce of strength

in my body, dragging my leg one step to the side so that he slipped, momentarily off balance, and in that moment, I drove my left elbow hard into his stomach and pulled my right arm free of his hold. When he staggered back, I pounced forwards, throwing all my weight at him. His feet scrambled against the ground, his arms flailing, and I felt him fall underneath me. His back thudded on to the earth.

The roar from the audience thundered across us. For a moment, I was locked in a strange intimacy with him, his body prone beneath me. Disbelief clouded his eyes; he was too stunned for rage. Gasping for breath, I sat back on my heels, looking up at the Argonauts, their arms held aloft, shouting in congratulation or anger, or some mixture of the two. I searched for Meleager's face. He was cheering too, but he looked slightly stunned, as though he couldn't quite believe what had happened.

I stood up, Argonauts converging all around me. In the melee, I found Meleager.

'Well?' I said, flushed with victory.

'Impressive,' he said. He smiled. 'Is there nothing you can't do better than anyone else?'

I laughed. 'Maybe not.'

Peleus hauled himself to his feet and marched away. His friends followed him, tight-lipped and frowning, but others clustered around me, generous with their praise: Orpheus, Euphemus and Idas most sincerely so. I basked in their celebration. I wondered briefly where Meleager had gone, but I was too elated to think more about it. I felt like my cheeks would split from smiling. I had spent so much of the past few weeks hoping that Artemis couldn't see me, that her eyes wouldn't fall upon me, that she might have forgotten she had sent me and turned her attention to other matters. But this, this I wished she could see. I had done this on my own, and I had done it for every nymph I'd shared the forest with.

16

My victory over Peleus was enough. I didn't take part in the rest of the games, content to watch them play out instead. Something had shifted; there could be no one left who would dispute my claim to be here now. After the games concluded, Ancaeus put himself forward to take Tiphys' place. He was a son of Poseidon, he declared, and he had an affinity with the sea that flowed in his blood. We had instructions from Phineus, and he was sure that he could steer us safely on to Colchis.

Jason assented, and so, with fervent prayers, we set forth again with Ancaeus at the stern.

He guided us faithfully, adhering to every direction Phineus had imparted. We sailed past long stretches of coast, rolling mountains, curving headlands, places where rivers ran into the sea, their waters mingling. We were careful not to seek shelter at Themiscyra, where the most hostile of the Amazon tribes had made their home, though I leaned out over the rail of the *Argo* and strained to catch a glimpse of the legendary women as we passed by. No member of our crew had ever travelled so far before; only Heracles had visited these lands, taking the girdle from an Amazon queen as his prize. I hadn't always cared to listen to his tales, which so often veered into bragging, but his knowledge might have helped us now, especially as we approached the Isle of Ares.

I noticed how Meleager watched alertly as it loomed larger ahead of us. This land was beloved by the war-god and inhabited by his creatures, the arrow-feathered birds of Dia. We'd heard how Heracles had driven such creatures away from the Stymphalian Lake with a bronze rattle so that they didn't attack.

'Phineus warned us about the birds of Ares,' Ancaeus called out. 'He told us we must frighten them off as Heracles did so that we can land here unharmed.'

The birds were clustered along the sparse branches of the spindly trees on the shore. I could make out the wicked curves of their long beaks. As we sailed closer, some of them began to notice us, ruffling their feathers and stretching out their necks. The first of them took flight, the wide span of its wings breathtaking.

'Their feathers are as sharp as any blade,' Meleager muttered to me. 'They'll shake them loose to strike us if they fly overhead.'

The bird glided towards the ship, its dark shape blotting out the sun as it swooped past.

'Raise your shields!' Ancaeus was shouting.

We were quick to lift them over our heads at once, the circular plates overlapping to make a roof. I could hear the beating of more wings and the hail of bronze feathers striking our shields.

'Make noise!' Ancaeus urged us and Meleager took up his spear, banging it against his shield. I did the same and, as everyone followed suit to raise the most alarming noise that we could, the birds joined in the clamour, shrieking in panic. The onslaught of feathers slowed and died away, and when we tentatively lowered our shields, we could see the shape of them in a vast formation across the sky, flying away from the island towards the distant mainland beyond.

The rest of the Argonauts cheered in celebration, but Meleager was quiet as we sailed on to make harbour on the Isle of Ares. What did he look for, I wondered. A bearded figure, helm flashing gold in the dying sun, eyes burning with the fire of every war that had ever raged? I couldn't picture what an encounter between them would be like, couldn't fathom what he might hope for from such a father.

As the *Argo* beached, the skies blackened, dark storm clouds gathering overhead. The wind whipped the water into foamy crests as we tethered the *Argo* hastily on the shore and found shelter as quickly as we could. There was no exploring, no searching for water or hunting for food. We scattered in every direction and, in the confusion and chaos, it was easy for Meleager and I to run together, away from everyone else.

Wary of lightning striking the trees, we searched in the gloom for a cave. The best we could find was an overhanging rock that jutted out from the cliff face along from the bay. Breathlessly, we squeezed in together underneath it. I stayed watchful in case any of the others stumbled past us, but as time passed, I started to relax. It was likely they'd all found somewhere to shelter by now.

'Don't worry, we won't be found here,' Meleager said. He pushed his rain-dampened hair back from his forehead, his breath warm against my cheek.

I wished I could feel as sure as he did. 'Do you think anyone suspects?'

He scoffed. 'Not at all.'

'What about Peleus?'

'He'd never dare say anything now, not after you humiliated him. He won't want you to do it again.'

'How can you be so sure?'

'Peleus has never met a woman like you before,' Meleager said. He laughed softly. 'There is no one like you. It's hard for him to understand – but I think he's got the message now. We all have.'

'We need to be cautious,' I said. This was just what Jason had suspected when he'd tried to refuse me my place on the *Argo*, and there was no way I was going to prove him right. For Meleager, though, discovery wouldn't matter so much. I had a sinking feeling none of the men would judge him the same way as they would me.

'None of them know,' he said. 'And I'll never breathe a word.'

I should have ended it. There were so many reasons why. Artemis and the Argonauts, the fears of either of them discovering us. But it was hard to think clearly with our bodies pressed so close together. The idea that the rest of the crew – intent as they were on drinking, fighting and heroics – would notice what was happening right in front of them seemed seductively improbable. I thought of Peleus and the rest of them huddling somewhere from the storm while we were here, sheltered together, and it made me smile.

We only had to keep our secret until the end of the voyage. Then Meleager would go home, back to his wife, and no one would ever know.

I let his confidence – or was it recklessness? – drown out my doubts, and I pulled him closer.

Above us, the winds howled like the unearthly screeching of restless spirits and the furious seas raged all night. When the dawn brought calm, I was the first to rise, leaving Meleager asleep. I looked around in the soft light to see what kind of place we had found ourselves in. We hadn't gone far from the beach, and so I walked down towards the bay where the *Argo* was moored.

I stopped dead. On the shore, four men I had never seen before lay exhausted, drenched and gasping for air.

'What's this?' a voice called out behind me.

I started. It was Jason. I wondered when he'd seen me.

'Who are you?' Jason demanded of the men.

Other Argonauts had heard and were coming too, gathering behind us.

One of the men raised his head. His soaked hair clung to his temples, his flesh bleached of colour and his whole body shivering.

Meleager was jogging over to us. I hoped Jason wouldn't notice we'd come from the same direction.

'Quickly, let's build a fire to warm them,' I said. 'They can't speak.'

Together, we helped the bedraggled quartet to where the *Argo* was moored, retrieving thick woollen blankets from the ship to drape over them as Orpheus and Acastus started a fire on the beach. We all gathered around it, letting the strangers sit the closest. Jason faced them, staring at them intently. As the warmth gradually returned to their bodies, their faces becoming pink once more, the first one spoke at last. 'I am Melas,' he said, 'and these are my brothers, Cytissorus,

Phrontis and Argus. Our ship was wrecked in the storm; we clung to the fallen mast and it washed up here.'

'Where have you come from?' Jason asked.

'Colchis,' Melas said.

'You have come from Colchis?' Jason repeated, disbelieving. 'Is it far from here?'

Melas shook his head. 'Perhaps a day's sailing, if the winds are kind.' He looked at us, one to the other, at the joy his words had sparked. 'What business do you have in Colchis?'

'Tell us first where you were going,' Jason said.

'We were sailing for Greece,' he answered. 'Before he died, our father had told us of the kingdom he left there, when he was carried away as a child.'

'Who was your father?'

'His name was Phrixus.'

Jason was exultant. 'The storm has brought us the sons of Phrixus! The gods must be smiling on us once more.'

Melas looked hesitantly pleased. 'Do you know of my father?'

'We are sailing to Colchis because of him!' Jason said. 'In search of the Golden Fleece.'

I saw a flare of worry in Melas' eyes, mirrored in his brothers' too. 'What do you want with the Fleece?' he asked.

'We have been sent to claim it,' Jason said.

'How do you hope to do that?' Melas' voice rose, perturbed. 'The Fleece is guarded by a serpent, surrounded by the magic of Aeetes – he will never let it go.'

Jason laughed. 'Look around you,' he said. 'Here is gathered the greatest collection of heroes the world has ever seen. We have joined forces to do the impossible, with the blessing of the gods.'

'What do you know of Aeetes?' Melas asked. In the silence that followed, he spoke again. 'He is our grandfather, the sorcerer-son of Helios, the sun god. His power is not like any you have known before.'

All of us were silent. Every eye fixed on Melas, every breath held so that we could hear his words.

'But you know him,' Jason said. 'And the gods sent the storm; they guided you here to safety so you could share that knowledge with us. Join us – help us to take the Fleece, and we will bring you back to Greece with us so that you can reclaim your kingdom.'

It was Cytissorus who spoke. He had a look of anguish on his face as he glanced at each of his brothers. 'We did make a promise to our father,' he said, and Melas dropped his face in his hands. Cytissorus carried on. 'We swore that we would take the throne that should have been his.'

'We can help you,' Jason promised. 'If you help us first.'

'I can see that you are strong, that your numbers are great,' Melas began. 'But the best advice I can give you is to turn back. Don't go on to Colchis; leave the Fleece to Aeetes. You can never defeat him; don't sacrifice yourselves for something that cannot be stolen.'

'We can do it,' said Jason. 'You are right that we do not know Aeetes, but he has never seen the like of us, either. We have come this far and conquered every enemy and obstacle in our path. We aren't afraid, and if you join us, you have no need to be either.'

They were afraid, it was evident to all of us. But their choice was a stark one. They could wait here, on this remote isle, and hope that another ship passed by, one that would risk the birds of Ares and give them safe passage to their long-lost kingdom, where they would arrive with nothing but themselves. Or they could join us.

Jason's confidence was swelling again. To find four young men with connections to Colchis, the grandsons of Aeetes himself, and to have them in our debt, was fortuitous indeed.

'This is the isle of the war-god,' Jason said. 'Let's find his temple, make sacrifice to him before we leave. We have the favour of many gods, you'll see.'

We made our way inland. I glanced at Meleager, wondering what this was like for him, if he searched the rock-strewn landscape for more than just his father's temple. It was so quiet, the air so still, and I thought I saw a tension in his shoulders as though he strained to listen for something. The temple of Ares, when we found it, was stark and simple. A tall, jagged black rock stood in the centre beneath the open roof, and outside was a small stone altar.

It was Meleager and I who were dispatched in search of sheep to slaughter. 'What do you think of these men?' I asked him as we wandered.

'That we're lucky to have them as guides,' he answered. 'Why, don't you trust them?'

I considered it. 'I think I do.'

'And I trust your judgement better than anyone's.'

'Why is that?'

'You see people as they are,' he said. 'Perhaps it's because you don't conceal anything about yourself. Artifice stands out to you.'

'Those men were near-drowned,' I said. 'They didn't have the wits about them to make up a lie.'

'They fear their king,' Meleager said. 'He is the son of Helios, after all.'

I glanced at him. 'You're the son of Ares. We have men among us fathered by Poseidon – by Hermes, too.'

'So you aren't afraid.'

'This is what we have been sailing towards,' I said. 'We're almost there. I'm not afraid. I'm ready; we all are. Aren't you?'

He caught my hand in his. 'Maybe I'm enjoying the journey too much to want to reach the end of it.'

I didn't know what to say. 'We're only halfway. We still have to sail home.'

Something shuttered in his eyes, just for a moment, at the mention of home. It was easier to live as though now was all there was, as though there was no one waiting for us at the end of this.

The sacrifices made, we feasted that evening and drank wine. If the war-god was pleased with our offerings, he sent us no sign. I wondered how disappointed that might make Meleager, but with the awkwardness of our previous conversation still hanging between us, I didn't ask. Instead, I turned my focus to what lay in front of us now. The air was rich with anticipation. Over the long voyage, we had set sail in giddy high spirits, full of optimism, sometimes trepidation, sometimes in grief or with regret or wistful longing. But early the next morning, when Ancaeus took up the steering oars, as we all took our places, as Jason stood at the helm with the sons of Phrixus, there was something else in the atmosphere. A solemn kind of weight, but not of sadness. Today we would reach Colchis; we would come to the furthest edge of the Black Sea, and we would find out at last what awaited us there.

Even Orpheus quieted his lyre as the waters stretched out in our wake. Ancaeus guided the *Argo* towards the broad mouth of the River Phasis, and we lowered the sail as we rowed in. The rolling ridges of a mountain range towered above us on one side, and on the other lay a long plain, gilded by sunlight. We all fell silent, only the splashing of the oars making a sound, while Jason filled a goblet with wine. He raised it in the air, his hand shaking just a little as he tipped it into the river. We watched the crimson liquid swirl away, our libation offered for the success of our venture.

'Anchor the ship in the marshes ahead.' Melas' voice was low and urgent. 'Hide it from sight of anyone keeping watch. You must leave it behind now, and go on foot to the palace of Aeetes.'

17

We kept quiet as we descended from the *Argo*, splashing lightly towards the grassy plain. I knew Meleager would be watching me from on board, and I wished he had been chosen to come with us.

Instead, it was me, Jason, of course, and the four sons of Phrixus. Jason would never have chosen me as his sole companion, but he had decided to trust in Melas and his brothers. Jason would present himself to Aeetes with just a woman and Aeetes' own grandsons. It was the least threatening approach, Melas had explained, with an apologetic expression.

It wouldn't just be Meleager's eyes on me from the ship, I knew. The other Argonauts were watching with a mixture of envy, hope and resentment, I was sure. Peleus, who had barely looked in my direction since our wrestling match, must be desperate for this to be a trap. The sensation of his glare burning into my back made me walk a little slower, luxuriating in the impotence of his anger.

'So, my first course of action is simply to ask him for the Fleece?' Jason asked.

Melas nodded. 'He will refuse, of course. He wouldn't surrender his Fleece, not for anything.'

'So why waste our time? Why not seize it before he even realises that we've landed?'

'His punishment would be swift and brutal if he caught you,' Melas replied. 'He wouldn't grant you the mercy of pleading your case; it would be immediate war. You are on unfamiliar ground, in a strange land, facing foes of which you have never dreamed. Trust me that this would be a foolish course of action.'

Jason bridled.

'But he respects the laws of Zeus,' Melas went on. 'Present yourselves as guests and he will be bound to offer you hospitality. He will expect no treachery if you're open and honest about why you're here. You know he'll refuse you, but it will give you time to resolve on a strategy. In his court, you might find that other ears are more sympathetic to your cause than the king's.'

'Is he so disliked, then?' I asked, intrigued.

A shadow crossed Melas' face. 'You cannot imagine.'

Above us, a dark shape swooped, and I spun to watch it, thinking for a moment it was one of Ares' bronze birds come after us. But its hooked beak didn't shine like theirs; despite its monstrous size, it wasn't one of the war-god's flock. Its wingspan cast shade up the slopes of the mountains beyond as it arced over their cloud-wreathed peaks.

'Listen,' Melas said.

A few moments passed, and then I caught it. A faint, hollow moan floating from somewhere in the mountains. Then the winds changed direction and I could hear nothing at all.

'What was that?' asked Jason.

It was Phrontis who answered. 'That bird was an eagle, sent by Zeus. It flies across our city every day, towards the Caucasus mountains where the Titan Prometheus is chained. Every day, the bird tears open his flesh and devours his liver. At night, his body heals and his liver grows anew and it comes back again, every day for the rest of time.'

Despite the blazing heat of the day, I shivered.

I had seen other cities on our journey, but none like Colchis. The city gates stood tall, flanked by even higher turrets, the walls smooth and shining. The light flooded everywhere, as the gates rolled open for the sons of Phrixus and us alongside them, and I was dazzled by the sweep and intensity of it. Colchis was a polished gem of a city, more fabulous than any we had visited, and in the heart of it all rose the palace of Aeetes.

His guards stepped aside for Melas and his brothers, and Jason and I walked in between them, through the graceful columns into a large courtyard. Vines wreathed around an arching trellis, and four springs bubbled from the ground in the very centre. I marvelled at the colours of the liquid gushing up: one pure white milk, another rich red wine, a third golden oil that released an intoxicating fragrance into the air. Only the fourth seemed to be water – crystal clear and fresh.

'My grandsons.' His voice was smooth, its tones deep and mellifluous. It made me think of a cold stream, flowing in an underground cavern. 'You have returned so much sooner than I expected.'

He stepped out from the shaded cool of the palace interior. He was tall, robed in fine purple linen, his bald head crowned with a shining golden band, upon which an orange jewel glittered. His eyes were a darker shade of the same colour, smoked bronze, contemptuous as his gaze swept over us. Behind him stood a cluster of men, finely dressed, though not so magnificent as him. There was a woman among them, her face still beautiful, though lined with worry and sadness. Her eyes were fixed, anguished, upon Melas, Cytissorus, Phrontis and Argus.

The four sons of Phrixus bowed their heads before their grandfather. Then Melas spoke. 'A storm wrecked us off the coast of the Isle of Ares. Our ship was destroyed, our crew lost to the raging sea.' He gestured to Jason. 'This man saved us, when we washed up on the shore where he had sought rest on his journey here to Colchis. In gratitude for our lives, we brought him back with us so that he could make his entreaties to you.'

The king's expression remained unreadable. 'Who are you, and what are these entreaties my grandson speaks of?'

Jason cleared his throat. 'I am Jason, son of Aeson. I was born in the city of Iolcus, ruled now by my uncle who has stolen the throne from me. To claim it back, I seek something that belongs to you – the Golden Fleece.'

Aeetes stared at him. The hush that followed was long and terrible. Then he shifted his eyes to his grandsons. 'Sons of Phrixus, is this why I took pity on your father when he arrived in my city, fleeing death at the hands of his own stepmother? Is this how I am repaid for my kindness, in letting him eat at my table, live under my roof, marry my daughter, Chalciope?' He inclined his head at the woman behind, and I understood now the reason for her despairing expression as she looked upon her sons. 'And now his sons bring an enemy right into my home, one with demands on the sacred Fleece we dedicated to the gods in gratitude for his safe passage?'

Jason opened his mouth to protest, but Aeetes carried on, his words as venomous as an uncoiling snake.

'I wonder what you have told this stranger about the Fleece, how many of our secrets you have betrayed already. Perhaps I should tear out your tongues before you let slip any others, and cut off your hands so that you can't show him the way to our ruin.'

Chalciope gasped, then pressed her hand to her mouth to stifle the sound.

His grandsons were frozen to the spot, unable to move, held fixed by the weight of his stare.

'I don't propose your ruin,' Jason said. 'I wouldn't take the Fleece without offering a fair exchange.'

Aeetes laughed, a sound utterly devoid of mirth. 'What could you offer me that would come close to its value?'

Jason glanced at me. 'I bring Atalanta, a champion chosen by Artemis herself, to greet you. But I have a party of men, more than fifty in number. Among them are sons and grandsons of the Olympians; men of power, strength and skill. Atalanta is the fastest runner and most formidable huntress the world has ever known, but she is only one of my crew. I have the sons of Boreas at my command, whose winged ankles mean they can rise into the sky and fly at their enemies. I have Ancaeus, son of Poseidon, who can steer any ship to safety. Meleager, son of the fierce Ares; Orpheus, whose skill with the lyre can soften any heart and draw tears from the cruellest of tyrants. We are blessed and favoured by Hera, Queen of Olympus, and Athena, whose wily strategy will bring us victory whatever we set our minds towards. If you bestow the Fleece upon us, you will have our gratitude as well as that of the gods. We will be your army, conquer any neighbouring tribes that you wish to bend to your rule. We can bring you glory.'

'And all these heroes, this unparalleled gathering you boast of, they all follow you?'

Jason nodded eagerly.

'You must be truly magnificent,' Aeetes said, 'if they call you leader and do as you command.'

'They do.'

'Then you can take the Fleece,' Aeetes said, and the air felt suddenly too thick to breathe. 'It is yours. All you have to do is prove yourself.'

'Of course, I will bring my Argonauts and you will see—'

'Not them.' Aeetes smiled, smug in his satisfaction. 'Just you.'

I thought that Jason would waver, but he stood stoutly, raising his face to the king. 'I will complete any test you set.'

'You must do what no man has ever succeeded in doing before. Only that will show you are worthy of the Fleece.' Aeetes brought his palms together, his fingers steepling. 'You mentioned that the gods show you favour, but they have not neglected Colchis either. Those springs you see flowing forth from my floor, they were built by Hephaestus, who owes a debt of gratitude to my father, Helios. So grateful was he to my father, that he gave me more gifts – a pair of bulls that breathe out fire and have hooves wrought in bronze. If you can yoke these bulls and drive them over the Plain of Ares, tilling the earth and sowing it with serpents' teeth, then I will hand you the Fleece myself.'

It was like a labour of Heracles, I thought despairingly, not something that Jason would ever be equal to.

Aeetes carried on, his smooth, cold words sliding into place one by one. 'If you fail' – he leaned forwards, his eyes like bright copper – 'then I will burn your ship and every Argonaut with it.'

And Jason looked at him, firm and direct, with more conviction than I'd ever seen him display. 'I'll do it.'

'Tomorrow,' Aeetes said. 'At sunrise, on the Plain of Ares.'

Jason nodded and I turned on my heel, desperate to get out of that stifling courtyard, as far away from the king as I could. Jason wasn't far behind me.

But as we hurried away, the king's laughter trickling through the air behind us, I caught a glimpse of another woman, half-hidden behind a pillar, watching us. She wore a dress of dark crimson, her hair piled up in a crown of braids, jewels sparkling at her throat and wrists and twined through her hair. Her eyes were steady, intent upon us – no, upon Jason – eyes that burned golden like Aeetes' did. I yanked at Jason's sleeve, pulling him away as he turned his head to look back at her.

Out of the city, gulping in the fresh air of the plains, I tried to shake off the lingering feel of that place. 'So, we have tonight to find and take the Fleece,' I said. 'Make sure we're gone before dawn.'

Jason was perplexed. 'What are you talking about?'

'You can't stay to attempt that task,' I said. 'He means to kill you – to kill all of us.'

'I gave my word,' Jason said.

'No one's word can mean anything to a man like that.'

'He'll have guards stationed all around the Fleece tonight,' Jason said. 'There will be no chance to take it.'

I blew out my breath, frustrated at our mistakes, at the stupidity of walking into the palace of such a king and laying out our desires so honestly. 'Then what?' Every instinct in my body rebelled against the idea of sailing away quietly in the night. We'd come here for the Fleece. We weren't going to leave without it. But for everything to come down to Jason, for the fate of our quest to be in his hands alone – I couldn't bear the thought of that either. A man who had done nothing to prove his merit so far, while the rest of us had conquered everything that had stood in our way. And yet he had the self-belief to think he could outwit Aeetes, that his strength could overpower two bulls imbued with power from the volcanic god, Hephaestus.

'Then we'll do as Aeetes has said.'

'You might die.'

He glanced at me. 'You were sent by Artemis. It was Hera, the queen of the immortals, who gave this task to me. I won't defy her.'

But Hera wouldn't save him, I thought. Artemis had shown me that the gods could be as ruthless to their favourites as they were to their enemies. Jason thought that Hera's blessing was the same as her protection. He didn't see that she had merely given him the chance to succeed. If he failed her, it would be better he die than survive long enough to face her disappointment. But he knew nothing of the gods. Jason thought the world was built for heroes. I knew we had to build it ourselves.

We were almost at the end of the meadows now. Further ahead, the land would become boggy and moist, giving way to the reed-fringed marshes; here, stooping trees leaned out over the water, their roots entwined in the earth but their leaves trailing over the rippling surface. I could still feel Aeetes' eyes burning at our backs, and I was grateful to slip into the cool green shade of the grove. I searched my soul for faith in Jason; a hope that this was indeed the moment of his becoming.

He stopped, transfixed, and in a moment I saw why. A figure, ahead of us, the branches curving above her head as though she were a statue in a high-domed temple. It was impossible that she was here before we were, but it was true. The woman who had watched us in Aeetes' courtyard.

Beyond the veil of hanging leaves, frogs croaked and long-legged birds bent to dip their beaks in the water. Insects hummed, lizards darted with a swish of their dry tails from rock to rock, and little currents of bubbles streamed upwards to burst on the surface.

She looked young, more so than I'd realised when I'd seen her in the courtyard. Out here, in the dappled glow, I could see the radiant bloom in her cheeks, the sheen of her skin and the polished smoothness of her hair. The glittering stones and shining gold that she wore were unnecessary adornments. I didn't think I'd ever seen anyone more beautiful.

'I heard you,' she said. 'What you asked of my father.'

Aeetes' daughter. I stiffened, and she noticed and laughed.

'You have nothing to fear from me,' she said. Despite her youth, she was entirely self-possessed, an imperious ring in her voice that reminded me of her father. 'I only want to help you.'

'Help us how?' It was Jason who spoke. He gazed at her as though she were Hera herself come down to guide him.

'And why?' I interjected. 'You heard your father's answer; why would you want to help us?'

'Because if you survive his challenge, you'll be sailing back to Greece. And you can take me with you.'

I heard footsteps behind; Melas and his brothers had caught up with us. I could see the words evaporating from their lips as they saw her.

'Why do you want to leave Colchis?' Jason asked.

'Ask them.' She nodded towards the four men. 'And then consider what it would be like to be his daughter, rather than his grandsons.'

'Would you really risk that, Medea?' Melas whispered.

'I'd be a fool not to.'

'Is there a trick?' Jason asked. 'The bulls that he says I must yoke – can it be done?'

She shook her head. 'He told you that no man could do it, and he spoke the truth.'

'So how can Jason survive it?' I asked. The feeling I'd had in his courtyard, that everything was pressing in upon me, was the same crushing sensation I'd felt when the clashing rocks had reared up on either side of me. Now I felt like it might suffocate me here in this grove.

'I've learned enough from my father,' she said. 'There is a salve, I can conjure it for you. Smear it on your body, and the fire that the bulls breathe won't touch you. Their horns won't be able to pierce your flesh. It will give you the strength to yoke them together. When you sow the serpents' teeth, dead men will rise from the earth, armed with swords and spears, intent on your blood. But hurl a rock among them and they will fight one another for it, forgetting that you are there at all.'

I felt the stirring of goosebumps across my arms at her words. But Jason was nodding, a feverish excitement racing across his face. I turned to the four brothers to see how they reacted to what she said. They looked more solemn than Jason did, but not so aghast as me.

'If he finds out what you have done . . .' Melas said to her. Their eyes locked and she smiled.

'Then I'll bring his wrath down on me now, rather than later,' she said. The weight had dropped out of her words; where she had sounded imperious and sombre, there was now a sweetness instead. 'We all know, all of us who live under his rule, that it's only a matter of time.'

'This salve,' Jason said. 'Do you have it?'

She shook her head. 'It can only be made from flowers that grow on the slopes of the Caucasus mountains, flowers that grow from the blood of Prometheus as it drips from the eagle's beak and claws when it soars away from him. They're scattered, up high and hard to find. Only I can find them.' The pride shimmered from her. 'They can only be cut in the light of the moon, only harvested if Hecate allows it to be done.'

'And if Jason doesn't have this salve?' I asked.

'The bulls' breath will burn him to ashes the moment he sets foot in their field,' Medea answered.

It made sense, of course, that the key to defeating the sorcerer-king was through magic. We'd seen unnatural things on our route – the shrieking Harpies with the faces of women, the rocks that crashed together, the six-armed giants that hurled boulders at our ship. I had grown up protected by the magic of Artemis, the bears' savagery blunted by her enchantment. But Medea's talk of blood-drenched flowers, gathered in darkness to defeat an army of the dead, chilled me in a way that nothing else so far had. It was this kingdom, ruled by a tyrant whose children spoke of him in hushed and dreadful tones. The darkness that lay beneath the wealth and golden light felt like a palpable thing, a menace surging like the blackest depths of the ocean.

'If you can bring it to me, we will take you with us when we go,' Jason said.

'I'll come to the *Argo* tonight, where you've anchored in the marshes,' she said, and I felt my eyes widen. Did Aeetes know where we were too? Was it all a trap?

'Don't worry,' she said, smiling right at me. She walked away, stepping between me and Jason, turning once to glance back at us, framed by the trees and haloed by the sun.

'What should we do?' I directed my question at the four sons of Phrixus, rather than Jason.

Melas looked contemplative. 'I believe she can bring you that salve. If anyone can mix such a thing, it would be Medea. I think her knowledge is second only to her father's in the whole kingdom.'

'But can we trust her?'

'Why not?'

'What if she's acting on her father's orders?'

Jason raised an eyebrow. 'Is that what you think?'

'Didn't it occur to you?'

Melas waved my suggestion away. 'Medea is young, the youngest of Aeetes' daughters by many years. She hasn't been hardened by his treatment – not yet. She's seen a chance to escape, the same way that we did.'

A soft wind blew up from the marshes, ruffling the leaves overhead, swirling up a peaty odour, a salt stink of fish and clouded water. I'd thought we would face a fight in the end, our forces against theirs, a test of strength and courage. Something clean and clear that I could understand. But the very ground beneath our feet here was treacherous, shifting and sinking.

'With her help, you can do it,' Melas said, and I could see that Jason was convinced.

'Let's go back to the *Argo*,' I said. I wanted him to put it to the others, hoping their reactions would reassure me that this was the right course, or else that they would make Jason see that to stay was madness.

'Come on,' he said. There was a firm decisiveness in his attitude now, a determined set to his broad shoulders, his upturned jaw. Something new, something I might have welcomed in other circumstances, but that now only made me feel even more apprehensive.

We stayed on board the *Argo* as night fell. The moon was full, a ghostly orb suspended in the sky above the dark peaks of the mountains. Some of the men laid blankets over the wooden benches and tried to doze. Orpheus sat alone, one hand tapping restlessly against his thigh. I knew he must be craving the release of his lyre, to soothe our anxious spirits with music, but none of us would dare to risk the noise. Jason was sitting at the prow, his legs stretched out in front of him, his head tipped back. Ancaeus and Acastus stood at the stern, alert to the sound of any approach.

Meleager and I sat together on the deck, squeezed between the rows of benches, our backs against the rail. To the sides of us, I could hear the regular, even breathing of the sleeping Argonauts. The wood was smooth and polished, but it jutted awkwardly into my shoulders. I was grateful that it stopped me sinking into sleep. I wanted to be awake when she came – if she did. We spoke in whispers, mindful not to disturb our slumbering companions.

'Do you think that can really be all it takes?' Meleager sounded doubtful. 'A magical salve and Jason wins the Fleece?'

'I thought there would be more to it than that.'

'I expected a battle,' he said.

'So did I.'

'Are you disappointed?' I heard a soft huff of laughter escape him.

'If anyone is, I'd think it would be the son of a war-god,' I whispered back, pointedly.

'There might be one yet, though. If what you say about the king is true.'

'He doesn't mean to let us take it, that's definite.'

'So neither of us might be disappointed.'

'But will the salve work?' I wondered. 'Or will Jason burn up in front of us all?'

'There – a figure – can you see?' Meleager sat up, pointing at something in the darkness, and I craned to see it too.

It was a figure, hurrying towards us, her white dress fluttering around her ankles as she emerged from the shadows like a spirit. She swung herself nimbly over the high side of the ship. Jason sprang to his feet and the sleeping men startled awake, hands gripping at spears and swords immediately, leaping up, on guard for an attack.

She looked unperturbed by the armed men surrounding her, standing lightly in the centre of a circle of spears and blades. 'I have it,' she said, holding out a little jar to Jason.

He took it from her uncertainly.

'Spread it across your skin,' she said. 'On your shield and your spear, too. The sap from the flowers of Prometheus is imbued with ichor, the blood of the gods. It will make you as indestructible as they are, for long enough to yoke the bulls and fight the earthborns.'

'Did you gather it on your own?' he asked.

She nodded. 'It could only be done by me. I waited for the sun to set, for the palace to fall dark and quiet, and then I crept out and climbed the mountainside. I knew where to look; I had already made my offerings and beseeched Hecate at her temple, and she guided me there. The flowers grow tall, their stems too thick to cut without her help. I called on her again, seven times, and from the Underworld she heard me, the mother of the dead, and the stems snapped in my fingers. The ground shook beneath my feet, I heard the Titan groan as though he felt it breaking apart his own flesh again, and the sap flowed.' Her eyes shone reverently, her tone as sincere and sweet as though she had been plucking wildflowers in a meadow.

Jason stared at the jar in his hands. 'Will there be enough?'

'Enough for what you need to do,' she said. 'And after it is done, my father will be furious. You will need to flee as fast as you can – I'll take you to the grove where the Fleece hangs, so we can escape while he summons his forces. He won't be ready; he will only have anticipated your death. You must seize the moment while he is surprised, it won't last long.'

All around me, everyone was hanging on her words. I looked at her delicate frame – how young and tender she appeared – and tried to imagine her climbing that mountain, alone, in darkness. I found it was easier than I'd thought. She had a core of determination; I could see it glinting from her, like bronze forged in fire. Something in her that I recognised.

She was as swift to leave as she had been to appear. She couldn't risk it being discovered that she had left her bed. She gave us her assurances that she would be watching tomorrow, would be there ready to lead us away in the confusion when it ended, and then she was gone.

No one slept any more that night. We waited until the skies lightened, the sun rising up to cast its glow across Colchis. Helios, father of Aeetes, drove it forwards through the air, and I could feel his glare upon us. We were spread beneath him with nowhere to hide as we unmoored the *Argo* and rowed down the river, towards the Plain of Ares.

18

The plain lay some distance from the city, but we could see as we approached that already the Colchians were gathered there, ready to witness the spectacle. As we brought the ship to a halt at the riverbank, Jason uncorked the jar that Medea had given him. The salve flowed like oil, thick and golden, and he smoothed it over his skin and then his weapons as she had instructed, all of us watching in silence. He closed his eyes for a long moment, his arms outstretched and his face turned up to the sky. I wondered if he could feel it, the strength flowing through his body, if he would know the moment that it took effect and transformed him. Perhaps he did, for he left his armour lying on the deck, only taking up his spear and shield before jumping down from the high sides of the *Argo*. His skin glistened in the sunlight as he walked away.

The Colchians were ranged along the edge of the field, King Aeetes at the centre. He turned to watch Jason's approach, his eyes unfathomable. At his side, a woman in long robes, presumably his queen, and beside her, Medea. She looked as she had done the day before, her hair braided around her head again, regal and dignified. No hint of wildness, only smooth composure.

And in the field, the two bulls snorted and pawed at the earth. I was fascinated by the sight of them: their immense size, the shine of their bronze hooves scuffing at the earth, the smoke wreathing from their nostrils, encircling their horns.

Jason kept striding towards them. A man detached himself from the group of Colchians, carrying an upturned bronze helmet that rattled as he hurried towards Jason. He handed it to him, and Jason took it with a nod before he entered the field and the bulls caught sight of him.

The yoke and plough were on the ground beside them, and it would have taken a brave man to approach such strong, furious-looking beasts even if they couldn't breathe fire. But Jason didn't falter. I thought perhaps the salve imbued him with fearlessness as well as its other properties, the same indomitable spirit that had sent Medea climbing through the night to tear up those flowers while the Titan groaned in his unrelenting agony.

The king craned forward, a malicious smile on his face, as Jason got closer and closer to the bulls. Their great eyes rolled up in their heads. One of them bellowed, the sound thundering across the plain, and as it did, a tongue of flame shot from its mouth, right at Jason. He walked on, undaunted.

On the *Argo*, we exchanged glances of mounting excitement. The fire had brushed his body, but he hadn't flinched. Now both of the bulls bellowed, and this time the flames surged forth, enveloping them and Jason together, and Aeetes looked triumphant, but through the smoke we could see him, reaching forwards and grasping the horns of the first bull. More flames soared up, the smoke streaming from the plain, and as it reached me, I could feel my eyes stinging. The Colchians, too, were spluttering and rubbing at their faces, but, almost indistinguishable through the fire, that bull was being forced to its knees, and somehow Jason was throwing the yoke over its neck, and that of the other bull too. Aeetes' face was drained of all emotion now; he watched blank-faced as the inferno died away, and through the billowing, ashy clouds, we all saw the impossible: Jason, driving the bulls forward, their huge heads bowed under the yoke.

The field was vast, and the bulls unruly, but Jason kept going, up and down, the soil churning in their wake. When he drew close to the end nearest to us, I could see there wasn't a mark on him, no trace of burns. Medea had kept her promise. He showed no delight in his prowess. His gaze was slack and dull, as though he moved in a trance. Medea's face was calm and perfect, betraying nothing, though her eyes never left him. I glanced between Jason's empty eyes and Medea's intense stare, and I felt a queasiness turning my stomach. On and on it continued, this strange feat, nothing like the heroics I had imagined. I itched to be in battle, clean and honest – anything rather than this impenetrable magic.

The day wore on longer than seemed possible, and when, at last, the ploughing was done, Jason lifted the yoke and the bulls stampeded away, far across the wide plains, trailing smoke behind them. He took up the helmet he had left lying on the earth and reached into it, scattering what lay inside across the freshly tilled ground. They were sharp, shining triangles. Serpents' teeth.

He had covered half of the ground when they began to rise. Where green shoots should spring forth, they clawed their way out from the bowels of the earth: warriors brandishing swords and shields, their skin smeared with dirt and hair clotted with mud, snarling as they heaved themselves up.

Jason did just as Medea had told him. He seized a rock from the ground and flung it at the emerging fighters. They shouted, staggering in confusion, swinging their swords frantically at one another. Jason began to run, the remaining teeth tumbling from his hand as he dodged nimbly across the rest of the furrows, and when he reached the end, he spun around and started to hack at those who were just pulling themselves up. He plunged his spear through the faces of the newest ones, before they could free their arms from the prison of the ground, leaving them mangled. If any managed to slice at him with their blades, he remained unhurt, the salve holding its impermeable sheen over his flesh.

It was over more quickly than anyone could have anticipated. So little spectacle for the gathering crowds; Jason stood triumphant, and around him, Aeetes' earthborn army lay dead and broken.

Jason turned towards the king. 'I have done as you asked,' he called out across the devastation. 'The Fleece is mine.'

Aeetes' face was transformed with anger. His jaw worked furiously, the words he sought choking in his throat, strangled by his rage. His robes swished out around him as he turned and stalked away, jumping into his chariot and yanking on the reins so that his horses whinnied shrilly and set off at a gallop. The rest of the Colchians milled about uncertainly, unsure of what to do next. Only Medea had purpose and direction, dashing towards the *Argo*, terror stamped across her face. Jason saw her and followed at once, so that both of them reached the ship together, he still smiling and full of self-congratulation, she in a disarray that shocked me.

'Go now, at once!' Her voice was ragged, urgent and desperate, and I felt my hands go to my oars instinctively. 'This way, along the river,' she ordered, and we began to row. 'He'll gather his forces, he'll be in pursuit of us as fast as he can muster them,' she was saying, the words spilling out over one another. 'Row faster, we have no time!'

We snapped into action, all of us pulling together as hard as we could.

'When we reach the Grove of Ares, I'll lead you to the Fleece,' Medea was telling Jason. 'It's guarded by a serpent, fearsome and terrible to you, but I can charm him to sleep. As soon as I do, you take the Fleece and we row back. If we can reach the open sea before my father does, we can escape.'

We hauled the ship on, down the wide river, past the grassy plains, until we reached the woods. Medea took Jason's hand and yanked him to the edge of the ship, more frenetic than we had ever seen her, and the two of them disappeared into the trees.

'What do we do?' I demanded.

'Wait for them,' Melas answered.

I shook my head, furious. 'I'll follow – see if they come to harm. If anything happens to them, we're just sitting here, a target for Aeetes.'

'You think you know better than his own grandson?' Peleus spoke up, his face twisted with contempt. 'I thought we were following Melas' advice. Hasn't it got us this far?'

'No, she's right,' Meleager said. 'I'll go too.'

The two of us jumped down on to the marshy shore, not wasting a second to see Peleus' reaction. Tree roots tangled in the water, the huge leaning cypress trees growing right out of the swamp. I cast a look upwards. Darkness fell swiftly here, dropping like a veil, and already I could see the bruised edges of the sky, the spreading indigo stain. All day, we had watched Jason at his toil. I wondered how long his invulnerability would last, if already the protective salve had been absorbed into his skin, the magic evaporated.

The trees thinned out; I could see Medea's dress streaming in the wind as she and Jason ran through the last of them into the clearing.

The Fleece was there, the object of our quest before me at last. I reached out my arm to halt Meleager but he had already stopped, staring at it, as transfixed as I was. My eyes struggled to make sense of it, the way that it glimmered fantastically in the remaining light, wide and rippling in the soft breath of the air, seeming to emit its own gentle glow as it hung draped over the branch of a tall tree that stood alone in the centre. Coiled around its trunk, the serpent. If the Fleece, with its shining gold surface, looked improbable, then the serpent was impossible. A monster beyond all imagining. I realised that what I had thought was the wind through the leaves was in fact its hiss. Jason was standing as though stunned before it, its enormous head weaving back and forth as its great, cold eyes fixed upon him.

And then Medea began to sing, her voice high and thin, and the monster turned its gaze to her instead. Step by step, she drew closer to it. It reared up as she advanced, its black tongue flicking through its fangs, but she kept walking, her eyes blank, the eerie keening of her song quivering in the air. Despite myself, I flinched as she reached the serpent, sure that it would strike, but instead it lowered its head to the ground at her feet. I watched, appalled and fascinated, as she reached out a hand and stroked the gleaming scales of its forehead.

Jason shook himself out of his trance, darting around the coils of the beast to the trunk where the Fleece was suspended just out of his reach. He pulled himself up, reaching out for it, and then he plucked it from its branch. Medea was still singing, the melody floating through the grove. The Golden Fleece was vivid in the dying light, and I couldn't believe it was done, our quest achieved. Jason jogged across to us and Medea lifted her hand away from the serpent, backing away gently and quietly until she was with us. 'Run,' she whispered, and we did.

I couldn't make sense of the hollowness inside my chest as we sprinted back to the ship, as we boarded again to gasps and cheers, as we took up the oars and rowed back in the direction we had come. This time, as the ship made its stately way back up the river, I could hear the pounding of hooves as they came cascading from the city: Aeetes' men on horseback, hurling spears at us as they advanced.

I threw down my oar, taking up my bow instead, firing a hail of arrows towards them as the crew rowed with all their energy. I leapt up on to a bench, aiming with precision, watching Aeetes' men topple from their horses every time I loosed the string and let my arrow fly. We were leaving the city in our wake, the horses that still pursued us rearing back and losing their footing in the mud. But rounding the bend just behind us was a warship, Aeetes at its prow. I had him in my sights, I fired, but my arrows veered around him, falling harmlessly at his feet.

The river widened, the sea just ahead, and although his ship was fast, the strength of the Argonauts was greater. We made it to the open water; Aeetes' ship was still in the river, and a gust of wind helped us surge ahead. The sail shuddered down from the mast, billowing out, and then he was only a tiny shape in the distance, screaming his curses at us.

We sailed on, through the darkness, guided by the stars. At the stern, Melas and Ancaeus were in an intense conversation. They were comparing possible routes, listing off islands and seas, rivers and channels, treacherous hazards and ways that Aeetes might seek to pursue us. Medea and Jason were at the prow of the *Argo* together. Jason was holding the Fleece before him as though he couldn't quite believe it, and she was looking up at him with the same expression on her face.

'He won't give up,' Medea said. 'His fleet will be spread across the Black Sea by now, searching for us.'

'We've escaped him once,' said Jason. 'We have what we came for. Let him try, let him come after us. We'll beat him again.'

The Argonauts were nodding, rumbling their appreciation and their agreement, but Medea's eyes were wide and bleak.

We sailed on through the night. The exhaustion was beginning to weigh upon us now; after a near-sleepless night at Colchis, the fiery burst of energy we had spent in fleeing was leaching from our bones now. My eyes were burning, my shoulders aching, and all the elation I was sure I should feel was absent.

I had left my forest for this quest, convinced it would be a feat of heroic glory. But the bulls, the earthborn warriors, the monstrous snake – none of it had been our battle. Somehow, we had been spectators to Medea's victory instead.

All around me, I could see that the rest of the crew were flagging too. But somewhere, across the dark water, the Colchian fleet was intent upon us.

'We'll keep going, on to the Brygean islands,' Melas was

saying to Ancaeus. 'If we can get that far, they're two islands both sacred to Artemis. If we rest on the first where there is a temple raised to her, we should find sanctuary there. No one would dare to defile it.'

Islands sacred to Artemis. Islands that meant something to her, places she loved now or had once. Islands that she might visit, for all I knew, when she was away from the forest. The thought of it should have brought me comfort, but I shivered, the cold night air prickling my bare arms. What glory had I won her? In the end, the Fleece was won by trickery, by Medea's witchcraft and nothing more. That was it, the reason for the unease I felt. And now the Fleece was ours – as long as we could defend it – and we were going home. Home had felt like an abstract vision, out on the seas, hazy and mostly forgotten. I'd let the far more urgent reality of my desires take precedence, and the images flashed through my mind again: my lips pressed to Meleager's, the heat of his body against mine on the floor of our hidden cave, the recklessness I'd felt leading him into the trees, away from everyone else, the nights we'd spent together, the secret glances we'd exchanged, a whole language that belonged to us alone. Now I had to wonder if I could go home to Artemis at all.

There were hours more to go, passing long stretches of coastline, circumnavigating countless little islands. Morning came at last, and I saw people on the shores gathering to watch us. I wondered if word had spread ahead of us, if any of them knew who we were.

The island of Artemis, when we finally reached it, was uninhabited, the only structure the temple built in her honour. I stood for a long time before her statue, looking up at the graceful folds of her sculpted tunic, the cold determination of her stone face, one arm raised as though about to pluck an arrow from the quiver at her back. Arcadia opened up around me; I was there again in an instant, the dogs surging around our feet and her laughter floating in the slipstream of wind behind us as we ran together. I swayed slightly. Perhaps it was the delirium catching up with me, a vivid snatch of a dream taking hold as sleep tried to sweep me away even as I stood.

It was Medea who stayed awake, perched on the high rocks overlooking the sea, staring out at the waves while the rest of us gave in to desperate fatigue. So it was she who saw the ship when it approached, she who watched it anchor at the neighbouring shore of the second island. While we slumbered, she formed her plan.

When I hauled myself up from my fractured sleep, my limbs still leaden, the Argonauts were circled around her, Jason at her side, and she was speaking rapidly.

'. . . my brother's ship.' Her hair was loose, but her eyes were bright and clear.

Meleager caught my eye and I dropped my gaze quickly to the sand.

'What are they waiting for?' I heard someone ask.

'We'll find out shortly.' That was Meleager's voice, and when I looked up again, he was gesturing out to the water, where a small boat was rowing towards us. Only one man was seated in it.

'A herald,' Medea said.

'Here to set your brother's terms?' Jason asked.

It was so. 'Jason, son of Aeson,' the herald called. 'I have a message from Apsyrtus, son of Aeetes.'

Jason strode down the beach towards him. 'What message?'

'The king accepts that the Fleece is yours. You fulfilled the challenge he set you and won the Fleece fairly,' the herald announced. A cheer went up around the Argonauts, elation lifting us out of our fatigue, delight and relief winning over the fear and anxiety that had beset us since we'd fled across the water from Colchis. But he had not finished. He raised his voice to be heard over us. 'You have his daughter, and that was never part of the bargain. He will not allow you to keep her. You must give her back to us so that we can return her to Colchis.'

I whipped my head around to look at Medea. The colour had drained from her face, but she held her chin high, her eyes fixed on the speaker.

Jason said nothing. I looked at him, trying to decipher his expression. I remembered Hypsipyle, how easily he'd forgotten the promises he'd made to her, and I wondered if Medea was about to discover the worth of this man's word.

She was faster than any of us, of course. 'Tell my brother we will meet his terms,' Medea called out. 'Tell him that Jason will prepare gifts to send back, in compensation for the valuable Fleece he's taken. But Apsyrtus must come for me alone. I wish to speak to him with no one else listening. The Argonauts will sail away, leaving me here. When you see them depart, my brother can come for me.'

The herald nodded. 'I'll deliver your reply to Apsyrtus.'

Jason's mouth hung open; he stared at Medea as the herald took up his oars again. 'You'll go back there?' he asked, and I saw her face twist from smooth composure to rage.

'Back to my father?' she spat. 'What do you imagine he would do to me on my return? He's lost his Fleece, his most treasured possession.'

'Then why . . .?'

'I gave up everything for your quest.' Her eyes were flames. 'I made myself a stranger everywhere in the world. I can never go home, never see my family again. I left a wealthy palace to flee on your ship, so that you could have the Fleece. Now it's yours and you can keep it; you can reap every reward while I lose everything I've ever had.'

The ragged edge of pain in her voice was excruciating.

'Do you want to return me to face my father's tortures? Can you sail away with the Fleece and abandon me to that? After I saved every one of you from death at his hands?'

'What do you want us to do?' Jason asked quietly. 'Why did you give that message to the herald?'

'My brother's crew aren't loyal to him,' Medea said. 'They're Colchian slaves, following his orders through fear of my father. If Apsyrtus is gone, they won't fight on his behalf. They'll scatter and flee, do their best to lose themselves in the islets and villages here. They only do as he commands for fear of what he might tell the king if they don't.'

I realised what it was that she intended then.

'So when your brother comes to collect you . . .'

Medea nodded. 'You will all board the *Argo*, all except Jason. He can hide here, concealed from my brother. Sail around the headland and wait. When we've dealt with Apsyrtus, we'll come to the other side to board. By the time the crew realises he isn't coming back, we'll be gone. They won't pursue us any longer.'

When we've dealt with Apsyrtus. Her voice was cold.

'And you're sure that the ship won't give chase?'

'Yes.'

We owed the success of our voyage to her. We did as she said, climbing back aboard the *Argo* and leaving her on the island with Jason.

'It's like the bulls and the earthborns again,' I muttered to Meleager. 'We're here, on the ship, just waiting. Following Medea's orders.'

He leaned back on his bench, resting his arm on the rail beside me. 'You don't like it.'

'It's not what I thought it would be.'

'Would you rather have stayed to fight?'

I drummed my fingers on the polished wood. Not in sight of Artemis' temple, I knew that much. We'd come here to avoid bloodshed; somehow we'd ended up orchestrating it. I worried that we would draw her eyes to us, and I quailed a little at the thought. 'Maybe not.'

'Don't worry.' The warmth in his voice was like honey in sunlight, his fingers brushing the nape of my neck. I felt a momentary burst of anger at him, that even with a wife waiting for him back home he never felt himself bound by rules or hampered by the promises he'd made. The rush of fury came from nowhere and died away again as quickly as it had come. It was the proximity I felt to Artemis here; it was making me anxious that even without marrying Meleager, I would still have broken my vow. I envied him his lack of care, even if I wondered how he could forget so easily.

'We still have to get home. There's plenty of time for battles,' Meleager said.

Plenty of time to win glory for Artemis. Perhaps that would placate her. Besides, even if I hadn't plucked the Fleece from the branch myself or cut down the earthborn warriors or yoked a fire-breathing bull, I had been part of the Argonauts, and we were returning victorious, however it was that we'd won our victory.

The moon was high above us when Medea and Jason

appeared, hurrying along the bay towards the ship. They splashed through the shallows to get to us. We tossed down a rope and they clambered up.

The silvery light fell across her, illuminating every deep, dark stain splattered across her dress.

'It's done,' Jason said, and he put his arm around her shoulders as he guided her to the prow.

The seas lay open ahead of us, the Fleece was safe on board, and we could turn the *Argo* homewards again. Victory shimmered, tangible as a jewel that we could pick up and hold, and although Medea's blood-soaked dress was a reminder of the price we'd paid, there was a tang of exultation in the air as we took up the oars again.

As we rounded the headland, something flew low and fast across the deck. All of us turned, searched the darkness behind us to see where it had come from, and I saw the shape of the Colchian ship looming. Another flew past, ruffling my hair.

'They're firing arrows!' I jumped up on to the bench, taking up my bow and returning an answering volley at the pursuing ship. Medea had been so confident there would be no chase, but she'd clearly underestimated either their loyalty or their fear.

Over the still waters, I heard the grunts and moans where my arrows connected, the heavy sound of bodies slumping on to the hard wood. Around me, half the Argonauts rowed furiously and the other half hurled spears and fired arrows of their own.

My blood was hot in my veins, my muscles singing, my mind as steady and focused as my arm. The enemy was falling behind; I could see the panic on board their ship as they scampered from end to end, dodging my arrows, and I felt a savage satisfaction.

I didn't even register the pain; I barely felt it when it hit. Only the horror in Meleager's eyes as he turned to me, and then I felt the blood trickling over my collarbone, down my chest, and when I looked down, it looked so absurd I couldn't understand at first what it was.

Sprouting from my chest, the end tipped with feathers, the sharp flint point buried deep in my flesh. It felt like a dream, the world around me tilting and tumbling, and I was sliding down and down, and everything turned black.

19

The fractured light of the moon over the waves. The sweep of her long dark hair across my cheek. Her hands, cool and soft on my skin.

I could feel the pain now, a throbbing agony deep in my shoulder. Slowly, the haze was receding, and the shapes around me resolved into something recognisable.

Medea was smiling down at me, and there was a sharp scent that reminded me of the depths of the forest. She pressed something into the pain, something cold and damp, that smell of the earth seeping from it, and I gasped as it froze and burned all at once.

I fought to sit up, to push her away, but there were other hands on me now, holding me down.

'She's healing you,' Meleager was saying, and I was writhing in pain, but even as I struggled, I could feel my vision clearing more and more as the cold fire raged through my wound, the agony dwindling in its wake.

She laid her palm on my forehead. 'You will live.'

More than that. I was frustrated at first, my arm bound in

linens so that I could only sit uselessly on the bench, unable to row. But whatever salve Medea had used, it worked quickly. In a few days, the pain lessened to no more than a dull ache, though Medea still shook her head when I asked to take up my oar again. 'Another week,' she said.

'A week?' I echoed. The prospect of it stretched ahead interminably, but she was immovable.

'If you open up the wound again and make it worse, you might never be able to shoot your arrows again,' she warned.

Reluctantly, I acceded. Meleager kept up hearty conversation with me, and Orpheus would sing stories when I asked. As Medea had promised, the wound knitted back together as though I had never been hurt at all.

'Your arrows took most of them down,' Meleager told me. 'Their final shot, the one that hit you, that was their last desperate attempt. We got away after that, thanks to you.'

There was a shift, I realised, in the way the rest of the crew regarded me now. That Peleus hated me still, I had no doubt. Jason had no more warmth towards me, either. I was quite certain both of them would have been glad if that arrow had struck with more lethal accuracy. They knew, though, as well as anyone else, that it was because of me that we had left the enemy behind us. It was the battle I had wanted for the entire voyage, and even with my injured shoulder, I only wished there had been more like it.

Our smooth sailing didn't last long. A gale spiralled up from the west, the clouds blotting out the sun, and once again we were thrown into chaos. Storms tossed the *Argo* across the wide seas, the winds blowing us in every direction until I thought it would never end. When at last we were washed into the great river Eridanus, it should have brought us relief, but here was the lake that Orpheus had sung of. It was the place where Phaethon, son of Helios, had fallen to his death. The boy had demanded that his father let him drive the chariot of the sun, but he didn't have the strength to control the horses, and he dragged the flaming sun down to the earth itself, scorching the leaves from the trees, setting the ground alight, leaving everything in his path dead and blackened. To stop the devastation, Zeus hurled his thunderbolt at the reckless boy and his body tumbled here. As we passed the spot, we could see the smoke rising from the surface of the water, the bubbling heat from his ever-smouldering body. The stench of burning threatened to choke us, already nauseated and weakened from the storms.

It was evident that we couldn't just sail away from the murder of Apsyrtus as though it had never happened. Medea had cut down her brother on the island of Artemis, and with every moment that passed, we risked the goddess's wrath for harbouring her. And if Artemis descended to punish us for that crime, what further punishment might she have in store for me? I quailed at the thought of our transgression summoning her here, of Medea's insult bringing her attention to us now.

It was Medea who had the solution, once again. We would make for the island of Aea, she told us, where her aunt dwelt. She had the power to carry out the rites that would cleanse Medea and Jason of the foulness they carried, to purify them of the murder of a kinsman. I wondered why the sister of Aeetes would help us, but Medea was unshakeable in her conviction.

And when it was done, she added, as though it were an afterthought, she and Jason would marry.

The winds quieted when she spoke, and we made swift progress once more. Only Medea and Jason disembarked at Circe's island. The air felt easier to breathe without them on board; the heaviness that had hung around us since they had killed Apsyrtus lifted away.

'So, there will be a wedding,' Meleager said to me as we watched the pair disappear down a winding path that led from the beach. The island was small; a solitary, peaceful place.

'Why would she want to marry Jason?' I wondered aloud. I knew it would amuse Meleager; I knew he liked my irreverence, my habit of saying the thoughts I might have learned to keep inside my head if I had grown up in a fine house or a palace like the rest of them. But I truly wanted to know.

'It's the second offer of marriage he's had on this voyage,' Meleager observed, wryly. 'Perhaps being the leader of such an expedition is impressive to some women. Not you, of course.'

'Not me.' I watched the cypress trees swaying gently in the fragrant breeze, the sun sinking into the basin of the sea, transforming the waters into molten gold. 'Hypsipyle, though, she was trying to secure the future of Lemnos. It was her duty as queen to try to persuade him to stay, along with as many others as she could.'

'So you don't think she pines for him, then?'

'I hope not.' If she heard of this, though, it would injure her pride, I supposed. That he had turned down the kingship of her city and brought home a foreign bride, a witch who had betrayed her father and murdered her brother. If Hypsipyle had waited for him to keep his promise and return to her, this would be a bitter blow. 'I wonder if it's crossed his mind at all, if he's given another thought to Lemnos since we left.'

Meleager shrugged. 'It doesn't matter now.' A narrow plume

of smoke rose from deep within the island. 'The Lemnian queen, she was trying to save her city. But Medea has no home. Marrying Jason will give her Iolcus.'

'You've seen what she can do. She doesn't need Jason to give her security. She could take anything she wanted for herself.'

'It might seem that way to you.'

'What do you mean?'

He met my eyes. 'You grew up free. You make your own choices, as easily as breathing. It's not the same for everyone else. Especially someone who has lived as she has, with a father like Aeetes.'

I was surprised by his insight. 'I didn't realise you'd thought about it so much.'

'I do think about you.' The intensity of his tone took me aback. I was used to an easy rapport between us. I didn't know how to respond when he was serious.

'Well, maybe she and I aren't that different,' I argued. 'We're the only women to join the Argonauts, after all.' I didn't really believe it, though. Our similarities ended there.

When Jason and Medea re-emerged from the thicket of trees, they walked with a new lightness. It seemed that Circe had obliged, and the pollution that had clung to them was gone. They were eager to put more distance between us and Colchis, to ensure we had slipped well beyond Aeetes' reach.

Some time later, as we sailed on, a snippet of song drifted across the waves to us, and I felt my head turn irresistibly towards its source. The wind changed, the melody disappeared, and I could see the rest of the crew looking frantically about to try to find it again. There was something utterly bewitching about the tiny fragment I had caught, and I felt a desperation to hear more, almost as if I could fling myself over the side of the ship and swim towards it to get there faster.

Orpheus leapt up from where he had been dozing, his lyre at his feet. He seized it and began to play a loud, rousing tune, stamping his foot in time as he sang. I was bewildered, irritated for a moment, and then my mind began to clear, the tendrils of fog that had crept in unnoticed dissipating once more. He played and sang, drowning out any other sound, and now when I looked out, I could see land – a golden beach, figures reclining on the sand. Their forms became clearer; they were women, but each one of them winged, a wide span of feathers arching from their backs. Their mouths were open, their faces contorted as we sailed by, and it wasn't until they were well out of sight again that Orpheus stopped singing, drew a long breath and explained.

'Sirens,' he told us. 'That's what they are. They were nymphs of Persephone once, but when she was stolen away by Hades, her mother, the goddess Demeter, gave them wings so that they could help her search for her daughter. She was below the earth, far out of their reach, and when at last they gave up, they made their home here. Their song is beautiful, more beautiful than any music I can play. It drives sailors to madness, making them plunge into the sea to get to them, but the waves are treacherous here and the rocks are sharp and jagged. Every man who attempts it is dashed to pieces before he reaches their shore.'

The mention of Persephone's name made me think of Artemis. I wondered if she knew her friend was grieved all the way across the seas. While I was thankful to Orpheus for protecting us from the lure of their song, I wished there was a way I could have seen them more closely. I felt drawn towards them by something other than their magic. It was their rage, I thought, the anger for their stolen girl that made them punish every man they saw.

That night, we stopped on the Phaeacian isle Drepane. Legend told that it was here the Titan Kronos had buried the sickle he had used to castrate his own father. It was here that Medea and Jason were to marry. I raised an eyebrow when I heard that. It didn't seem to bode well for their union.

The townsfolk were friendly and welcoming when we landed, bringing us food and wine. Nymphs came, too, from the rivers and the woodlands, their sweet faces shining, everyone eager to hear our stories and lay eyes on the glittering Fleece.

Medea held it, gathered in her arms, the bright gold wool catching the sun's rays, its radiance reflecting back on her face. She was so vibrant and vivid, glowing with ripe satisfaction as she called me over. 'Atalanta, come with me, help me to prepare.'

I went. Such was the effect she had. She led me down the shore to the bank of cliffs that rose beyond, stepping lightly through the tall grasses. A hum of bees rose as we walked; they were everywhere I looked, fat and contented, tumbling dozily out of bright blooms and hovering over luscious, velvety petals.

She led me to a cave, sandy-floored, flowers growing in abundance all about the entrance. 'What's this?' I asked.

'It's where I want to make the bridal bed.' She stroked the Fleece in her arms, a dreamy smile playing on her lips. 'Isn't it beautiful?'

It was. But the look on my face must have betrayed my feelings. I couldn't believe that a woman as powerful as Medea could bind herself to a man like Jason, that she would willingly reduce herself to be his wife.

'I always thought that when I married, I would have my sister and my maids to prepare with me,' she said. 'That they would help me dress in some golden gown, hang my necklaces, slide glittering bracelets on to my arms and crown me with jewels.' She took my arm, guiding me into the cave. The light was soft and dim, and there were flowers scattered all about the cave interior, stems wreathed together, fiery hues of red and orange. A simple wooden bed stood in the centre, draped over with woollen blankets. 'The nymphs,' she said, nodding at the bed and the flowers. 'They made it ready for me. And you are the only other woman here with me.'

So I would have to do. 'I know nothing of weddings,' I told her.

'And you wonder what the reason is for this one.'

I pressed my lips together.

She gestured to me to take one edge of the Fleece and she stepped back, holding the other, so it stretched out between us. It glimmered, unreal, as though it was infused with starlight, something otherworldly and impossible. She shook it slightly so that it rippled, sending shimmering waves over its tufted surface, and laid it down across the bed. I let my edge fall too so that it lay flat. I couldn't resist resting my palm on it one more time, feeling its softness.

'I swore never to marry,' I said at last.

'And you're happy to keep that vow?'

'Of course I am. Why would I want a husband?'

She laughed. 'Most of us never imagined a life without one. What does your father think of your promise?'

'My father left me on a hillside when I was born,' I said. 'He hoped a wolf would come for me, or that I would starve or die from the cold.'

'And you survived.' Her face darkened as she spoke. 'Better the wolf or the freezing cold than a father like mine.' And then the darkness passed, like a summer storm, and she was smiling again. 'So we have that in common, Atalanta. Fathers who didn't care for us. Who never felt a moment of love for anyone else in their lives.'

'I don't know,' I answered. 'I never knew him. I only know that he didn't want me.'

'I knew it too, every day that I lived with mine. We aren't the only girls with fathers like these. They're more common than you might think. He told me the stories, like different fathers might spin tales of love and happiness. Nycteus, who threatened his lovely daughter with fearful punishments when she was raped by Zeus. Danaë, another of Zeus' victims, another whose father blamed her and cast her and her baby off to sea inside a sealed chest, hoping it would be her tomb. Echetus, who blinded his daughter for the crime of looking at a man. That was the kind of husband my father would have chosen for me, if he had had the chance.'

'But you aren't in your father's power anymore,' I said. 'You can choose your own husband – or you can choose to have none at all.'

'And if I chose that life, would I be like you?' Medea asked. 'An adventurer, setting out with heroes, fighting battles and sleeping on the hard ground?' She lifted her hands, a rueful tilt to her mouth. Her soft skin, her dimpled cheeks, her shining hair and the finery of her dress, even if it wasn't the golden bridal gown she'd dreamed of – it was true that she didn't look like a warrior. But then, I'd seen what she could do.

'Why not?' I asked. 'You have the courage and the spirit for it.'

She shook her head. 'I've been fighting every day of my life. I don't want to tussle with enemies anymore; I don't want to face pain and suffering and death. I am tired of battles. When your ship came to Colchis, I saw another life. A man not like my father, not a cruel tyrant, not a sadistic torturer. A man who can give me a home and children, a life without fear.'

I saw her, squashed into such a life as she described, and however I imagined it, I couldn't make it fit. A woman who could scale a mountain in the dead of night to conjure her potions; a woman who could tame a mighty serpent, take charge of a ship full of men, plot the death of her brother and carry it out without a shudder of remorse – she wanted to bear Jason's children and live quietly for the rest of her years? 'Jason isn't a man like your father, or mine, maybe, or any of the others you describe. But that doesn't mean he's the man you should marry.'

'But how would you know?' Determination settled across her features; I could see that my words fell on stony ground. 'You said yourself, you know nothing of weddings or husbands or marriage. So how can you say my choice is wrong?'

'That's true, I don't know.' I only knew what I felt, as certain as the earth beneath my feet. The life she described was one I knew I never wanted. It was the reason I felt relief when I remembered that Meleager had a wife already, that he was never going to ask it of me.

'Perhaps I haven't picked the right bridal attendant.' She laughed softly as she said it, though; there was no recrimination in her voice. 'But will you at least wish us well?'

In all honesty, I thought the words might stick in my throat if I tried. It wasn't that I disliked her; I didn't want to offend her or make her sad. 'He promised another woman he'd come back and marry her, you know,' I said.

'But he has chosen me instead.'

Had he? She had chosen him, that was certain. But he let himself be carried along with the tides, allowed them to swing him this way and then another. And one day he might look around and ask how he ended up where he did, as though he'd had no way to prevent it. 'I hope you aren't disappointed,' I said.

'You can go, Atalanta. I don't need you to help; I can manage alone.' Still, she spoke without rancour, though she'd have every right to take umbrage at my phrasing, my inability to make my words more palatable. I was glad to be released, to leave her with her shining bed, lost in her own reverie.

That night, a sheep was led to sacrifice, the wine was mixed, and we took up torches, singing for the marriage of Jason and Medea. I sang with the others, hoping that the gods would bless them, doubting that they would.

We stayed there for three more days. Medea and Jason were in no hurry to relinquish the comforts of the hospitality we enjoyed. It reminded me uncomfortably of Lemnos, but this time I could sense a similar impatience from more of the Argonauts. The quest was done and most were eager to return home. When Jason and Medea acceded, however, and we left, we sailed straight into another storm, a howling gale that swept us for days across the seas, into a seaweed-smothered gulf cloaked in mist, where the *Argo* ran violently aground. When we climbed down, weak-kneed and shaken, the grave expression on Ancaeus' face told us what we needed to know.

We were stranded. The tides here were too unpredictable, the land desolate and sparse, a blank void of drifting fog.

'Let's walk,' I urged Meleager. 'We can search for food, for people, for anything that might help.'

'Atalanta and I will go,' he called out. 'We'll get the lie of the land and come back with what news we can.'

It didn't seem to cheer any of our companions. I felt fiercely that I needed to bring them back some kind of hope. They longed so much for a smooth journey home now, and here we faced yet another setback.

We searched for hours. Even Meleager's indefatigable optimism had drained away by evening, when all we had found was a seemingly endless wasteland, veiled in a haze that never lifted.

Impossibly, we heard a clattering of hooves just as we reached the Argonauts again. A huge horse, its mane bright gold, galloped past us – it had come from the sea, the Argonauts clamoured, a sign from the gods. We would follow its tracks in the sand; it would lead us to safety.

We had to drag the *Argo* along with us, heaving it behind us with great ropes. I'd grown used to the burn in my shoulders from hours of rowing, but this was a new suffering entirely, and the traces of hoof-marks in the earth seemed such a flimsy thing to pin all our hopes upon. It led us through the fog, however, across sandy plains so dry and dusty that our throats were parched and croaking, until at last we came to a vision indeed. An orchard with a fresh water spring, where we could greedily slake our thirst.

At the centre of the orchard, a snake lay dead, its lifeless coils encircling a tall apple tree. A vast, thick-bodied serpent, nearly as great as the one Medea had charmed in Colchis. This one's diamond-patterned scales were punctured by a hail of arrows, its wounds oozing with some foul and reeking substance.

Beside it grew three different trees: a poplar, an elm and a willow. I stared at the third, sure that I could see a flicker of movement, and then she stepped forwards, slender, shy and delicate. A dryad, so timid she hardly looked any of us in the face.

'What happened here?' Medea asked.

'A man, a trespasser here in the Garden of Hesperides, intent upon the Golden Apples,' the dryad whispered. 'It was our task to tend them, but his to steal them. He slew the serpent with his poisoned arrows, beating its head with his giant club as it died. He was ferocious, unstoppable.'

My eyes widened. 'What did he look like?'

She shrank in on herself. 'Huge. Bearded. He wore a lion skin draped over his shoulders.'

'Heracles!' The shout went up around our circle, the noise startling her, and she darted away, lost between the trees as though she had never been there at all.

The serpent was newly slain, and we searched for our lost companion, but it seemed he had made away already. It heartened the crew, though, to know that he was travelling still, that he must be once more engaged upon his own quests. This task was so similar to ours: a golden treasure, guarded by a monstrous snake. It made me wonder what Heracles would have made of the way in which Jason had won the trials in Colchis. The same thought might have occurred to Jason; he merely scowled as the others cheered.

Beyond the orchard was a bay, the waters calm and the air clear and sparkling all the way to the horizon. We launched the *Argo* again, with lighter hearts. The south wind propelled us on, towards home.

The end of our voyage was in sight. As the last of the starlit nights that we would share together passed, I found myself choosing my words to Meleager with more circumspection than before. We both knew this was coming to an end, and neither of us wanted to speak of it. We had rarely talked of home, but it loomed larger ahead of us, our silence on the subject filling all the space between us, until at last Ancaeus shouted out that Pagasae was in sight. The voyage of the Argonauts was over, we had won, and despite my joy, I felt more unsure than I had done when we embarked from that harbour into the unknown; more rootless and unmoored than when we had sailed for the edge of the world. We were home, but I wasn't the same woman who had left, and in my heart I wondered if I could step back into the life I had always led, if it waited there for me, or if the forest had grown over my absence as if I had never been there at all.

20

There was no one there to welcome us at Pagasae. We beached the *Argo* in the harbour from which we'd sailed so many months before. I'd expected a crowd drawn by the sight of the *Argo*, eager to see the Fleece with their own eyes, gathered to hear the tales of our voyage. Instead, we splashed through the surf on to a deserted beach.

'We'll make our way to the palace at Iolcus,' Jason declared. 'My uncle has not come to greet us. Perhaps he's disappointed that we have succeeded. We'll make him stick to the terms he set: we have brought back the Fleece and the throne is mine, however reluctant he might be to hand it over.'

I wasn't watching Jason as he delivered this speech. My eyes were on Medea. Her face was cool and unreadable, but something about her expression made me nervous. She, an exile, had thought she was arriving a queen. I doubted that Jason's show of determination had her convinced.

'Perhaps they're preparing a feast in your honour,' she said smoothly. 'To celebrate their new king and all the brave Argonauts.'

It was in mixed spirits that we reached the palace on foot. As we'd neared land, there had been much excited talk on board of the celebration anticipated tonight. I knew the crew had expected to boast of our adventures and enjoy the comforts of a rich palace and the attentions of eager admirers before returning to their own kingdoms for more of the same. Instead, when we arrived, the tall oak gates were closed and bolted. I glanced up at the high walls, the tall watchtowers at the corners. I could see a flash of sunlight striking a bronze helmet, the sharp head of an arrow aimed down at us. There would be no triumphant return for us.

Medea had turned away from Jason. It was Acastus caught in her gaze now. 'What kind of a man is your father?' she asked. Her voice was calm and sweet, but he quailed a little in the bronze flame of her stare. 'Is he a man of his word?'

Before Acastus could answer, we heard the heavy sound of the bolts being drawn back. The gates began to swing open, and I tensed in readiness for whatever awaited us on the other side.

Pelias, crowned and cloaked, flanked by guards. His smile was thin and stretched. His eyes went straight to the Fleece in Jason's arms.

On the periphery of my vision, I watched the archers on the top of the wall for any sign of movement. At my side, Meleager had his hand on his sword. Before, I would have relished this. Even in the aftermath of my injury, I'd only lamented we hadn't had more battles to fight. But the prospect of a war to put Jason on the throne didn't excite me.

There was no outbreak of hostilities at the gate, however. Pelias gave us words of welcome and offered us hospitality. I was sure he would rather have cut us all down where we stood. He clicked his fingers to summon slaves to show us to the chambers they had prepared, promising baths and wine and feasting later. No mention of making his nephew king.

I cast a glance back at the trees beyond the city walls, the wide sweep of forest and the mountains ranged against the sky. The urge to run was almost irresistible. To the west, far behind those mountains, lay Arcadia. To the east, the sea surged out towards distant shores and countless islands, fed by cold, deep rivers that could carry you to the depths of the earth they girdled.

'Come on, Atalanta,' Meleager said, and I realised the rest of them were walking through the gates. I shook myself and followed behind.

The courtyard was scattered with straw, and a whiff of manure lingered in the air. Dogs whined and barked and women hurried past bearing heavy pots and piles of folded cloth. We were being led into the building, and I made sure we were well out of Medea's view when I pulled Meleager out of the wide corridor into a small room on the side. 'Are you going to stay?' I whispered urgently.

'What do you mean?' Meleager looked around. We were in some kind of storeroom, lined with wide earthenware jars standing half as tall as us.

'We've won the Fleece,' I said. 'That's what Artemis sent me to do. Isn't it over now?'

He looked dubious. 'Pelias won't give up without a fight.'

'I won't fight again for Jason.'

'Where will you go?'

'Home, of course.' I was surprised by the question. 'I'll give the news to Artemis. And then . . .' I trailed off. Then what? The gnawing uncertainty I'd felt on board was growing worse with every passing hour. Would she welcome me back to my old life? Would she send me on another quest? Or would she see everything I'd done and find me unworthy to be her champion again? I had no idea.

'Is this really Atalanta, the only woman of the *Argo*, turning down the prospect of a battle?' His voice was light with gentle mockery, but there was a hint of sadness in his eyes.

'You don't want to be a part of this, do you?' I asked. 'The quest is done.'

'Let's just wait another night,' he said. 'See what Jason's plan is.'

I snorted. 'It doesn't matter what Jason's plan is. It's Medea's that counts.'

'Just promise me you won't sneak off under the cover of darkness,' Meleager said. 'Pelias might be reasoned with yet. He made the promise to Jason in front of his entire court. If he doesn't break his word, you should be part of the celebrations. You earned your place.'

It was true. 'I'll give it tonight,' I said. 'Then I'm leaving.'

Later, we slipped away together from the feasting, escaping the crowded hall that was thick with smoke from the tapers mounted on the walls and rowdy with song and laughter. At the centre of it all, Pelias held court, talking expansively of family with his three daughters clustered around him, lies falling from his lips while his eyes darted back and forth between us and the Fleece. The guards lining the walls, silent and watchful, spears at the ready. Jason, brooding and uncertain, waiting for an outright declaration of refusal. And Medea, her face a mask of smiling calm, her golden eyes smouldering with quiet determination.

I didn't care what they did. Inside the unpainted walls of the little stone chamber I'd been shown to earlier, there was only us. The room was shadowed, the air still and warm, the only light the pale glimmer of stars visible through the narrow slit of a window. Only us and a new urgency, a desperate sense of longing, a need to imprint this on my memory while I still could.

Later, he slept beside me, his heartbeat steady and even under my hand. I looked up at the strip of sky and felt a soft breeze rippling through like the breath of the forest, fresh and green with the scent of spring, the way I remembered it in my cave. It felt so close now, a call I couldn't ignore. I looked at Meleager's face, browned from the sun, and lifted his hand, the calluses on his palm from the oars matching mine, and I wondered how Persephone felt when she stepped between her two worlds. If, when she came back home, she ever missed what she had left behind.

The palace was roused by the sound of screaming. A chorus of wails, lifting higher and higher into the air. Meleager and I leapt up, a flash of understanding passing between us as we reached for our weapons. Pelias must have decided to flout the sacred law of hospitality; he must have launched his soldiers against the Argonauts while we slept. I hadn't wanted to fight for Jason, but if we were under attack, there was no other way.

It wasn't what I thought. The screams were those of grief, not warning. As we ran down the corridors, searching for the fray, words began to take shape. 'The king is dead!' I slowed, stopping at a corner, a sick sense of realisation settling upon me.

In the throne room, the three daughters of Pelias were weeping. The room was full of men, nobles and advisers to the court, striding back and forth, wringing their hands. And Acastus, in the middle of it, his face graver than I had ever seen on even the darkest days of our travels.

He saw us and spread out his arms, beckoning us to him.

'What happened?' I asked.

'It was Medea.'

That was what had been in her eyes the previous night. 'Where is she now?' I asked.

'Gone. Her and Jason both, with the Fleece.'

Meleager interrupted. 'They didn't stay to take the palace? Then why—'

The daughters' grief was rising to fever pitch, the sound of their moans keening painfully in the crowded space, echoing from the walls and ringing in my ears.

'My guards went to seize them, when we realised—' Acastus was saying, but the chaos made it hard to hear. More Argonauts were arriving, dishevelled from their beds, reeking of wine from the night before.

It took the morning to restore some sense of calm and to find out what had taken place.

'I was disappointed that my father did not keep his promise to Jason,' Acastus told us. 'I hoped I could persuade him to keep his word. But before I had the chance, Medea found my sisters. They'd heard about the witchcraft she learned in Colchis, how she used it to help Jason. She said she hoped to win my father's gratitude, so that he would give Iolcus to Jason peacefully. She showed them a trick, leading them out to the stables late in the night while the feasting was still taking place. There, she killed an old ram and brought it back to life with its youth restored. She promised them she could do the same for Pelias, so they would lead her to his chamber when he slept.'

We stared. It was plain what had happened next.

'When he was found this morning, his throat slit, my sisters knew they had been fooled.' Acastus took a long, shuddering breath. 'He broke his promise to Jason. He never dreamed we would come back with the Fleece. He was wrong, I won't deny it, but still, I am his son. He was killed by treachery and deception. I couldn't allow his murderers to stay and take the kingdom like that. I took the palace guards with me to confront Jason and Medea. I offered them a ship, told them to sail away now, and in return, I would attempt no revenge for my father's death.'

And it worked out well for you, I thought. Acastus, who had fought alongside Jason, his father's rival, and still ended up with the royal sceptre. I glanced down at the smooth scar on my shoulder, where Medea had applied her healing balms and saved my life. I wondered where they had run to, she and Jason, and if she could find the life she had so desperately sought; if they could find somewhere to take them in. I realised that I hoped they would.

Acastus asked us to stay for the funeral rites. Bulls were led to sacrifice, their horns draped in ribbons and the thigh bones burned in honour of the gods, while the rest of the meat was roasted for the mourning citizens. That evening, Meleager and I took a jug of wine from the palace and walked through the city, taking long swigs. I hardly cared now about us hiding from the rest of the Argonauts, those that were still here. I remembered how it had felt when he'd led me through the same streets towards Pagasae to join them. The forest I'd met him in had been bright with the blooms of late summer, the air a golden haze on the edge of autumn. Now we were back as the earth was awakening again to springtime. It didn't seem that enough time had passed for everything to change as much as it had. I thought back to how things had been before. Before I'd heard the stories of Heracles, the crimes he'd committed and the labours he did in penance. Before I knew what kind of man Jason was, a hero whose feats had been won by his wife, who had promised himself to one woman and then another, as carelessly as a child turns from one toy to the next. Before I knew even Meleager, who forgot his wife to lie with me. And what about me? I had been caught up in the adventure, and now it was almost over.

'A herald from Calydon came today,' Meleager said, tipping the last of the wine into his mouth. 'He arrived in the middle of all the confusion with news from my father.'

'Has he heard already that we're back? Is he calling for you to return home?' I felt a twinge of sadness, though what else had I expected?

'He says a ferocious boar is rampaging throughout the town. It's bigger than any that has ever been seen before. They're saying that Artemis has sent it in punishment.'

Alarm rose up in me. 'Punishment for what?'

'My father neglected her worship in his harvest sacrifices. He has sent out a call for hunters, and luckily it's coincided with our return home. The beast's tusks and its pelt will be rewarded to anyone that can bring it down.'

'So, you'll return to hunt it?'

'Atalanta.'

I looked up at the stars, my head swimming pleasantly from the wine. 'You can't think I would go.'

'My father, the king, is calling for the best hunters across the land. That's you, and you know it. Why wouldn't you go?'

I traced the shapes of the constellations, letting my vision blur, letting them swirl and shimmer into one another until I couldn't bear the silence any longer. 'How can I come to Calydon with you?' I let myself look at him. I had always been able to read every emotion on his face; he never said one thing and meant another. 'That's your home. That's where your wife is.' Shame prickled at me as I said it. I never thought of her. That was how it worked. We were far from home, far from the promises we'd made to others. We'd never made any promises to each other.

He took my hand in both of his. 'What if it wasn't?'

'What do you mean?'

'What if I had no wife?'

I shook my head, confused. 'But you do.'

'I could leave. With you, both of us together. After the boar hunt.'

I pulled my hand free. 'What are you talking about?'

'I love you.'

The air felt heavy with the words he'd kept unspoken, that I'd hoped he'd never say. 'I swore to never marry.'

'We'd both be breaking an oath.'

I took a deep breath. 'I can't.' I looked down. I didn't want to see the hurt in his face.

'Can you truly imagine going back to the forest again?' he asked.

I didn't answer.

'I'd give up my kingdom,' he said. 'I'd leave my family behind. We could go somewhere far away, anywhere we could be together.'

There was an upsurge in the breeze, a fresh current breathing from the wooded mountains behind the city, carrying the earthy fragrance of oak and cypress. 'No.'

The silence that followed was painful. When we met, he had told me the story of his mother's dream, the log she had seized from the fire to give him invulnerability. Maybe swords and spears and arrows would bounce off his flesh, but here was a wound I'd never expected, splitting him apart in front of me.

'I'll come to Calydon, for the boar hunt.' It was all that I could think to offer him. 'But after it's done, I'll leave.'

He swallowed. 'And if I wasn't married?'

I kept the images of Hypsipyle and Medea at the fore-front of my mind, a shield from Meleager's face. I remembered how much I had admired Hypsipyle's strength and courage in fighting to claim the city as her own, but then she had offered it up to Jason. Medea had the power to charm monsters and heal mortal injuries, magic that laid the world at her feet, and yet she tried to shrink herself down to a life at his side. I wasn't going to do that. 'It would be the same.'

The pause that followed was more terrible than anything else I'd faced on our voyage. In all of those dangers, I'd had something to fight and we'd faced it all together. Now it was me who'd dealt the blow, and only me who could assuage it – and I'd chosen to turn away instead.

'Then my father will be grateful for your service in tackling the beast,' Meleager said at last. 'All of Calydon will be.'

I nodded, my eyes stinging.

'Some of the other Argonauts have agreed to come, too. We'll set off tomorrow. It will be a long journey. We should sleep tonight.'

I hated the stilted tone of his voice, but I knew there was no one to blame for it but myself.

'I'll go and round them up, stop them from drinking too much,' he went on.

'That sounds wise. Unlikely, too.'

His smile was weak, the moment painfully at odds with the easy flow of our usual conversation.

'Tomorrow, at sunrise then,' he said. 'At the city gates.' And with that, he turned and slipped away through the streets, his cloak swinging behind him.

I made my way back to the palace alone. Although my body betrayed me, yearning to invite him back to my chamber again, I felt released too.

Behind the safety of the bolted door, I would let myself feel pity for both of us, just for tonight. But tomorrow would be the start of something new.

21

In the morning, the wagons were loaded, horses whickering and scuffing at the earth with their hooves, and several Argonauts gathered at the city gates. Castor and Polydeuces, Idas too, Telamon, Eurytion, Echion and Ancaeus. No sign of Orpheus, I noted with a pang of regret, but Peleus was there, glowering. I was shocked to see him, but Meleager seemed unconcerned, giving instructions at the front as though he didn't have a care in the world.

I wasn't going to let Peleus' presence make me waver. There was a snap in the air that felt invigorating in my lungs, a bright clarity to the day that seemed full of energising purpose. It would take several days to reach Calydon, Meleager was explaining, but the terrain was familiar. There were no giants or sorcerers or storms to throw us off course.

I wondered if it would be better if there were. I worried about the tedium of the journey without the easy companion-ship from Meleager I'd grown to rely on. At first it felt that way. I walked at the back, behind the carts, looking up at the towering mountain range ahead, remembering how I'd raced through the thick forests clustered on the slopes on my way to Pagasae. I drank in the scents and sounds and sights, the feeling of being near home again more overwhelming than I'd expected.

It didn't take long for Meleager to fall into step with me, as he'd always done. For a while, we didn't talk, but when I glanced sideways at him, he looked contemplative and calm, not as though he was harbouring resentment or about to launch into any further declaration. The tension loosened from my body; I was glad to be outside, to be moving, to hear birdsong and feel the gentle warmth of the sun on my back.

At last, I broke the silence. 'Tell me what to expect in Calydon.'

'It's beautiful,' he said. 'I think it's the loveliest place I've ever known. The plains are always fruitful, the crops growing as far as the eye can see. Our vineyards are blessed, our animals graze contentedly, the forests are abundant and the rivers full of fish.' I could tell he was choosing his words carefully; there was a formality in his manner that was new and jarring. But as he talked, he began to relax, and I felt some of the old ease creeping back in. 'From the reports my father has sent out, the boar has laid waste to much of it. It's trampled everything in its path, gored the livestock, wreaked havoc everywhere.'

'I can't wait to arrive,' I said.

He laughed. 'Everyone there will be very glad when you do.'

We stayed in hamlets along the way as we travelled. I didn't miss hauling in the ropes to secure the *Argo* every night, or the ache in my shoulders from rowing, or my cheeks raw and stinging from wind and spray. Wherever we stayed, we were greeted with warm smiles, hosts ready to share what little they had in exchange for our stories.

Meleager didn't ask me again to leave with him. I started to wonder if he'd come to the same conclusion as me; that what we had shared had been left behind across the waves, something that already felt as though it had been a dream. Then I'd catch his eye across the circle and a flash of memory would unsettle me, like a stone dropped into a still pond.

After several days and nights, we woke on the final morning to Meleager telling us that Calydon was near. We'd be there by nightfall.

It was only then that I began to feel some degree of nervousness. I didn't fear the boar. I did fear meeting Meleager's family; what would it be like to set eyes on his wife after all this time?

It was clear when we were approaching the town. The trees lining the track were scored, great gouges carved into ancient bark. Some were toppled entirely, split apart by tusks far bigger than any I'd seen before.

As we walked, the scope of the devastation loomed larger. The fields that Meleager had told me of, that should be filled with waist-high crops, were flattened, half-ripe corn torn up from the earth and scattered across the mud churned up by the monster's hooves. In the vineyards, the vines were pulled down, the grapes split open. Cattle lay dead or dying, blood drying in the sun over their savage wounds, flies buzzing in thick clouds around them, rising up as we passed and then sinking back down to continue their feast.

Hurrying to meet us, wringing his hands in agitation, was the king, cloaked and crowned and surrounded by attendants. There was nothing about this drawn, anxious man, weighed down with worry, that reminded me of his adopted son. Meleager clasped his arms around the king, greeting him warmly. I took the moment of their reunion to observe his companions. There was a woman at his side whose cold, regal beauty momentarily froze me. She reached out for Meleager, pulling him into an embrace, and when he stepped back, I saw his face alight with joy.

'My father, King Oeneus,' he said, 'and my mother, Queen Althaea.'

'We're so glad of your return,' the king said. 'So glad you've brought your companions to rout out this scourge on our kingdom.' He looked out at us, no doubt assessing our number and strength. He paused when he saw me, but said nothing. 'Other heroes have answered my call,' he went on. 'There are more great men to add to yours, skilled and powerful hunters, though the boar has proven too crafty and too strong for them so far.'

'With Meleager to lead them, they will have no trouble,' the queen said. Although her words were confident, her stare bore into me, radiating doubt and, I thought, a little contempt. Then she tilted her head and smiled at Meleager. 'Your uncles, Plexippus and Toxeus, have volunteered to help you.'

Two burly men stepped forwards, clapping their hands on Meleager's shoulders.

'Thank you, Uncles,' he said, grinning back at them.

The men the king had spoken of were approaching now, a group of them bristling with blades. Swords and spears glinted in the afternoon sunlight, and a pack of hounds ran at their feet.

'Meleager,' the foremost of them said as they reached us. 'We came at your father's summons. We've tracked the boar and found its lair. We have tried to flush it out, but each time it has evaded us. With more men' – he saw me and hesitated – 'we can trap it.'

Meleager nodded. 'Thank you.' He swept his arm towards us and listed off our names. I watched for their reaction when he came to me. Most of the men looked surprised, confused for a moment as they realised he was including me in the group of hunters rather than as a companion. One of them curled his lip in derision, flicking his eyes over my short tunic, lingering on my bare calves.

'My name is Caenus,' said the original speaker. 'Here are Leucippus, Hippothous, Dryas, Phyleus, Nestor, Lelex, Panopeus, Hippomenes, Pirithous and Theseus.' It was the last of them who stared at me with that mingling of disdain and desire, but it was the name Hippomenes that caught my attention.

He was partly hidden towards the rear of the group, but as they fanned out, I saw him more clearly. It had only been a fleeting encounter, so long ago now, but I called up the memory of a young man, his skin smeared in ash, the trees around us burning, flames shooting into the dark sky. A spark of recognition in his face confirmed it. He knew who I was. He remembered.

'There are still enough hours left of daylight for us to drive it out,' Caenus was saying, looking up at the clear sky.

'Then we'll go now,' Meleager said.

'Are you sure?' his father asked. 'Would you prefer to dine with us, to rest tonight and wake up refreshed and ready in the morning?'

Meleager laughed. 'We're ready now,' he said, and we all nodded in agreement. We were far from tired from the journey; all of us were keen with anticipation, eager to do what we had come for.

'We'll lead you to its den,' Caenus said.

We gathered weapons from the carts we'd brought, each of us equipped with both sword and spear. Meleager pulled down hunting nets, rolled loosely into bundles. The dogs were keen, ears pricked and eyes alert, noses high in the air as they awaited our commands.

'This way.'

We set off where Caenus pointed. Meleager was at my side, but I was conscious of Hippomenes behind us. I wanted to speak to him, to ask him how he came to be here, but it wasn't the moment. We were focused, intent on the task at hand, and as we drew closer to the forest, I forgot everything else. There was only the hunt.

The forest was cool and dim, the light falling in soft, green shadows. We took care to tread quietly up the slopes, through the close-growing plants, and then I saw them: tracks, pressed deep into the soft ground. We were on the boar's trail.

In silent agreement, we formed a long line, hunting nets spread, weapons in hands. Those leading the hounds let them loose, and the dogs hurtled forwards, the quiet forest echoing with the chorus of barking. Birds startled from the trees, and then, from the far side of the ditch, I heard the furious bellow of the beast. It surged towards us with incredible speed, slamming its tusks into slender willows, sending them hurtling to the ground as it tossed its head and charged right through the pack of dogs. The hounds were flung into the air, huge and strong as they were, yelping as they hit the ground. Spears whizzed overhead, and still the boar was coming. It loomed larger than the mightiest of bulls, its small, blank eyes tinged red, and froth bubbling from its jaws. It crashed from side to side, spears embedding into tree trunks behind it, the ones that hit it bouncing uselessly from its thick, bristled hide. Enraged, it lunged straight towards Hippasus, and I saw him crumple, his screams rising to mingle with the boar's grunting and the dogs' howling. He was on the ground, his body contorted in pain, his hands clutching at his thigh, blood streaming through his fingers. The chaos was overwhelming, the noise deafening, and panic threatened to scatter our wits.

The boar charged again, men diving out of its way as it thundered between them. Its massive bulk swung around, knocking four of them to the ground, and it reared back, about to trample them, when Hippomenes leapt forwards, hurling his spear. Though it bounced off the beast's side, it distracted the creature long enough for Hippomenes to help the men scramble, breathless and panting, to their feet again.

I ducked behind a fallen trunk, my palms slipping across the polished surface of my bow. I forced myself to breathe, to quieten the thunder of my pulse. Now I had my bow, steady and reassuring in my hands, and I clambered up on to the log, centring the boar in my eyeline. The cacophony died away; nothing existed but me and the arrow I was fitting to the bow, the string that I pulled back, the boar's throat.

The arrow flew, whistling through the air. It struck the animal just under its ear, and with a rush of triumph, I saw the blood begin to flow from the wound. It shook its huge head, dizzied and stumbling for a moment. Ancaeus took advantage of its confusion, lifting his axe and letting out a wordless battle-cry as he plunged ahead.

The boar lifted its head and charged. The cruel, sharp point of its yellow tusk thrust deep into Ancaeus' belly and I saw his face twist, his eyes stretched wide as he fell backwards.

Pirithous ran forwards, but Theseus shouted at him to get back, to throw his spear from a safe distance. Plexippus threw his; it ricocheted off the boar's flanks and fell uselessly to the ground, followed swiftly by Toxeus'. I hurled mine, but the beast swerved and it hit the tree behind instead. Before I could move, Meleager leapt ahead of me into the boar's path, closer than anyone else dared. He threw one spear, hard enough that it lodged into the beast's back, stopping it short, and nimbly he dashed closer, shoving his second spear hard into its neck.

Froth erupted from its jaws, a torrent of blood and foam, as it wavered and then crashed hard on to its side. Too stunned to cheer, I stared at its body, unsure for a moment if it would drag itself up, but its heaving chest stilled and silence fell across the grove.

As it sank in, one by one, the hunters came forwards, tentatively at first. Each man stabbed his own spear into the carcass, holding the bloodstained points aloft. I yanked my spear from the tree trunk, approached the body, and did the same. As I did, Meleager caught my arm and lifted my hand to the sky. Planting one foot on the boar's head, he called out to the rest of them, 'Atalanta drew first blood! The hide and the tusks of this beast belong to her!'

'Are you mad?'

The queen's brothers were before us, faces red with fury.

'Every one of us weakened the beast before you struck it down! This girl did nothing special!' Plexippus wiped the spittle off his beard, his broad shoulders shuddering with rage.

Toxeus spat on the ground. 'It wasn't what she did in the hunt, it's how he hopes she'll thank him for it later; that's why he wants to give her the prize. You're an idiot, nephew, you always were, but we won't let you humiliate us and yourself by giving the glory to her.'

A moment ago, everything in me had been focused on

bringing down the boar. Now, my bloodlust seethed again and I longed to drive my fist right into Plexippus' face. 'My arrow pierced its hide,' I said. 'Your spears glanced off it; it barely noticed them at all.'

'Shut your mouth,' Plexippus hissed, at the same time as Toxeus snarled, 'How dare you answer me, woman?'

I tried to snatch my arm away from Meleager's so that I could get to them, but his grip was like iron around my wrist as he stared at his uncles in disbelief.

Some of the others were rumbling their assent, nodding self-righteously and jeering at Meleager. I looked for support from my fellow Argonauts. Poor Ancaeus was dead, his entrails spilled across the forest floor.

'Toxeus is right about them,' Peleus sneered. 'I saw them on the *Argo*; I know why he's favouring her now.'

'Atalanta pierced its hide first; she's a skilled huntress,' Castor protested, but some of the others who had come with Caenus began to jeer, drowning him out, Theseus and Pirithous the loudest among them.

The sun was sinking rapidly, shadows reaching out like dark tendrils across the clearing. I could still hear Hippasus groaning faintly; it was Hippomenes who was at his side, sponging the dying man's head with his tunic, his eyes frantically darting between his bleeding friend and the argument boiling over where the rest of us stood. The dogs were slinking back and forth, unsettled by the turn in atmosphere.

'It was Atalanta who made it bleed first.' Meleager's voice was firm. 'Atalanta's arrow gave it the first wound. I killed the boar; I decide who takes the spoils.'

This was too much for Plexippus; he let out a roar and sprang at me. I didn't see it coming, and Meleager was still holding my wrist, so when Plexippus barrelled into me, the force of his weight knocked me off balance and I tripped, sprawling on the earth. Plexippus was on top of me, his meaty fists grabbing at my throat, squeezing the air from my windpipe. But before I could jam my knee into his belly and free myself, his face sagged in astonishment. His crazed, bloodshot eyes went blank as his hands fell away from my neck and his head dropped.

I shoved him away, frantic with disgust, and I saw what had happened at the same moment as Toxeus did.

Meleager was standing over Plexippus' body, his sword buried in his uncle's back.

Toxeus charged at Meleager. I could see it happening like a dream unfolding. Meleager, how laughable to think he could be Oeneus' son, this man of fierce grace, tall and powerful, throwing back his head, his face upturned to the sky. All the savagery and strength of his father, Ares, was at once embodied in him as he yanked the sword from his uncle's body and thrust it, already crimson with Plexippus' blood, smoothly into Toxeus' heart.

The quiet was broken by the trill of a distant nightingale. A bank of tiny white flowers breathed their sweet scent towards us. There was no other sound save the final gurgles of Hippasus before his eyes fluttered to a close.

Four of our men were dead, along with half a dozen hounds. The monstrous boar lay, bloated and grotesque, in the centre. The dying rays of the sun illuminated Meleager's face.

I took a cautious step towards him and his eyes met mine. My chest ached with compassion at the stark despair I saw in him.

'Come,' said Castor. 'We must go back to the town, deliver

the news.' His voice was flat and sombre. 'The boar is dead, its destruction ended.' He swallowed. 'These men were wrong to deny Atalanta's victory.'

At that, some of the others scoffed, a harsh and scornful sound.

'It's true,' said Polydeuces. 'And they've paid the price for it.'

Theseus turned on his heel, stalking away between the trees. His friend Pirithous followed, and a couple of the others went after. Peleus cast me one last hostile glare and followed, leaving Ancaeus' corpse where it lay. My face was hot, my anger unabated, but I felt a desperate urge to undo what had happened, to go back and make my body move faster, to deflect Plexippus' attack and stop it all from unfolding.

Hippomenes spoke up. 'They're jealous – bitter that a woman was first. They didn't know what she can do.' He got to his feet. 'We can all bear witness for Meleager.'

My mind was moving so sluggishly, I hadn't even thought about the consequences for Meleager. I hadn't considered that he was guilty not just of murder, but of killing his own kin.

The boar was too vast for those of us left to move. Others would have to come back for it. My body revolted against the thought of taking the tusks and the pelt as promised. I never wanted to see any part of it again.

The others took hold of the bodies, lifting them gently to carry back to the town. I walked at Meleager's side, behind them. He didn't speak a word until we were almost at the edge of the forest.

'I'd do it again,' he said, stopping while we were still among the trees. It was hard to make out his expression in the darkness. His voice was hoarse. 'They deserved to die.'

I couldn't bear his pain. I wanted to hold him, to ward off the hurt and give him comfort. But I didn't want to cause him any more suffering, either. I didn't want to offer him love only to take it away again. More than anything else, I wished he hadn't awarded me the prize. As passionately as I'd wanted it, as fervently as I'd known it was mine by right, I would have given anything now for him to be returning with his victory unmarred. That way, when I left, I would leave him with a triumphant memory, instead of this terrible, tarnished disaster. 'You heard what Hippomenes said.' My words felt inadequate, a scrap of driftwood in a raging storm. 'He and the others will tell what happened, how you had no choice.'

'I know that's true,' he said. 'But my father—'

'You're the saviour of Calydon,' I insisted. 'You slew the boar; no one else in that grove could do it.'

'I saved them from the boar and I killed the queen's brothers,' he said. 'My own blood.'

'Everyone who came on the hunt knew it could cost them their lives.'

'From the boar, yes; even from a badly thrown spear. Not like this.'

'Your mother loves you,' I said. 'She will prize the life of her son more greatly than those of her brothers. She'll understand you had to do it.' I remembered the cold sweep of her gaze, the chill I'd felt under her stare, and I shuddered, doubting my own words even as I spoke them. 'Come on.' I took his arm. 'Come back to the town, kneel at your father's feet and explain what happened. You will be forgiven.'

And I led him out, across the ravaged fields, towards the burning torches of the town.

*　　*　　*

Outside the royal house, there was chaos. The bodies of Plexippus and Toxeus were laid in front of the colonnaded entrance, wrapped in cloaks. A crowd had gathered, and in the centre, Meleager's father clutched at his head and his mother knelt by her dead brothers, her body gripped by violent tremors as she sobbed.

With every step we took, I felt the urge to flee. Meleager held his head high as we approached, though his face was a blank mask that made him seem like a stranger.

The crowd fell quiet when they saw us, an eerie silence descending, broken only by the queen's weeping.

'Meleager.' The king's face had caved in upon itself.

The queen jerked her head up. When she'd greeted us before the hunt, her imperial dignity and beauty had elevated her, made her superior and imposing. Now, I stepped back in shock to see her: the ragged scratches bleeding across her cheeks, where she'd dragged her fingernails through her smooth skin, gouging and tearing. Her eyes flashed with a furious passion that made her look like a cornered animal. 'Is it true?' she hissed. 'You killed them?'

Meleager was staring at his mother. I was used to seeing his face split by his wide smile, so young and handsome and kind – now it was stark, horrified, pale with grief and fear. My heart clenched for him. I longed to defend him from their condemnation, but I was sure that if I spoke, it would only make things worse. 'They tried to steal the prize from Atalanta,' he began, and I flinched at the quiver in his voice.

'So it was for her.' The queen spat out the words as though they might choke her.

'I—' Meleager began, but she leapt to her feet. There was a fervent madness seething within her, something primal and raw that rooted my feet to the ground, and Meleager too, it seemed, for he froze, speechless.

'You murdered my brothers. Stole my father's sons from him, blighting his old age. Robbed Calydon of its finest men. You aren't my son, you can't be.' For a moment, a terrible vulnerability shattered her façade, and then she hardened again, ice and stone once more. 'I should have let the fire burn that log to ashes when you were a baby. I should never have tried to cheat the Fates. I should have let you die.'

Her dress flared out behind her as she swung around and fled between the columns. I feared to look at Meleager's face.

The king bowed his head. 'You cannot return here.'

There was a gasp from somewhere in the melee around him; someone was fighting their way to the front. It was a woman, rich and lovely, her fine dress threaded with gold falling to her ankles, a necklace shining at her throat, her face streaked with tears and her eyes frantic. 'No,' she begged. 'Please have pity for us, for your son, for me.' Her eyes darted from the king to Meleager, back and forth.

I felt a sickening lurch as I realised who she must be. When we had first arrived in Calydon, I'd readied myself for her, but she hadn't been there to greet us. She must have been waiting instead for her husband's victorious return from the boar hunt, never anticipating it would end like this.

She ran to Meleager, throwing her arms around his neck, weeping into his shoulder. I watched him wrap his arms around her, how he stared over her head at his father. 'I killed the boar,' he said. 'Let me explain what happened after; let me tell my mother how her brothers were the first to turn on us – if I can make her understand, if I can seek forgiveness from the gods—'

Tears were falling down Oeneus' cheeks now. 'If the gods will pardon you—' he began and for a moment, I felt hopeful.

But Meleager staggered backwards, his face contorted all at once in agony. His body doubled over and he fell to his knees. I heard his wife screaming, shrieking to know what was happening. He was writhing on the ground, and she threw herself down, trying to hold him still, but he jerked back and forth, a stream of words flooding from his mouth. *Burning*, I heard, *I'm burning*, and I could see it, how he desperately fought to escape the flames that weren't there, how he was consumed from the inside out, rolling over on the ground, trying to extinguish the inferno that no one could see, until at last he was motionless, limp and silent, his eyes rolled backwards into his head.

His wife seized his shoulders, pleading with him to wake, but it was no use.

The queen had had her vengeance.

Meleager was dead.

22

I ran. In the forest, the cold silver light was swallowed up by the shadows that stalked me as I hurtled over the tangled roots, branches whipping at my face. My breath came in desperate gasps, not enough air to fill my lungs, not enough distance behind me to cleanse the images from my head.

They flashed before me, over and over. His wife, prostrate over his body, how they'd come with gentle hands to move her and she'd fought them off. His father, sinking down, unable to withstand another blow, his courtiers rushing to catch him. The other Argonauts, their faces bleak.

And Meleager, thrashing in agony in his final moments. Meleager, grey and unmoving. Meleager, disappeared from his own body, just an empty shell lying in the dirt.

Meleager, flushed with victory, his foot on the boar's head. Singing on board the *Argo*. Lighting a fire in the darkness of another night, far away from here, drawing me into his arms underneath the stars. The weight of his body, the softness of his hair tangled in my fingers, his broad, joyful smile. I couldn't stop seeing him, tears blinding me. I thought if I ran fast enough, I could escape it.

Even I could not run forever. At last, I was forced to acknowledge the ache in my legs, the burn in my chest; at last, I had to slow down, to steady my pace and to finally look around to see where I was.

I didn't know. I'd run blindly, recklessly away, only thinking how I wanted to be gone from that terrible scene. Now I had no idea where I was, and there was no navigator, no Tiphys at the helm, no one to study the sky and plot my course. I drew to a halt, turning in a circle where I stood, looking up through the branches at the stars.

Where was I supposed to go? The Fleece was won, whatever victory I could call it. The monstrous boar no longer ravaged Calydon; it had cost Meleager his life and brought me nothing. The glory I had sought in the company of brave men had been no more than a glittering mirage, something that collapsed down to nothing whenever I drew close.

I was alone in the forest, as I had always been.

I took a long, shuddering breath and closed my eyes. The image of the bleeding boar rose up, the sound of Meleager's screams ringing through my mind, but I pushed them away. I let the soft sounds of the forest filter in: the rustle of leaves and the quiet rush of air as an owl swooped from a high branch; the faraway trickling of a stream over rocks; a scuffle as something pounced and its victim darted away. I opened my eyes again and looked at where the moonlight fell, discerning what tracks I could make out, which way I could follow that might lead me to water, to the safety and survival I had always secured for myself. I let my instincts blot out the horror and the shock, and I walked on.

* * *

There was no purpose to the following days. I walked. I found what sustenance I needed. I thought only about putting one foot in front of the other, continuing. I recognised the signs of other hunters, and I followed them all the way to a village. It wasn't Calydon; that was all I cared about. I presented myself at the first house I saw, the custom of hospitality demanding that I was offered food and a bed before anyone could ask me questions, before they could give voice to the curiosity I sparked. Why I'd sought out the company of other people wasn't something I even considered until I heard myself asking them in which direction lay the Arcadian forest.

I felt a bone-deep weariness I'd never known before. The boundless energy that had always driven me on had deserted me, and left in its place a sick, heavy fatigue. I couldn't seek out adventure, couldn't strike out on my own or search for another band of travelling companions. An unfamiliar sadness within me, a well of grief, sent tears rolling down my face as I trudged on, day after day.

And I didn't think it was just grief for Meleager. As painful as it was to think of the manner of his death, I had already said goodbye to him; I had sent him back to his wife, and it hadn't broken my heart to do it. I wished that he was alive still. I wished I had never gone to Calydon. But I never wished he was with me.

I didn't know how to make any of it better: the sadness, the exhaustion, the fog that had settled in my brain. So I followed the directions I was given by my hosts and I followed the impulse that propelled me onwards, even though I had no idea what I would do when I got home.

As I walked on in solitude, I bargained with myself in my head. Artemis might be merciful, I told myself; she might overlook the vow I had broken in favour of what glory I did bring back for her. If her pride in my exploits outweighed her anger at my disobedience, I could return. Then, surely, I would shake off this malaise and begin again, find another quest: a better one this time, one more worthy of me.

Although this plan took shape in my mind, it didn't energise me as I'd hoped. Aches besieged me, my body felt like it wasn't my own anymore. When I woke, I found it hard to peel my eyes open, to tug myself out of the thick, dreamless sleep that submerged me nightly but never refreshed me. I forced myself to eat, but everything that crossed my lips made my insides revolt.

I ignored it, as though my strength of will would be enough to command my body to behave, to act as it had always done. But time was passing. The green shoots in the earth had long since flowered into a profusion of colour. The days lengthened, the sun blazed down on me as I hauled myself on and on, and at last I could not ignore it any longer.

The leaves were on the cusp of turning when I stood on the high ridge, looking down at the canopy that was still mostly green, but interspersed with gold, crimson and orange. I stared down for a long time. Deep in its heart, my cave lay waiting for me. I could smell the velvety moss on the stony sides, hear the deep croaking of the frogs in the still pool. It was so vividly alive to me.

I rested a hand on my stomach as I looked. Further still, hidden to all but the most determined, were Artemis' sacred groves. Her hounds would lie panting in the shade at the base of the wide, towering trees, exhausted from the hunt. The nymphs would be perched on the rocks, laughing and singing as Artemis shrugged off her tunic and slid into the cool, clear water. The flat, muscled planes of her body: her long thighs, her smooth belly, her small breasts. My body had mirrored hers, but no longer.

On my long journey back, the exhaustion and the unrelenting rumble of nausea had lessened in time, only to give way to something much worse. As some vestiges of my energy came back and the sore tenderness in my breasts dissipated, the suspicion that something was still very much wrong only intensified.

I thought of Althaea while I stood there, seizing the charred wood she'd guarded all those years, hurling it into the flames and watching it spark and crumble into ash. I thought of Artemis, letting me be raised in her forest, satisfaction writ across her face when she told me of Arethusa's spring, when she transformed Callisto, when she demanded my promise and sent me away. I thought of the bear who had taken me from the mountainside, how when she wanted rid of the cubs she'd nurtured, she turned on them, chasing them away so that she could be free. I thought of the queen who had given birth to me, but hadn't fought to keep me. Those were the mothers I knew.

I felt the movement beneath my palm, the surge from inside answering the touch of my hand.

I had been the fastest, the strongest, the best of them all. It was why Artemis had chosen me as her champion. I'd sailed across the world, fought monsters, faced death. I did everything the men alongside me could do and more.

But it was this, this neat round swelling cupped beneath my hand, that would be my undoing.

* * *

She emerged from the forest, as swift and unpredictable as always. I couldn't believe I'd ever thought she moved like a mortal. I'd spent time now among humans, the finest heroes the world had to offer, and none could match her agile stride and effortless power. Everything about her gleamed silver and strange.

She took me in, the sweep of her measured stare like cold fire over my body. She paused on the unfamiliar curve of my midsection, but her eyes betrayed nothing. If she had known already, if she'd seen me coming, I'd never know unless she chose to tell me.

I wouldn't cower. I held my chin high, not letting my gaze falter. 'We won the Fleece.' My voice was steady.

'And Hera's favourite has fled to Corinth with his witch-bride, stained with the blood of his kin,' she said. How had I forgotten the music of her voice? The whisper of rustling leaves, the mellifluous flow of water over rock, every wild echo of the forest overlapping in her tones. 'Zeus' proud hero dropped away from the quest and labours for an inferior king once more.' She met my eyes. I felt it like the first chill of a cold breeze fluttering before a storm. 'The son of Ares died by his mother's hand.'

'And I've come back to you.'

'The promise you made?'

'I never married.'

For a split second, I thought I saw a flicker of surprise at my daring. Had she expected me to fall at her feet and weep? Did she think I would beg for her forgiveness? Surely she hadn't forgotten so much about me as to think I would.

'Did you forget to heed my warnings?' she said. I could hear in her voice a threat of distant thunder. 'When I told you how women suffer, when I ordered you to stay away from men?'

'You sent me on a ship with fifty men.' The heat was rising in my chest too. 'I spent months among them, sharing food and drink with them, facing storms and battles together. I fought for your Fleece and we brought it home. I would have died to get it, so that you could have your glory.'

There was a sizzle in her eyes, a surge of contempt. 'When I heard the *Argo* had returned victorious, I awaited your return to the forest at once,' she said. 'That you flouted me to go after the boar I had sent to Calydon, that was my first inkling of your disobedience. I watched the hunt. I saw what happened.'

I felt the sear of her disappointment, the only moment when I thought I might break apart. 'Why didn't you come to me then?' I whispered. I pictured her cold stare, watching me flee Calydon. How broken and alone I had been. And she was there, all along.

'I let you make your own way back,' she answered. There was no mercy in her; I'd learned that long ago. 'To see that you would return to me. Perhaps I would have shown myself to you on your journey – except that I saw before you did the unmistakeable signs of what else it was you had done.' She dropped her gaze to my swollen middle, her meaning clear. I braced myself for what was coming, for whatever she was to inflict on me.

'The nymphs can never know what you have done,' she said, and I didn't close my eyes or plead or tremble. The mountains behind her were silent, the night dark and uncaring. There was no circle of anguished women around us to watch how she punished me.

I breathed in the familiar green scent of the air I loved. I was thankful she had not sprung upon me as I made my way home, that at least I had made it back here once again.

'Stay hidden, Atalanta,' she said.

I stared, uncomprehending.

'Let everyone think you perished after the boar hunt.' Her face was tight with determination. 'You cannot bring a baby into the forest, I cannot allow it. My nymphs must keep their vow. They cannot see you go unpunished for breaking it.' She turned her face, as though listening for something in the forest, and my heart jumped at the reprieve I'd never expected and the fierce beauty of her profile in the moonlight. 'But you won the Fleece, and for that, I'll let you go free.'

The earth felt unsteady beneath my feet as she glanced back at me one more time.

'You can live as you are, Atalanta. But you have lost your place among my nymphs.' She paused, and everything was still as though the forest around her quieted itself to listen. Her face was devoid of any trace of pity as she uttered her final words to me.

'You can never come home again.'

After she disappeared, I stood there until the dusk gathered, watching the shadows lengthen down the sides of the mountain and the colours fade and merge into shapeless grey. As hungrily as my eyes raked the dark forests at my feet, as eagerly as I dreamed of running through those trees again, to be as fast and free and powerful as I had been when I was here last, I had come back only to see it from this distance.

If it wasn't for this, the undeniable proof of my broken promises, I could tell myself that Artemis would have welcomed me back, that I had achieved enough for her to forgive me for Meleager, or even that she might never have known about us. But I couldn't take my place among her retinue like this; I couldn't bathe in the streams alongside the others and recount my stories. I had feared the journey would change me too much to go back, that I would outgrow the home I'd always loved, that I would crave so much more. And that would have been true, if it wasn't for this. The very thing that made me want the comfort of the old and familiar, the quiet safety and simplicity of the days before, was the reason I couldn't return.

There was no place for me anymore.

PART IV

23

Artemis had banished me, and I couldn't defy her, but I couldn't undertake another long journey, either, even if I could think of somewhere to go. I wasn't sure how long I had left before the birth and I was horribly aware of my new vulnerability. I couldn't run and fight like I always had. Without realising it, I'd made my choice when I ventured back. I would have to find somewhere here, at the outskirts of the Arcadian woods, close to my home but forever barred from entering.

I might be more ungainly, less fleet-footed than I had been before, but I could still hunt in the forest fringes, staying well away from any places the nymphs could see me. I had the strength to gather and chop firewood, to fetch water and carry out whatever other tasks might be needed. I could find a place to stay, I decided, until the baby was born, and then . . . and then I wasn't sure.

I glanced up at the encircling mountains, wondering on which bare stretch of rock my parents might have left me. I tried to picture it, not through the bleary eyes of the squalling baby, but as the person who set the infant down and walked away. I wondered how long it had taken for the cries to die down.

I imagined the other Argonauts and what they were doing now. Returning to their kingdoms or finding new quests. I could picture Heracles, the Golden Apples he'd stolen from the Hesperides thrown in a sack over his shoulder. That's what heroes won: shining trophies they could hold before the world to prove their courage and endurance. I had fought at their sides; I was better than them. I'd conquered every doubt and misgiving that anyone could have held about me, but this is what I'd brought back – no golden fruits tended by immortals, no glorious prize, but an encumbrance nurtured by my own body, the body that had never let me down before. It made me seethe, and I vowed that I would not be ruined by this. I was even angry at Meleager, for dying and leaving me with this burden. Who could count the number of babies my travelling companions might have left in their wake? And not one of them would ever give it a second thought. So why should I?

The fury kept me going. I found a village, and there I found a ramshackle home where an ageing huntsman lived with his wife. I made them a bargain. I demonstrated my skills, offered to take on the more strenuous of the household tasks that they were becoming too frail to manage, and in exchange they gave me a bed in their cottage and a share in their meals. They were grateful, having had no children of their own to care for them in their later years, so grateful that they were easily discouraged from asking questions about my swollen form.

For the infant's sake, and indeed for Meleager's too, I had found it a home. I wouldn't leave his child on the hillside.

I found it strange at first, to sleep under a roof every night, even one as worn and tired as this. I missed the spread of the

sky above me. Sometimes, as I lay awake, I yearned so power-
fully for freedom, for the dark silhouette of the *Argo* blotting
out the stars behind it, the promise of another journey and
another land with every sunrise, that the resentment churned
my stomach, its bile scalding my throat.

The day that he was born, I felt an unfamiliar terror, a
deep and primal horror opening up inside me as I looked out
towards the trees beyond our shack. Artemis came to help
women in childbirth; I feared to see her shape materialise,
to see her running gracefully from the cover of the woods to
come to the aid of a desperate mother, only to see my face.
But the trees remained still and silent, only the gentle breath
of the wind ruffling their leaves. I gritted my teeth through
the surging pains, the floor rough against my knees as I kept
my eyes fixed on the dark, distant forest interior where the
branches twined together, wishing I could feel that cool, damp
air on my face, the moss-tinged green freshness.

She never came. I told myself she had no need to, that I
didn't struggle in labour. That I could do it without her guidance or her help, even if she had been willing to offer it. He
was born and I watched the huntsman's wife lift him in her
arms, her face shining with delight. She pressed his warm,
round cheek against her rough, wrinkled one. I saw that his
eyes were like Meleager's and, too exhausted to cry, I turned
away from them both and slept.

I named him for the mountain I didn't leave him on, Parthenopaios, and I left his mothering to the old woman. He slept in
a hut, not a bare hillside. He knew human parents, not the wild
beasts of the forest. I looked at his chubby fists waving from

his crib and I wondered if one day the black-eyed war-god would guide his grandson into battle, if he would live up to the formidable destiny that should be his: my warrior blood and Meleager's mingling in his veins.

Far beyond where the village stood, I could see the slopes where Artemis dwelt, but, mindful of her edict, I always stayed on the outskirts. As Parthenopaios grew stronger, able to go longer without my milk, I roamed further away. Over the months that passed, I found the freshest spring where the coldest, clearest water flowed. I hunted, the huntsman's dog at my heels. She loved to run with me, going further than he had ever let her, across the furthest ridges we could see, but always on the fringes, never into the wild heart. The greater the distance between me and the dim interior of the hut, filled with Parthenopaios' shrill cries, the more I felt my old self return. Running with Aura, the rhythmic thump of her paws against the earth behind me, the shaggy ruff of fur at her neck rippling in the wind, the eager nudge of her head into my palm when we stopped for breath, it could feel so much like the days before the *Argo* that sometimes I would be confused for a moment. I'd turn, looking for the way back to my cave, listening for the soft laughter of a nymph, and I'd have to shake myself back to the present.

When the light drained from the sky, we'd return to the village, bringing back whatever we'd gathered – a bloody bundle of prey, a brimming cask of water, a bag of ripe fruit. I'd watch Parthenopaios cramming handfuls of berries into his mouth, the sweet red juices smeared across his face as he perched contentedly on the old woman's lap, tilting his head back to look up at her, winding a lock of her grey hair through his sticky fingers. I let myself imagine that Meleager could see his son, how proud he might be of the little boy we'd made together, and I was glad, glad that he thrived here. I was even more grateful, though, for every dawn that heralded my freedom from him again.

My strength had returned and my energy too, and I could feel the faint stirrings of hope. Artemis had not come to punish me further. Perhaps her ongoing silence was her punishment. As cruel as it felt, I still had my human shape; I still had my life. That was something.

I saw the tracks of the other hunter immediately. Aura and I usually had the mountainside to ourselves. I'd chosen the least hospitable slopes, those with the most perilous faces, the most dense and prickly shrubs, where shade was hardest to find. Where we wouldn't be disturbed by anyone else.

Whoever it was hadn't left many traces, but enough for me to recognise at once. I slowed my pace, coming to a halt and turning slowly, checking every direction for where he might be. Aura sat poised on her haunches, nose to the air. She whined a little at something, some remnant of a scent maybe. I held out my hand to her, a silent command to stay still. Then I nodded and she slunk forwards, both of us treading as silently as we could.

I was curious to know who had made it up here, who else would venture so far when the lower reaches of the forest were home to a wealth of scampering animals, ripe fruits and cool water. Up here, you were more likely to encounter a prowling lion than a deer. I wasn't afraid – whoever it was, it didn't matter. But I could feel something poised in the air, a moment suspended, the last breath before everything would be different. I'd felt this before, before I joined the Argonauts. It gave me misgivings. I didn't trust in the future the same way I had back then.

I drew it in, a deep inhalation, steadying myself as I came to a rocky outcrop just below the highest peak. This wasn't somewhere you would stumble upon by mistake. Whoever it was must know me, might even have been tracking me, and there was virtually no one alive and mortal I could think of who could do such a thing.

I breathed out, braced my shoulders and stepped around the jutting rocks.

My eyes widened in surprise.

'It's you,' I said.

24

He held himself tentatively, a wariness in his posture as though I was something unpredictable. I stared at him, outlined against the sky, his shock of dark hair, his rich brown eyes staring back at me. Memories of the last time I'd seen him flashed in my mind: the iron scent of the boar's blood hanging heavy in the clearing, exultation turning so swiftly to horror. Meleager, writhing on the ground, burning to death from the inside while we watched, powerless.

'Atalanta, I didn't know if you'd remember—'

'Hippomenes,' I interrupted him. The set of his shoulders was broader now, bulkier with muscle, and the clean lines of his jaw were shadowed with a dark beard. 'Have you followed me?'

He dropped his eyes. 'After the boar, I came back here. I have friends not far away. I heard rumours, stories about a woman in the woods, one too fast for anyone to catch more than a glimpse of. I knew it must be you.'

'Did you stay long?' I stumbled over the words. 'In Calydon, I mean. After . . .'

He shook his head. 'There was talk that Meleager was gathering another group of fighters, that there was going to be another quest, even greater than the Argonauts. That's why I went there in the first place. After Meleager died, the queen killed herself. The town was in mourning; the men who'd joined the hunt disbanded. No one wanted to stay.'

I swallowed. It was hard to remember Meleager's hopefulness before the hunt, and how it had all fallen apart so quickly. 'Why come up here?' I asked him. 'Why would you search me out?' I was impressed that he'd managed it.

'The heroes of the *Argo* have gone their separate ways, back to their homes,' he said. 'They throw feasts in their fine houses, where the poets sing about how they won the Fleece. The stories spread faster than plague or wildfire; we hear them everywhere we go.'

'So?'

'I got tired of hearing the same tales over and over. I don't want to sit in a hall listening to wine-soaked reminiscing of how brave they all were. I remember how it was in the boar hunt, the way they ran when you fought. That's why I came to find you.'

I felt like his words were pressing on a bruise. Instinctively, I wanted to be away from him, from the pain his presence caused and the feelings he evoked.

'Why would you think I'd want to see you?'

It worked. My hard tone deflated his enthusiasm – just a little, but enough for me to take a certain satisfaction in it. 'When I heard that you were here, back in Arcadia again, I thought you might be preparing for something else, that maybe Artemis would send you somewhere again – and if you needed a crew ...'

It angered me, to hear him describing something I'd dreamed about all those nights in that stifling hut, listening to the sound of a baby crying, something private and secret that I'd never speak aloud to anyone. I shook my head. 'There's nothing. No new quest, nothing to seek. I'm a huntress, just as I was before, and I don't need anyone to help me with that. Certainly not you.'

He was silent. I let my words sink in, and then I turned to Aura, who had sat patiently at my side through the whole conversation. 'Come,' I said to her, and she jumped up, eager to run again.

'They don't mention you.' His voice reached me when I'd already turned away, about to disappear back into the trees where he'd stand no chance of finding me again. I paused. I was desperate to get away, but this piqued my curiosity, despite myself.

'In their songs. They don't say that a woman went with them, most of the time. They leave out your name when they reel off their list of heroes – and that's now, when the *Argo*'s voyage is still fresh in people's memories. What will they say in years to come? Will anyone remember you were there at all?'

I stiffened. 'How dare they leave me out?'

'None of them wants to remember. None of them wants it immortalised in their halls that Atalanta was one of their number. That a woman was as good as them, certainly not that you were better. They say that you asked to go but were refused, that Jason wouldn't allow it, so you gave him a cloak to take with him instead, that only an emblem of you went with them.'

I tried to wipe my face clear of anger before I turned back to face him. I held my voice as cool and steady as I could. 'You know they're lying. Others will, too.'

'People remember what they want. They'll lap up the tales of the *Argo* and be all too happy to forget you were ever there. If you're living in obscurity, hunting in this forest, all that will be left will be rumours. No one will know who you were or what you did.'

I could feel my fists curling, the overwhelming temptation to stop his words with them, to pummel him to the ground. 'Leave this mountain,' I told him. 'Don't try to find me again.'

He opened his mouth to protest, but the flash of my eyes silenced him.

'Don't come back,' I warned him, and I ran.

Even Aura struggled to keep up as I fled across the uneven slopes. The thought of my former comrades lounging in their great halls, letting the praise roll over them – praise for my deeds, which they took as their due – made fury drum inside me until I thought my chest would burst. They were grateful for my skills when I was firing arrows at our enemies, but now they would pretend I'd never been there at all, that they'd survived on their own wits, as if they had enough. Without me, they might never have left Lemnos, never reached Colchis and the Fleece at all. I ground my teeth together. This ugly inferno of emotion was something I didn't want Hippomenes to see, didn't want to show to anyone. Because the heroes of the *Argo* could say whatever they wanted, and there was nothing I could do. Artemis had abandoned me, as surely as my father had when he gave the order for my infant body to be tossed out on the hillside. There would be no other quests, not from her.

I stopped, my breath coming hard and fast. Anger still

surged through my body, but I heard Hippomenes' words again in my head, and now that the shock of indignation had passed, I heard them settle differently in my mind.

Instead of heralding my triumphant return, instead of setting me a new task, Artemis had left me to flounder in ignominy, to be forgotten, as the Argonauts were so clearly happy to allow. She wasn't my mistress any longer; she wasn't determining what I would do next.

I wasn't bound by any promises I'd made to her or anyone else. Seeing Hippomenes again had reminded me of what I'd lost, but it also made me think about what I'd gained in return. I'd made a life for myself and my son, and from now on, it would be up to me to decide my own fate.

I'd told Hippomenes not to come back, but I looked for him over the next few days all the same. I wandered further, staying away from the cottage for longer, sometimes spending nights in caves or under the shelter of trees. Sometimes I woke in the darkness, thinking I was back on a faraway shore, expecting to hear Meleager breathing beside me. I found myself wondering how the tales of the Argonauts were being told, which episodes were embroidered and which I would recognise as truth. Since the horror of the Calydonian boar hunt, I'd pushed so many of those memories aside. I hadn't wanted to dwell on any of it. I hated that I couldn't think of our adventures without seeing Meleager, fresh and vital in my mind's eye, how the image gave way every time to the desolation of his death. Even the happy recollections I might have had of our voyage had been clouded for so long with my guilt at the way everything had ended. The pain I'd caused him before the hunt. How it had been my presence there that had sparked his uncles' rage and triggered the bloodshed. My anger that he'd been so foolish to proclaim me the victor in front of them all.

But now, stepping out into the fresh dawn after rainfall, the world made clean and new once more, I tried to let myself remember without pain. I saw myself the way Hippomenes had described me. He'd searched for me as a heroine of the *Argo*, someone with cause to feel pride, not shame. Instead of the inhospitable mountainsides, I took Aura in a long, meandering loop through woods and meadows. At one long, flower-strewn stretch, I stopped and shrugged the bow off my back. Aura paced around in a circle, then flopped down on to the grass, head on her paws, her dark liquid eyes watching me as I fitted my first arrow. Narrowing my eyes, I aimed at a distant tree and loosed it. Quivering, it stuck in the very centre of the trunk, and I felt a little unfurling of exultation deep in my belly. It had been a while since I had done target practice just for the joy of it.

I lost myself in the rhythm of the familiar motion. Behind me, Aura yawned, baring her teeth and pink gums. Her eyelids drooped, the haze of gentle sunlight and the contented buzzing of insects among the blooms soothing her to sleep.

I jogged over to the tree trunk to gather up the arrows. Ingrained in me was the instinct to leave behind no trace of myself, to ensure no one knew that I'd been here. I yanked hard on one arrow that was deeply embedded into the wood, and the slender shaft snapped in my fist, splintering my palm. I cursed under my breath, blood seeping from the broken skin.

Somewhere through the trees, I could hear the faint trickling of water over rocks. I followed the sound of it, eager to bathe the wound.

He was at the bank of the pool when I found it, his knees drawn up and his elbows resting loosely on top of them, watching the ripples on the surface, seemingly lost in his thoughts.

I cleared my throat, feeling almost awkward, and he looked up at me, surprised. 'Don't worry,' I said. 'I'm not here to chase you away.'

He raised an eyebrow. 'I haven't followed you. I didn't know you were here.'

'I know.' I knelt down and dipped my hand into the water. The cold stung the raw flesh of my wound then gave way to a numb throbbing. Pink tendrils of blood spiralled into the stream and vanished.

'What happened?' he asked.

'Splinters – a broken arrow. What are you still doing here? Is your home nearby?'

'Not far,' he answered. 'But I've been travelling for a while now, and I thought I'd stay a little longer before I move on.'

I wondered why he didn't want to go home. 'Do you miss it? The place where you're from?'

'Sometimes, a little. Not enough to return. Do you want something to bind your hand?'

I lifted it up, shook off the water and saw the blood start to swell up in little round beads again. 'Yes, thank you. Why don't you want to return?'

He handed me a square of fabric tucked into his belt. I took it, noticing its smoothness, the heavy fall of its drape, how it slipped between my fingers. It was finer cloth than I was used to. I bound it around my hand, little crimson spots seeping through from my palm.

'Why not return? I don't want to go back and settle there,' he said. 'Before I know it, twenty years will have passed, and I'll have seen barely anything beyond our city walls.'

'So you're still searching out a quest? A journey?'

'Have you changed your mind?'

'Hardly.'

'So you've come back home to stay?'

'This isn't my home.' A vision of my cave swam up before my eyes. I rocked back, crouching at the water's edge, halfway between pushing myself up to standing and leaning back to sit on the ground. Somehow, I found myself wanting to carry on talking to him.

'Don't you want to go somewhere again?' he asked. 'Set sail and find something new?' The words spilled out in a rush, and he looked as though he regretted them. Perhaps he thought I might storm away like I had done before.

I sat back, settling myself on the soft earth. 'Not like the Argonauts,' I said. 'Not that again.'

He looked interested. 'Really?'

I wrinkled my nose. 'It wasn't as heroic a quest as you might think. Medea won the Fleece with her magic. We were just there to watch. It was artifice, whatever they're singing about it now.'

I saw the disappointment on his face. 'But surely, just to get to Colchis must have been a feat?'

I nodded. 'I suppose so. That's true.' I tangled my fingers in the reeds growing beside me, twisting them out of the ground. 'I thought it was the start of something, that on my return there would be another quest, a better one. But the boar hunt happened and then . . . Then I came back here.' I tried not to let my face betray me, not to give any hint of what had happened next. 'Maybe you shouldn't be so eager to go. You might find it isn't what you expect.'

'The centaurs would have killed me if it wasn't for you,' he said, a sudden intensity in his tone. 'It's why I didn't believe any of the stories about the *Argo* that denied you. I was saved by Atalanta before any of them.'

I laughed. 'You tried to save me first, I recall.'

I saw a hint of colour rising on his cheeks. 'It didn't prove necessary.'

'Centaurs are strong, and those two were crazed with drink. You were mad to try – brave, but mad.'

'Well, I didn't want to find myself in such a situation again. I went away, learned better fighting skills and got stronger.'

'And now you want your chance to prove yourself?'

'Is that any different to what the Argonauts were doing?'

'No, I suppose not. But that's exactly what I mean: I thought I would prove my strength by going, and it ended in trickery and disgrace. Jason was exiled. Meleager died. And I'm not even in the songs. It makes me wonder what the point of it was.' I paused. 'I'd never join someone else's expedition again.'

Before he could say anything else, Aura came padding into the clearing. She looked between me and Hippomenes, her lip curling back as she stared him down.

'Don't worry, Aura.' I patted her on the head and turned back to Hippomenes. 'It'll be dark before long.'

I saw him look up doubtfully at the clear blue overhead. But I still had to collect water and firewood to take back to the huntsman's cottage.

'If you're going to be here longer, I'll see you again. I'm out here every day, somewhere in the vicinity at least.'

'I'd like to.' He sounded eager. I hoped he wouldn't try to persuade me again to run off on some dreamed-up quest. But I hadn't minded having someone to talk to.

I left him there, taking a long detour back to the village to gather what I needed. The shadows were drawing in by the time I reached the familiar tumbledown shape of the hut.

The huntsman's wife was watching for my return, Parthenopaios fretful in her arms. His cheeks were blazing red, his small brows drawn together. 'He has teeth coming through,' she explained. She looked weary, her hair coming loose from its twist at the top of her head.

I set down the logs I was carrying in one hand and held out the cask of water I'd brought back with the other. 'Do you want me to hold him for a moment?'

She nodded gratefully, taking the water, and I accepted the weight of my son in exchange. He was so much heavier now than he had been the last time I'd held him, something I rarely did since he was able to stand and totter about himself. His big eyes were wary; he turned his head to track her, not totally resistant but not comfortable in my arms.

I worried he was about to wail in protest, so I walked him back to the path I had just come from, keeping up a stream of nonsensical chatter to divert him from his grievance, pacing this way and that. The sun was dipping behind the mountains in a blaze of crimson; I pointed it out to him and he turned his face to look at it, the fiery glow illuminating his stern expression.

And then I heard it: the flight of footsteps coming down from between the trees, the shape detaching itself from the darkness and his voice ringing out in surprise. 'Atalanta?'

I closed my eyes for a moment, fervently wishing him

gone. Then I turned, the child in my arms now clearly visible to him, and I saw the shock in his eyes, his mouth gaping around the words that had deserted him as he stared at Parthenopaios.

25

It was the huntsman's wife who broke the silence between us. Her kindly and hospitable nature rescued me from any immediate questions or explanations; she saw Hippomenes and at once invited him to sit beside the fire and share in our repast. Host and guest alike were gracious, their polite conversation filling up the small space while I said nothing. I saw Hippomenes' gaze return to Parthenopaios over and over, lingering on my son's dark eyes and serious expression, so unlike his father's easy smile.

Hippomenes was gentle, not demanding of the child's attention or loud in a way that would disconcert him. I watched, a shadow on the edges of their chatter, until I saw the boy smile at him. The smoke from the fire felt stifling, the walls too close around me, and I jumped up, striding out into the welcome cool of the evening.

He wasn't far behind me. I wheeled around to face him. 'Did you follow me here? After I left you in the woods, did you track me?'

He held up his hands. 'No, I didn't.' He looked a little taken aback by the savage edge to my tone, but I could detect a slight defensiveness there too. He'd come looking for me, I was sure of it, and I was angry that he'd discovered precisely what I wanted to hide. I'd liked talking to him before; it reminded me of the carefree early days of the voyage, or even of a time before, when I'd had nothing more urgent to do than sit in a grove with Callisto or one of the other nymphs, even Artemis herself. A time with no complications, no responsibilities. Now he'd crossed over, into the other part of my life, and there would be no going back from it.

I scoffed. 'So you just stumbled across me by accident?'

'Not by accident, no. I was looking for you.' He ran his hand through his hair, pushing it back from his face in frustration. 'I didn't know about any of this; I just heard you lived in one of the villages down here and I needed to find you again.'

'Well, you did.' This was the consequence of the compromise I'd made, giving my son to villagers to be raised. When I'd lived out in the wild, I'd been nothing more than a myth to passing hunters. But however quickly I might flit through the woods here, I returned to the same place. I was weighed down by it, anchored to the mortal world, trying to repay my debt to the couple who had taken him in.

'I didn't mean to intrude into your life,' he said. 'I've just had news, something I thought you'd want to hear.'

'If it's news of some quest or some other gathering together of heroes or the like, I think you know now why I can't go.'

He nodded slowly, though he still looked confused. 'Why didn't you say anything about Parthenopaios before?'

I sighed. The scent from the jasmine that the old woman tended so carefully spilled out on the breeze, the delicate star-shaped flowers opening to the darkness. The soft peace of the night, the ancient wild I'd once felt so much a part of, was completely at odds with the jangling discord I felt now. 'Let's walk,' I said, preferring to get away from the hut, from the smoking chimney and the cultivated flowers, out beyond the bounds of the village.

He walked at my side, not pushing for my answer. It was easier to talk this way, not looking directly at him.

'He is Meleager's son,' I said. 'After I left Calydon, I came back here. I'd thought perhaps I could come back to Artemis, but when I realised I was with child, I knew that I couldn't. I forfeited her protection and her patronage.' I took a long breath. 'My father left me to die not far from here when I was born.'

'I know that,' he said.

I glanced at him, surprised. 'I didn't want to do the same as my father had done. I found Parthenopaios a home and willing parents. I help them in exchange, until he's older and I can leave again. But that's why I can't set out on some new venture – Artemis has no more plans for me. I'm not her champion anymore.'

'What if you could do it in your own name, rather than hers?'

Irritation bubbled up in me again. 'You've seen the shack where my son grows up. You know the palaces and the wealthy houses the other Argonauts hail from. Ships are expensive. Without Artemis to guide me, I can't go on my own, and I won't join another band of men.'

'You could have taken him back to Calydon,' Hippomenes said. 'Given the king his grandson to raise. Oeneus has gold and treasure.'

'The Queen of Calydon killed her own son.' I shook my

head. 'I couldn't leave Parthenopaios there any more than I could leave him on a hillside. Besides, you said yourself that the town was in chaos when you left.' The thought of Meleager's wife rose up as well, what vengeance she might harbour in her heart if she knew. 'It was safer for him to grow up here.'

Hippomenes nodded slowly. 'The reason I came to find you ... I heard news. I'm not the only person looking for you now.'

I stiffened. 'Who else?'

'I went back to my friends after I saw you today. They told me that news was spreading of a message from King Iasus. Your father. He's put out word that he wants to find you.'

I spluttered. 'My father? Doesn't he think I'm dead?'

'He must have heard differently. Even if the Argonauts are all telling their own versions of the voyage, there are people who saw you sail from Iolcus, who are sure they caught a glimpse of a woman with braided hair and a short tunic on board the ship. Together with the rumours there have always been about a huntress in these forests, the stories have trickled back to him. He's heard that his daughter survived, and that she accompanied Jason. Whether he believes it's really true or not, I don't know, but he's sent out heralds to spread the message that he wants you to come home.'

'Home? He cast me out to die. I had no home with him; I only had the home that Artemis gave me. Why does he think I'd go back?' I turned away from the sympathy in Hippomenes' eyes, looking out into the dark trees.

'I didn't know if you'd want to hear it, I just thought you should know. But now that I've seen you here, with the child, doesn't it give you another choice?'

'A choice to go to the man who tried to kill me? What for?'

'You said that you never want to be a part of someone else's expedition. That Artemis won't help you and that you have nothing. But you do; you're the daughter of a king, and now he wants to recognise you.'

I laughed, surprised at how bitter it sounded. I hadn't thought I cared enough to resent my father; I'd barely thought of him at all. 'He thinks I'll do instead of a son, if the rumours about me are true. He's heard he has a warrior for a daughter.'

'He wants to know if he does. He wants you to go to the palace; he's promised that he'll acknowledge you now. If you go, he'll see that you are the Atalanta some people are saying you are – equal to the heroes of the *Argo*. If not, maybe he'll think the other versions are the truth.'

'Why would I care? It doesn't matter what he thinks of me.'

'If you go back, everyone will know who you are. And you'll have the backing of a king for whatever you do next.'

'I don't want his backing. I don't want anything he has to offer me.' The thought of it revolted me. 'Thank you for telling me. I'm glad I heard it from you. I'll be careful not to be seen.'

I could feel his frustration, how carefully he was searching for more to say, but he held it in. 'I won't tell anyone that you're here.'

'And—' I hesitated.

'I'll say nothing of Parthenopaios either, of course.'

'Thank you.'

He couldn't stop himself from speaking again. 'Can I come back here – can I see you again?'

'If you make sure you aren't followed.'

'Of course.'

I was unaccountably relieved that he wasn't going away. There was more comfort than I'd realised in having someone here who linked me to my life before, even in such a small way. Someone who had known me briefly in the other lives I'd led. It was a lonely feeling, knowing that the nymphs would reject me, that I'd face the wrath of the goddess who had once taken pride in me if I tried to go back to them. But Hippomenes didn't stand in judgement over me. There was something pleasant in anticipating that I would see him again and that I wouldn't have to hide my responsibilities to my son.

That night, though, I didn't sleep. Despite myself, I let Hippomenes' words slink back into my mind. I despised my father, of course I did. The thought of presenting myself to him, of him thinking that my deeds could reflect on him, was repulsive. That he thought I would do as a substitute for the son he'd never had, that he imagined I would go back and take that place. I flung the thin woollen blankets aside, thinking I would set out into the darkness, outrun my anger until I was gasping and breathless. But somehow, my feet took me to Parthenopaios. I looked down at him, his limbs flung out like a star, the soft rise and fall of his chest and the curve of his rounded cheek.

I was better than my father, a hundred times over. I had done my duty towards my son, however much my instinct had rebelled against it. But if I tried to set aside my hatred of the father I'd never known, I wondered if Hippomenes might have been right that he had something to offer me.

I had no interest in inheriting the throne. But that didn't mean Iasus had nothing I wanted. The huntsman and his wife were old already. Their poverty was evident in the rough, torn blankets I'd cast aside, the meagreness of their shack, their thin, papery cheeks and the weariness in their eyes. Iasus' wealth could give them comfort, provide for them until Parthenopaios was older.

It would mean that I could leave, with no guilt or concern for what I left behind.

I didn't know exactly what Iasus wanted with me. But as I watched the child sleep, I started to think it could be worth finding out.

'So, why did you change your mind?' Hippomenes was full of energy, striding forwards, his eyes shining whenever I looked across at him.

'I want to know what the king is offering me,' I answered. I kept looking back, expecting to see Aura at my heels, but I'd left her at the hut. It was a wrench, kissing her goodbye and leaving her sitting so obediently where I'd told her to. I didn't know how long I would be gone, and I wanted her to stay to protect the old couple and Parthenopaios while I was away. I felt a pang every time I turned and felt her absence again.

I wondered that it felt harder to leave my dog than my son, but I reasoned that this journey was for his benefit.

'As you said, he's a rich man,' I continued. 'It never mattered to me before. I had everything I needed in the forest. But Parthenopaios can't live as I did. My son has the blood of Ares. If he has a king's wealth, too, he can do whatever he wants.' And if going back to Iasus meant that news of me would spread across the land, countering the stories the poets were telling about the *Argo*, then Artemis might hear of it, too. It could be enough to help me win back her favour.

We lapsed into silence as we walked. When I looked across at Hippomenes, his expression was thoughtful.

'How far do we have to go?' I asked eventually.

'It isn't so far in distance. It's mountainous, though; it slows us down.' He glanced at me. 'Or it slows me down, at least.'

'They didn't take me very far away then, to leave me.'

'Your father's town is in the shadow of Mount Parthenius,' Hippomenes said.

I had travelled such vast distances across the sea, but I knew so little of the land where I had grown up. 'How do you know?' I asked.

'I've spent so long travelling around this region,' he explained. 'I left my father's home and set off, explored what I could of the forest, learned to hunt and survive whatever is out there – except perhaps for centaurs.' He smiled ruefully at that. 'I wanted to learn the skills I needed.'

'Why did you need to leave to learn them?'

A shadow crossed his face. 'My brother died. It was painful for everyone, and I didn't want to stay.'

'I'm sorry.' I remembered the restlessness I'd felt after losing Callisto. I could understand why the loss had driven him to find somewhere else, where there would be no reminder of grief.

The vertiginous terrain began to level out, the downward scramble becoming gentle and easy. We reached dirt tracks, fields dotted by the woolly backs of sheep, the sight of buildings in the distance.

'It's ahead of us,' Hippomenes told me. 'We'll reach your father's palace by evening.'

My stomach clenched in anticipation. It was building the same way as when we had approached unknown shores, when we'd cast out the mooring ropes and leapt off the ship, not knowing what might greet us. I didn't know what it would be like to see the face of the man who had tried to kill me and failed, the man who saw nothing in me but disappointment, the man who had given me over to the elements and unwittingly given me a life unlike anyone else's.

It was dark when we arrived, but the palace was lit by flaming beacons all around. The shadows danced across the smooth stone walls and at the gates, where two sentries held long spears, the tips glimmering viciously. 'Who are you?' one of them demanded. His voice was low and suspicious.

Beside me, I felt Hippomenes tense.

I stepped into the light so they could see me clearly, as tall as any man but with braids wrapped around my head. I saw their eyes widen and I spoke, my voice clear and ringing. 'Tell the king that his daughter has returned.'

I saw the surprise flooding across each of their faces.

I smiled. 'He has sent out word for my return, so tell him I am here. Tell him I am Atalanta, the huntress of Arcadia and heroine of the *Argo*.'

26

King Iasus' throne room was a vast, gleaming hall. Fires burned in shallow bowls, the aroma of scented oils hung thick and sweet in the air, and the walls were a riot of colour – bright painted friezes depicting endless scenes of battles and gods, wild animals and sword-wielding heroes. The floor tiles shone, the long tables were heaped with golden platters and goblets, and my father sat upon his throne, a rich purple cloak draped across his shoulders and jewelled rings on his fingers. His chin rested on his hand as he studied my face. I couldn't tell what he was thinking.

I was standing before him, Hippomenes at my side, the words I'd just spoken seeming to hover between us. I had spoken without rancour: a calm presentation of the facts of my life and my feats. I kept any recrimination out of my voice, letting only pride infuse my speech as I held my head high and recited it all. The hall was full – richly dressed nobles seated at the tables, slaves serving them, a musician with a lute whose song was thin and quavering compared to Orpheus' glorious harmonies. All of them had fallen silent at my declaration, and all of their eyes were on me now.

At last, Iasus spoke. 'And your companion?'

Hippomenes glanced at me before he spoke. 'I am Hippomenes, son of King Megareus of Onchestus. I brought Atalanta the news of your message and I guided her here.'

I couldn't hide the shock on my face. Son of a king? He shrugged slightly, as if it was of no consequence at all.

Iasus waved a hand at the slaves at his side. 'Prepare chambers for our guests,' he said. 'They have journeyed far. Fetch water so they can bathe. First, Hippomenes and Atalanta, sit and eat with us.'

The king gave no acknowledgement that he believed what I had said; he made no speech of acceptance of my identity. His bland courtesy grated on me, the kind of hospitality he might offer to any traveller that came. Perhaps it shouldn't surprise me that he gave so little away. The kind of man who could choose the fate of his own infant so coldly was surely a calculating one, someone who would keep any emotion locked firmly away behind an impenetrable mask. I took a seat beside Hippomenes. The platters of roasted meats smelled enticing after a day of walking, the crumbling cheeses and dark ruby wine too alluring to resist.

My father wanted me back here for a reason. I'd come here to discover what I could take, how my blood could benefit me at last. But of course, he had his own intentions, and it didn't seem that he was going to reveal them until he was satisfied – that I really was his daughter, that I would prove useful to him.

Cold settled into my bones. I'd never met anyone related to me before; it had crossed my mind that maybe there would be some kind of pull, but I felt nothing.

'Where is my mother?' I asked. My tongue tripped over the word.

Iasus looked coolly across the table at me. 'The queen died, some years ago.'

I felt a dart of concern from Hippomenes, but why would I grieve a woman I'd never known?

Iasus took a long sip of his wine, setting down the goblet with careful precision. 'So, Atalanta,' he said. 'Tell me about the voyage of the *Argo*.'

It was long into the night when I finally made my way to the bedchamber that had been prepared for me. As promised, a bath had been filled with warm water and scented oils, and I pulled off my tunic and slid into it gratefully. Iasus had heard my stories; all the men around our table had craned their heads to listen. I was fairly confident that I had them all convinced.

I let the water soothe my tired muscles, steam rising in fragrant tendrils around me. Although my body was pleasantly fatigued, my mind was still racing. When the water began to cool, I climbed out and wrapped a soft blanket around myself, loosening my hair from its tight braids and letting it fall down my back. I noticed that a dress had been left for me, draped over a stool. A small lamp burned low, its light sparkling off the smooth lines of a crystal vase. I shook out the dress. It was like nothing I had held before. It reminded me of Hypsipyle; a similar deep shade of blue to the one she had worn, fastened with a shining silver clasp, falling in thick drapes all the way to the floor.

I dropped it back over the stool, and put my tunic back on. Then I went to find Hippomenes.

*　　*　　*

He was startled to see me at his door. 'What are you doing here?' He looked up and down the corridor as though worried we might be seen.

'I want to talk to you. Come on, let's walk.'

'Now?'

'Yes, now.'

He looked as though he might argue, but thought better of it. He threw a cloak around his shoulders and followed me.

We slipped out of the quiet palace, into the gardens. I knew why Hippomenes was cautious. This was his world, not mine. In the forest, I could wander wherever I liked. With the Argonauts, it was the same. Here, if Iasus were to hear that the woman purporting to be his daughter was taking late-night strolls with a man, it would be enough for him to cast me out again – if not worse. *Let him try*, I thought, *I've been cast out before*. Of course, I wanted to get what I'd come for, and for that reason I moved stealthily, flitting between the shadows as we hurried out of the torchlight into the darkness. I let the fresh night air fill my lungs. I was so glad I hadn't grown up within these walls.

'So, what do you think of Iasus?' Hippomenes asked.

Somewhere in the garden, a fountain tinkled. We stood where the shadows pooled together. I couldn't make out his expression.

'Not much,' I replied.

'He seemed to believe you when you were talking about the Argonauts.'

I nodded. 'It probably helps that I've brought a prince along with me, to vouch for me. Why didn't you tell me your father is a king?'

He sighed. 'I told you that my brother died. He was killed by a lion, one that harassed our town relentlessly. Like the boar in Calydon. He'd set out to try to kill it, but it brought him down instead. My father was devastated. He offered the throne and my sister as a prize to anyone who could kill the lion and avenge his son.'

'The throne that you should inherit?'

He was quiet for a long moment. 'I had a different mother to my brother and sister. My father raised me in his palace, but it was never the same. I went out with my brother, the day that he died. I couldn't save him. When I came back to tell them he was dead and the lion still on the loose, I knew what a failure I was in my father's eyes. I left. I wanted to get stronger, and I never could have done it if I'd stayed there, where everyone thought I should have been the one who died.'

I remembered Medea in the bridal cave telling me I was like her, that we were both children of fathers who didn't want us. I'd pulled away from her, not wanting to find any similarity between us. I found more sympathy in my heart for Hippomenes. Maybe it was his open honesty, or maybe I had softened since then. 'He should have been grateful you survived,' I said.

He laughed softly, without bitterness. 'It doesn't matter now.' Swiftly, he changed the subject. 'I think Iasus will acknowledge you tomorrow.'

I snorted. 'He might acknowledge me. I'll never acknowledge him.'

'But he'll be useful to you. And your son can live a better life.' He started to say more, then hesitated. 'Can I ask you a question about Parthenopaios?'

The breeze lifted my hair, grazing the back of my neck. 'I asked you about your past, you can ask about mine.'

'It's not so much about Parthenopaios, really,' he said. 'I

wondered, if Meleager hadn't died – what would have happened?'

I wrapped my arms around myself, glad of the dark that
shielded me from his eyes. 'I was leaving Calydon after the
boar hunt, whatever the outcome.'

'Did you love him?'

I wondered if he'd have had the boldness to ask me that
if we were inside the palace. 'I never did. All the time, on
the *Argo*, I was glad that he was married. I was glad that he
would go home to his wife at the end of it, that I knew there
was an end.' I wondered if that made me sound cold-hearted.
'I thought he felt the same, but he said he would leave her. I
told him no.'

'Why?'

'Artemis warned me before I left the forest that there was a
prophecy: if I was ever to marry, I would lose myself. I promised that I wouldn't. I never intended to, anyway; it didn't feel
like any kind of loss.'

'But Meleager—'

'I would never have married him, prophecy or not.' It had
been a reckless, joyful abandon that I'd gambled on getting
away with. 'So many of the Argonauts were married, so many
of them must have left children in their wake. I didn't behave
any worse than any of the men. Better, in fact, because I didn't
leave Parthenopaios.'

'You're better than your father, too,' he said gently.

'And you're better than yours. There are few men who can
kill a lion single-handedly. You must have been young, untried.
It wasn't your fault.'

'Thank you,' he said. He paused and then went on. 'The
lion wouldn't have given you any trouble, of course.' It was

the kind of thing Meleager might have said, only he would have been laughing. There was something sweeter about Hippomenes, an honesty that was as gentle as it was disarming.

'Of course.' Any remnants of tension between us had dissipated. I was fervently glad that he had come with me to this strange place that could have been my home. 'I think I can sleep now. Let's go back inside.'

We were as soundless on our return as we had been leaving. I bid him goodnight and crept back to my chamber. The bed was too soft, the coverlets too luxurious. Nothing felt right. I fell into a fitful sleep until dawn washed into my room.

I squinted at the painted wooden targets in the distance, then looked back to King Iasus. He was flanked by lords, a cluster of noblemen gathered to watch. He held up his hand for quiet, and his voice boomed out across the open courtyard.

'The rumours of Atalanta reached our palace some time ago. There were those who insisted that a woman had gone with the brave Argonauts, that her skill with the bow was unrivalled, even among the men. No one like her had ever been seen before. The explanation for her strength and abilities was that she had been raised far away from human eyes, under the cover of the forest, with the goddess Artemis as her teacher. When my wife gave birth to a baby girl, we left her on the slopes of the mountain that overlooks that forest. We needed a son to inherit my throne, so we left the daughter to her fate. Now, a woman stands before us claiming that she is Atalanta, that she sailed on the *Argo* and accompanied Jason on his quest for the Golden Fleece – and that she is my daughter. No son has ever been born to me, but it seems the

Fates may have sent me a daughter who is equal to any son I could have been blessed with.' He paused, letting the dramatic silence build. 'Here is your chance to prove that you are truly Atalanta and my daughter, the woman who can shoot arrows better than any other mortal, second only to Artemis herself.'

There was a rustling of anticipation among the crowd.

His speech rankled. How easily he spoke of leaving me to die. My life had been worth nothing to him until now, when he thought he could turn me into a spectacle for his audience, that I would perform for them to prove my value. I let the anger rise and cool, hardening into resolve instead. They weren't prepared for what I could do. They had no idea who I really was.

'Artemis showed me how to carve this bow myself,' I answered, slipping it off my shoulders and holding it aloft for all of them to see. 'She taught me how to use it.'

I looked at Hippomenes, who smiled back. I could feel his faith in me, warm and steadfast. Then I turned, fitting the arrow to the string and pulling it taut. I held it still for a moment, following Iasus' example of a powerful silence. I could feel how they held their breath.

I let it fly, its arc true and sweet, all the way to the centre of the first target. Smoothly, I slipped the next arrow from the quiver, aimed it and fired. Again and again, the motion so practised and expert I barely noticed it. My body was fluid, controlled, moving with the instincts I'd been honing since I was a child.

It was over in a flash. Each of my arrows was driven deep into the heart of a target. When I turned back again, I could see the exultation on Iasus' face and the stunned shock of the crowd he'd gathered.

Euphoria was tingling through me; after so long spent on solitary runs with Aura, it had felt like my days of public victory were behind me. So I didn't flinch away when Iasus seized my wrist and raised it in the air, the two of us side by side in front of the crowd.

'No other woman in the world could perform such a feat,' he declared, and I wanted to tell him there was no man that could match me either, but I bit my tongue. 'She is undoubtedly Atalanta of the Argonauts, champion of Artemis, and so I believe her claim to be my daughter. I accept her as mine – my only child, blood of my blood.'

There was a storm of applause. I caught Hippomenes' eye. He looked slightly worried at Iasus' words, perhaps anticipating my anger. But this was what we had come for. I had the status of his name, access to his privilege and power, just as I'd wanted.

He hadn't finished.

'Whoever marries my daughter will inherit my kingdom,' he said. And with these words, I began to realise how badly I had miscalculated. 'Send out the heralds with the news: I seek a husband for the bold and beautiful Atalanta.'

I wrenched my wrist from his grasp, more forcefully than I intended, and he stumbled a little. My chest was still heaving from the elation I had felt only moments before, the thrill of my own strength, the rush of my own fearlessness. 'I've sworn I'll never marry,' I said, my voice carrying loud and clear to all the assembled listeners. 'There is no man that can ever match me.'

I could see Iasus gathering his composure. 'In the forest, maybe, you could live like that. But you've come back here, wanting to claim your birthright. As the daughter of a king, that birthright is marriage. We will have to comb the length and breadth of Greece to find a suitor worthy of you' – he sneered – 'but be assured that we will.'

It felt as though everyone watching held their breath, the silence between us as sharp as a blade.

I made myself just as composed as him, a taunt lacing the edge of my words as I spoke. 'Find a man that can outrun me – that's the only man I'll marry.'

And he smiled. He turned to the crowd, held his arms out in an expansive gesture. 'Let that be the message you take from here,' he commanded. 'We will hold a footrace – the man that can run faster than Atalanta will win her.' He lingered over the next words almost lovingly. 'Any man who loses the race will lose his life. Let that be the challenge. This is how we'll find a husband deserving of my daughter.'

There was a buzz of excited chatter. Iasus strode away from me, but I stood frozen, staring at Hippomenes, wondering what I should do now.

27

'I'll leave,' I muttered to him. We were walking through the palace orchards, fruit trees laden with ripe pears and apples growing in abundance, bright red pomegranates hanging heavy. Dust kicked up in clouds around my worn sandals with every agitated stride. I yearned to go faster, to be among trees that grew freely, not trapped amidst this carefully tended luxury. 'It was foolish to come here in the first place.'

'We can go now, before any hopeful suitors arrive,' Hippomenes said. 'Let's just run.'

The image of Iasus' smug face rose up in my mind. I clenched my jaw. 'Does he get to outwit me that easily?'

Hippomenes cast me a look of surprise. 'If you go, he doesn't get what he wants.'

'Maybe he does. Maybe it's just a game to him. He thinks that he either gets to put me up as a prize in his contest, or that he's made me run away, too scared to compete.'

'If he thinks you're too scared to compete, he has no idea who you are.'

'No man can win against me,' I said. 'Perhaps he won't find anyone who'll risk it.'

'They'll come,' said Hippomenes. 'Everyone will want to see the woman who claims to be an Argonaut.'

And every man will want to beat me, I thought. It was an opportunity they'd relish. A chance to put me in my place, to show the woman who thought she was as good as the heroes that she couldn't keep up. 'I'll race.'

'Really?'

'What do I have to lose? I'll beat any man stupid enough to try.'

'Iasus will kill them all.'

'It's their choice to run. I'll show Iasus that no one can defeat me. He'll see I'm not a daughter he can control.'

Hippomenes looked troubled. 'I don't trust the king. What if he finds some way to sabotage you?'

I shook my head. 'He's underestimated me. He thinks I'm not fast enough. He doesn't realise what I can do, even after I showed him.'

'And when he runs out of suitors willing to risk their lives?'

'Then I'll set my terms.' I started to feel a ripple of excitement. 'This is better than anything I could have asked for. This race will prove me, beyond any doubt. I'll be legendary across Greece. If Iasus is desperate for an heir, well then, I already have a son.'

Hippomenes hesitated. 'Will he accept Parthenopaios?'

'He will when I've defeated every competitor he can find and he understands what I am.'

'So you aren't going to leave? You'll stay and race?'

I stopped walking. In the distance, I could see men working in the vineyards beyond, heaving heavy baskets of grapes under the baking sun. Further still were the mountains, and far behind them, I knew the vast sea would be glittering in the golden light, the waves frothing in foamy white peaks. A whole world beyond, waiting to be conquered.

'I'll race.'

'Then I won't wish you luck, or the favour of the gods,' Hippomenes said. 'You don't need it. You'll beat them all.'

I knew he believed what he was saying, so I wondered why he still looked worried as he said it.

In the days that followed, I would slip outside the grounds before dawn, jogging until I was far enough away that I knew I wouldn't be spotted by anyone in the palace. Then I would give myself free rein to run, to push myself further and faster until it felt like my feet were flying across the earth, as though I could leap the craggy faces of the mountains and skim over the surface of the seas.

Only Hippomenes knew where I went. He'd wait for me to return to my starting point, holding a flask of fresh, cold water that I'd gratefully swig, pouring what was left over my sweat-drenched forehead, laughing and exhilarated. I knew that he was anxious, that he suspected some kind of trickery from Iasus, but I knew there was nothing to worry about.

I was confident there would be a fair number of suitors; this was the kind of challenge that would speak directly to their egos. When they started to arrive, they were just as I'd expected. Vigorous, healthy men who glowed with vitality; men who had been brought up with tutors to teach them sword-fighting, the kind of men who'd come in parties to hunt in my forest, blaring their horns and letting their dogs run free. Men who thought the world belonged to them, who imagined I was just another trophy that they could win.

When two dozen were assembled, Iasus gave the order that the first race would be held the next morning. They should split into two groups, he commanded. The most eager would race on the first day. Any man who couldn't keep up with me would lose his head at the finishing post. If there was no winner among the first twelve, the second group would have their chance the following day.

I noticed those who clamoured to be in the first group, who pushed themselves forward. The loudest ones, the brashest, whose voices rang across the great hall each night as they competed to tell the most impressive stories.

'It's decided.' Iasus' voice boomed out across them. 'You will race at dawn.'

I slept soundly that night. When I stepped out under the feathery pink-tinged skies the next day, it looked as though the suitors had too. None of them betrayed any nerves; no dark shadows under their eyes gave away a night spent tossing and turning.

A racetrack had been laid out, tall posts sunk into the ground to mark the course. It would take us through a long, green valley, the mountains rearing up around us, ferocious and craggy. There would be nowhere to flee once they started to realise the hopelessness of their task. The spectators took their places, a hum of expectant chatter rising, good-natured speculation on which of the men would be the victor.

The suitors began to take their places. I'd seen them as a braying mass before, an interchangeable group of pampered, arrogant men, but now I started to notice the differences between them: this one whose smile was easy and whose nose had clearly been broken before; this other with a haughty expression and a jawline so sculpted he might have been carved from marble; another whose eyes were warm and hopeful, and one with a jagged white scar slashed across his arm. These men were young, no doubt convinced by their previous exploits that they would be successful. Out of nowhere, I felt pity for them.

Before Iasus could speak, I raised my arm, calling for their attention.

'This is your last chance,' I said. 'I was one of the Argonauts, I ran alongside the greatest living heroes of our lands, men who were the sons of gods. Not one of them could catch me; I was faster than them all. Please heed my warning; none of you has to run this race. Go home now, before it's too late.'

In the brief quiet that followed, I thought I had been heard. But only moments later, laughter broke out among the men, making its way to the gathered spectators. Only Hippomenes remained grave.

I remembered the story the nymphs had told me of Artemis, righteous and avenging, how she'd transformed the hunter Actaeon into a stag so that his own dogs would tear him apart in punishment for his insolence to her. I could taste blood in my mouth. 'I won't even start running until the last of you reaches the halfway post,' I spat. 'You still won't stand a chance.'

They only laughed harder.

Iasus raised an eyebrow. 'Atalanta has offered a generous advantage. The first of you to reach the finishing line before her will be my son-in-law. If she reaches it first, you will die.'

They all dropped into position. The horn blared. They shot across the valley, legs pumping, leaping across the ground in long strides.

I stood and watched. I felt Iasus' eyes on me, curious. I smiled, letting the anger surge through me, molten in my veins. The group of runners were tight together, a knot of them equally matched. As they approached the halfway post, ready to turn, I sank into a crouch. The earth was soft beneath my toes, the breeze warm in the early rays of the sun. As the last of them rounded the corner, I sprang forwards.

The scenery shot past me in a blur. I saw a glimpse of their faces as they sprinted back down the valley towards the finish, a flash of open mouths and staring eyes. Effortlessly, I increased my speed. I darted around the halfway stake, the cloud of dust behind the runners' legs just ahead of me, and then I was in the thick of them, slipping through their barging elbows and frantically racing legs, breathing in the heat and sweat for a second before I was out in the clear air once more, the urgent thunder of footsteps receding behind me. At the forefront of the crowd, Iasus' jaw dropped as he saw me pull ahead, the desperate men lost in my wake.

I whirled around at the finishing post, flushed with triumph. The horror of their situation struck the runners, and they began to scatter, the men who just moments before had scoffed at the idea that they would be afraid.

Iasus' soldiers advanced remorselessly. I glanced over at the king, his face now impassive as he watched the exhausted suitors scrambling for escape, only to be seized one by one by the guards.

Morning light spilled into the valley as the sun rose over the trees. From their leafy perches, the birds began to sing. The sobs and anguished pleas made a discordant counterpoint to their chorus.

The man with the broken nose twisted free of a guard's grasp and he hurled himself away, the sound of his breaths sharp and ragged as he ran. Another guard launched his spear, piercing the man's shoulder. I heard cheers from the spectators as he fell.

I saw Hippomenes look away, but I couldn't tear my eyes from the boulder where each of them was hauled and forced down, the tender napes of their necks bared. The axe blade glinting in the sun as the executioner lifted it high. The sickening sound it made as it sliced through flesh and bone.

I'd seen men die; I'd fired the fatal arrow myself on more occasions than I could count. In the heat of battle, I'd never flinched. But never before had I witnessed such a cold-blooded parade of killings. Still, I'd wanted them humbled; I'd wanted them punished.

Iasus was unmoved. If he was angry that I'd proven myself right, he didn't show it. When the last of the suitors was dead, he turned to the crowd. The jovial atmosphere had given way to something darker, something savage.

'We'll display their heads outside the palace,' Iasus announced. 'If no man wins tomorrow, we'll do the same with theirs, as a warning to future challengers. These men thought the task before them would be easy. Those that run tomorrow know now that it is not. The man who defeats Atalanta must be far greater than today's competitors; he must be a man of extraordinary skill and speed. Send out word again! Spread the news of what has happened here today. No ordinary man can beat my daughter. My son-in-law must be one of the most powerful heroes in all of Greece.'

If I'd hoped that this would be enough, that these twelve deaths would show Iasus the futility of his plan, I knew now I was wrong. This would only spur him on, only make the contest more alluring.

I thought of doing this over and over. Of how many deaths I would have to watch before he gave up.

Iasus stalked away. His cloak, vivid and crimson, flowed

behind him. The crowd began to disperse and the guards to gather up the bodies of the suitors.

I started to walk along the racetrack. I wasn't sure where I was going, but I couldn't bear to return to the palace.

Hippomenes' touch was light on my shoulder. 'You told them not to race you,' he said. 'They knew the penalty.'

'I know.'

I leaned against a rock and turned my face to the sun. 'Maybe Iasus overestimates how many more will be willing to try.'

'There are always men who want to make a name for themselves. Maybe not so many like these were, young and arrogant and deluded. It will be the ruthless ones, who'll stop at nothing to secure their immortality in the legends – brutal men, seeking glory, men who want to be as famous as Heracles, whatever the cost.'

For Heracles, it had cost the lives of his wife and daughter. Innocent lives, women whose names would never be remembered like his, sacrificed in the flames that forged a hero's destiny.

'So, men who know the stakes,' I said.

'Does that mean you'll carry on racing? Is it worth it?' I could hear a faint sadness in his voice. It was likely he'd hated to see the executions even more than I had.

'Is it worth it, to buy my freedom and my son's security? I think so.' I paused, trying to squash down the niggling question of whether this was the world in which I wanted Parthenopaios to grow up.

My head ached. I might wish now that I'd never come here, but here I was, and it was too late to leave. And I knew that whoever came, they could never outrun me. If every hero of Greece had to die here, then so be it.

I wasn't going to forfeit. I was going to win.

My resolve carried me past the grisly display that Iasus had ordered outside the palace when I returned. It wavered, just a little, when I saw the faces of the second group of suitors in the great hall. They were seated around one long wooden table, the food before them untouched, none of the camaraderie or laughter of the previous night. I halted before I'd fully entered the hall and turned on my heel. I wasn't going to eat in there.

Out in the courtyard, statues of young men were ranged around the edges, each of them holding aloft a burning torch. The columns were twined with flowers and, above me, the stars sparkled in the sky. It was so peaceful.

I heard soft footsteps behind me and I turned, expecting it to be Hippomenes. Instead, it was one of the suitors, his face wretched.

'What are you doing here?' I asked.

'I couldn't stay in there.' His face in the firelight looked painfully young.

'Why did you come here at all?'

He shrugged. I could see his shoulders trembling even as he attempted some façade of bravery. 'My father sent me,' he said. 'I'm his youngest son, he has no use for me. "Go and make a good marriage," he told me. "Or else don't come back at all."' His mouth twisted. I thought perhaps he was trying not to cry.

'Just go,' I urged him, my voice low. I darted my eyes around to make sure that no one had seen us. 'Run, now, while they're feasting.'

'The king has posted guards on every road out of this town after what happened today, otherwise he would have no competitors left at all. Besides, where would I go? My father won't have me back if I fail. And – and I will.'

'Atalanta?'

It was Hippomenes, coming up from the garden towards the courtyard where we stood.

'You'd better go back,' I told the young man. 'Before someone notices you're missing.'

He swallowed, a painful gulping sound, and then squared his shoulders. He nodded at me and walked away.

'What was that about?' Hippomenes asked.

'He didn't even want to race.' I drummed my fingers on the lip of the low stone basin beside me. 'His father made him come.'

'It could be true of some of the others in there, too,' Hippomenes said. 'None of them volunteered to be in the first group. If one of those men had won, these men could have gone home.'

'If they were allowed back without having succeeded.'

He gave me a half-hearted smile. 'There have to be losers. It's a competition.'

'And I won't be one of them.' I threw up my hands. 'What else am I supposed to do?'

He rubbed the back of his neck, and I noticed how the muscles in his upper arms shifted smoothly under the skin. His strength was quiet and understated, not like the suitors flexing and stretching before the race this morning, strutting in front of the crowd like Hera's beloved peacocks. He looked tired, more profoundly worn down by the day's events than I'd realised, but still he searched for the right thing to say, for some kindness. 'I thought you'd decided what to do. Has anything really changed?'

I pressed my lips together, thinking. A bat flitted overhead, crickets chirped in the long grass. I wished that I could be out there, away from the brightness of the torches and the finely decorated sculptures. Out there, where the darkness was a familiar friend. Not like here, where horrors took place in the clear light, where monsters smiled behind human faces. 'I think it would be better for Parthenopaios to grow up penniless than to grow up to be a man like my father. But . . .' I looked away from Hippomenes, into the featureless blank of the dark gardens. 'I can't let them say that Atalanta ran away from the competition. My name is out there, just as I wanted it to be. I have to race. They'd say I was a coward, that my woman's temperament couldn't stand up to the challenge. It's worse than being forgotten. I'd be disgraced.' I let out a long sigh. 'I do wish they didn't all have to die.'

He reached out and rested a hand on my shoulder. 'It isn't your fault.'

His touch was warm.

'There's a temple of Artemis, down the track that runs beyond the orchards,' I said. 'I saw it earlier. I'm going to go there now.'

'That's a good idea.'

'I'll see you at sunrise,' I said, and I hurried into the darkness. The further away from the palace I got, the more the beacons were swallowed up by the night, and the better I felt. I made my way down the dusty track, past the fruit trees, until I saw another light ahead. The flame burning outside her temple.

It was a modest building, simple and unassuming. I'd glanced within when I'd passed it before, but I'd held back from entering. It was deserted now, the single flame dancing in its low bowl, moths fluttering in the warm glow.

I slipped between the pair of stone columns at the front. Inside, the air smelled of cedar, woodsy and comforting. A statue of Artemis stood in the centre. It was a little clumsy in its execution, but I felt the twist in my heart nonetheless. It felt a whole lifetime since I'd seen her last. I didn't know if I would ever lay eyes on her again.

I knew what she would do if anyone was foolish enough to challenge her. She would have no mercy.

I waited there a long time, standing in the shadows, gathering my resolve. I had been among too many people, living according to their rules for too long. It was clouding my vision, gnawing away at my confidence and certainty, making me doubt the instincts that had kept me alive all these years. I needed to remember who I was, who I had always been. A woman who was unafraid.

I woke with no sense of anticipation or excitement, only inevitability. I would do what I had to do, but it gave me no pleasure to send twelve more men to their deaths.

Down at the racetrack, the same crowd was gathered, the same line of guards, the same axe laid across the flat boulder, which still bore the dark stains from yesterday.

The twelve men were there too, a quiet, subdued group, each lost in his own intense concentration. Some of them cast their eyes up to the sky, calling on the gods maybe, while others stared down at the ground.

I jogged from foot to foot where I stood, too full of nervous energy to be still. I was eager to have it over with.

When Iasus stepped forwards, I felt a sense of relief. He made his declarations, reminding us of what had taken place yesterday, what a mighty task lay ahead of the suitors.

But this morning, just as the runners took their places to the side of me, and the heralds raised the trumpets to their mouths to signal the start, another voice called out.

'I challenge Atalanta too! Let me run as well.'

The voice was familiar, but it was impossible that it could be so. Dread kept me from turning around to confirm it.

There was a ripple of laughter in Iasus' voice as he spoke. 'Hippomenes? You put yourself forward as a potential husband?'

'I do.'

I closed my eyes, willing him to stop with every sinew in my body.

'I'm a worthy suitor for your daughter,' Hippomenes said. 'I'm the son of a king. I was part of the famed Calydonian boar hunt.'

'And can you run?'

There were sniggers from the spectators.

'I can.'

But I knew, and so did he, that I'd outrun him countless times.

'And if I win,' he went on, 'I demand that you let the other suitors go unharmed.'

'I accept your challenge, Hippomenes. Maybe the gods are smiling down on you today.' Iasus' voice was smooth as honey.

And to my disbelieving horror, Hippomenes came forwards to crouch at my side.

The shout came before I had a chance to do anything.

'Competitors, ready!'

28

'What are you doing?' I hissed in the frozen seconds that followed.

'This way, no one has to die.' His eyes held mine for an agonising instant, a bright flash of connection before the trumpets sounded and the runners hurtled forwards, as though propelled like arrows from a bow. I rocked back on my heels, watching the dust billow up around their ankles. I felt as though the air had been knocked out of my chest. What could have possessed him? His words repeated in my mind: *No one has to die.* Did that mean he thought I'd let him win? Was he so sure of our friendship that he would gamble his life on it?

Hippomenes was swifter than the rest of them, smoothly taking the lead. The pack receded and I trained my gaze on them, watching for the instant they rounded the halfway post. My body thrummed with anticipation, my mind emptying of any thought except to run.

I launched myself forwards, my strides long and light, the trees and mountains rushing past me faster than ever before. The wind roared in my ears; there was nothing in the world but me. I barely noticed as I drew level with the runners, as I darted around them to the figure in front, closing the gap between us effortlessly.

Just as I was about to pass him, I saw in the corner of my vision that he fumbled for something, and I slowed just a fraction to see what he was doing. A cloth bag was tied at his waist, there was something shining gold in his hand, and then he flung it, right across the path in front of me. I felt the shudder of air as it flew past my face, and I couldn't help it. I turned to see what it was.

It had rolled to the edge of the track, incongruous against the dirt and dust. It gleamed so brightly, it looked as though it didn't belong to the human realm at all.

Impulse seized me. I darted back, plucked it from the ground and ran again, catching Hippomenes with ease. I glanced down at the golden bauble I held, smooth and curiously heavy. It wasn't a sphere, as I'd first thought; there was a dimple at the top, from which emerged a golden stem and a leaf, carved with delicate incisions to trace the veins.

An apple, made of gold, startlingly beautiful. I knew it meant something, that there was a story I'd heard before, and just as the memory slid into focus, I saw him, at my side, reaching back into the bag to toss a second apple. His arm was stronger this time; it flew further than the first.

The finishing line was in sight, the faces of the crowd a blur of screaming mouths, a delirious frenzy. I clenched my jaw, surged forwards again, leaving Hippomenes behind me, and the apple too.

But I could still win easily, I told myself. It wasn't a conscious decision; my feet veered off in pursuit of the second apple. Now I knew what they were: the Golden Apples of the

Hesperides. We'd come across the devastation Heracles had left when he'd plundered the sacred garden to seize them. I remembered the weeping dryad.

Nimbly, I leapt back over on to the track again. Hippomenes' legs were pumping furiously. I sprinted across the empty space between us, his back within touching distance, and then I was past him again.

I looked back, for the briefest glimpse. The sheen of sweat on his forehead, the determination in the set of his jaw, the purpose in his eyes – something that he wanted me to know, some message he was giving me with these Apples that I couldn't understand.

The third rolled past my feet and off the course.

I forced myself to think. These Golden Apples were a trophy presented to Hera, Queen of the Olympians, on her marriage to Zeus. Heracles wanted them like Jason wanted the Fleece; an emblem of his legendary status, proof to the world that he was the greatest of heroes, that he could take what no ordinary mortal could ever hope to possess.

And now, they could be mine.

The tumult among the spectators was incredible as I shot sideways, off the track, chasing the final Apple as it rolled to a halt well away from the course. I seized it, pressing all three awkwardly to my chest, racing back to where Hippomenes was now within touching distance of the end. Time seemed to slow, he was inches away from me, his elbow just in front of my arm; he was beside me; we were both about to reach the post and I was just ahead of him, the din of shouting echoing from the rocky mountainsides, reverberating all the way to the heavens.

And just before I got there, with immense effort, I pulled

myself back. Hippomenes hurtled past me and, in a flurry of motion, past the final stake. He flung himself on the earth, then rolled on to his back gasping desperately, staring at the sky. Iasus was raising his fists in elation.

The other runners were struggling on, but the joyful realisation was dawning across their faces. The crowd was chanting Hippomenes' name, he was being hauled to his feet and crowned with a wreath of twisted branches and leaves. He was the winner, not me, and the others did not have to die.

He broke free from the press of well-wishers and made his way across to where I stood, my hand still on the finishing post.

'I wanted to explain.' His voice was low so that we wouldn't be heard, but his breath was still coming in fast, juddering gasps from the exertion. 'I couldn't tell you about the Apples, I promised—'

I shook my head. 'I didn't understand, at first.'

'You could have beaten me easily, even with the Apples,' he said.

'And let you die?'

'If you'd wanted to. I only wanted to give you the choice.' His eyes were earnest, fixed on mine, his words coming faster now. 'You could have still won and taken the Apples. Winning those and the race too would prove you equal to Heracles, it would give you all the fame you could want. You could have left here with no shame; you could have beaten me and taken the Apples and no one would have dared to race you again. Iasus would have no willing competitors, so he would have no hold over you or Parthenopaios. Your reputation would have been unblemished.'

I smiled. 'What would my reputation be worth if I let my friend die? What kind of a hero would I be?'

He shrugged. 'The usual kind. I'm glad you're different. I hoped – I hoped that you would be. Because, you know we don't have to get married on Iasus' orders. We can walk away from here. You don't have to go through with the bargain; you can do whatever you want now.'

'You didn't do this to be my husband?'

His cheeks, already flushed from the race, flooded with a darker red. 'Of course not. You told me about the oracle. You told me you'd never marry. I wanted to help you find a way out of the bargain, without any needless deaths, without you having to compromise your fame.'

'But how did you get the Apples?'

Iasus was descending upon us, his arms outstretched. Hippomenes spoke more rapidly still. 'When you went to the temple of Artemis, I prayed to Aphrodite for help. She heard me. It was the goddess who gave me the Golden Apples. Why, I don't know.'

I hesitated, confused. Iasus reached us, clapping Hippomenes on the shoulder, glowing with triumph. I was too preoccupied to feel any irritation, far less the humiliation he no doubt intended.

Why Aphrodite? I knew of her rivalry with Artemis, the hatred she felt for the goddess who demanded her followers turned their back on the kind of passion and desire that Aphrodite revelled in. I wondered why Hippomenes would have turned to her, and why she would have deigned to help him.

The stories the nymphs had told me were flooding back. Aphrodite and Artemis had quarrelled over mortals before, each of them resentful of the other encroaching upon their devotees, each of them determined to gather more worshippers for herself. I knew that; I remembered them telling me of

Persephone and how Artemis had taken her revenge through Adonis. What a prize for Aphrodite if she took Artemis' own protégée.

And Aphrodite responded to entreaties born of love. For her to grant Hippomenes' request for help, she must have seen into his heart and knew what he felt, whatever he said about our friendship. He'd risked his life for the sake of my pride. He was prepared to die so that I could succeed.

And now, he risked everything again. A thwarted goddess would be merciless if she didn't get what she'd demanded. And as far as I could see, she could only have demanded one condition from Hippomenes in exchange for the Apples.

I was certain of it now. Aphrodite would have given him these trophies on the promise that I would be married, to ensure that Artemis could never claim me again. If, instead, I left here with the Apples and no husband, it could be enough to win my patron's favour back, and maybe I could belong to Artemis once more. But I had no doubt that Hippomenes would pay a terrible price for it – and he must know it too, even as he urged me to go.

Iasus was staring at me expectantly. Whatever he'd said, I hadn't heard it over my racing thoughts. 'What?' I asked.

There were hands on my shoulders, a cool weight placed on my collarbones. I looked down to see a string of polished stones that someone was fastening around my neck.

'The marriage will take place at once,' Iasus was saying.

Hippomenes was shaking his head. 'But, the rituals – nothing has been observed, there hasn't been any preparation, any sacrifice. How can a marriage take place like this – a royal marriage, at that? Surely we should wait, make proper arrangements.' He was babbling desperately. Trying to save me again.

I put my hand on his arm. 'What preparations do we need?' I said, and his mouth dropped open, his bewilderment almost comical. A laugh rose up in my chest, a sudden swoop of merriment.

I turned to the king. 'Nothing about this situation is usual. I made a bargain with you, and I'll honour it. We'll get married here.'

I took a long breath. The air was quiet and still. No divine wrath, no signs of Artemis' fury descended in the wake of my revelation.

I cleared my throat. 'Now.'

29

It was a rushed affair, so hasty it felt tinged with panic. I suppose that Iasus feared I might disappear. After all, I'd demonstrated well enough that no one would be able to catch me if I fled.

A fine drizzle hung in the air, enveloping the tops of the mountains in swirling clouds. My hair was damp, loose tendrils clinging to my face and the nape of my neck, cold droplets tracing down my spine. Our feet were still bare from the race, our legs coated in the dust that stained the hems of our tunics. I was aware of Hippomenes' hands encircling my wrists, the bleating emanating from the sheep that were led up from the nearby fields for sacrifice in the hope that the gods would look kindly on the union. Libations poured, Iasus' gleeful smile, the delirious relief on the faces of the young men who had been allowed to live. The Apples shining on top of the flat stone where, today, no one had needed to die.

I thought about the man who had walked away from the crying infant on the hillside. The mother bear, weary of her cubs, snarling at them to be gone. The silence from the forest when I returned from my adventures, sore and tired and hopeless, craving sympathy from Artemis that never came. Her face, cold and empty when she told me never to return. The loneliness after I gave birth.

And now, Hippomenes, with his gentle, self-sacrificing love. Facing the penalty from Iasus or Aphrodite, whatever it took to let me be free.

On the racetrack where we were married, I said goodbye to the conditions Artemis had placed on my life and to the demands my father had made. For the first time, the choice was mine. Let Iasus think he'd made it for me; what did it matter?

I didn't have to be an obedient follower of Artemis, jumping to serve her every command; I didn't have to be a hero in the mould of Jason or Heracles or the angry boar-hunters at Calydon. I wasn't going to try to shape myself to be like one of them, a ruthless, self-serving, glory-seeking man. I was something different to them all.

The drizzle gave way to a downpour, a sudden torrent that scattered the crowd. I laughed, watching them disperse, Iasus holding his cloak over his head as he ran. Hippomenes and I were left alone, the track churning up into thick mud under the relentless hammering of the rain.

'Don't you want to follow them?' Hippomenes asked me. 'Go back to the palace?'

I shook my head.

His smile dawned, a slow sunrise, chasing the last of the shadows away. 'What about Iasus? What about claiming what's yours?'

'There's nothing I want from Iasus,' I said. 'I've seen enough of his world to know I should never have come here at all.'

'And Parthenopaios?'

'He's better off staying where he is.'

'So, that's it? You're leaving with nothing?'

'Not quite.'

I took his face in my hands and kissed him. His lips were soft and warm against mine; he smelled of rain and earth, the fresh pine of the forest, a crystal-clear stream, bright and cold and reviving.

He drew back a fraction, his forehead touching mine, a gasp of half-laughter escaping. 'Since I saw your face after the centaurs knocked me unconscious, I've thought of nothing but you.'

I knew it was true. I hadn't admitted to myself that I loved him too until now. I hadn't been holding any part of myself separate from our kiss; I wasn't fearful of the tenderness, of the emotion between us. With Hippomenes, I could let myself feel it all – the passion and the love, together. I caught his hand, twining my fingers through his. 'Let's go.'

He glanced back as I led him up the slope heading away from the valley. 'What about the Apples?'

I stopped. I looked back at them, glowing golden through the damp mist, seeming to pulse and shift with a thrumming energy. A prize that could prove a hero's worth to the world.

My steps were steady, pulling me towards them like a thread being wound back up into a spool. I reached out to touch the foremost of them, its smoothness hard and unyielding.

I pushed it away, letting it roll to the lip of the rock, where it hovered for a moment, before falling on to the grass with a gentle thud.

'We'll leave them, too,' I said.

The clouds gathered above our heads as we hurried back along the road that had brought us into the town, past the palace, from where rhythmic drumbeats accompanied the loose scatter of notes falling from a lyre, shouts of laughter, bursts of song, voices lifted up to celebrate a wedding feast with no bride or groom. I wondered how long it would take Iasus to realise that his prize had slipped away, that he had no daughter to boast of anymore. Whatever he might have given us – treasure or ships or quests – anything I did with his resources would have been in his name, and I would never let that happen. It was nothing to me if my name was forgotten in halls like his, left unspoken by men like him, if it faded away from the songs and memories of men whose opinions were worthless to me. It had taken the sight of the Golden Apples for me to realise, but I knew it now.

We ran on through the rain, beyond the limits of the town, into the wilderness together.

The temple was overgrown, ivy climbing over its ruined walls, moss smothering the stones and briars tangling across the entrance. We'd stumbled into the grove where it stood, deep in the forest, illuminated by a pale beam of moonlight. The dark skies had cleared and the air was utterly still, heavy around us, thick with a strange heat and suffused with the cloying scent of the honeysuckle vines that grew rampant throughout the grove.

The last trails of our laughter were dying behind us, the ferns trampled in our wake, our chests bursting with exhilaration, until we'd come to a stop here, as though mutually agreed that it was our destination. The overwhelming perfume of the flowers dizzied me; the warm, fragrant air clouding my senses as I breathed it in, slow and stupefying.

'Come on.' I tugged at his hand, leading him to the open

doorway, not caring if the thorns scratched my calves. It was like a dream, a flow of euphoria surging in my veins, not just the joy of running or the thrill of our escape. There was something else in the forest, some presence in the grove unlike any I'd known before. Something that drew me into that tumble-down shrine, where I pressed my hand against the cool stone, seeking out something to steady me, to wake me back up to myself. It was so unlike the breath of wind that would carry Artemis, fleet-footed, tunic streaming behind her, into her sacred groves, the forest stirring to life at her presence. This, whatever it was in the grove with us, was drifting, soft and sweet and dangerous, something ancient and seductive that had us in its grasp. The scent of roses, thick and cloying, like the ones that had marked Aphrodite's meadow all those years ago. *Why would Aphrodite be here?* I wondered. And the answer surfaced in my mind.

The Apples, I thought, *the gift of Aphrodite that we left behind us, that we tossed into the mud.*

But I couldn't hold the thoughts clearly enough, they were too slippery, arching free from my grasp like the fish I tried to pluck from the river as the bears did all those years ago.

I shook my head, trying to clear it. Hippomenes' eyes were dreamy and unfocused, succumbing to the same trance as me. Aphrodite's trance, Aphrodite's bewitchment, that she cast on us now in punishment for the Apples we had disdained. Somewhere in my mind, the lucid part of me screamed in warning, but I couldn't fight against it, and neither could he.

'Rhea,' he said, gesturing at a carving on the wall, dragging his thumb over the shapes standing out in relief. I peered at them through the shifting shadows. Rhea, the goddess that Artemis had told me of once. Rhea who had ruled this forest before anyone else. Rhea, the mother of gods, mother of mountains, mother of the world. She was outlined in gold, glinting in the dim light, her high crown and flowing dress, stone lions prowling at her feet. So, this had been her temple, her sacred place of worship. It seemed right that it was so nearly swallowed up by nature, that the vines and plants had taken it back, working between the stones, claiming it back to the earth again, making it wild.

'We have to get away,' I mumbled. 'Hide in here.'

And he nodded, dazed.

The heavy fragrance of the roses receded as we made our way further inside. Now I breathed in Hippomenes again, the fresh mountain-scent, the earthiness of the temple interior, moss and stone. I barely thought of where we were, of the wooden carvings of ancient deities standing like guards around the ruined walls, Rhea taller than any of them, her painted eyes on us.

I kissed him right in front of her, lightning sparking behind my eyes, an eager intensity that burned away any other thoughts in my head. The thought I'd tried to hold on to, the worry that a vengeful Aphrodite was leading us into a trap, it didn't matter now. That fear drifted away like a wisp of cloud as I pulled him closer to me, his hands sliding down my back, his hair tangled in my fingers, nothing else existing in the world but the two of us.

The flames roared through me, an inferno obliterating any coherent deliberation, anything that could have held me back from him. If it was Aphrodite's spell that had us ensnared, our wits clouded by her magic, we were caught in it together. The night beyond the temple's walls was still poised and watchful, but within its dark sanctuary, we were all that mattered.

* * *

Afterwards, we lay breathless on the bare floor, a breeze at last trickling in through the open doorway. The foreboding heat that had hung so heavy in the air was burned out, dissipating in the gentle flutter that brushed the curled-up leaves that were scattered around, lifting them slightly and then settling them again.

I propped myself up on one elbow, my hair tumbling loose, running my other hand over the smooth white scar where the centaur's spear had pierced Hippomenes' shoulder the night we met. I was about to speak when the wind hissed through again, louder this time, the leaves jumping in its path. I felt a prickling down my spine, a sudden alertness catching hold.

Again, a swell of air surged through the temple, and I sat up, my hair blowing back behind me as another gust whistled past and I heard her voice.

Low and primal, a voice as ancient as the universe. Rhea.

'Animals,' she rasped, and the words layered one over another, like waves crashing and receding. 'Like animals ... my temple ... in my sanctuary ... so brazen.'

Hippomenes grasped my arm, his hand tight around me. The enchantment had dropped away; I saw it now and so did he. Aphrodite had led us in here, into Rhea's temple, and let passion overwhelm us. Artemis had told me that Rhea had left these woods, but she was here and she had seen what we did. We stared at each other, wordless, as the wind roused again, a discordant shriek that grew louder and louder until we pressed our hands over our ears and I clamped my eyes shut, trying to drive it out. The leaves were whirling, flying around us as she raged, and then, abruptly, they dropped. Everything was motionless, the goddess herself holding her breath for an instant.

I felt it on the back of my neck first: a scratching sensation, something tiny twisting its way out of me, through my skin, a thousand little pinpricks. Then a ripple that shuddered through my whole body, that seized it in a powerful convulsion. I thought that the goddess had me in her grip, that she was tossing me from side to side, but the movement was coming from my own body – a body that didn't feel like mine anymore, the shape of my limbs unfamiliar, a pressure building to an unbearable intensity, the sudden hideous conviction that I was bursting out of my own flesh, that I couldn't be contained. A howl tried to force its way out of my throat, but it was a grumbling, thunderous sound, guttural and raw, unrecognisable.

I was not what I had been. And as I lifted my head, the weight of it different now, the arching of my neck strange and new, I searched for Hippomenes in the gloom. The eyes that stared back at me were greenish-gold and rimmed in black, fixed on me with the same panic I felt.

But the terror of a moment ago was melting away. A flood of new sensations was rushing in. My legs, always strong and muscled before, now tensed, ready to spring with a new kind of force. *Power*, thrumming through every part of my body, greater than anything I'd ever felt before.

I felt the goddess strike my head, her palm reverberating against the golden fur that cloaked me now. I saw her fingers twisting in the tawny mane of the lion at my side, my lover, but it was joy that pulsed through me as she commanded us to run, a pure animal joy that eclipsed any I had felt before.

We fled into the night together.

EPILOGUE

I nuzzle my face into his thick, shaggy mane. He throws back his head, throat to the sky, his jaws stretched open, his fangs glinting in the low-slanting rays of the sun. He sinks down, his brindled muzzle resting on huge paws that look so soft, aside from the dark claws nestled in among the fur.

I lean back on my haunches, feeling the delicious stretch in my front legs, luxuriating in it for a long moment before I release the coiled energy and leap forwards. My body is low to the ground, my paws thundering on the earth, the long grasses that surround me waving as I surge through them. I'm running with a fluid grace and speed greater than any I'd ever achieved in my life before, my form lithe and sinuous and in perfect harmony with the world around me. My muscles roll smoothly under the silken fur, easy and effortless as I bound past the trees on the edge of the forest, streaking past the village where Parthenopaios lives. He grows strong and healthy, gaining an uncommon skill in fighting and hunting, never missing the life I once sought for him. His destiny awaits him one day; for now, he plays at swords with the other boys, using branches to practise; he patiently carves away at the shape of a bow, angling it this way and that, narrowing his eyes at an imaginary target; he heaves sacks of barley and casks of water, building his strength, honing his determination. When he catches a glimpse of the lions surging past, he doesn't run in panic like the other villagers. He lifts his face to us, fearless.

I run on, through the fragrant air of evening, across the steep sides of the mountains. Ahead of me, I see Artemis driving her chariot forwards, the bright fawns in front, her bow catching the fiery light of the sun as it dips below the horizon in a triumphant blaze of orange. She reaches out her hand as I approach, her anger at the woman I once was spent now that I am something else, caressing the top of my head, the base of my ears, the tingle of her touch running the length of my spine, all the way to my swishing tail, so that a low growl of pleasure escapes me, and I run again, faster still, to the highest summit, where I can see the world spread out beneath me, wide and limitless.

The oracle warned that I would lose myself, but the opposite is true. I am more myself than I have ever been. I am wild, I am free.

I am Atalanta.

ACKNOWLEDGEMENTS:

Writing this novel has brought me so much joy and, as ever, I couldn't have done it alone. Thanks go first of all to Juliet Mushens, my agent / fairy godmother / good witch who continues to work her transformative magic on my life. I'm also eternally grateful to everyone at Mushens Entertainment for all their support and kindness.

My editors, Caroline Bleeke and Flora Rees, have challenged and inspired me to make *Atalanta* the very best it could be. Their encouragement has always revived my enthusiasm and love for writing and given me so much confidence and courage to push myself further, while their insight and wisdom have instilled me with purpose and clarity to see the way forwards. I'm really proud of where we ended up!

I feel extremely lucky to have the opportunity to work with everyone at Wildfire and Flatiron and to have such amazing teams championing my books in the UK and US. Thanks in particular to Alex Clarke, Elise Jackson, Caitlin Raynor and Amelia Possanza but also to everyone involved in every stage of the journey from drafting to proofing to publication and beyond! And I remain forever grateful to Tara O'Sullivan for copy-editing so meticulously.

The most rewarding stage is always when I hold the book in my hands at last, and it's made all the more special because I have the best and most talented cover designers – Micaela Alcaino for the UK covers and Joanne O'Neill for the US covers. Their work is spectacular and breath-taking every time and it is always so thrilling to see what they come up with – I think on *Atalanta* they have both outdone themselves again! (And special thanks to Micaela's own greyhound Jojo for being the most beautiful cover muse.)

Atalanta is such a special heroine of Greek mythology – a fearless, skilled and ambitious woman who is a force to be reckoned with but full of heart and compassion too. I was drawn into her story by the image of the infant snuggled up with her adopted bear-cub siblings and as I discovered more about her, she really wove her own spell of wild magic around me. I loved writing her back into the legend of the Argonauts and I hope this novel gives others the chance to fall in love with her the same way that I did. Thank you to all the booksellers, book-bloggers and readers who have got in touch, pressed my books into other people's hands, taken beautiful photographs and responded in so many heartfelt and lovely ways to my novels – I truly appreciate it every day. To all my family and friends who have always supported me, thank you.

Read on for an exclusive essay from
Jennifer Saint:

ARTEMIS

ARTEMIS

Artemis, goddess of the hunt, looks down at the smudge on the gleaming tile where her dusty sandal has scuffed the polished stone. The dirt from the forest clings to her – not to the honey-gold skin of her bare calves of course, it wouldn't dare sully her immortal flesh – it adheres instead to the linen of her short tunic, staining the hem and gathering grime in a faint layer on the quiver strapped to her back. The arrows within the quiver though, and the bow she carries loosely in one hand, glow as gold and pristine as she does. Back in her forest, she strikes fear and admiration into the heart of any beholder in equal measure. But on Mount Olympus, where she so rarely visits, she stands out for a different reason.

This is the home of the reigning immortals; a gorgeous palace hidden in the clouds that wreathe the mountain's peak. From here, they can watch the mortals. They will see battles surge, kingdoms rise and fall, they will watch plagues spread and droughts decimate the land and they will savour the smoke that spirals up from the altars that burn in their honour.

It bores Artemis. She pities her Olympian family: enthroned

and cut off from the world. They don't know the joy of a forest morning: the cool stillness of dawn when curling tendrils of mist unfurl around the gnarled roots of the trees, when the pearl-grey skies are streaked with rosy dawn, and the crisp air hums with vitality.

Hera, her father's wife and the queen of the Olympians, reaches out a slender hand and plucks something from the heavy braid of hair that Artemis wears coiled around her head. Before she crushes it to dust, Artemis can see it's a leaf. Hera's hair falls about her shoulders in a shining river of curls. Her dress falls in a long white column, the fabric pooling at her feet, a glittering clasp holding it at her shoulder.

'So that's why Zeus is so angry?' Artemis asks.

It's what's brought her here today. Zeus' storms have raged for longer than usual. Wild gales have stripped leaves from branches. The thunder has growled from each end of the horizon, making Artemis' dogs whine and huddle close to their mistress. Torrents of rain have swollen the rivers she bathes in, whipping their waters into foaming waterfalls that turn the grassy banks to mud. The final straw was her favourite tree, a beautiful wide-spreading oak, split apart by lightning, toppled to the ground, its magnificent crown trailing in the sodden earth.

Hera sighs, but Artemis can see that she can't quite suppress a smile. 'He's very upset about it,' she agrees. 'Zeus is annoyed that his son, Heracles, is being humbled. Being made to perform impossible labours for a mortal king when he could be bringing glory to Zeus.'

'Why does he care so much about Heracles?' Artemis asks. 'Zeus has other sons.'

Hera bristles. She hates reminders of her husband's many

illegitimate children. 'Never mind about them. The world is full of strong, young mortal men,' she says. 'There are far worthier champions to choose.'

Artemis looks hard at her. 'What do you mean?'

'Heroes who can bring us glory,' Hera explains. 'I've been looking myself, for one I can send on a quest so that he can win success in my name.'

'Why a man?' Artemis asks.

Hera looks blank. 'He has to achieve great feats to honour me. That's the point.'

'Yes, but why not choose a woman?'

'What could she achieve? She could give birth to a hero, of course, but what else?'

Artemis draws herself up. 'My forest nymphs are better huntresses than any man. They are faster, stronger, more accurate. I would choose one of them.'

Hera laughs and Artemis' blood simmers. She can't bear it here a moment longer. Her chariot awaits outside the ornate palace; beautifully carved and light, pulled by her prized pair of golden does. They speed her away, down through the ragged pines dotted across the snow-scattered slopes, towards the verdant green of the forest far below.

Breathing in the fresh scents of oak and fern, of velvety moss and damp earth, she is herself again. Zeus' storms have quieted, at least for now. And then she hears it. A sound that she has never heard in the forest before. A shrill, piercing cry.

Artemis lifts her hand and the does, perfectly attuned to her every movement, slow to a halt. She looks around for the source of the noise and there it is, utterly impossible but real. A newborn baby, swaddled and laid on the bare ground.

Exposure, they call it. Artemis has seen it before. A baby

girl, torn from the arms of her mother and left on a hillside to die for the crime of not being born a son. She furrows her perfect brow. Not to die, she corrects herself. Left to the mercy of the gods.

Artemis may be unlike her fellow Olympians, but she is a goddess, and there is precious little mercy in any immortal. So she doesn't move, and while she's thinking, something else does.

A bear, shambling through the trees, lifting her nose to catch the unfamiliar scent of the infant. This bear has cubs back in her cave, brand-new hungry little creatures. She whines softly, looking back the way she came, anxious to return to them. But she's hungry herself, so hungry. Those ravenous little mouths have drained her of milk and she needs to nourish herself to keep them alive.

The infant cries out again, her small face screwed up. Artemis watches as the mother bear's ears prick up. She moves differently now, more intent as she comes closer to the child. Artemis is spellbound, an unfamiliar tension seizing her heart as the bear looms over the baby and the baby snuffles into silence. Artemis grips the edge of the chariot, leaning forward as the baby turns her head and opens her eyes. She doesn't cry out again. She looks into the bear's eyes and her gaze is not fuzzy and unfocused like any other newborn's, but clear and fearless.

The bear lowers her head, her nose brushing the baby's, and she opens her vast jaws. Gently, she catches the swaddling cloth between those sharp teeth and lifts the baby. She could easily have punctured that tender flesh, but she doesn't. The cloth could unravel, and the infant fall, but it doesn't. Artemis watches closely as the bear paces away, the precious bundle safe in her grasp.

The goddess has made her choice.

'Take care of her.' Her words are so quiet, no mortal could hear them, but it will be enough.

She speaks again, the name she has chosen for the child, for the champion she will become. The name means 'equal in strength', for this is what she'll be: equal to any hero that any other god chooses.

She takes a long moment before she pronounces it, and it seems that the whole forest holds its breath in anticipation before she smiles, and says it aloud.

'Atalanta'.

If you loved *Atalanta*, look out for Jennifer Saint's first novel, *Ariadne* – the mesmerising retelling about the woman at the heart of one of Ancient Greece's most famous myths…

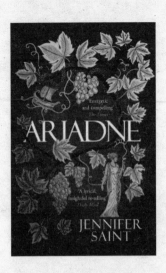

Ariadne, Princess of Crete and daughter of the fearsome King Minos, grows up hearing stories of gods and heroes. But beneath the golden palace something else stirs, the hoofbeats and bellows echoing from the Labyrinth below. Every year its captive, the Minotaur – Ariadne's brother – demands blood.

When Theseus, Prince of Athens, arrives as a sacrifice to the beast, Ariadne sees in him her chance to escape. But helping Theseus kill the monster means betraying her family and country, and Ariadne knows only too well that drawing the attention of the mercurial gods may cost her everything.

In a world where women are nothing more than the pawns of powerful men, will Ariadne's decision to risk everything for love ensure her happy ending? Or will she find herself sacrificed for her lover's ambition?